[redacted]

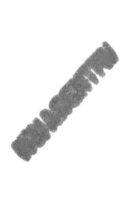

Serenity

宁静 **FIREFLY CLASS 03-K64**

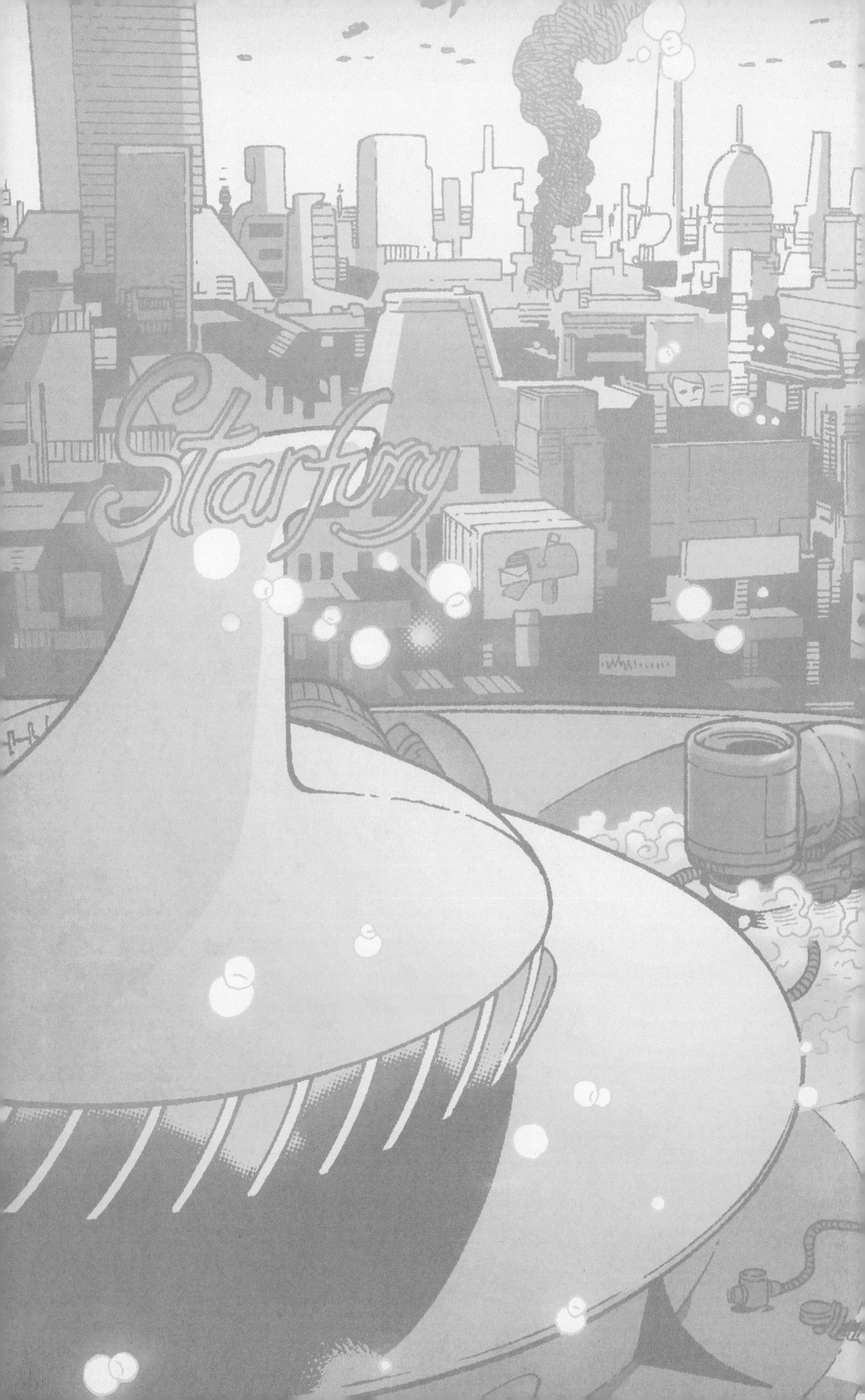
Starfury

Serenity
宁静 **FIREFLY CLASS 03-K64**™
···

— NO POWER IN THE 'VERSE —

CHRIS ROBERSON
GEORGES JEANTY
STEPHEN BYRNE

EXECUTIVE PRODUCER
JOSS WHEDON

FRONT COVER AND CHAPTER BREAK ART
DAN DOS SANTOS

DARK HORSE BOOKS

PRESIDENT & PUBLISHER
MIKE RICHARDSON

EDITORS
**FREDDYE MILLER, SCOTT ALLIE,
JIM GIBBONS, SIERRA HAHN**

ASSISTANT EDITOR
KEVIN BURKHALTER

COLLECTION DESIGNER
PATRICK SATTERFIELD

DIGITAL ART TECHNICIAN
CHISTIANNE GOUDREAU

SPECIAL THANKS TO NICOLE SPIEGEL AND CAROL ROEDER AT TWENTIETH CENTURY FOX, DANIEL KAMINSKY, BECCA J. SADOWSKY, RANDY STRADLEY, SPENCER CUSHING, AND MEGAN WALKER.

———————

NEIL HANKERSON Executive Vice President • TOM WEDDLE Chief Financial Officer • RANDY STRADLEY Vice President of Publishing • MATT PARKINSON Vice President of Marketing • DAVID SCROGGY Vice President of Product Development • DALE LaFOUNTAIN Vice President of Information Technology • CARA NIECE Vice President of Production and Scheduling • NICK McWHORTER Vice President of Media Licensing • MARK BERNARDI Vice President of Book Trade and Digital Sales • KEN LIZZI General Counsel • DAVE MARSHALL Editor in Chief • DAVEY ESTRADA Editorial Director • SCOTT ALLIE Executive Senior Editor • CHRIS WARNER Senior Books Editor • CARY GRAZZINI Director of Specialty Projects • LIA RIBACCHI Art Director • VANESSA TODD Director of Print Purchasing MATT DRYER Director of Digital Art and Prepress • SARAH ROBERTSON Director of Product Sales MICHAEL GOMBOS Director of International Publishing and Licensing

This volume collects the miniseries *Serenity: No Power in the 'Verse #1–#6*, originally published October 2016 through March 2017, and the short story "The Warrior and the Wind," from *Free Comic Book Day 2016*.

Published by Dark Horse Books
A division of Dark Horse Comics, Inc.
10956 SE Main Street
Milwaukie, OR 97222

DarkHorse.com

To find a comics shop in your area, call the
Comic Shop Locator Service toll-free at (888) 266-4226.
International Licensing: (503) 905-2377

First edition: July 2017

ISBN 978-1-50670-182-0

1 3 5 7 9 10 8 6 4 2
Printed in China

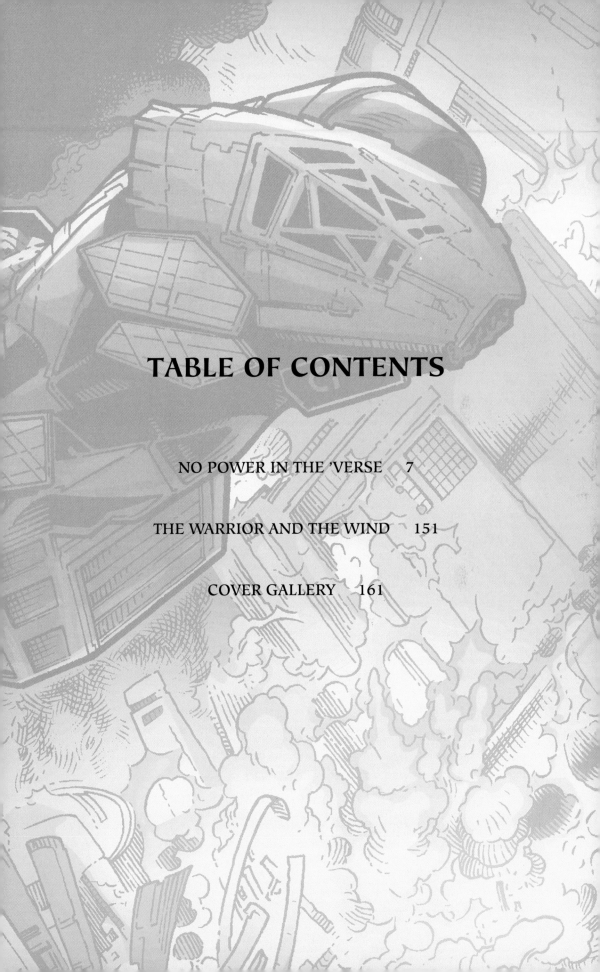

TABLE OF CONTENTS

Illustration by Adam Hughes

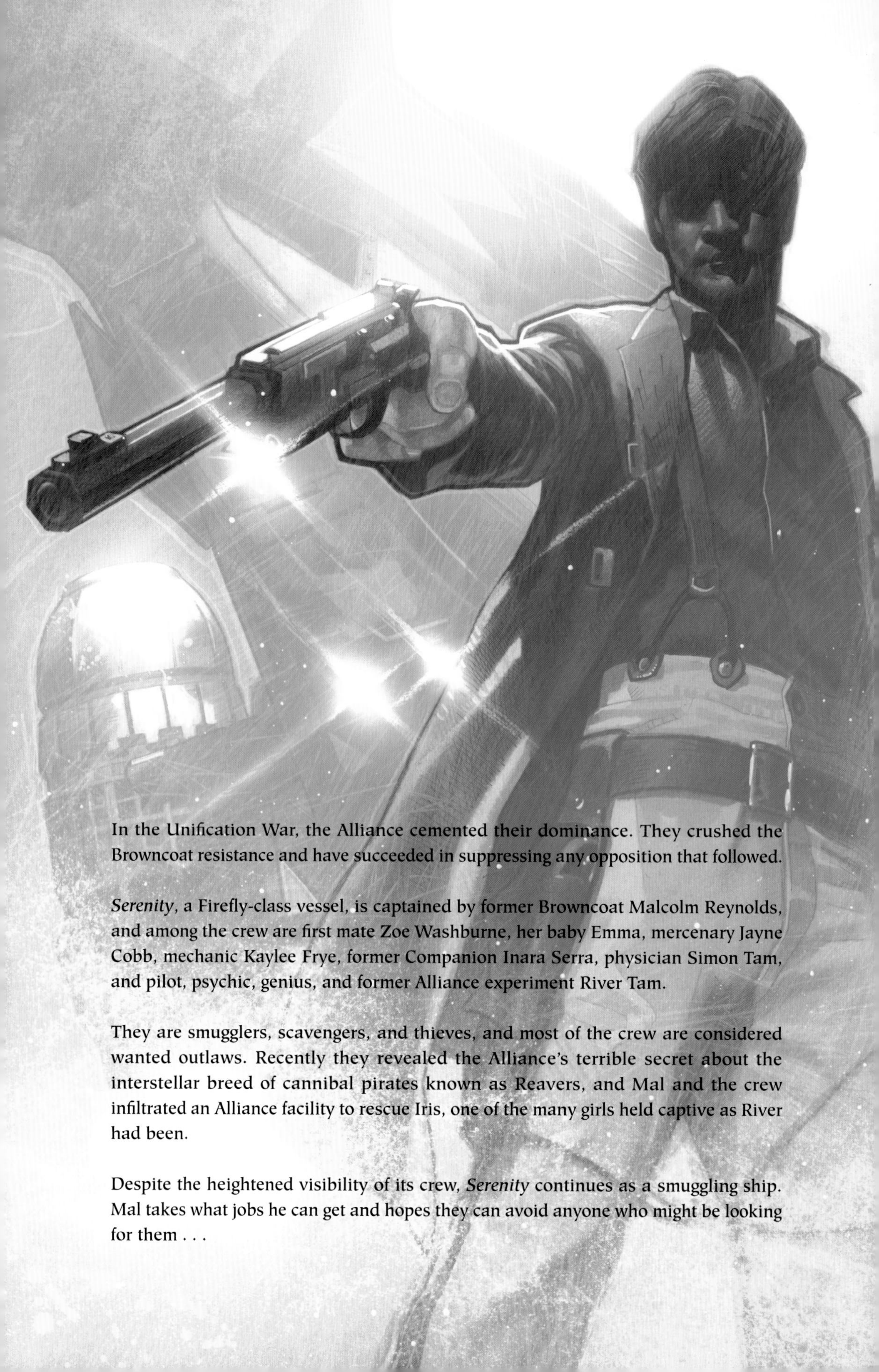

In the Unification War, the Alliance cemented their dominance. They crushed the Browncoat resistance and have succeeded in suppressing any opposition that followed.

Serenity, a Firefly-class vessel, is captained by former Browncoat Malcolm Reynolds, and among the crew are first mate Zoe Washburne, her baby Emma, mercenary Jayne Cobb, mechanic Kaylee Frye, former Companion Inara Serra, physician Simon Tam, and pilot, psychic, genius, and former Alliance experiment River Tam.

They are smugglers, scavengers, and thieves, and most of the crew are considered wanted outlaws. Recently they revealed the Alliance's terrible secret about the interstellar breed of cannibal pirates known as Reavers, and Mal and the crew infiltrated an Alliance facility to rescue Iris, one of the many girls held captive as River had been.

Despite the heightened visibility of its crew, *Serenity* continues as a smuggling ship. Mal takes what jobs he can get and hopes they can avoid anyone who might be looking for them . . .

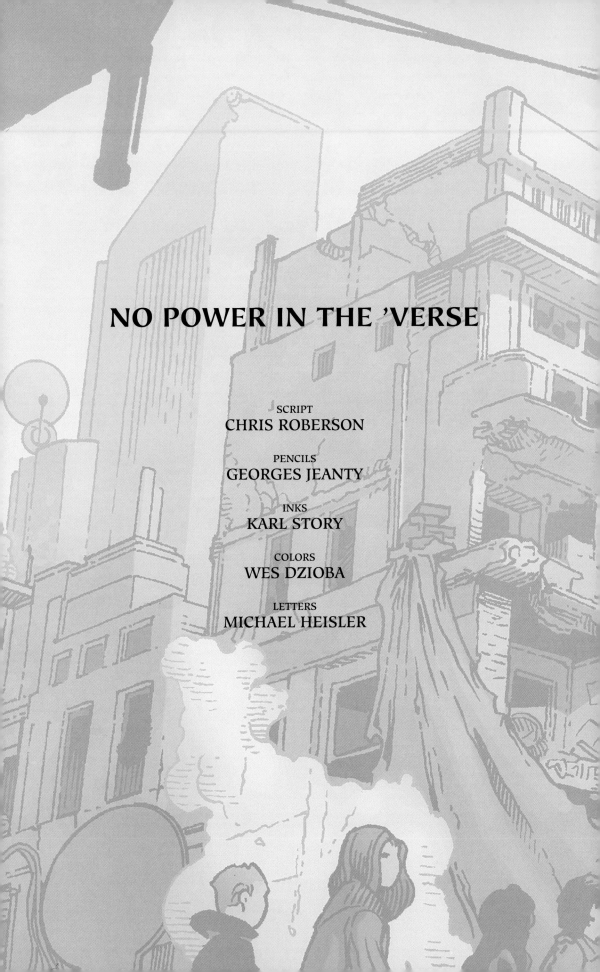

NO POWER IN THE 'VERSE

SCRIPT
CHRIS ROBERSON

PENCILS
GEORGES JEANTY

INKS
KARL STORY

COLORS
WES DZIOBA

LETTERS
MICHAEL HEISLER

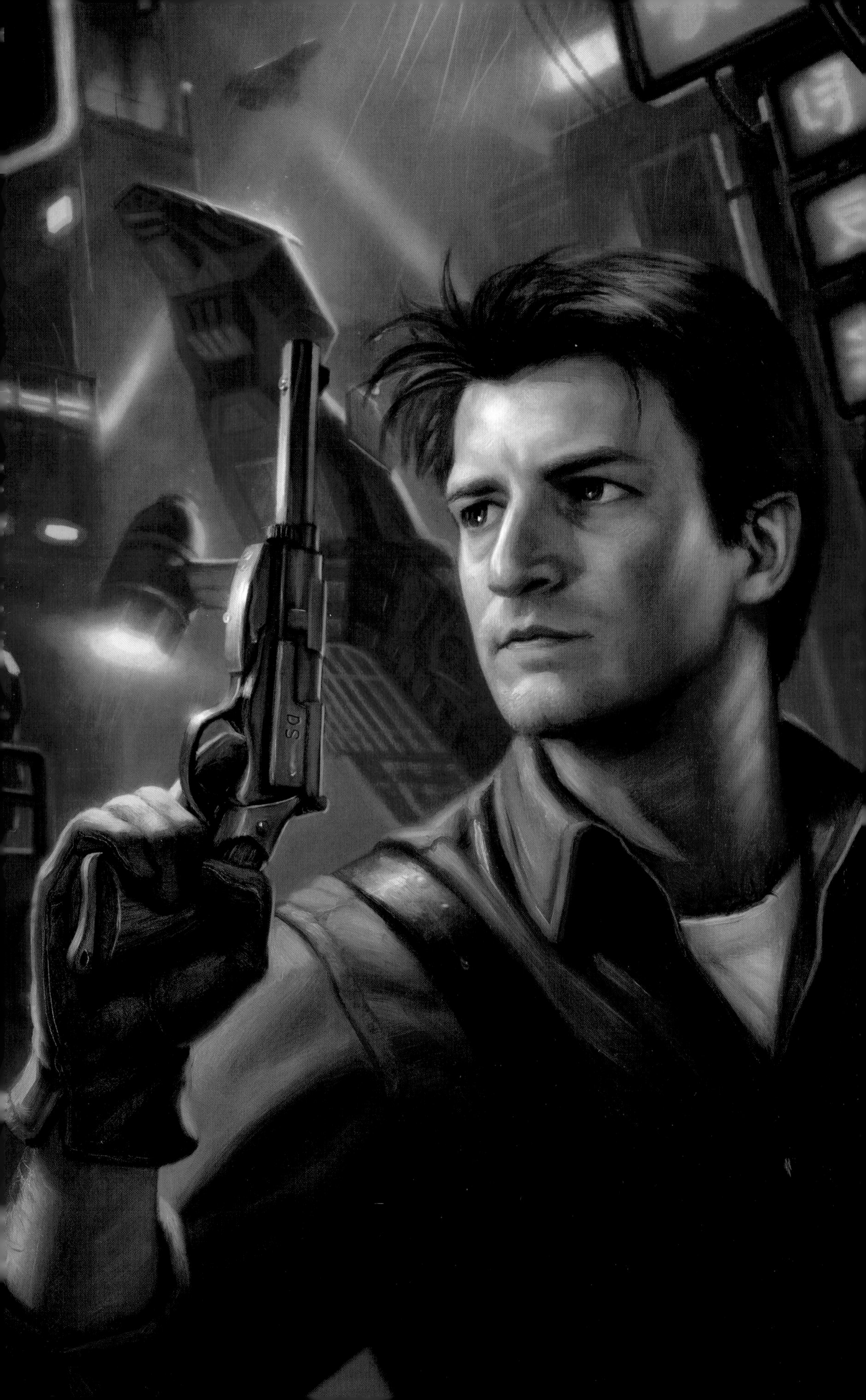

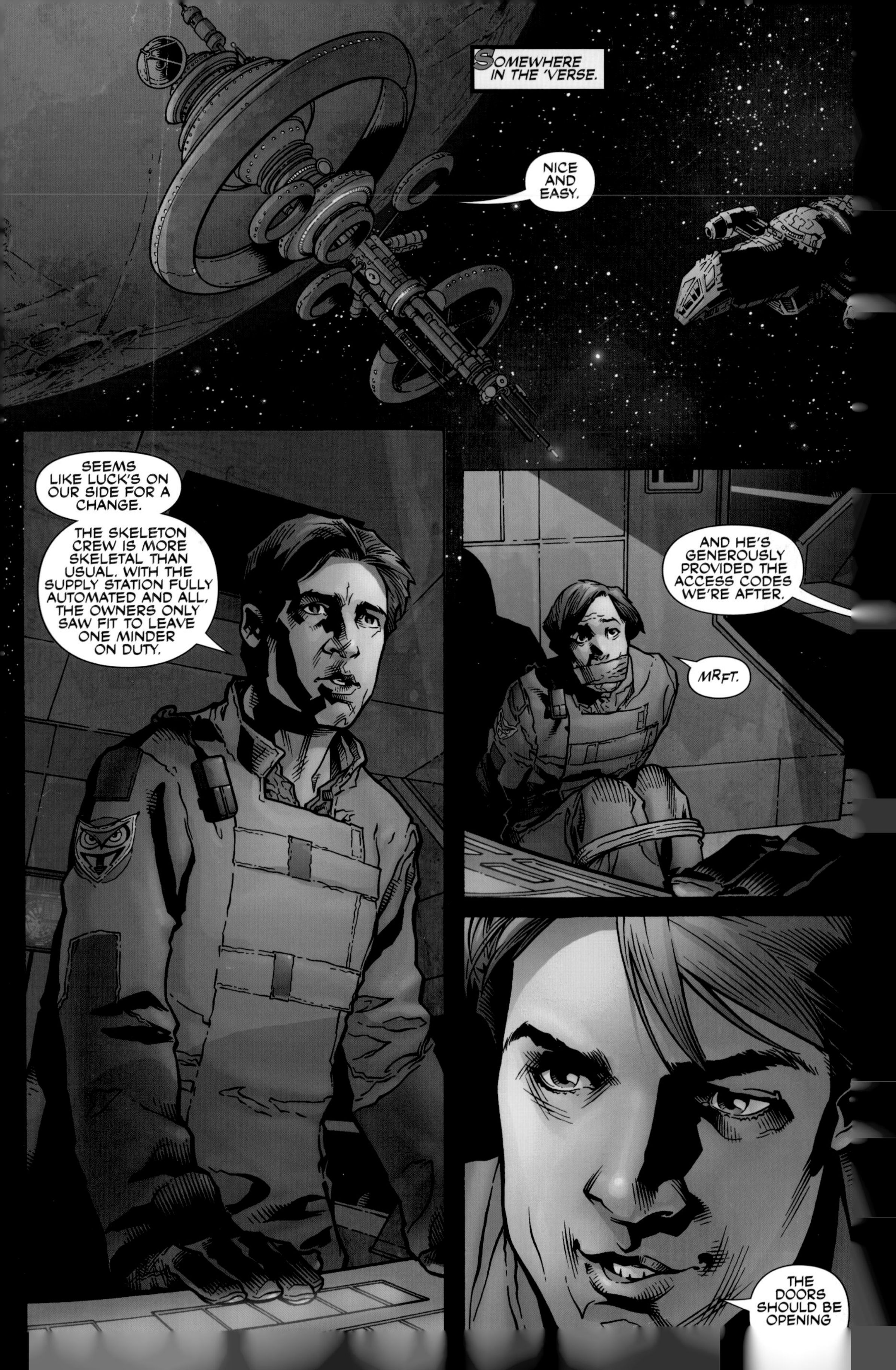
SOMEWHERE IN THE 'VERSE.
NICE AND EASY.
SEEMS LIKE LUCK'S ON OUR SIDE FOR A CHANGE.
THE SKELETON CREW IS MORE SKELETAL THAN USUAL. WITH THE SUPPLY STATION FULLY AUTOMATED AND ALL, THE OWNERS ONLY SAW FIT TO LEAVE ONE MINDER ON DUTY.
AND HE'S GENEROUSLY PROVIDED THE ACCESS CODES WE'RE AFTER.
MRFT.
THE DOORS SHOULD BE OPENING

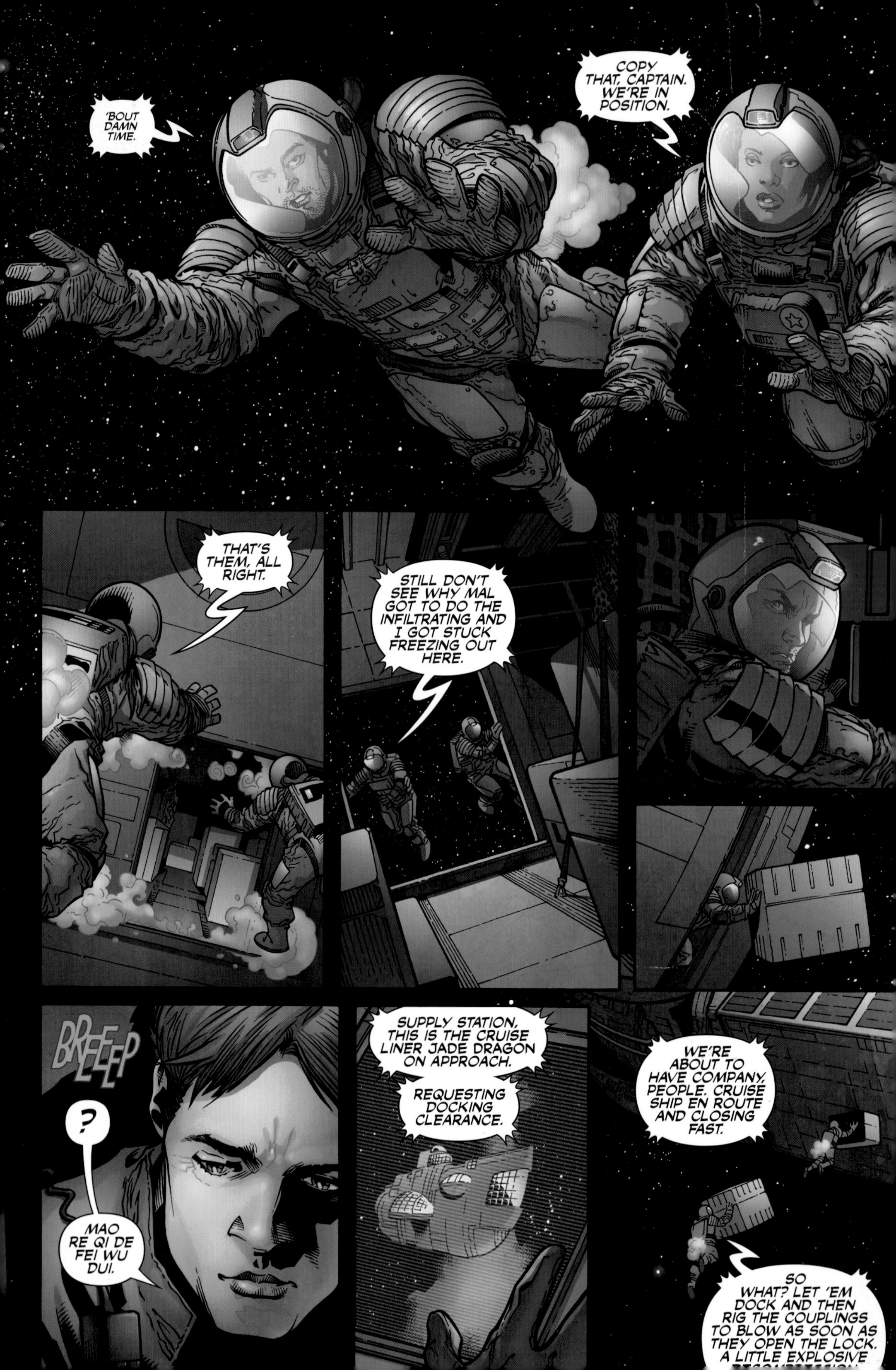
'BOUT DAMN TIME.
COPY THAT, CAPTAIN. WE'RE IN POSITION.
THAT'S THEM, ALL RIGHT.
STILL DON'T SEE WHY MAL GOT TO DO THE INFILTRATING AND I GOT STUCK FREEZING OUT HERE.
BREEEP
?
MAO RE QI DE FEI WU DUI.
SUPPLY STATION, THIS IS THE CRUISE LINER JADE DRAGON ON APPROACH.
REQUESTING DOCKING CLEARANCE.
WE'RE ABOUT TO HAVE COMPANY, PEOPLE. CRUISE SHIP EN ROUTE AND CLOSING FAST.
SO WHAT? LET 'EM DOCK AND THEN RIG THE COUPLINGS TO BLOW AS SOON AS THEY OPEN THE LOCK. A LITTLE EXPLOSIVE

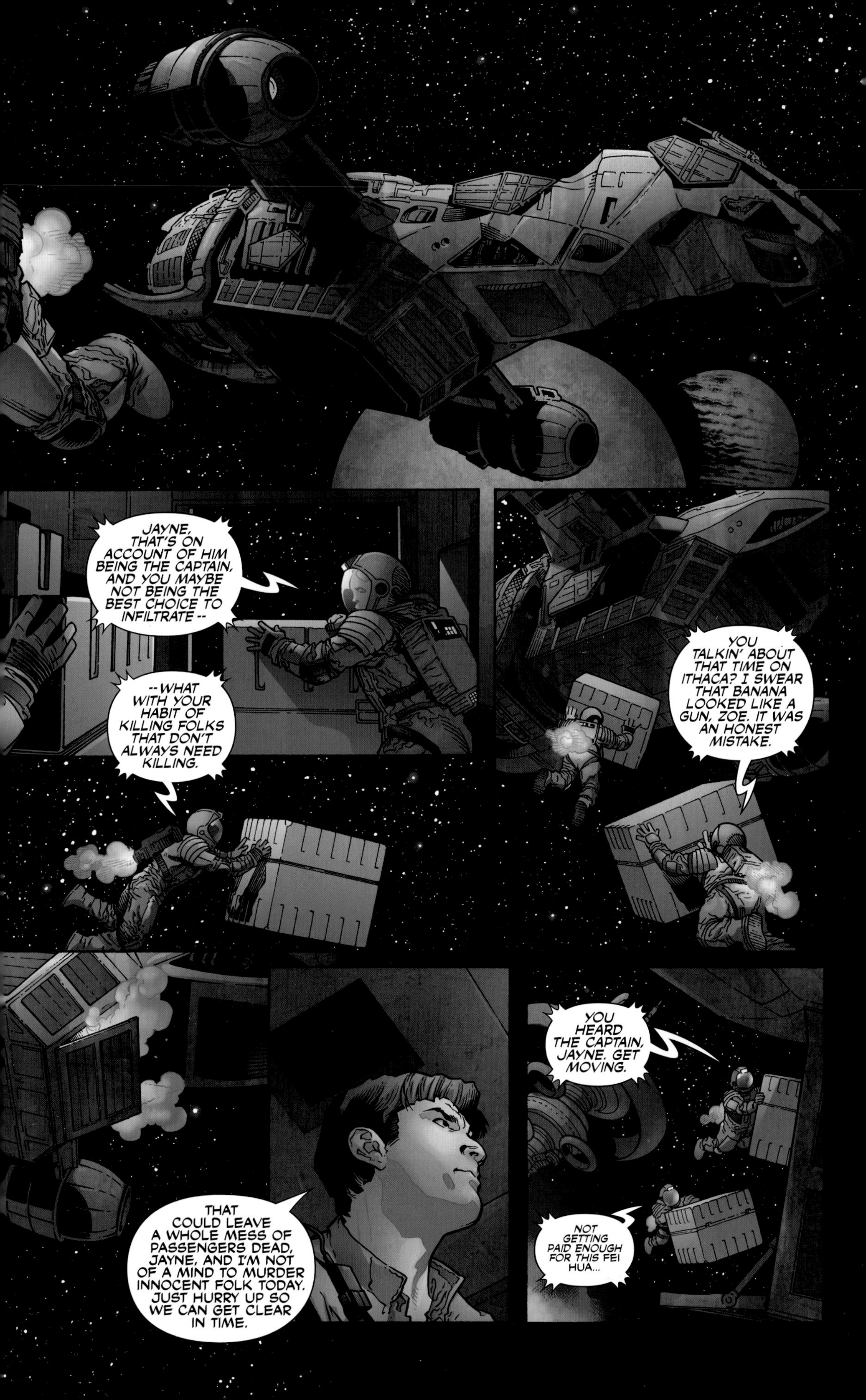
JAYNE, THAT'S ON ACCOUNT OF HIM BEING THE CAPTAIN, AND YOU MAYBE NOT BEING THE BEST CHOICE TO INFILTRATE --
--WHAT WITH YOUR HABIT OF KILLING FOLKS THAT DON'T ALWAYS NEED KILLING.
YOU TALKIN' ABOUT THAT TIME ON ITHACA? I SWEAR THAT BANANA LOOKED LIKE A GUN, ZOE. IT WAS AN HONEST MISTAKE.
THAT COULD LEAVE A WHOLE MESS OF PASSENGERS DEAD, JAYNE, AND I'M NOT OF A MIND TO MURDER INNOCENT FOLK TODAY. JUST HURRY UP SO WE CAN GET CLEAR IN TIME.
YOU HEARD THE CAPTAIN, JAYNE. GET MOVING.
NOT GETTING PAID ENOUGH FOR THIS FEI HUA...

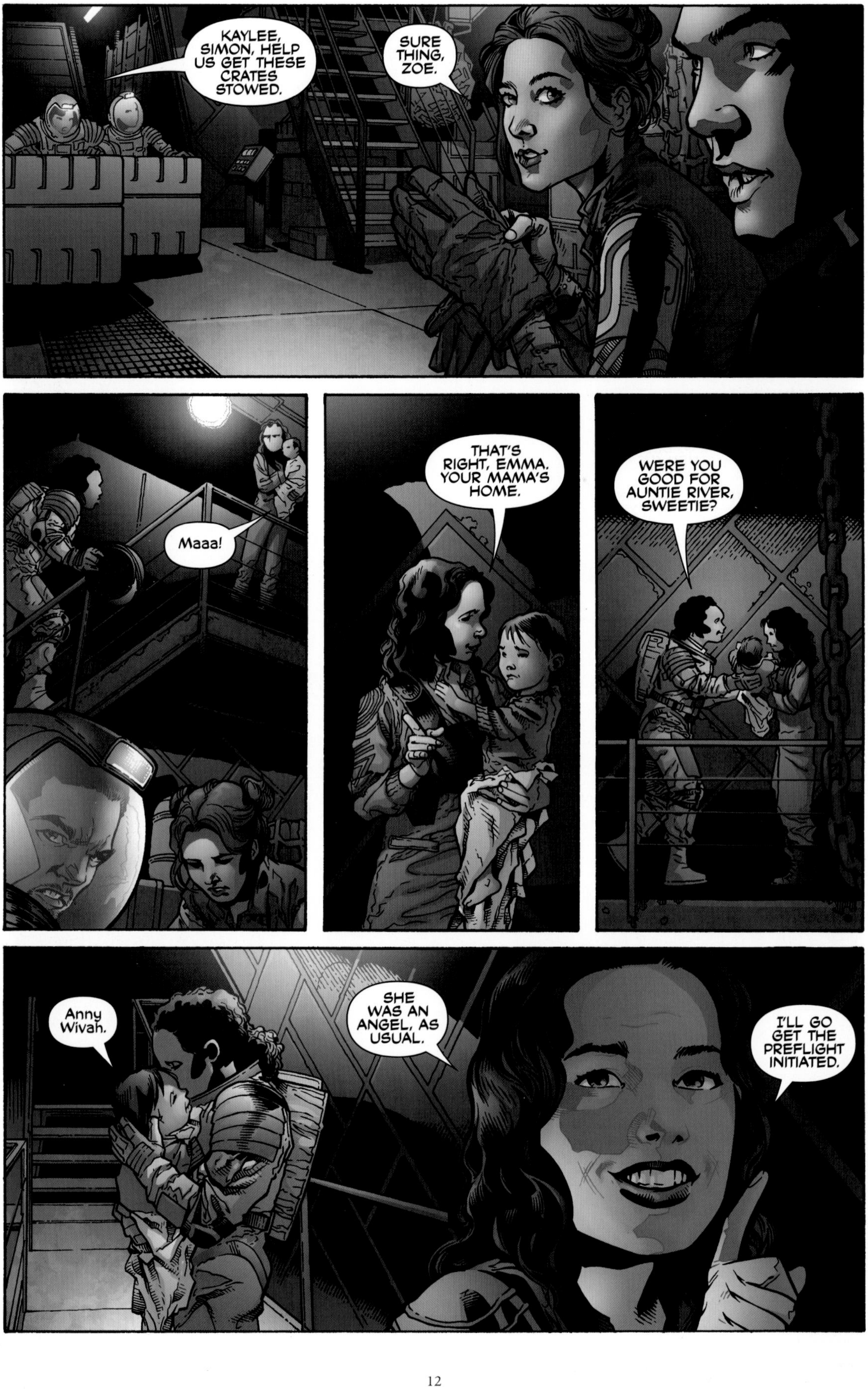
KAYLEE, SIMON, HELP US GET THESE CRATES STOWED.
SURE THING, ZOE.
Maaa!
THAT'S RIGHT, EMMA. YOUR MAMA'S HOME.
WERE YOU GOOD FOR AUNTIE RIVER, SWEETIE?
Anny Wivah.
SHE WAS AN ANGEL, AS USUAL.
I'LL GO GET THE PREFLIGHT INITIATED.

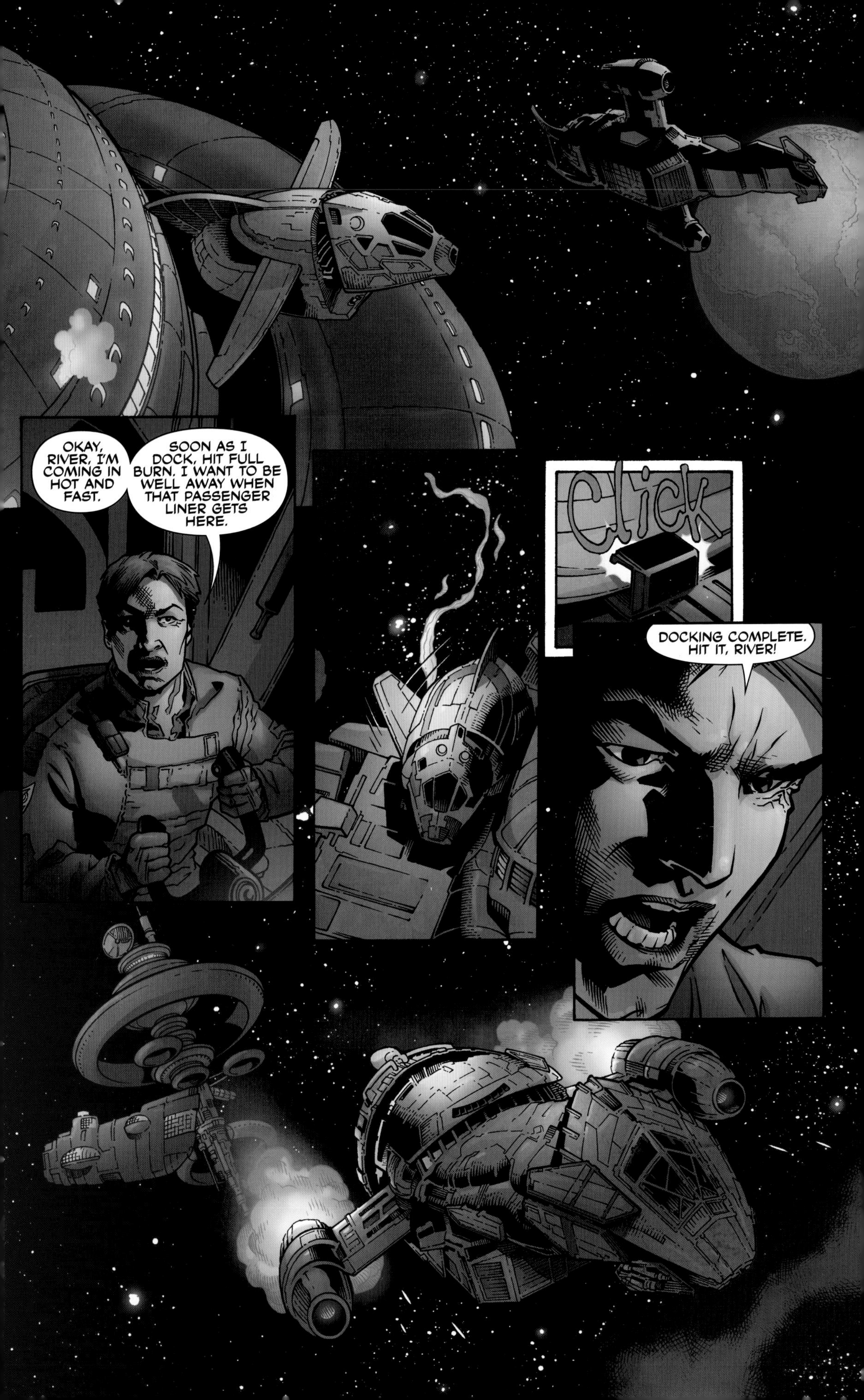
OKAY, RIVER, I'M COMING IN HOT AND FAST.
SOON AS I DOCK, HIT FULL BURN. I WANT TO BE WELL AWAY WHEN THAT PASSENGER LINER GETS HERE.
CLICK
DOCKING COMPLETE. HIT IT, RIVER!

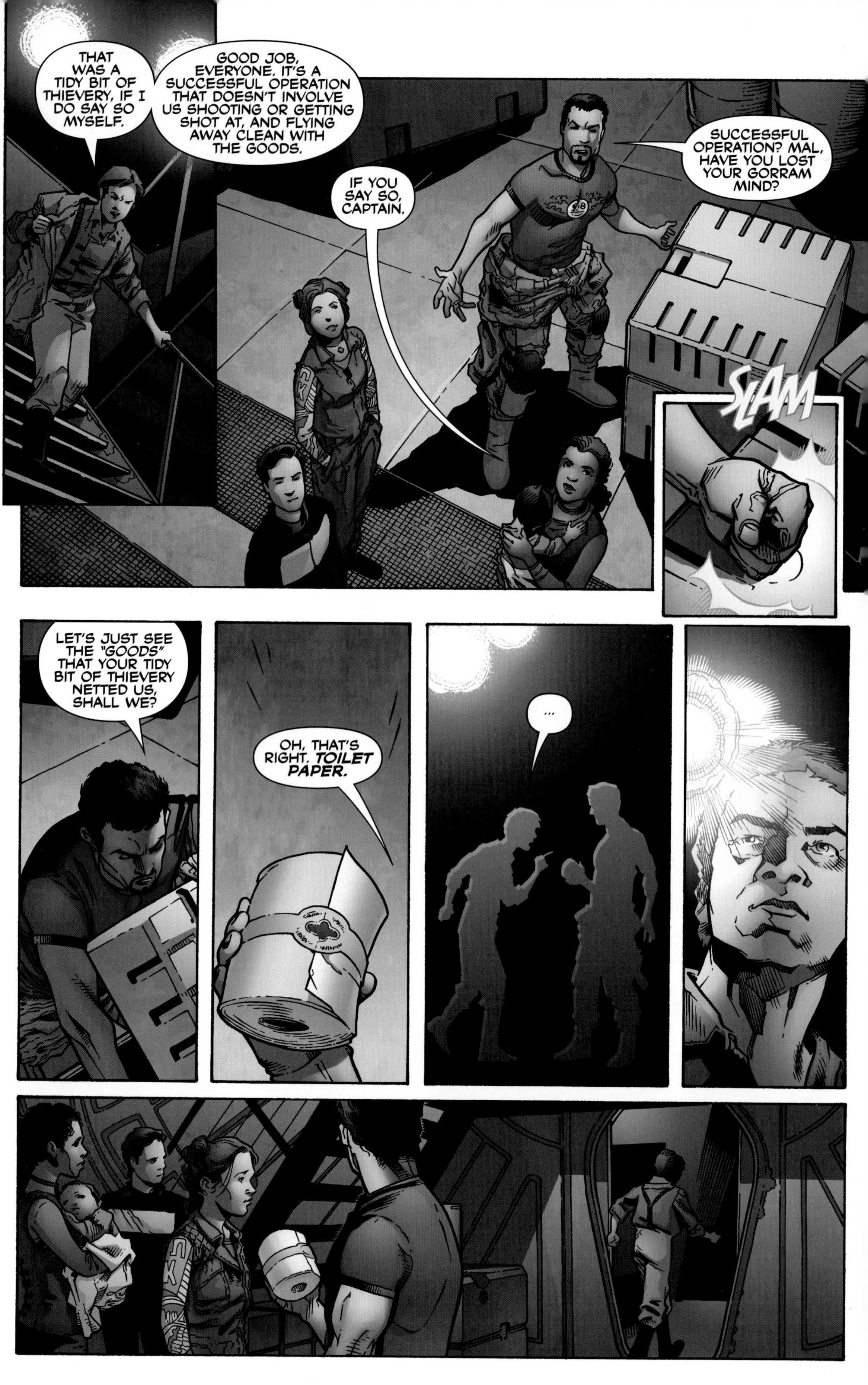
THAT WAS A TIDY BIT OF THIEVERY, IF I DO SAY SO MYSELF.
GOOD JOB, EVERYONE. IT'S A SUCCESSFUL OPERATION THAT DOESN'T INVOLVE US SHOOTING OR GETTING SHOT AT, AND FLYING AWAY CLEAN WITH THE GOODS.
IF YOU SAY SO, CAPTAIN.
SUCCESSFUL OPERATION? MAL, HAVE YOU LOST YOUR GORRAM MIND?
SLAM
LET'S JUST SEE THE "GOODS" THAT YOUR TIDY BIT OF THIEVERY NETTED US, SHALL WE?
OH, THAT'S RIGHT. TOILET PAPER.
...

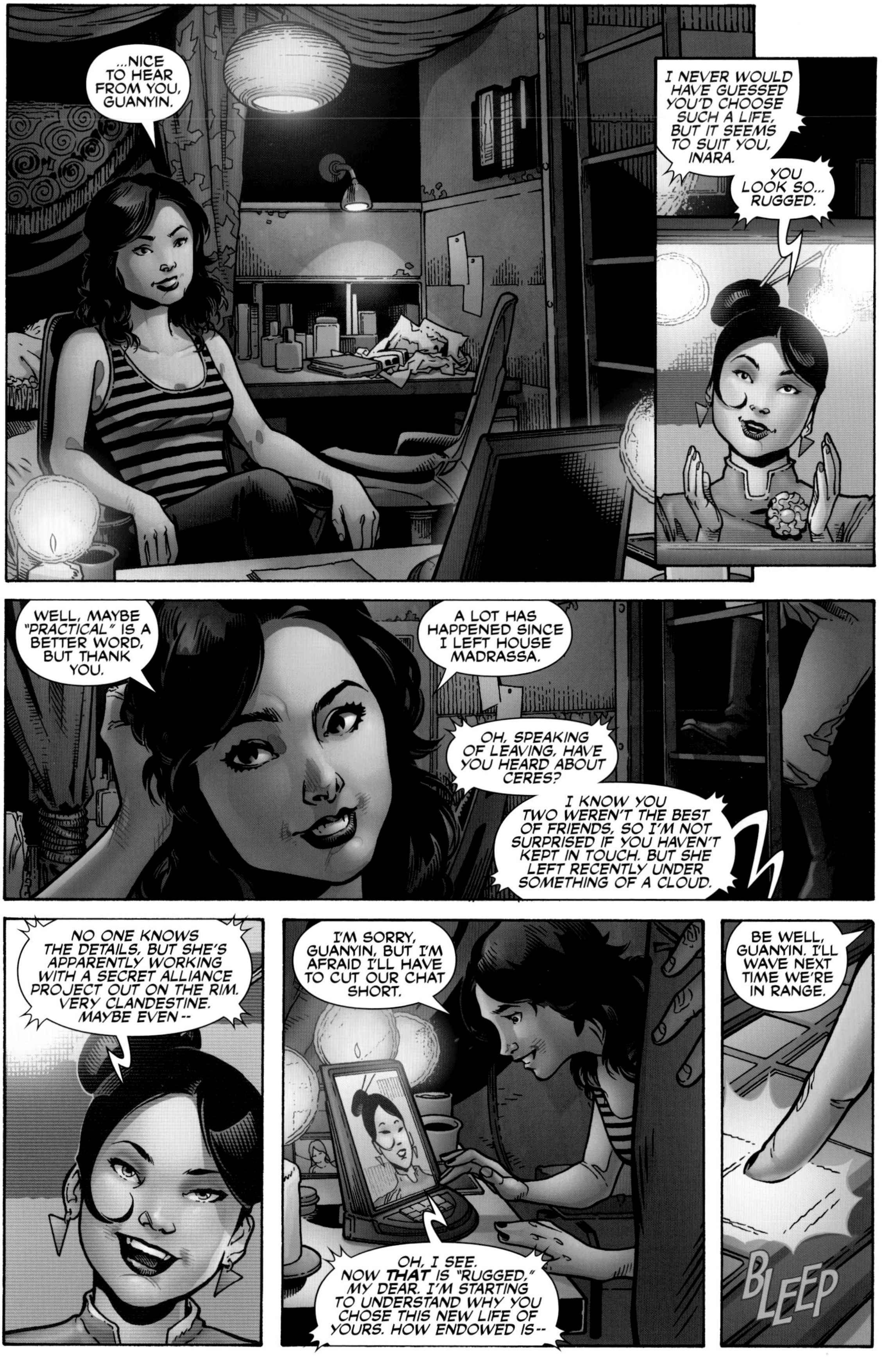
...NICE TO HEAR FROM YOU, GUANYIN.
I NEVER WOULD HAVE GUESSED YOU'D CHOOSE SUCH A LIFE, BUT IT SEEMS TO SUIT YOU, INARA.
YOU LOOK SO... RUGGED.
WELL, MAYBE "PRACTICAL" IS A BETTER WORD, BUT THANK YOU.
A LOT HAS HAPPENED SINCE I LEFT HOUSE MADRASSA.
OH, SPEAKING OF LEAVING, HAVE YOU HEARD ABOUT CERES?
I KNOW YOU TWO WEREN'T THE BEST OF FRIENDS, SO I'M NOT SURPRISED IF YOU HAVEN'T KEPT IN TOUCH. BUT SHE LEFT RECENTLY UNDER SOMETHING OF A CLOUD.
NO ONE KNOWS THE DETAILS, BUT SHE'S APPARENTLY WORKING WITH A SECRET ALLIANCE PROJECT OUT ON THE RIM. VERY CLANDESTINE. MAYBE EVEN --
I'M SORRY, GUANYIN, BUT I'M AFRAID I'LL HAVE TO CUT OUR CHAT SHORT.
OH, I SEE. NOW **THAT** IS "RUGGED," MY DEAR. I'M STARTING TO UNDERSTAND WHY YOU CHOSE THIS NEW LIFE OF YOURS. HOW ENDOWED IS --
BE WELL, GUANYIN. I'LL WAVE NEXT TIME WE'RE IN RANGE.
BLEEP

DIDN'T MEAN TO INTERRUPT. WHAT WAS THAT ABOUT "ENDOWED"?

OH, NOTHING. JUST TALKING TO AN OLD FRIEND BACK ON SIHNON.

HOW DID THE JOB GO?

A ROUSING SUCCESS. WE SHOULD BE ABLE TO UNLOAD THE GOODS WITHOUT TROUBLE NEXT RIM WORLD WE HIT.

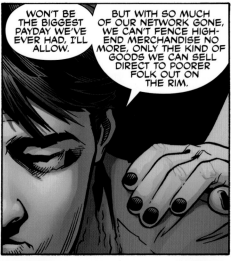

WON'T BE THE BIGGEST PAYDAY WE'VE EVER HAD, I'LL ALLOW.

BUT WITH SO MUCH OF OUR NETWORK GONE, WE CAN'T FENCE HIGH-END MERCHANDISE NO MORE, ONLY THE KIND OF GOODS WE CAN SELL DIRECT TO POORER FOLK OUT ON THE RIM.

LIKE TOILET PAPER?

EVERYBODY'S GOT TO WIPE, AND THERE'S MANY WHO'LL PAY FOR THE PRIVILEGE.

BUT THESE SMALL-TIME JOBS AREN'T CUTTING IT.

WE NEED A *BIG* WIN, SOMETHING THAT WILL KEEP FOOD ON THE TABLE AND MY BOAT IN THE SKY.

LUCK'S GOT TO TURN SOONER OR LATER.

MAL, TALKING WITH MY FRIEND JUST NOW...IT MADE ME THINK...

I'VE NEVER TOLD YOU THE REASON WHY I LEFT SIHNON.

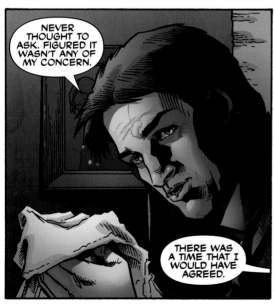

NEVER THOUGHT TO ASK, FIGURED IT WASN'T ANY OF MY CONCERN.

THERE WAS A TIME THAT I WOULD HAVE AGREED.

BUT THINGS HAVE CHANGED BETWEEN US, AND I FEEL LIKE YOU HAVE A RIGHT TO KNOW THAT--

SLAM

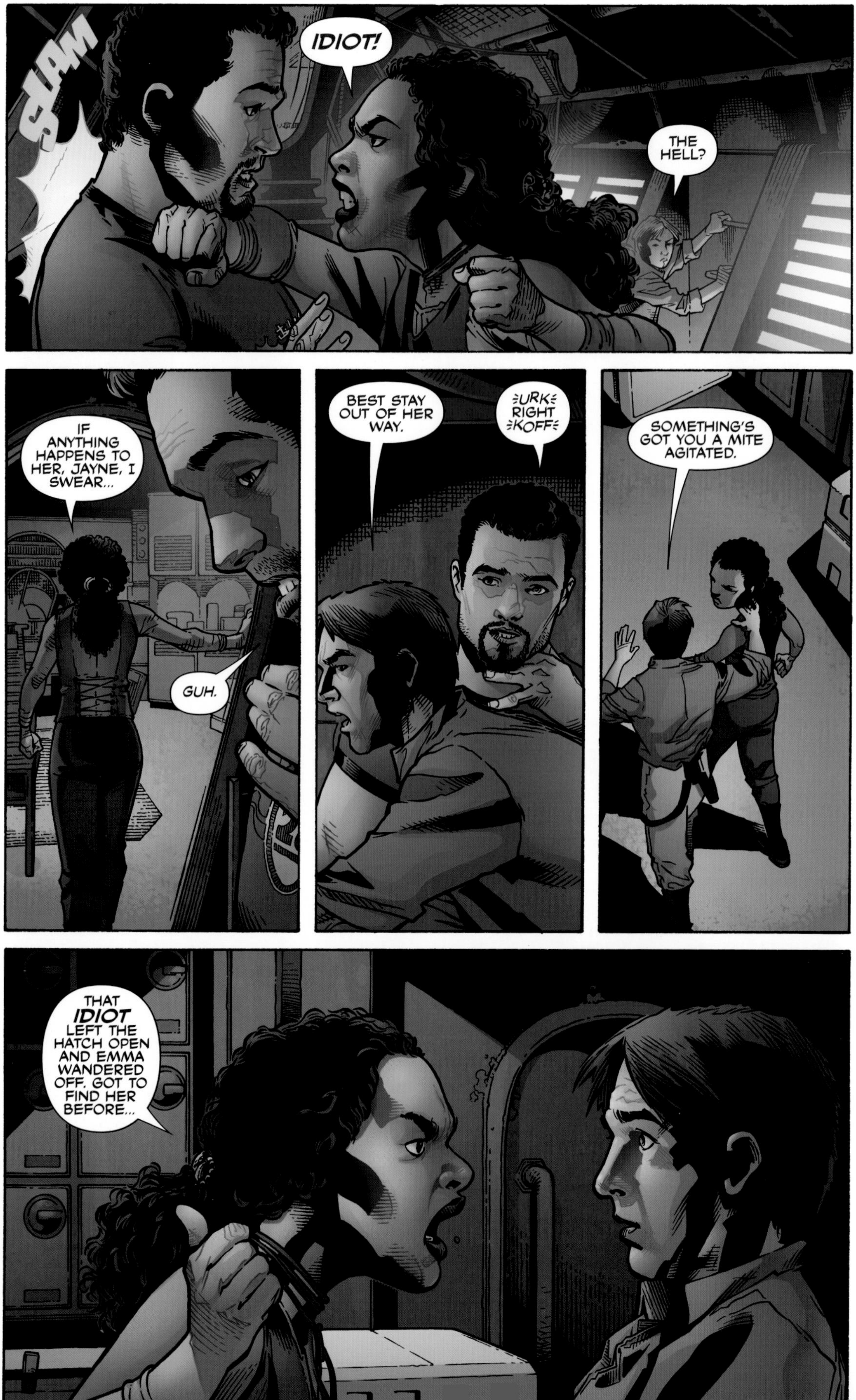
SLAM
IDIOT!
THE HELL?
IF ANYTHING HAPPENS TO HER, JAYNE, I SWEAR...
GUH.
BEST STAY OUT OF HER WAY.
URK RIGHT KOFF
SOMETHING'S GOT YOU A MITE AGITATED.
THAT IDIOT LEFT THE HATCH OPEN AND EMMA WANDERED OFF. GOT TO FIND HER BEFORE...

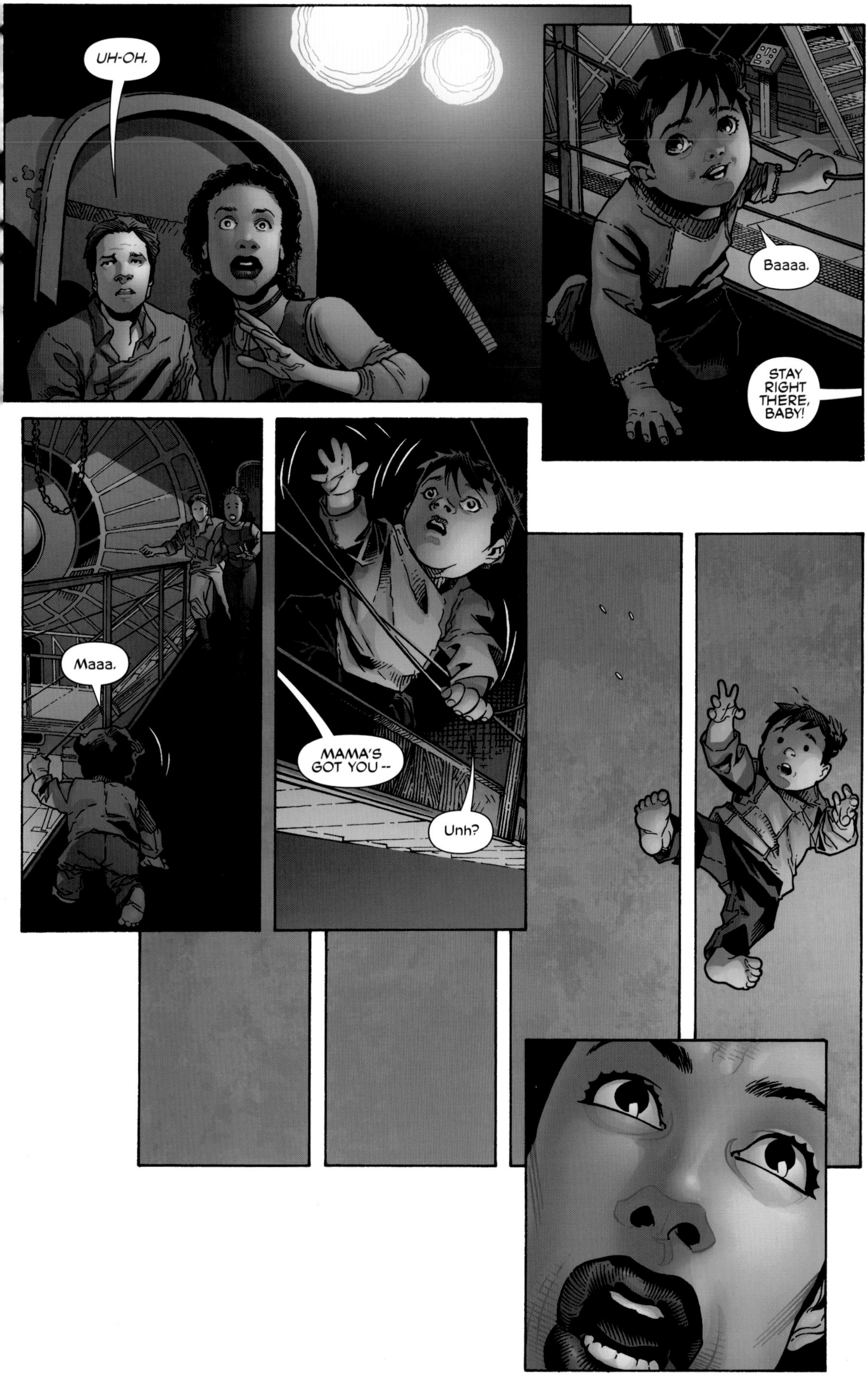
UH-OH.
Baaaa.
STAY RIGHT THERE, BABY!
Maaa.
MAMA'S GOT YOU --
Unh?

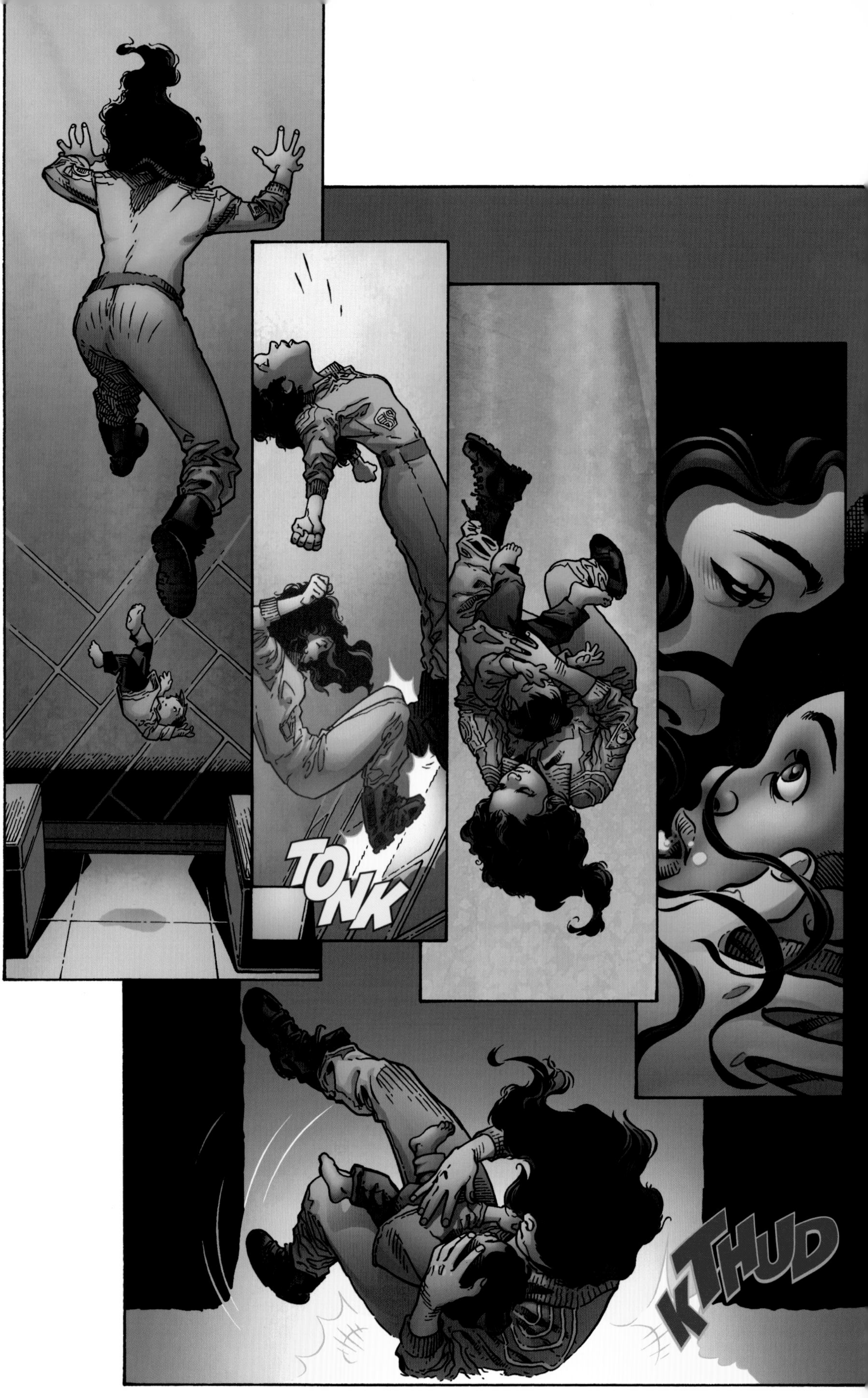
TONK
KTHUD

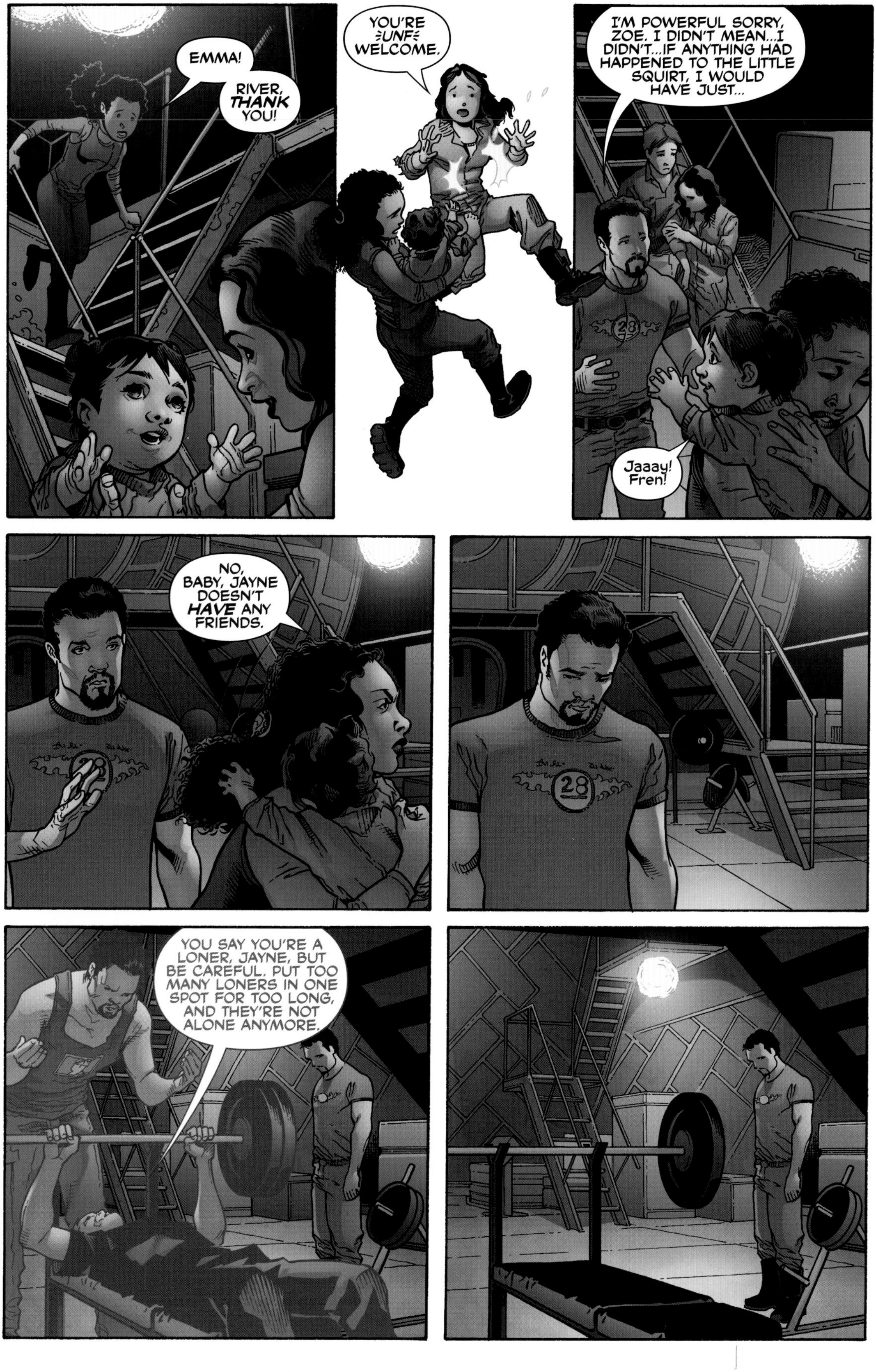
EMMA!
RIVER, THANK YOU!
YOU'RE =UNF= WELCOME.
I'M POWERFUL SORRY, ZOE. I DIDN'T MEAN...I DIDN'T...IF ANYTHING HAD HAPPENED TO THE LITTLE SQUIRT, I WOULD HAVE JUST...
Jaaay! Fren!
NO, BABY, JAYNE DOESN'T HAVE ANY FRIENDS.
YOU SAY YOU'RE A LONER, JAYNE, BUT BE CAREFUL. PUT TOO MANY LONERS IN ONE SPOT FOR TOO LONG, AND THEY'RE NOT ALONE ANYMORE.

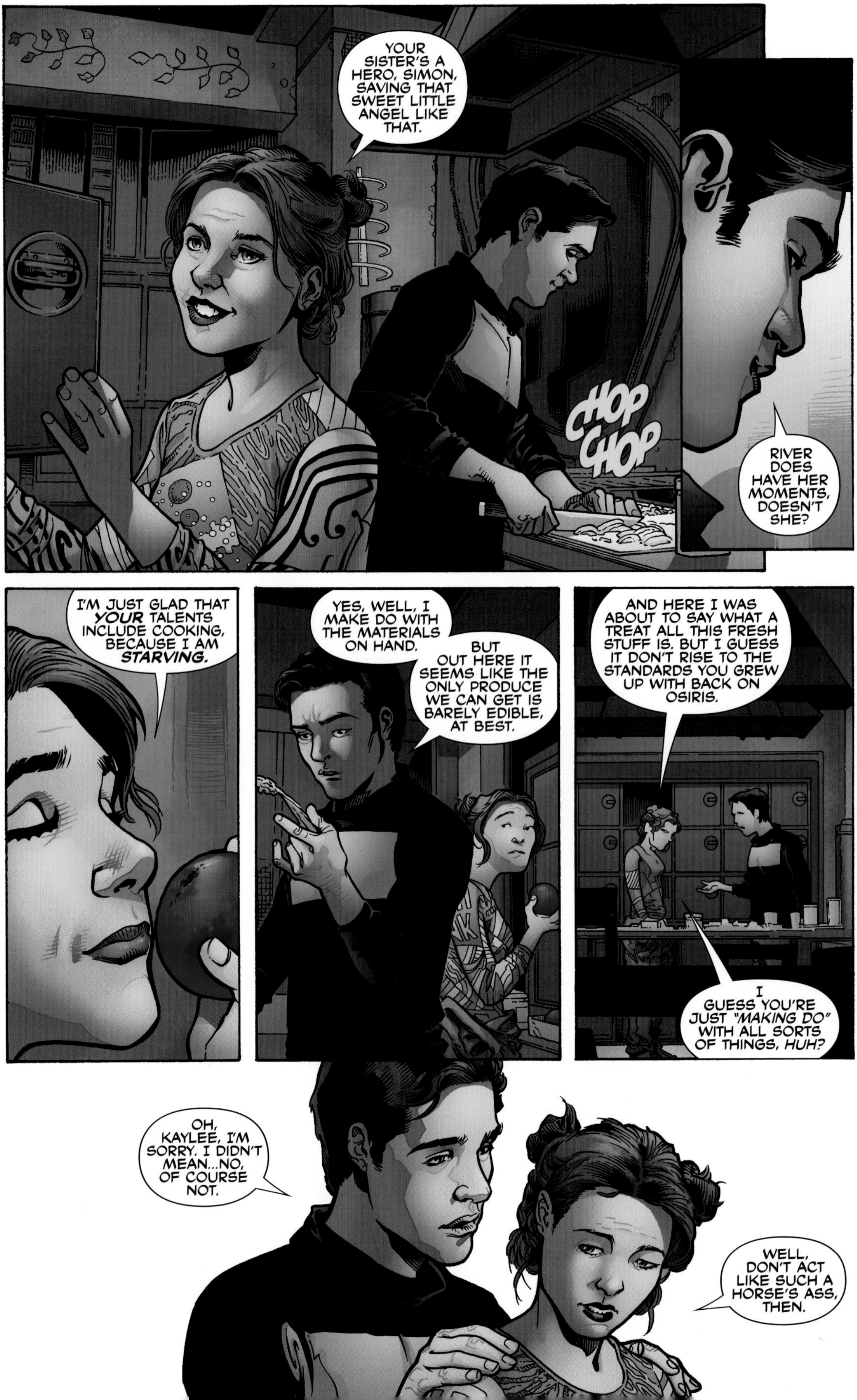
YOUR SISTER'S A HERO, SIMON, SAVING THAT SWEET LITTLE ANGEL LIKE THAT.
CHOP CHOP
RIVER DOES HAVE HER MOMENTS, DOESN'T SHE?
I'M JUST GLAD THAT *YOUR* TALENTS INCLUDE COOKING, BECAUSE I AM ***STARVING.***
YES, WELL, I MAKE DO WITH THE MATERIALS ON HAND.
BUT OUT HERE IT SEEMS LIKE THE ONLY PRODUCE WE CAN GET IS BARELY EDIBLE, AT BEST.
AND HERE I WAS ABOUT TO SAY WHAT A TREAT ALL THIS FRESH STUFF IS. BUT I GUESS IT DON'T RISE TO THE STANDARDS YOU GREW UP WITH BACK ON OSIRIS.
I GUESS YOU'RE JUST *"MAKING DO"* WITH ALL SORTS OF THINGS, *HUH?*
OH, KAYLEE, I'M SORRY. I DIDN'T MEAN...NO, OF COURSE NOT.
WELL, DON'T ACT LIKE SUCH A HORSE'S ASS, THEN.

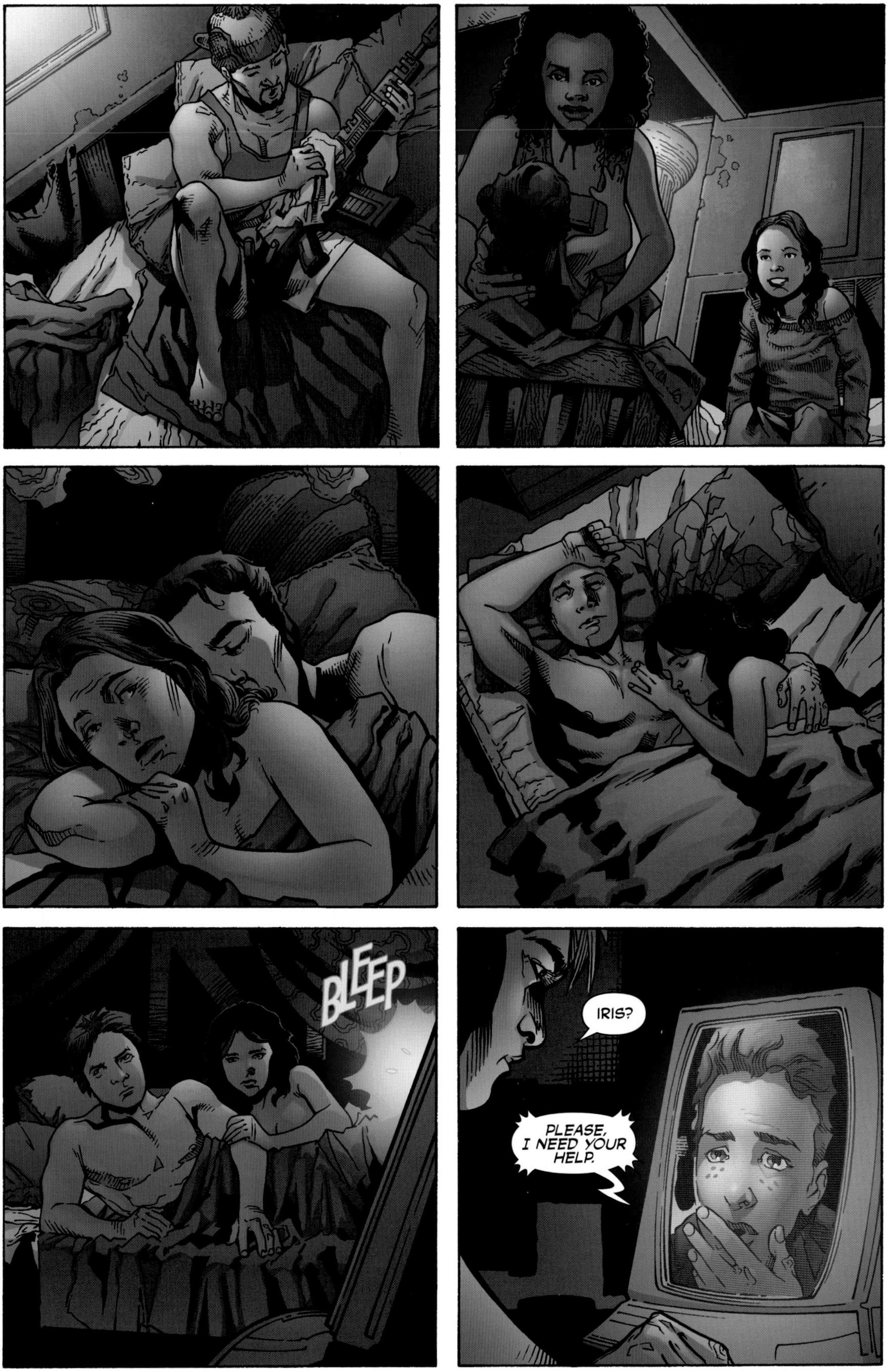
BLEEP
IRIS?
PLEASE, I NEED YOUR HELP.

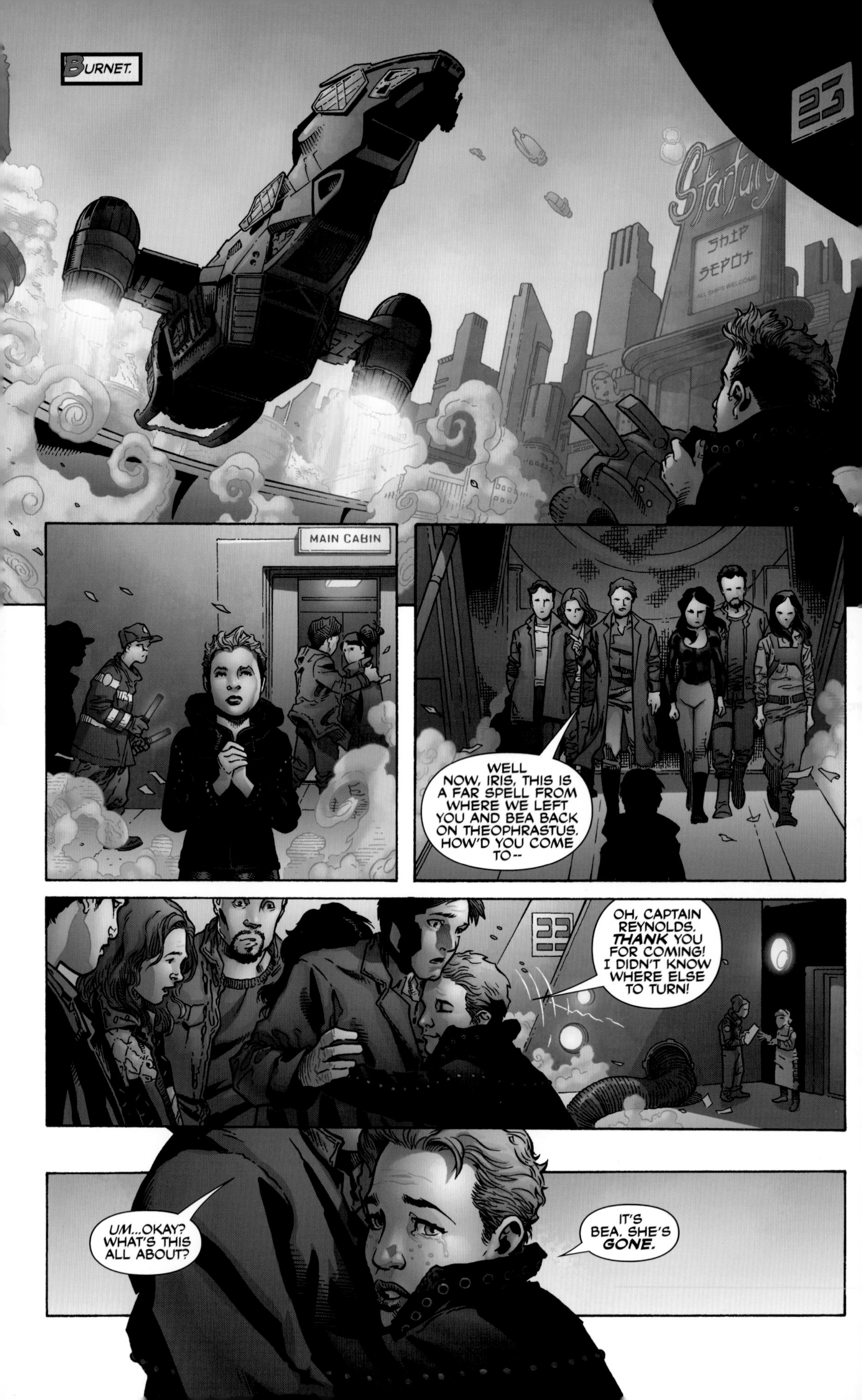
BURNET.
Starfury
SHIP DEPOT
ALL SHIPS WELCOME
MAIN CABIN
WELL NOW, IRIS, THIS IS A FAR SPELL FROM WHERE WE LEFT YOU AND BEA BACK ON THEOPHRASTUS. HOW'D YOU COME TO--
OH, CAPTAIN REYNOLDS. THANK YOU FOR COMING! I DIDN'T KNOW WHERE ELSE TO TURN!
UM...OKAY? WHAT'S THIS ALL ABOUT?
IT'S BEA. SHE'S GONE.

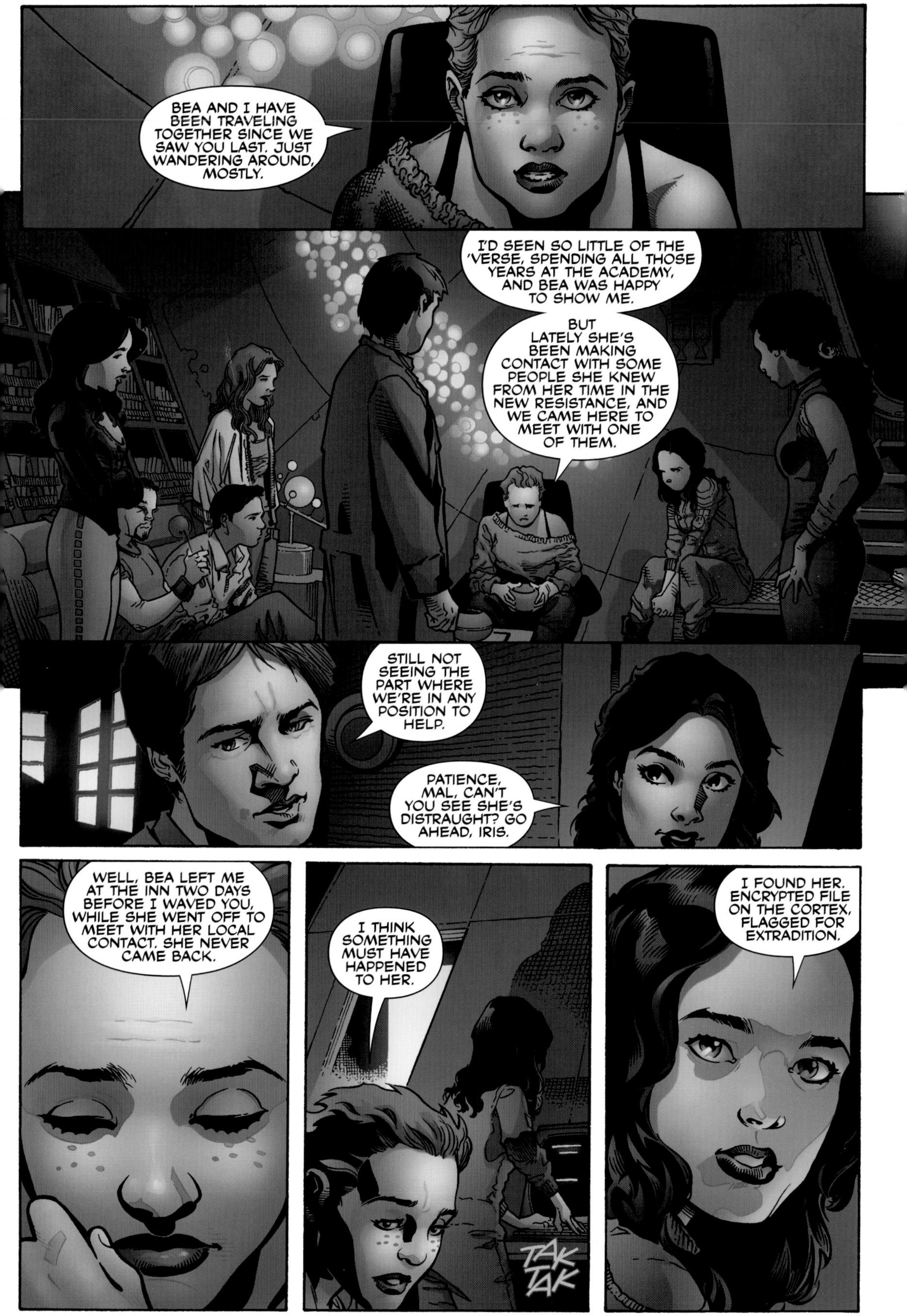
BEA AND I HAVE BEEN TRAVELING TOGETHER SINCE WE SAW YOU LAST. JUST WANDERING AROUND, MOSTLY.
I'D SEEN SO LITTLE OF THE 'VERSE, SPENDING ALL THOSE YEARS AT THE ACADEMY, AND BEA WAS HAPPY TO SHOW ME.
BUT LATELY SHE'S BEEN MAKING CONTACT WITH SOME PEOPLE SHE KNEW FROM HER TIME IN THE NEW RESISTANCE, AND WE CAME HERE TO MEET WITH ONE OF THEM.
STILL NOT SEEING THE PART WHERE WE'RE IN ANY POSITION TO HELP.
PATIENCE, MAL, CAN'T YOU SEE SHE'S DISTRAUGHT? GO AHEAD, IRIS.
WELL, BEA LEFT ME AT THE INN TWO DAYS BEFORE I WAVED YOU, WHILE SHE WENT OFF TO MEET WITH HER LOCAL CONTACT. SHE NEVER CAME BACK.
I THINK SOMETHING MUST HAVE HAPPENED TO HER.
TAK TAK
I FOUND HER. ENCRYPTED FILE ON THE CORTEX, FLAGGED FOR EXTRADITION.

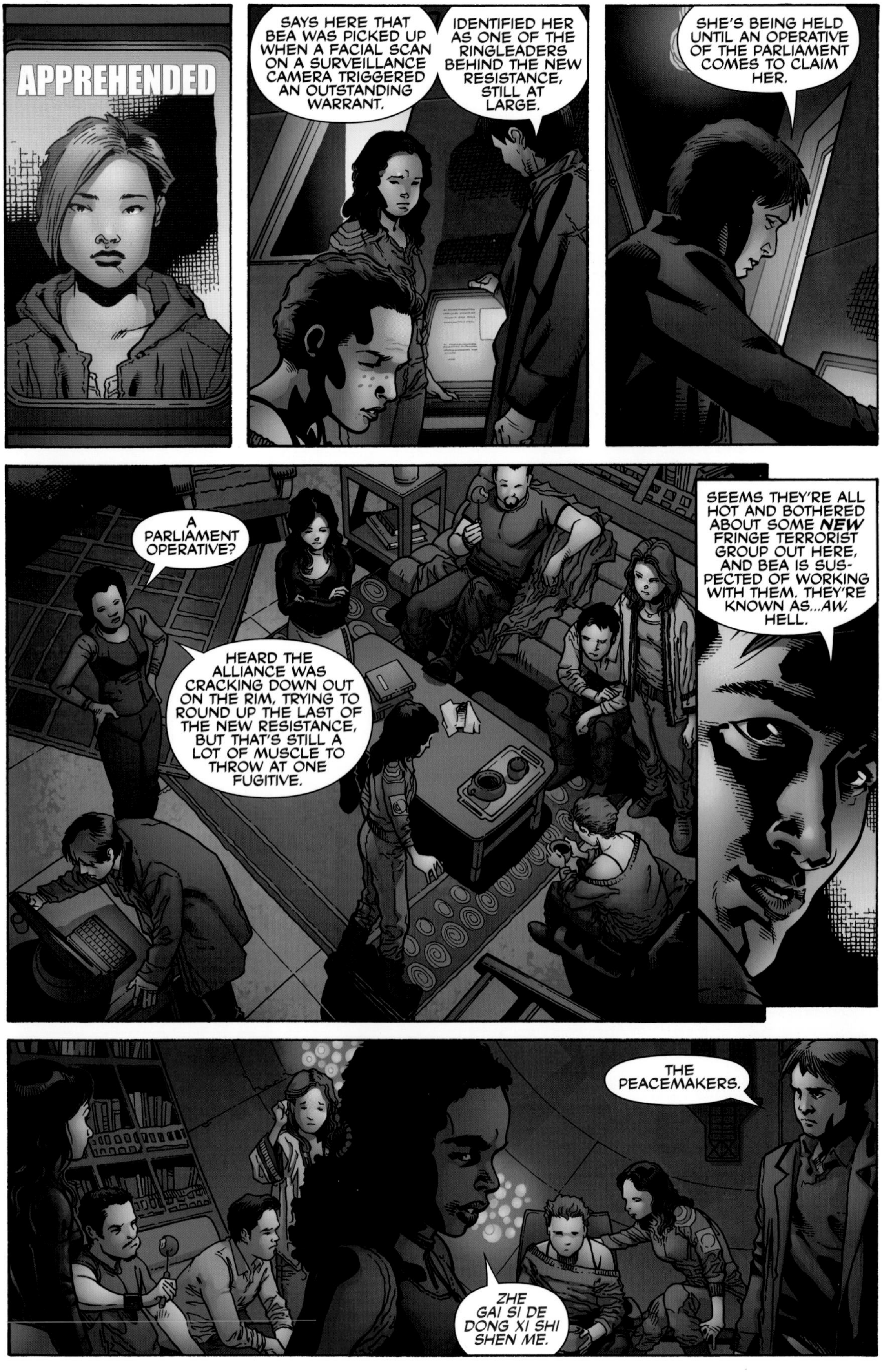
APPREHENDED
SAYS HERE THAT BEA WAS PICKED UP WHEN A FACIAL SCAN ON A SURVEILLANCE CAMERA TRIGGERED AN OUTSTANDING WARRANT.
IDENTIFIED HER AS ONE OF THE RINGLEADERS BEHIND THE NEW RESISTANCE, STILL AT LARGE.
SHE'S BEING HELD UNTIL AN OPERATIVE OF THE PARLIAMENT COMES TO CLAIM HER.
A PARLIAMENT OPERATIVE?
HEARD THE ALLIANCE WAS CRACKING DOWN OUT ON THE RIM, TRYING TO ROUND UP THE LAST OF THE NEW RESISTANCE, BUT THAT'S STILL A LOT OF MUSCLE TO THROW AT ONE FUGITIVE.
SEEMS THEY'RE ALL HOT AND BOTHERED ABOUT SOME *NEW* FRINGE TERRORIST GROUP OUT HERE, AND BEA IS SUSPECTED OF WORKING WITH THEM. THEY'RE KNOWN AS...*AW, HELL.*
THE PEACEMAKERS.
ZHE GAI SI DE DONG XI SHI SHEN ME.

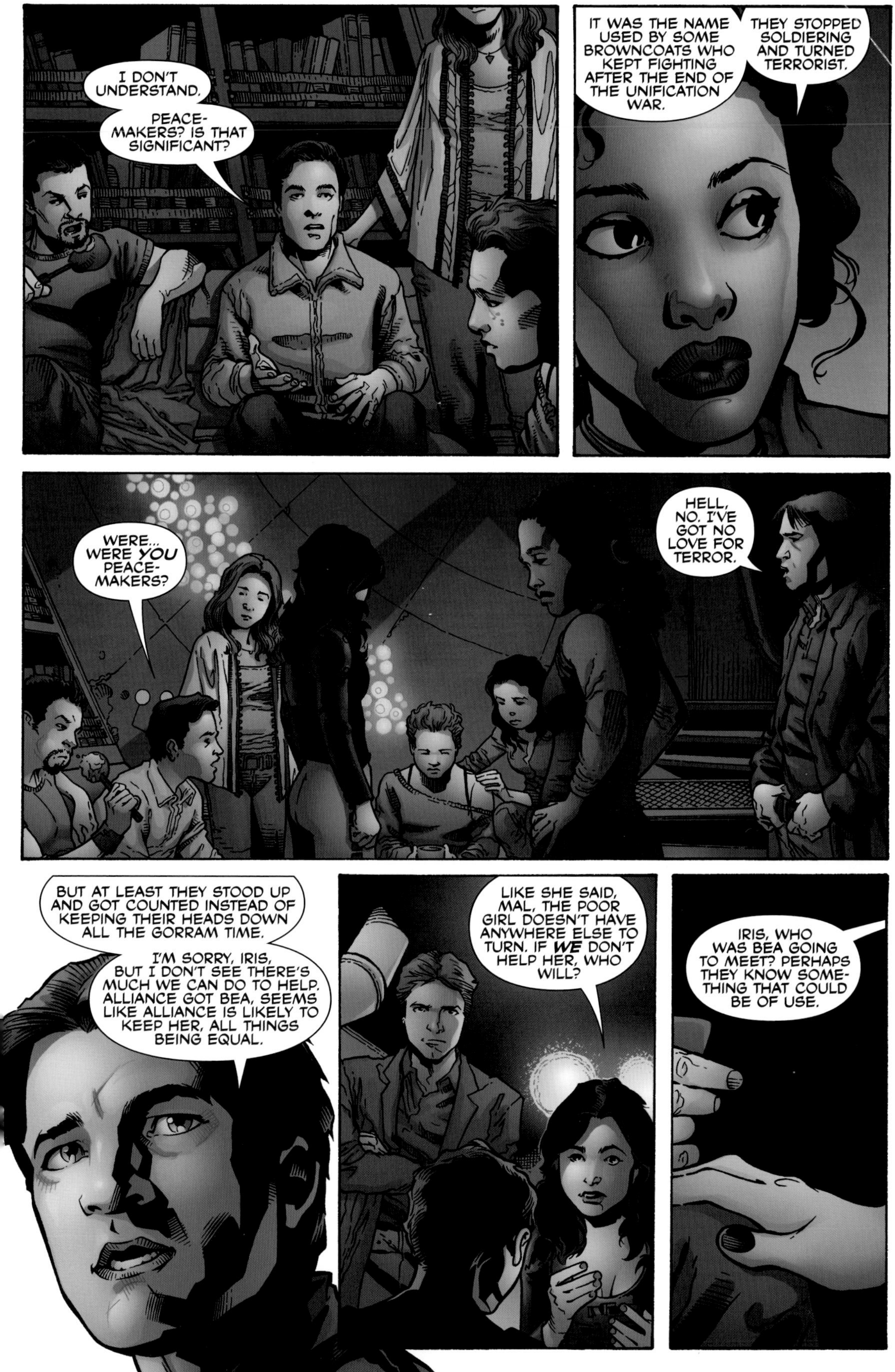

I DON'T UNDERSTAND.
PEACE-MAKERS? IS THAT SIGNIFICANT?
IT WAS THE NAME USED BY SOME BROWNCOATS WHO KEPT FIGHTING AFTER THE END OF THE UNIFICATION WAR.
THEY STOPPED SOLDIERING AND TURNED TERRORIST.
WERE... WERE *YOU* PEACE-MAKERS?
HELL, NO. I'VE GOT NO LOVE FOR TERROR.
BUT AT LEAST THEY STOOD UP AND GOT COUNTED INSTEAD OF KEEPING THEIR HEADS DOWN ALL THE GORRAM TIME.
I'M SORRY, IRIS, BUT I DON'T SEE THERE'S MUCH WE CAN DO TO HELP. ALLIANCE GOT BEA, SEEMS LIKE ALLIANCE IS LIKELY TO KEEP HER, ALL THINGS BEING EQUAL.
LIKE SHE SAID, MAL, THE POOR GIRL DOESN'T HAVE ANYWHERE ELSE TO TURN. IF *WE* DON'T HELP HER, WHO WILL?
IRIS, WHO WAS BEA GOING TO MEET? PERHAPS THEY KNOW SOME-THING THAT COULD BE OF USE.

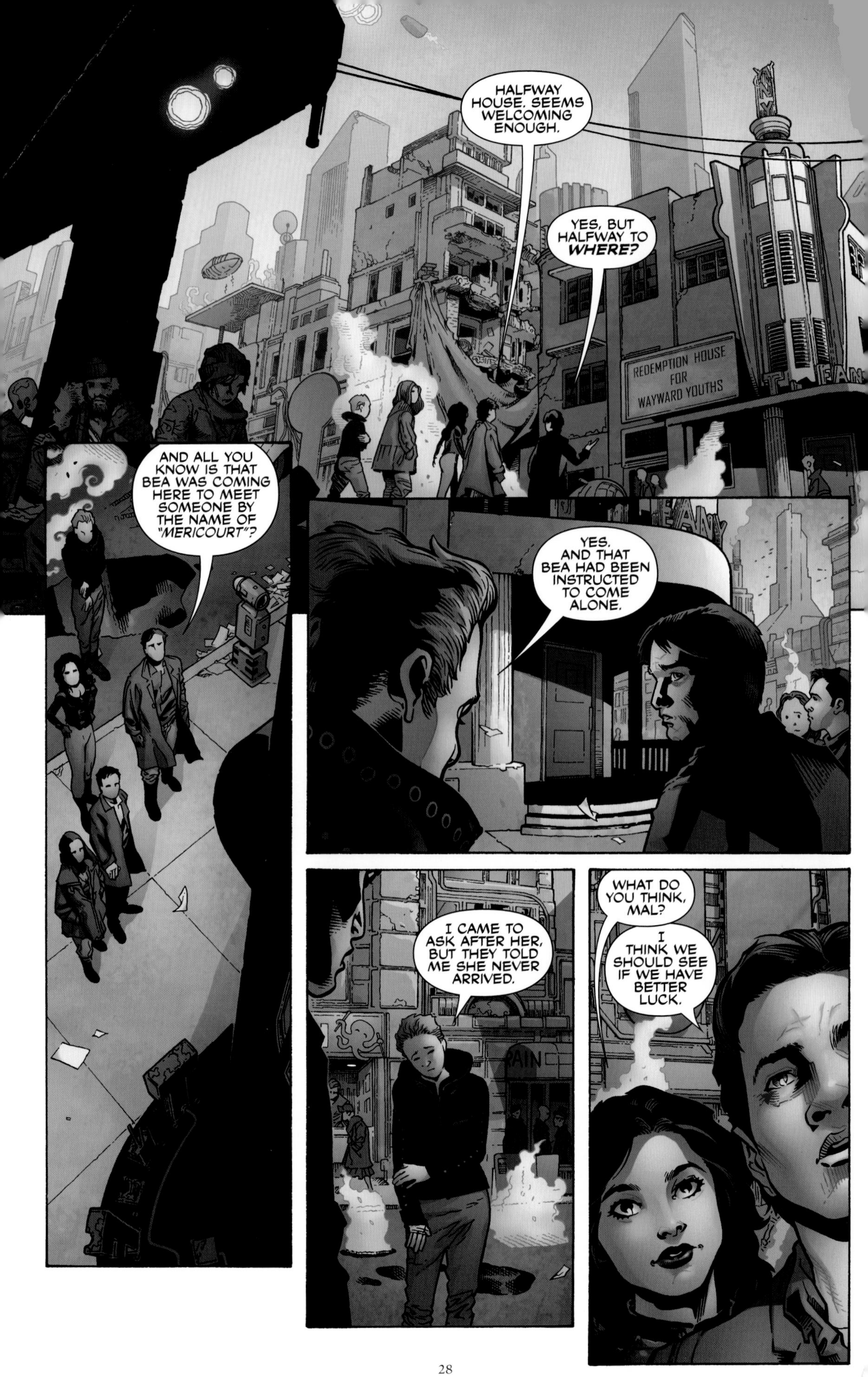
HALFWAY HOUSE. SEEMS WELCOMING ENOUGH.
YES, BUT HALFWAY TO *WHERE?*
REDEMPTION HOUSE FOR WAYWARD YOUTHS
AND ALL YOU KNOW IS THAT BEA WAS COMING HERE TO MEET SOMEONE BY THE NAME OF *"MERICOURT"*?
YES. AND THAT BEA HAD BEEN INSTRUCTED TO COME ALONE.
I CAME TO ASK AFTER HER, BUT THEY TOLD ME SHE NEVER ARRIVED.
WHAT DO YOU THINK, MAL?
I THINK WE SHOULD SEE IF WE HAVE BETTER LUCK.

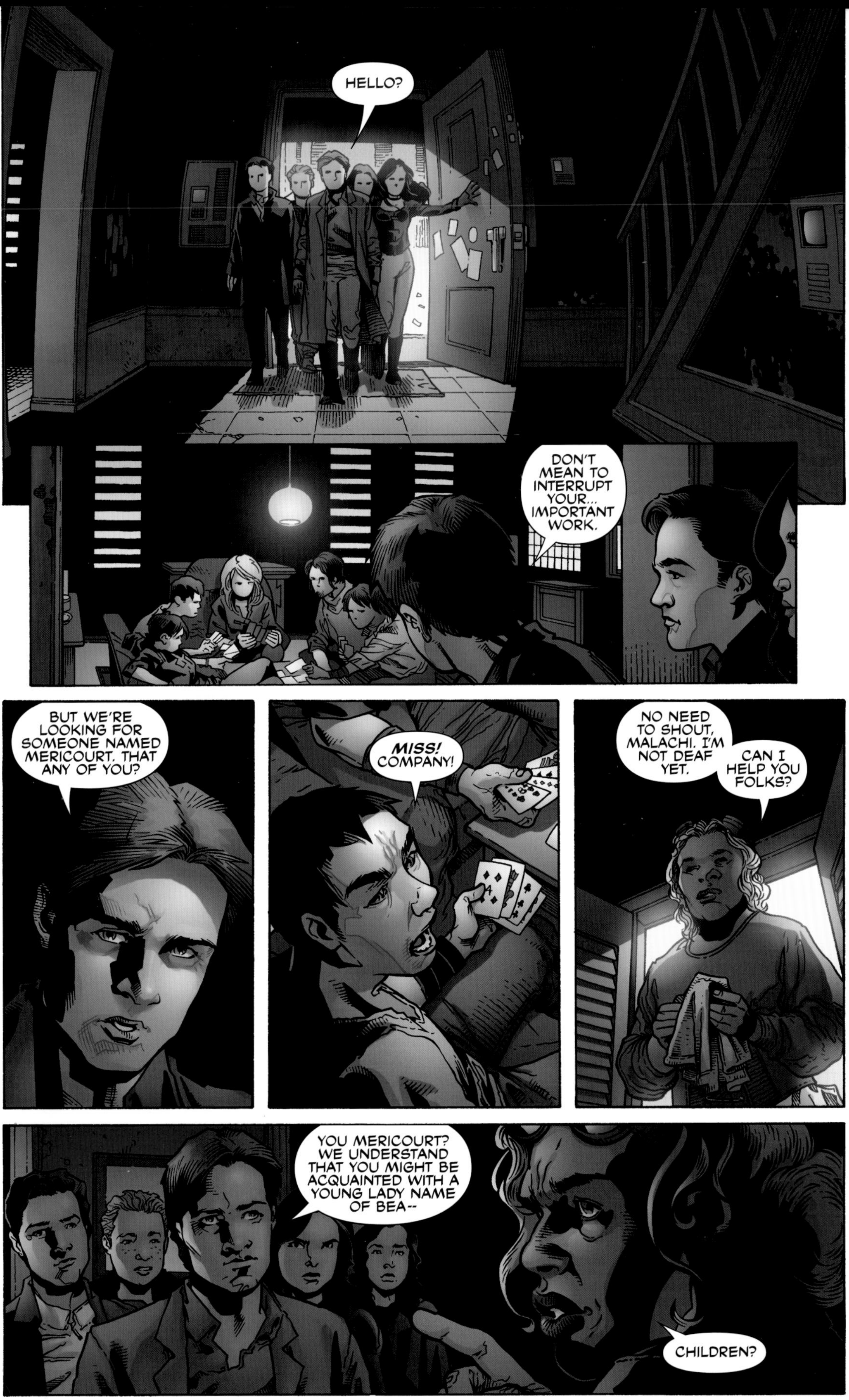

HELLO?
DON'T MEAN TO INTERRUPT YOUR... IMPORTANT WORK.
BUT WE'RE LOOKING FOR SOMEONE NAMED MERICOURT. THAT ANY OF YOU?
MISS! COMPANY!
NO NEED TO SHOUT, MALACHI. I'M NOT DEAF YET.
CAN I HELP YOU FOLKS?
YOU MERICOURT? WE UNDERSTAND THAT YOU MIGHT BE ACQUAINTED WITH A YOUNG LADY NAME OF BEA--
CHILDREN?

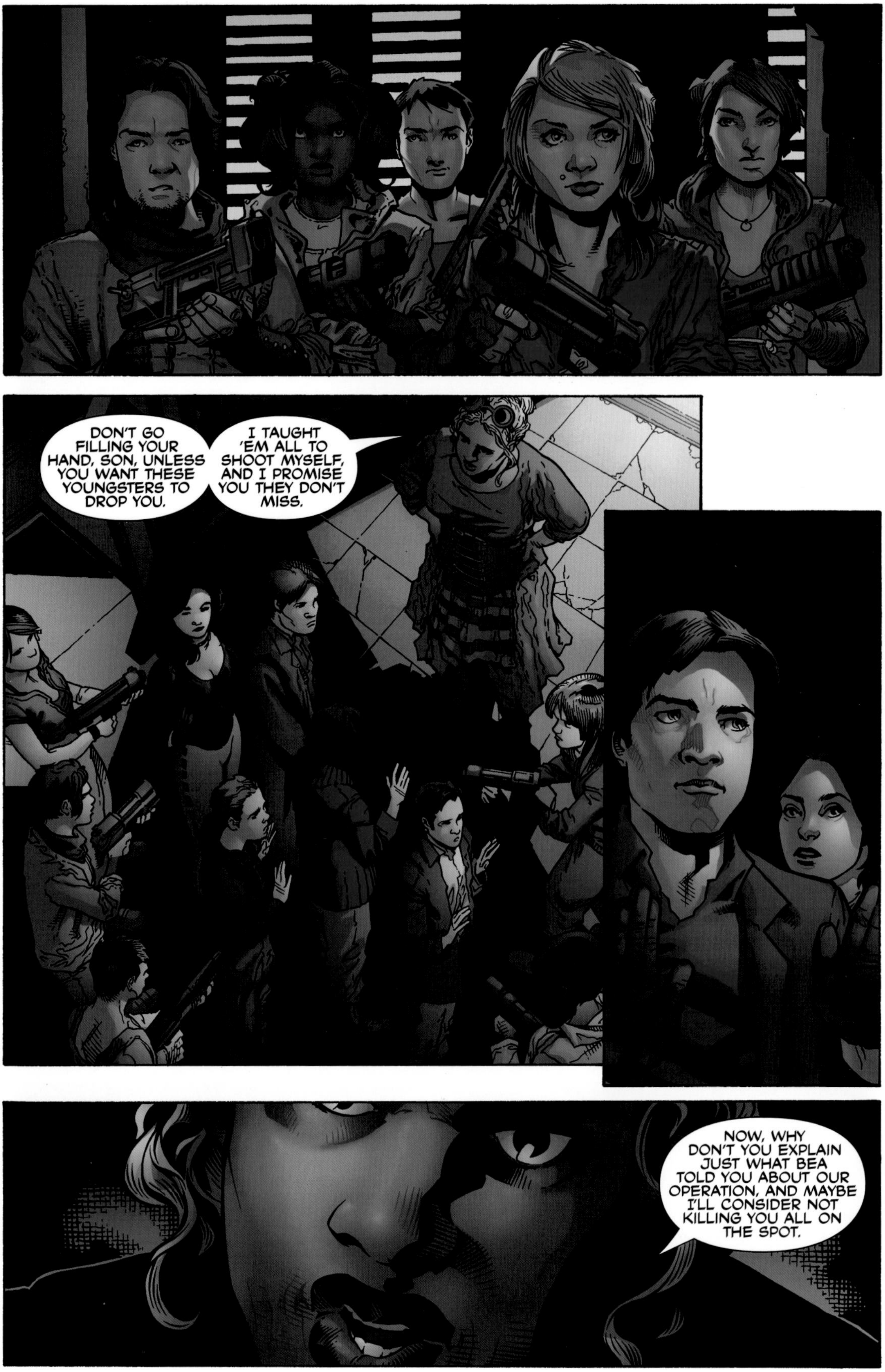
DON'T GO FILLING YOUR HAND, SON, UNLESS YOU WANT THESE YOUNGSTERS TO DROP YOU.
I TAUGHT 'EM ALL TO SHOOT MYSELF, AND I PROMISE YOU THEY DON'T MISS.
NOW, WHY DON'T YOU EXPLAIN JUST WHAT BEA TOLD YOU ABOUT OUR OPERATION, AND MAYBE I'LL CONSIDER NOT KILLING YOU ALL ON THE SPOT.

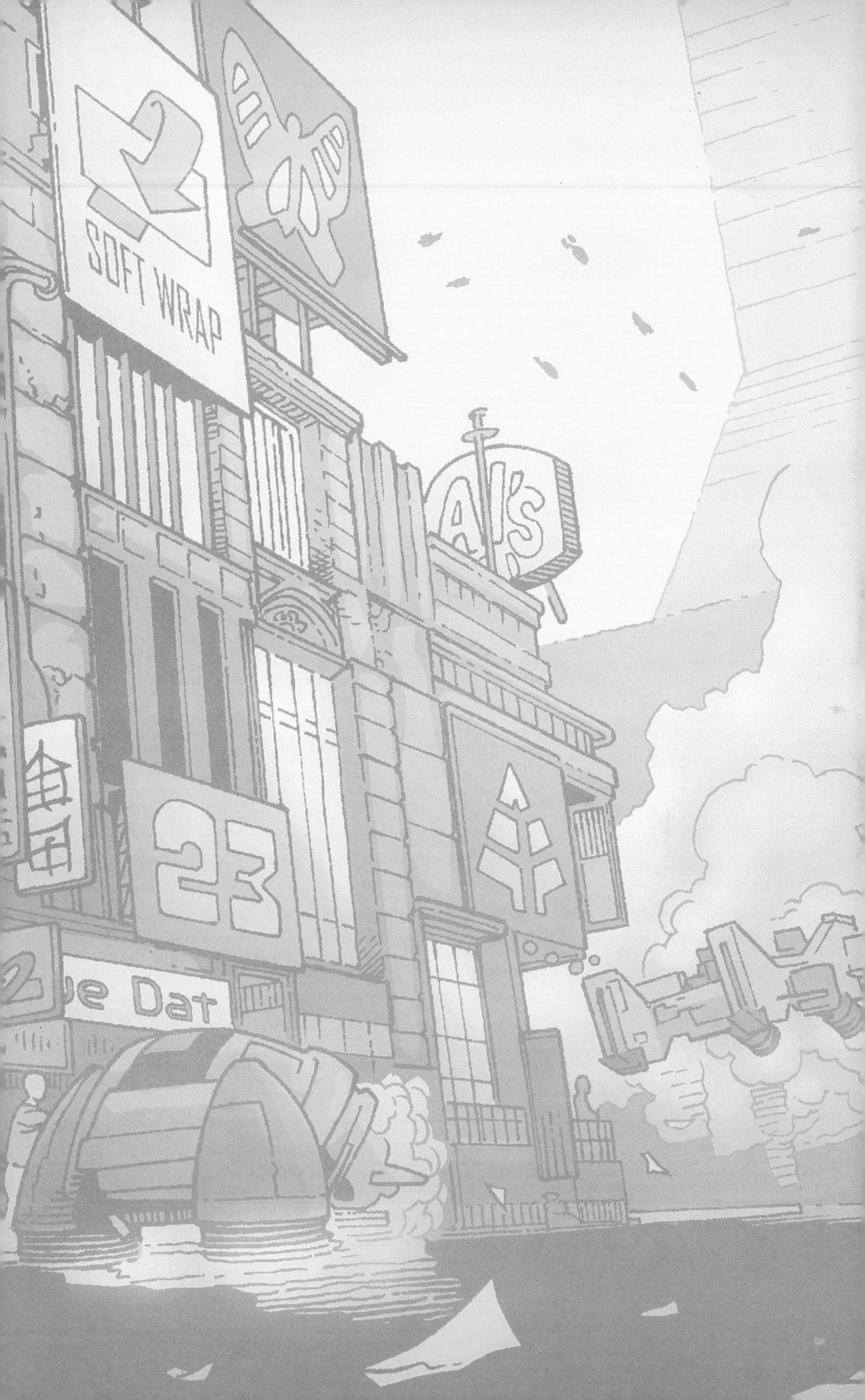
SOFT WRAP
Al's
23
ue Dat

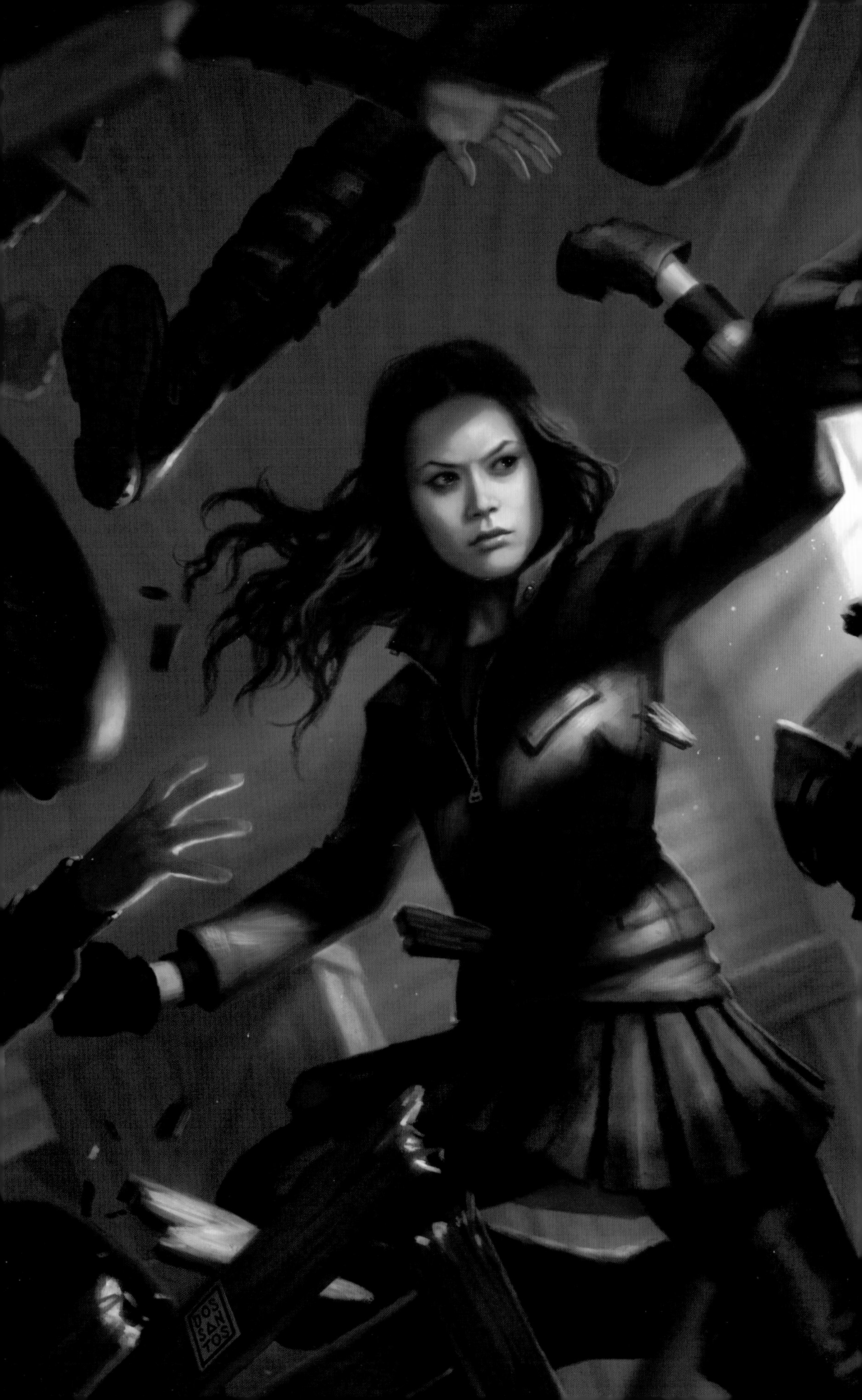
DOS
SAN
TOS

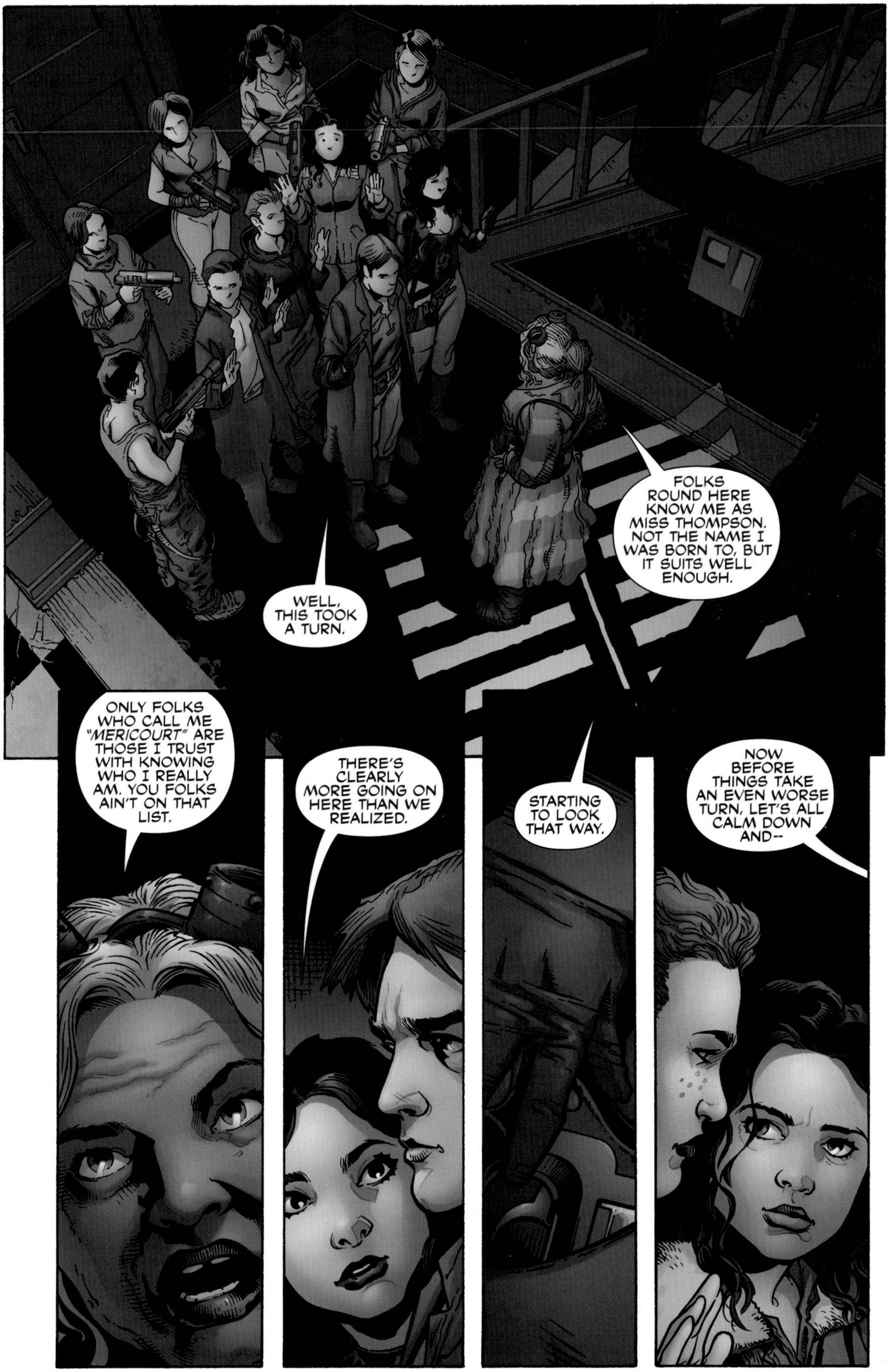
FOLKS ROUND HERE KNOW ME AS MISS THOMPSON. NOT THE NAME I WAS BORN TO, BUT IT SUITS WELL ENOUGH.
WELL, THIS TOOK A TURN.
ONLY FOLKS WHO CALL ME *"MERICOURT"* ARE THOSE I TRUST WITH KNOWING WHO I REALLY AM. YOU FOLKS AIN'T ON THAT LIST.
THERE'S CLEARLY MORE GOING ON HERE THAN WE REALIZED.
STARTING TO LOOK THAT WAY.
NOW BEFORE THINGS TAKE AN EVEN WORSE TURN, LET'S ALL CALM DOWN AND--

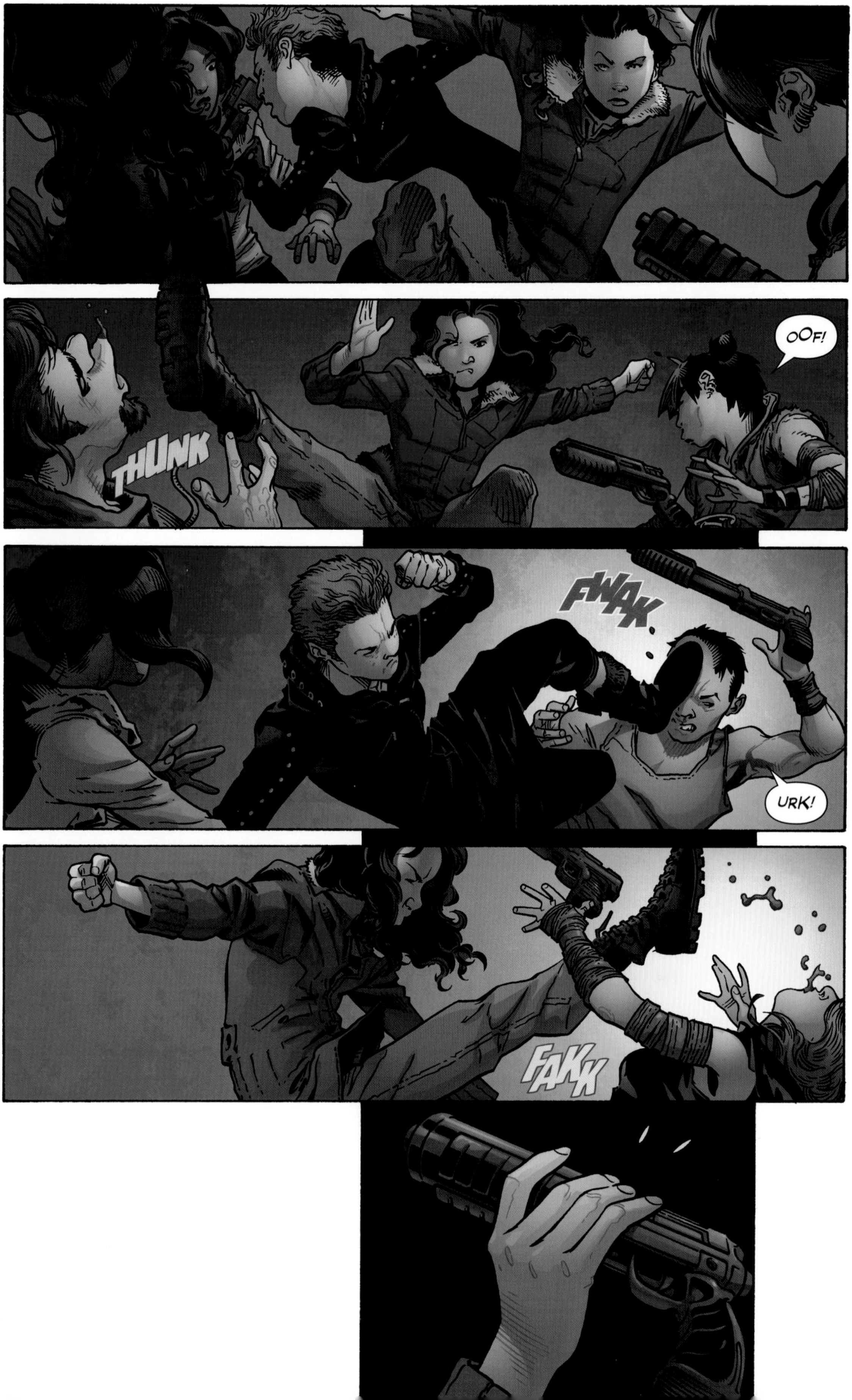

OOF!
THUNK
FWAK
URK!
FAKK

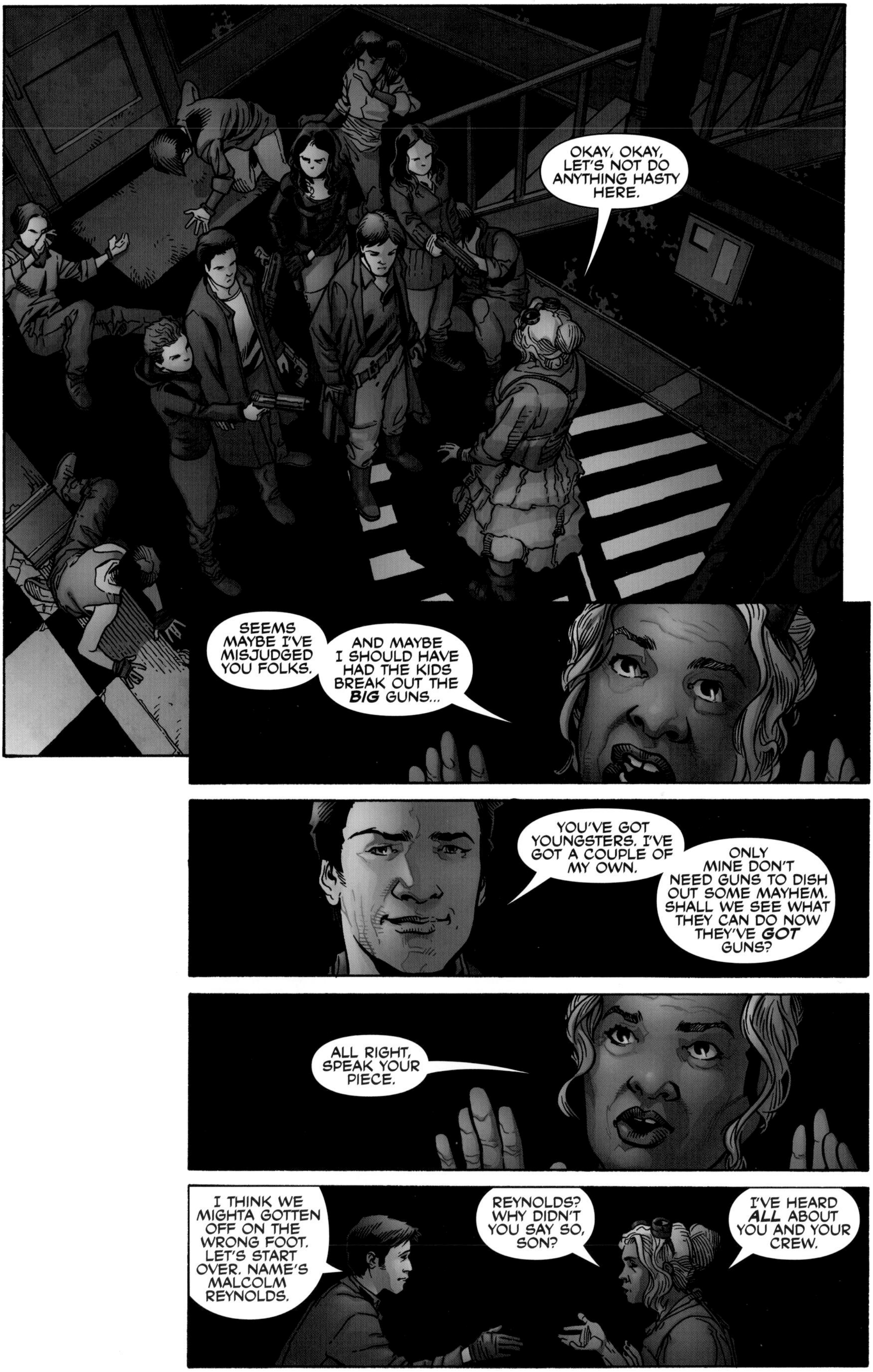
OKAY, OKAY, LET'S NOT DO ANYTHING HASTY HERE.
SEEMS MAYBE I'VE MISJUDGED YOU FOLKS.
AND MAYBE I SHOULD HAVE HAD THE KIDS BREAK OUT THE *BIG* GUNS...
YOU'VE GOT YOUNGSTERS. I'VE GOT A COUPLE OF MY OWN.
ONLY MINE DON'T NEED GUNS TO DISH OUT SOME MAYHEM. SHALL WE SEE WHAT THEY CAN DO NOW THEY'VE *GOT* GUNS?
ALL RIGHT, SPEAK YOUR PIECE.
I THINK WE MIGHTA GOTTEN OFF ON THE WRONG FOOT. LET'S START OVER. NAME'S MALCOLM REYNOLDS.
REYNOLDS? WHY DIDN'T YOU SAY SO, SON?
I'VE HEARD *ALL* ABOUT YOU AND YOUR CREW.

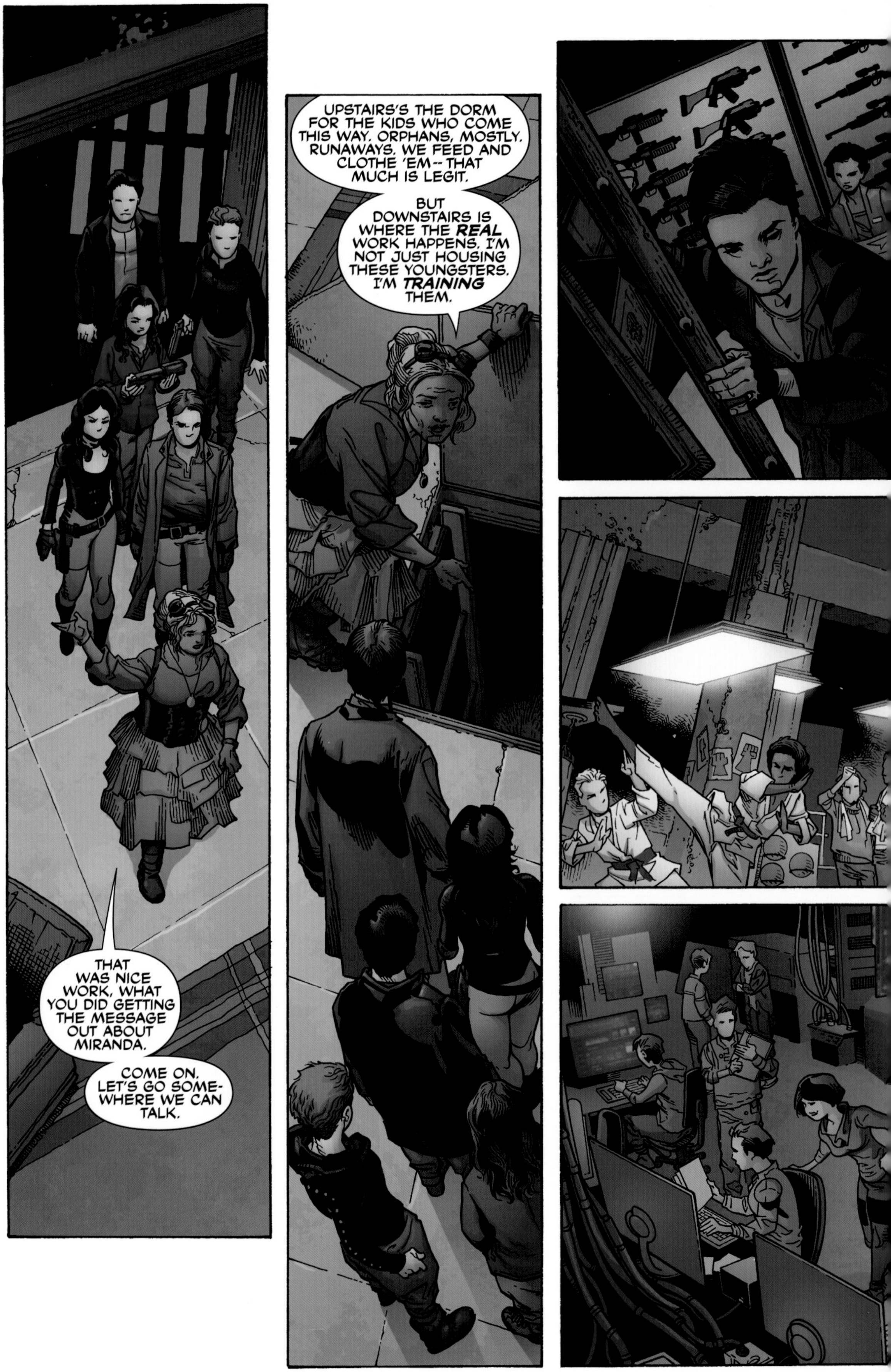
THAT WAS NICE WORK, WHAT YOU DID GETTING THE MESSAGE OUT ABOUT MIRANDA.
COME ON. LET'S GO SOME-WHERE WE CAN TALK.
UPSTAIRS'S THE DORM FOR THE KIDS WHO COME THIS WAY. ORPHANS, MOSTLY. RUNAWAYS. WE FEED AND CLOTHE 'EM-- THAT MUCH IS LEGIT.
BUT DOWNSTAIRS IS WHERE THE ***REAL*** WORK HAPPENS. I'M NOT JUST HOUSING THESE YOUNGSTERS. I'M ***TRAINING*** THEM.

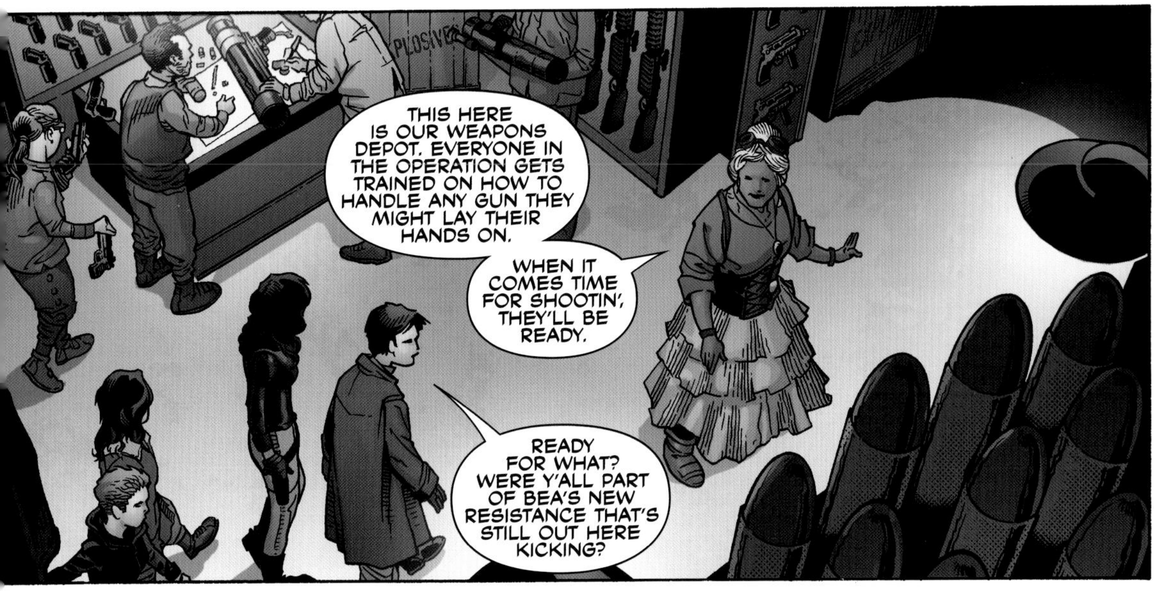
THIS HERE IS OUR WEAPONS DEPOT. EVERYONE IN THE OPERATION GETS TRAINED ON HOW TO HANDLE ANY GUN THEY MIGHT LAY THEIR HANDS ON.
WHEN IT COMES TIME FOR SHOOTIN', THEY'LL BE READY.
READY FOR WHAT? WERE Y'ALL PART OF BEA'S NEW RESISTANCE THAT'S STILL OUT HERE KICKING?

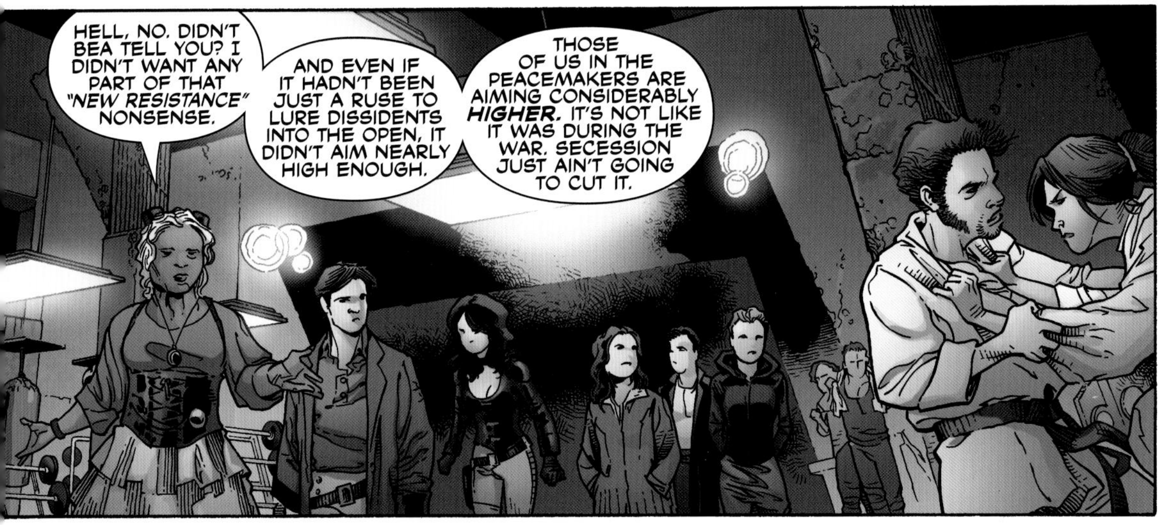
HELL, NO. DIDN'T BEA TELL YOU? I DIDN'T WANT ANY PART OF THAT *"NEW RESISTANCE"* NONSENSE.
AND EVEN IF IT HADN'T BEEN JUST A RUSE TO LURE DISSIDENTS INTO THE OPEN, IT DIDN'T AIM NEARLY HIGH ENOUGH.
THOSE OF US IN THE PEACEMAKERS ARE AIMING CONSIDERABLY ***HIGHER.*** IT'S NOT LIKE IT WAS DURING THE WAR. SECESSION JUST AIN'T GOING TO CUT IT.

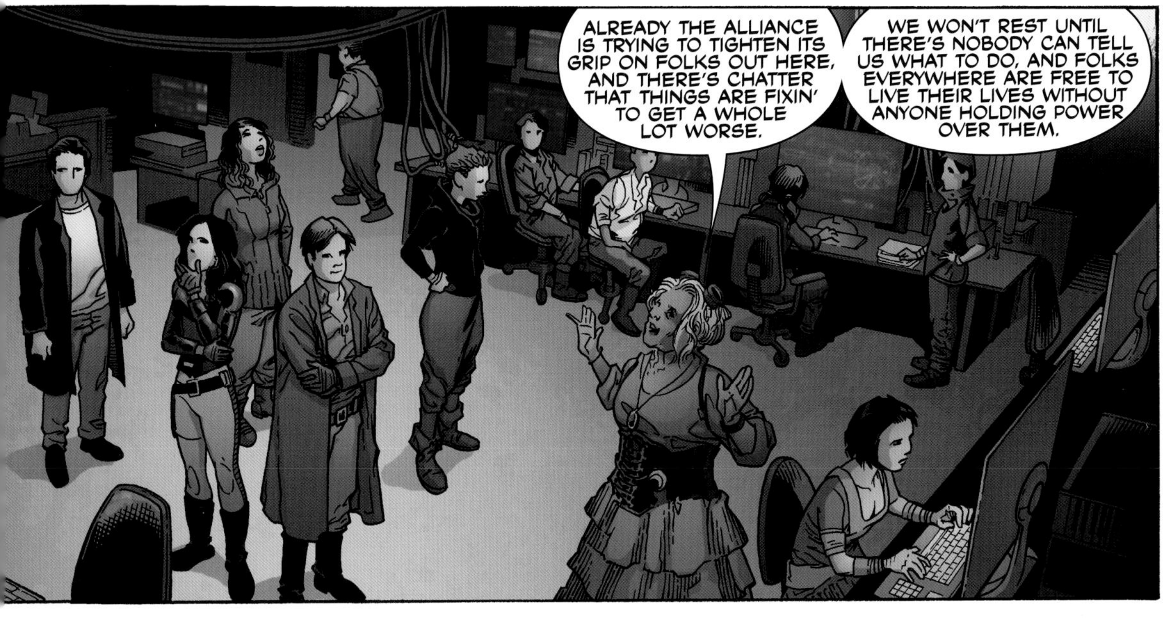
ALREADY THE ALLIANCE IS TRYING TO TIGHTEN ITS GRIP ON FOLKS OUT HERE, AND THERE'S CHATTER THAT THINGS ARE FIXIN' TO GET A WHOLE LOT WORSE.
WE WON'T REST UNTIL THERE'S NOBODY CAN TELL US WHAT TO DO, AND FOLKS EVERYWHERE ARE FREE TO LIVE THEIR LIVES WITHOUT ANYONE HOLDING POWER OVER THEM.

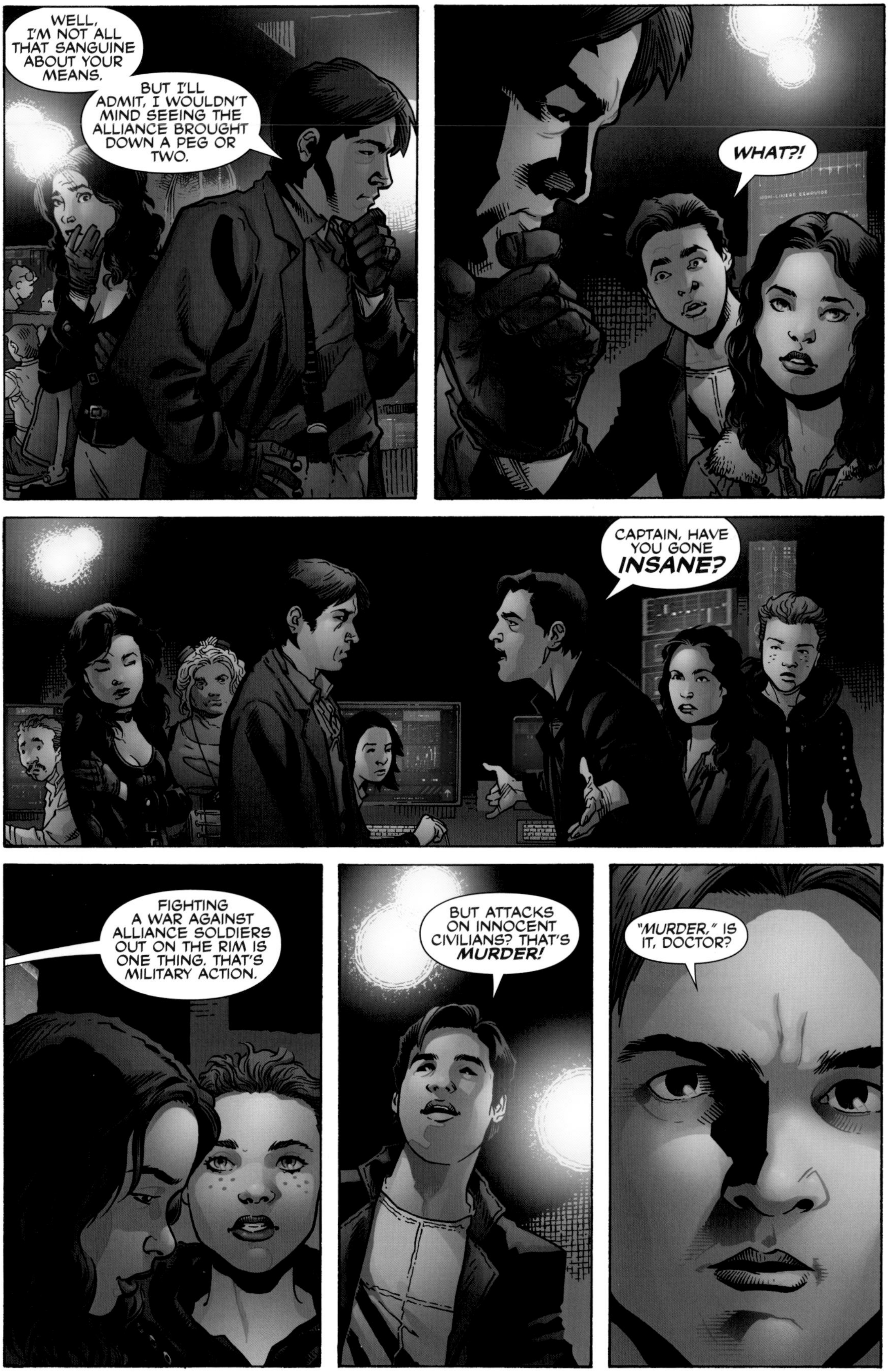
WELL, I'M NOT ALL THAT SANGUINE ABOUT YOUR MEANS.
BUT I'LL ADMIT, I WOULDN'T MIND SEEING THE ALLIANCE BROUGHT DOWN A PEG OR TWO.
WHAT?!
CAPTAIN, HAVE YOU GONE INSANE?
FIGHTING A WAR AGAINST ALLIANCE SOLDIERS OUT ON THE RIM IS ONE THING. THAT'S MILITARY ACTION.
BUT ATTACKS ON INNOCENT CIVILIANS? THAT'S MURDER!
"MURDER," IS IT, DOCTOR?

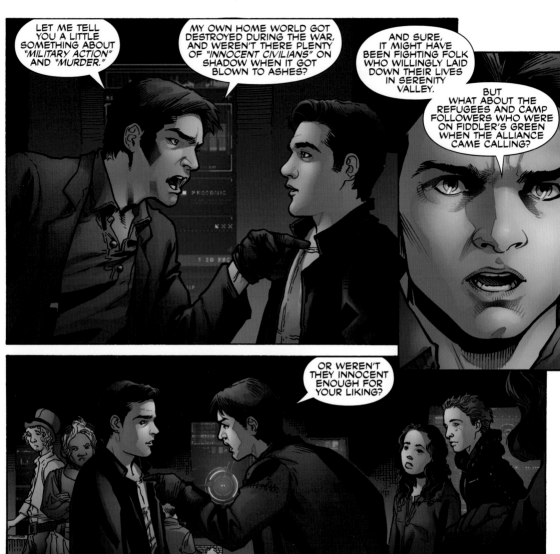

LET ME TELL YOU A LITTLE SOMETHING ABOUT *"MILITARY ACTION"* AND *"MURDER."*

MY OWN HOME WORLD GOT DESTROYED DURING THE WAR, AND WEREN'T THERE PLENTY OF *"INNOCENT CIVILIANS"* ON SHADOW WHEN IT GOT BLOWN TO ASHES?

AND SURE, IT MIGHT HAVE BEEN FIGHTING FOLK WHO WILLINGLY LAID DOWN THEIR LIVES IN SERENITY VALLEY.

BUT WHAT ABOUT THE REFUGEES AND CAMP FOLLOWERS WHO WERE ON FIDDLER'S GREEN WHEN THE ALLIANCE CAME CALLING?

OR WEREN'T THEY INNOCENT ENOUGH FOR YOUR LIKING?

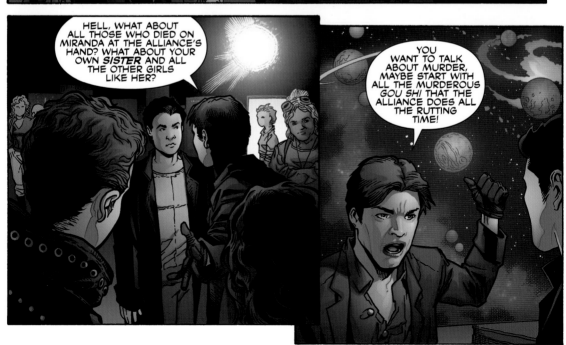

HELL, WHAT ABOUT ALL THOSE WHO DIED ON MIRANDA AT THE ALLIANCE'S HAND? WHAT ABOUT YOUR OWN *SISTER* AND ALL THE OTHER GIRLS LIKE HER?

YOU WANT TO TALK ABOUT MURDER, MAYBE START WITH ALL THE MURDEROUS *GOU SHI* THAT THE ALLIANCE DOES ALL THE RUTTING TIME!

NOW, NOW, YOU COME ASKING AFTER BEA.

SHE'S NOT A PEACEMAKER, BUT SHE'S GOT TIES WITH A LOT OF OUR PEOPLE, AND SHE GOT WIND OF AN OPERATION WE'VE GOT PLANNED.

SHE HAD WAVED SHE WANTED TO MEET IN PERSON TO TALK ABOUT IT, AND THEN NEVER SHOWED.

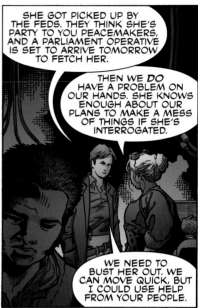

SHE GOT PICKED UP BY THE FEDS. THEY THINK SHE'S PARTY TO YOU PEACEMAKERS, AND A PARLIAMENT OPERATIVE IS SET TO ARRIVE TOMORROW TO FETCH HER.

THEN WE *DO* HAVE A PROBLEM ON OUR HANDS. SHE KNOWS ENOUGH ABOUT OUR PLANS TO MAKE A MESS OF THINGS IF SHE'S INTERROGATED.

WE NEED TO BUST HER OUT. WE CAN MOVE QUICK, BUT I COULD USE HELP FROM YOUR PEOPLE.

I CAN FIND OUT WHERE SHE'S BEING HELD, BUT I'LL NEED SOME UNFAMILIAR FACES TO GET PAST THE FRONT DESK AT THE ALLIANCE HEADQUARTERS HERE.

I'VE GOT AN IDEA ON THAT SCORE. BUT WE'RE IN POWERFUL NEED OF SUPPLIES. IF YOUR PEOPLE COULD SEE FIT TO LENDING US SOME...

WE CAN GET YOU ANYTHING YOU NEED FROM THE GENERAL STORE.

I CAN SHOW THEM THE WAY, MISS.

SIMON, RIVER, YOU TWO GO WITH THIS GAL HERE.

IRIS, HEAD BACK TO THE SHIP AND TELL KAYLEE AND JAYNE TO MEET AT THE STORE WITH THE MULE AND OUR SHOPPING LIST.

INARA AND I'LL STICK AROUND AND PLAN SOME MISCHIEF WITH MERICOURT HERE.

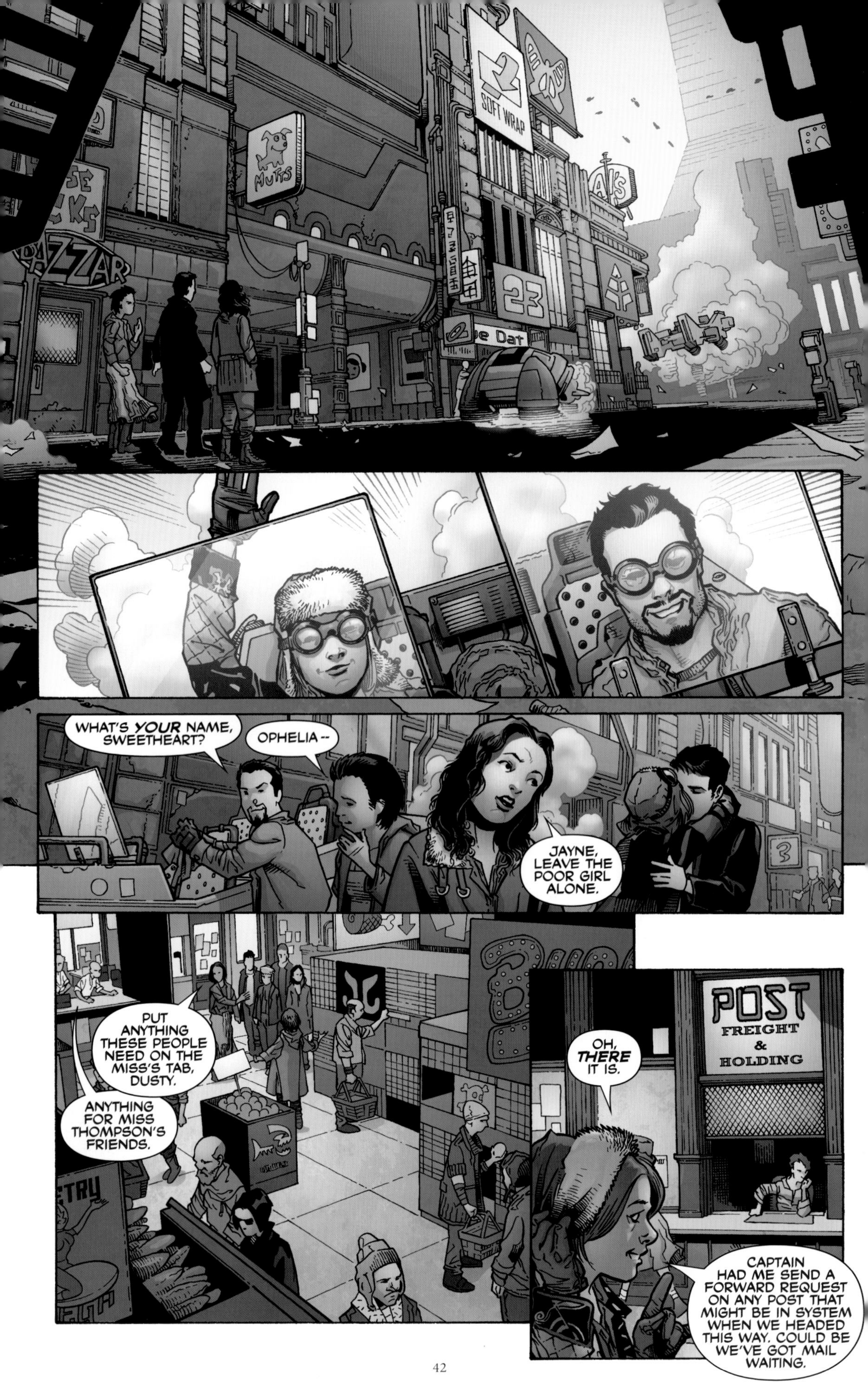
SOFT WRAP
MUTTS
23
WHAT'S YOUR NAME, SWEETHEART?
OPHELIA --
JAYNE, LEAVE THE POOR GIRL ALONE.
PUT ANYTHING THESE PEOPLE NEED ON THE MISS'S TAB, DUSTY.
ANYTHING FOR MISS THOMPSON'S FRIENDS.
POST
FREIGHT & HOLDING
OH, THERE IT IS.
CAPTAIN HAD ME SEND A FORWARD REQUEST ON ANY POST THAT MIGHT BE IN SYSTEM WHEN WE HEADED THIS WAY. COULD BE WE'VE GOT MAIL WAITING.

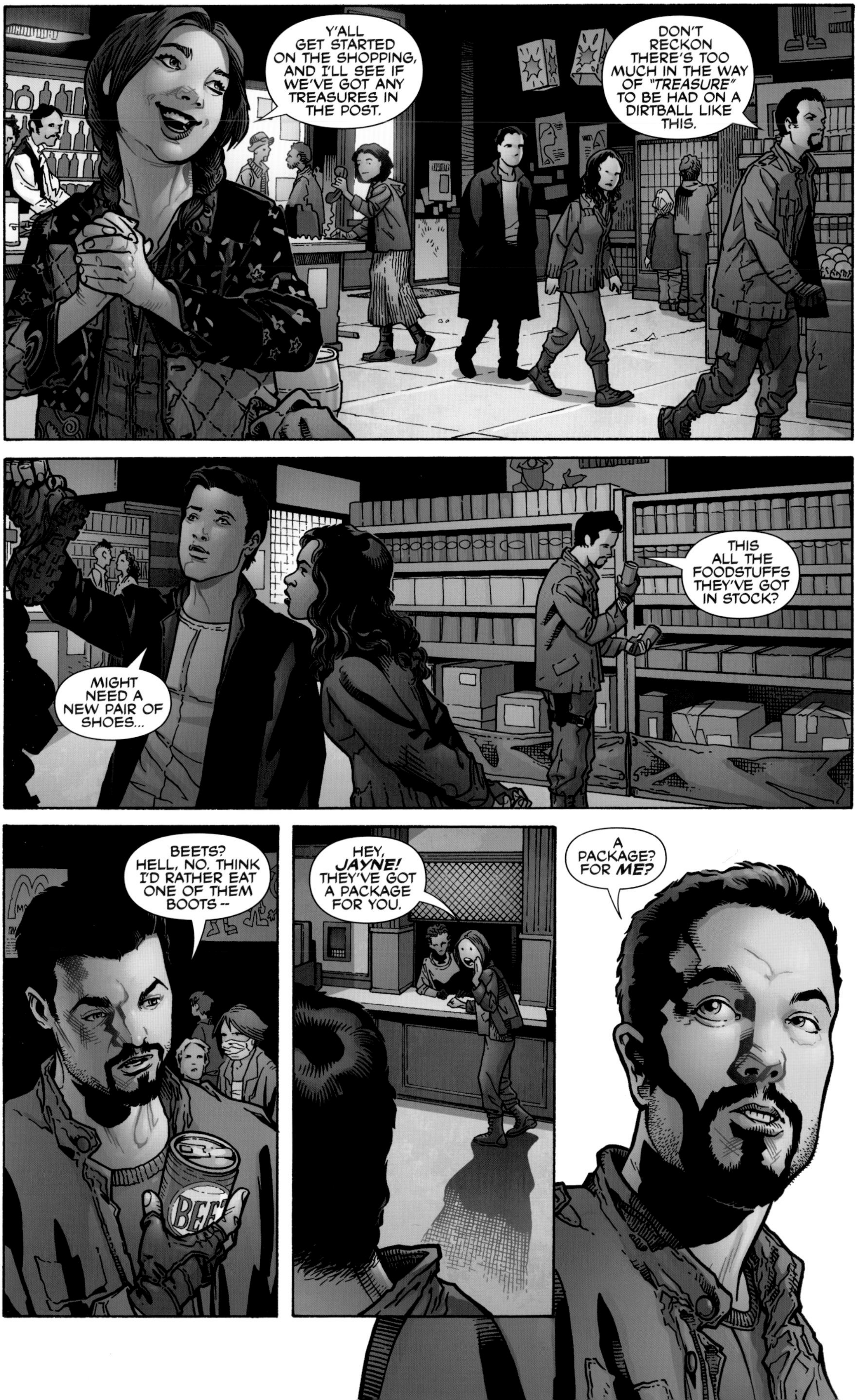
Y'ALL GET STARTED ON THE SHOPPING, AND I'LL SEE IF WE'VE GOT ANY TREASURES IN THE POST.
DON'T RECKON THERE'S TOO MUCH IN THE WAY OF *"TREASURE"* TO BE HAD ON A DIRTBALL LIKE THIS.
MIGHT NEED A NEW PAIR OF SHOES...
THIS ALL THE FOODSTUFFS THEY'VE GOT IN STOCK?
BEETS? HELL, NO. THINK I'D RATHER EAT ONE OF THEM BOOTS --
HEY, ***JAYNE!*** THEY'VE GOT A PACKAGE FOR YOU.
A PACKAGE? FOR ***ME?***

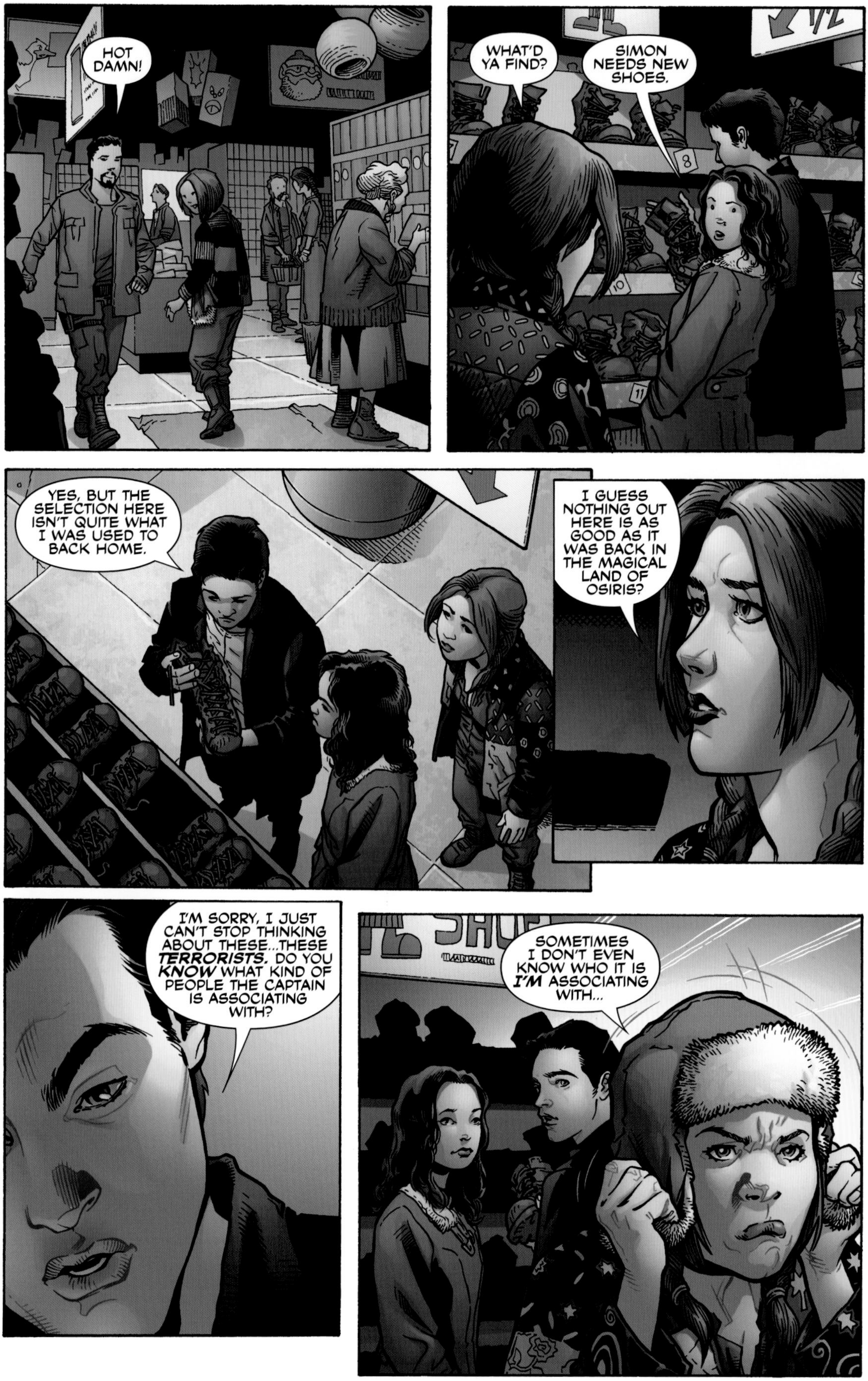
HOT DAMN!
WHAT'D YA FIND?
SIMON NEEDS NEW SHOES.
YES, BUT THE SELECTION HERE ISN'T QUITE WHAT I WAS USED TO BACK HOME.
I GUESS NOTHING OUT HERE IS AS GOOD AS IT WAS BACK IN THE MAGICAL LAND OF OSIRIS?
I'M SORRY, I JUST CAN'T STOP THINKING ABOUT THESE...THESE TERRORISTS. DO YOU KNOW WHAT KIND OF PEOPLE THE CAPTAIN IS ASSOCIATING WITH?
SOMETIMES I DON'T EVEN KNOW WHO IT IS I'M ASSOCIATING WITH...

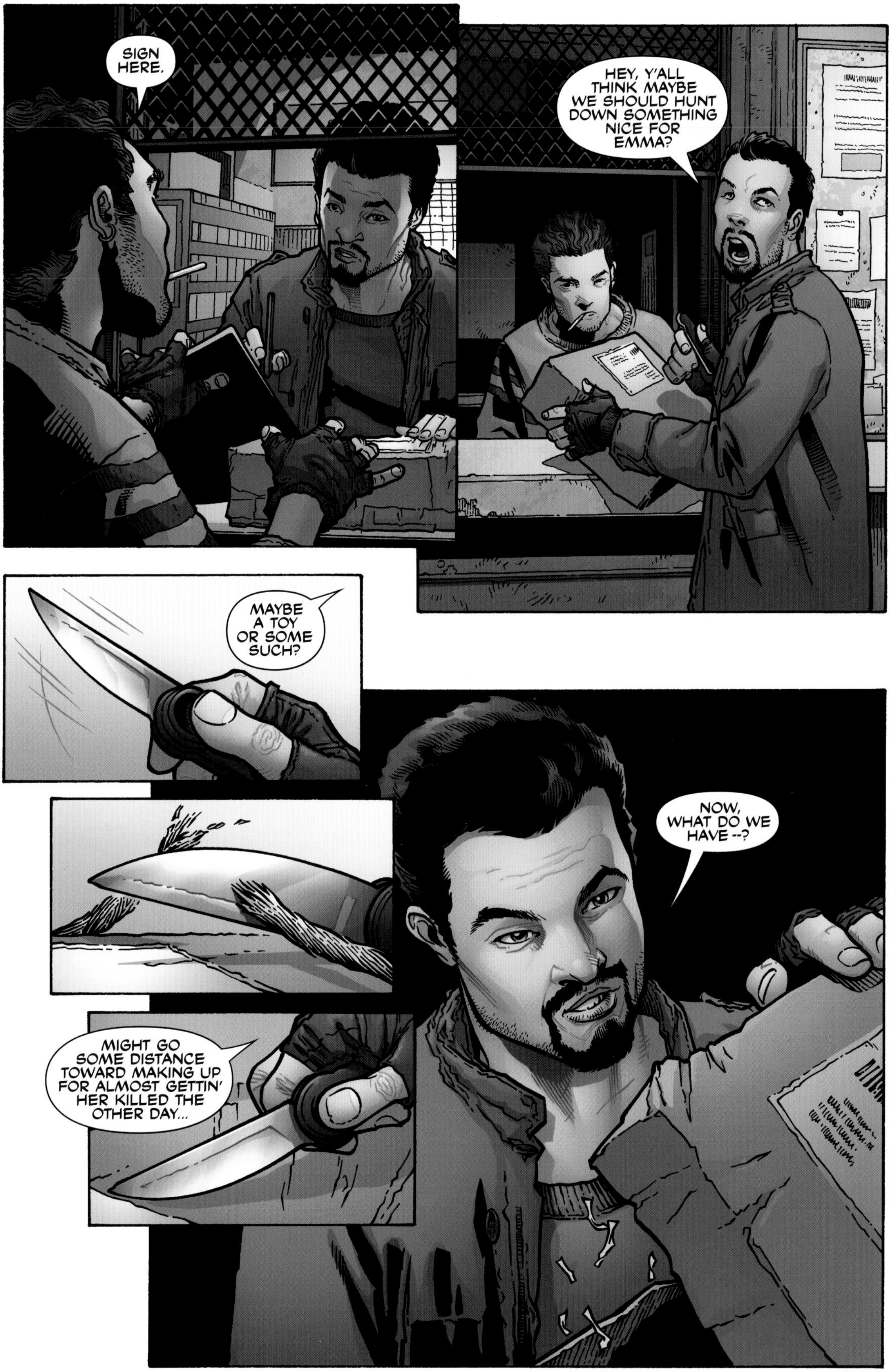
SIGN HERE.
HEY, Y'ALL THINK MAYBE WE SHOULD HUNT DOWN SOMETHING NICE FOR EMMA?
MAYBE A TOY OR SOME SUCH?
MIGHT GO SOME DISTANCE TOWARD MAKING UP FOR ALMOST GETTIN' HER KILLED THE OTHER DAY...
NOW, WHAT DO WE HAVE --?

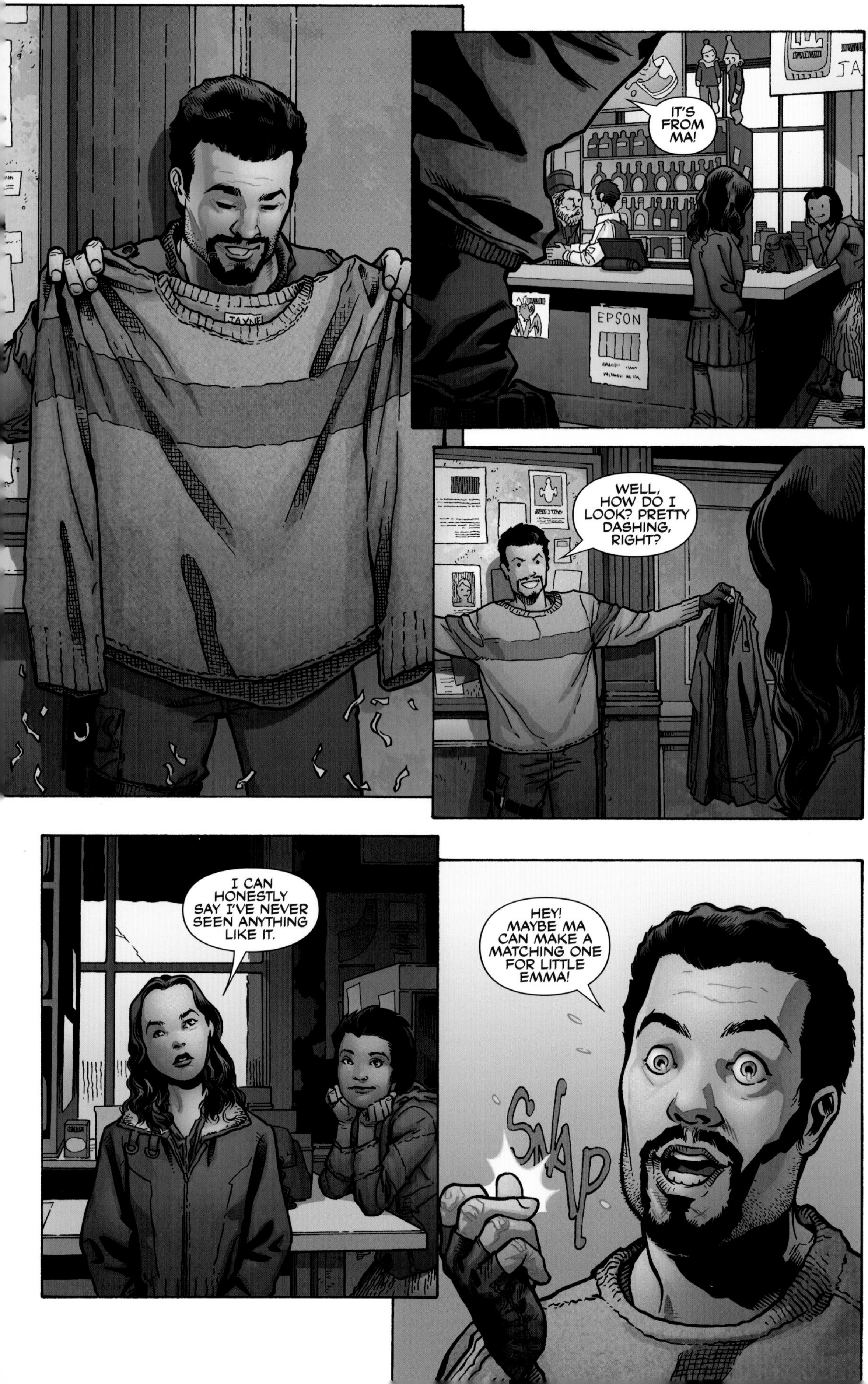

JAYNE
IT'S FROM MA!
EPSON
WELL, HOW DO I LOOK? PRETTY DASHING, RIGHT?
I CAN HONESTLY SAY I'VE NEVER SEEN ANYTHING LIKE IT.
HEY! MAYBE MA CAN MAKE A MATCHING ONE FOR LITTLE EMMA!
SNAP

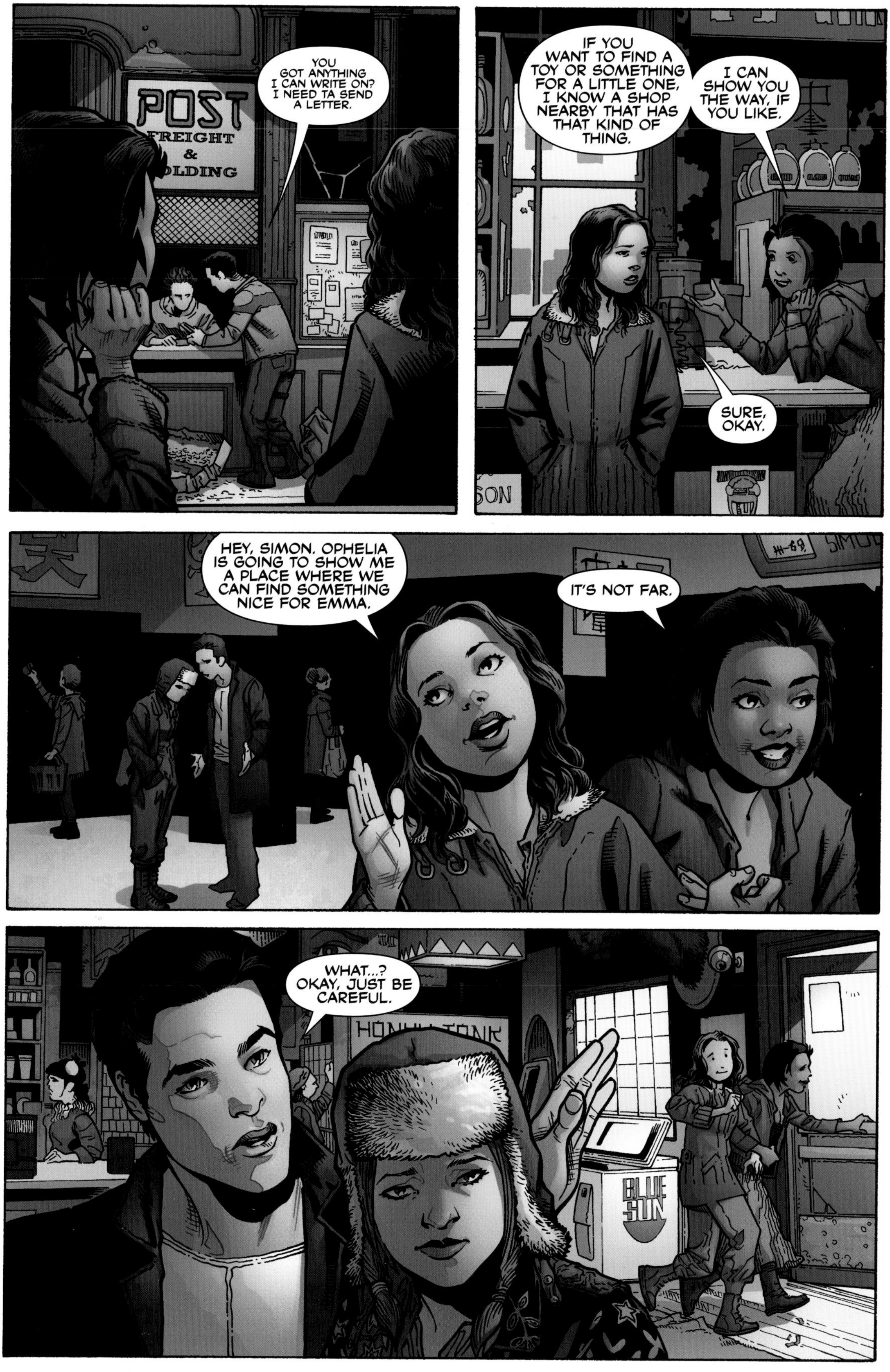
POST
FREIGHT
&
YOU GOT ANYTHING I CAN WRITE ON? I NEED TA SEND A LETTER.
IF YOU WANT TO FIND A TOY OR SOMETHING FOR A LITTLE ONE, I KNOW A SHOP NEARBY THAT HAS THAT KIND OF THING.
I CAN SHOW YOU THE WAY, IF YOU LIKE.
SURE, OKAY.
HEY, SIMON. OPHELIA IS GOING TO SHOW ME A PLACE WHERE WE CAN FIND SOMETHING NICE FOR EMMA.
IT'S NOT FAR.
WHAT...? OKAY, JUST BE CAREFUL.
BLUE SUN

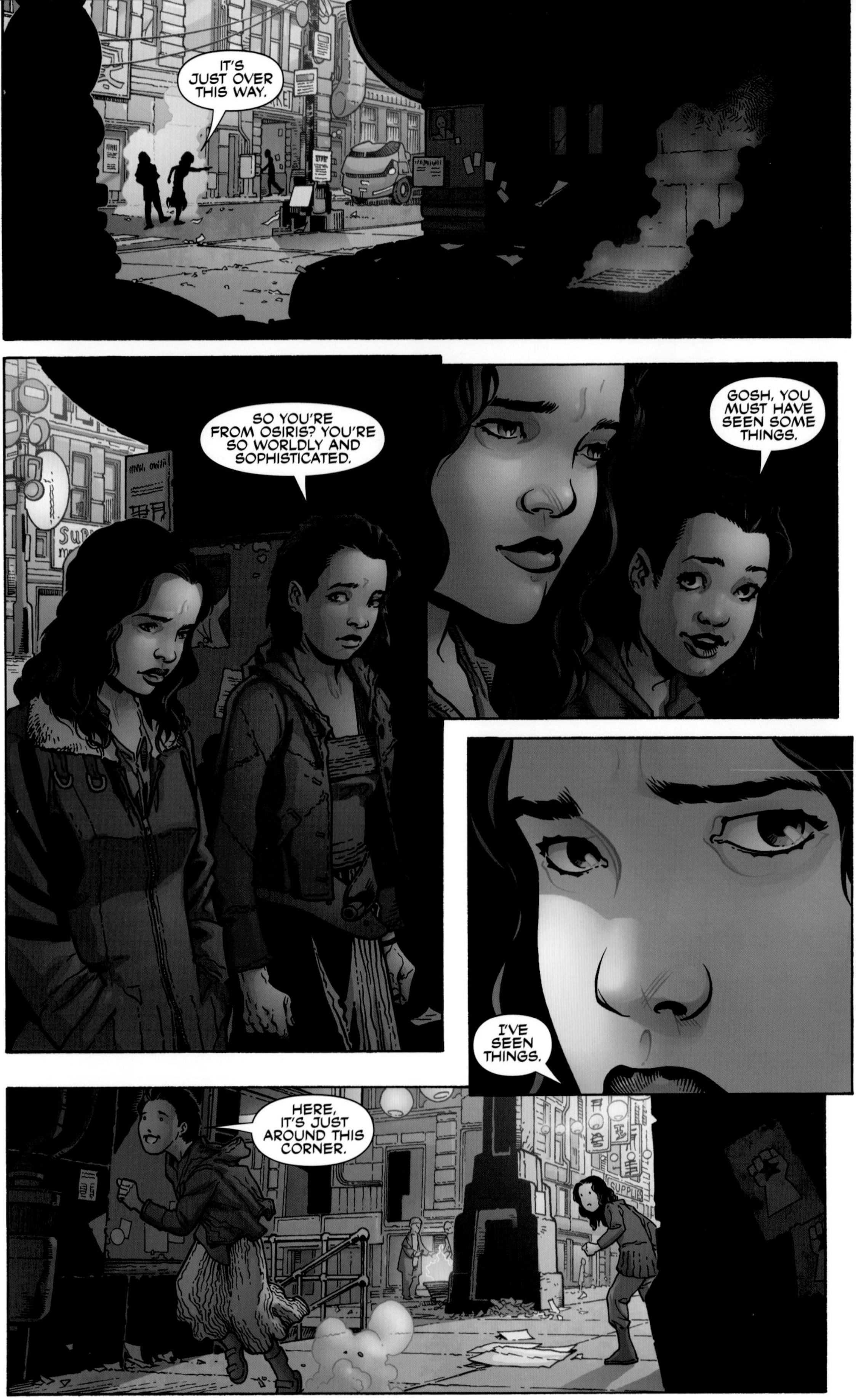
IT'S JUST OVER THIS WAY.
SO YOU'RE FROM OSIRIS? YOU'RE SO WORLDLY AND SOPHISTICATED.
GOSH, YOU MUST HAVE SEEN SOME THINGS.
I'VE SEEN THINGS.
HERE, IT'S JUST AROUND THIS CORNER.

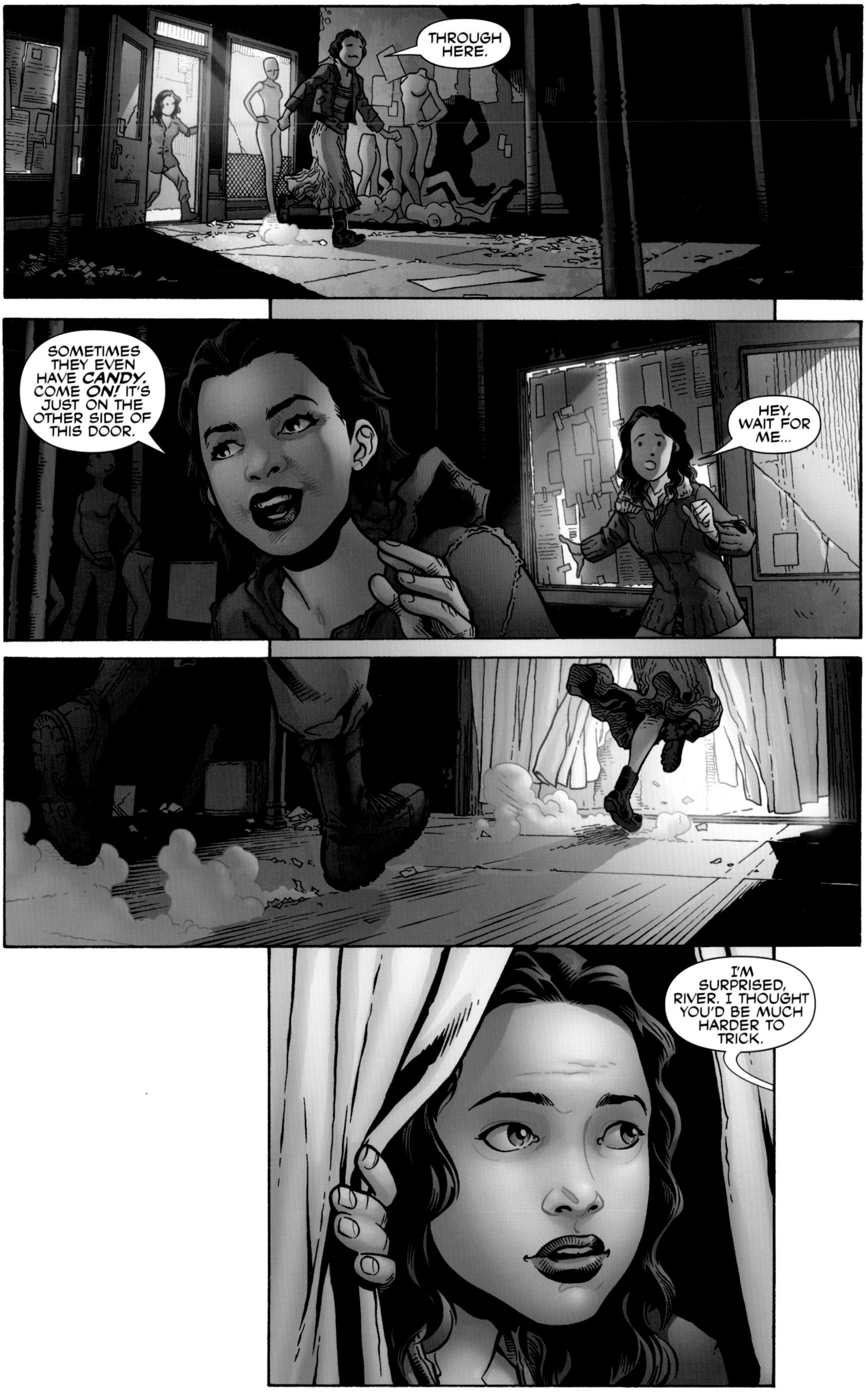
THROUGH HERE.
SOMETIMES THEY EVEN HAVE CANDY. COME ON! IT'S JUST ON THE OTHER SIDE OF THIS DOOR.
HEY, WAIT FOR ME...
I'M SURPRISED, RIVER. I THOUGHT YOU'D BE MUCH HARDER TO TRICK.

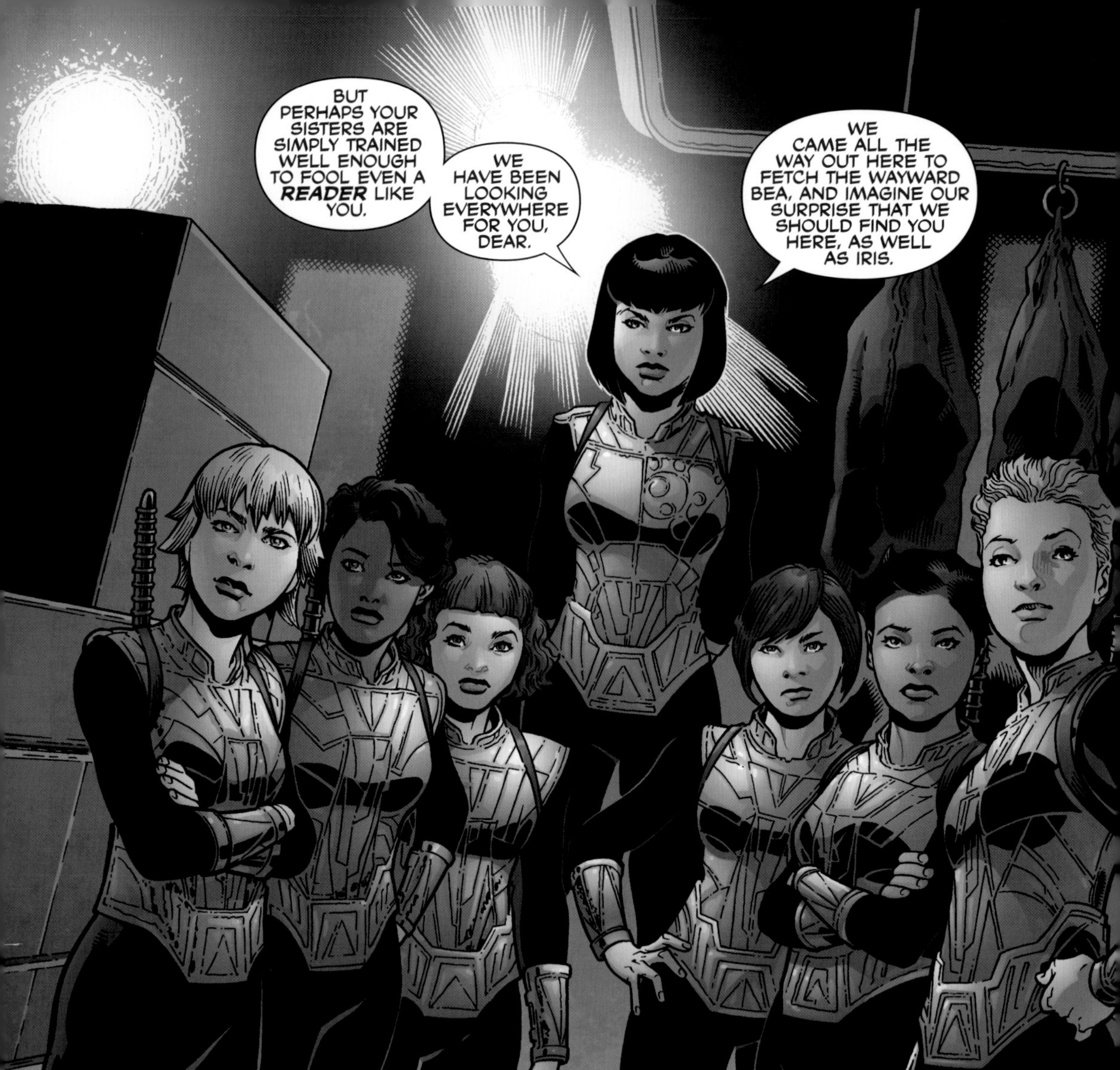
BUT PERHAPS YOUR SISTERS ARE SIMPLY TRAINED WELL ENOUGH TO FOOL EVEN A **READER** LIKE YOU.
WE HAVE BEEN LOOKING EVERYWHERE FOR YOU, DEAR.
WE CAME ALL THE WAY OUT HERE TO FETCH THE WAYWARD BEA, AND IMAGINE OUR SURPRISE THAT WE SHOULD FIND YOU HERE, AS WELL AS IRIS.

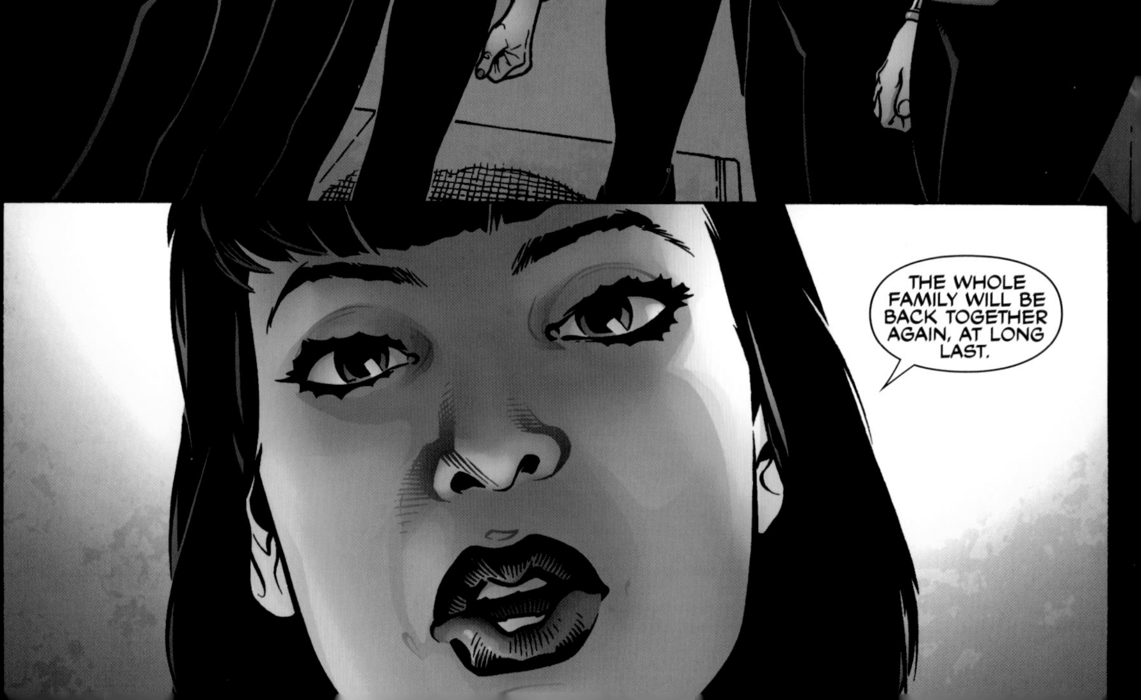
THE WHOLE FAMILY WILL BE BACK TOGETHER AGAIN, AT LONG LAST.

I'LL SKIP THE REUNION IF IT'S ALL THE SAME TO YOU, KALISTA.

YOU'RE CONFUSED. YOU WERE TAKEN FROM THE ACADEMY BEFORE YOUR TRAINING WAS COMPLETE. BUT COME WITH ME AND I CAN MAKE IT ALL BETTER.

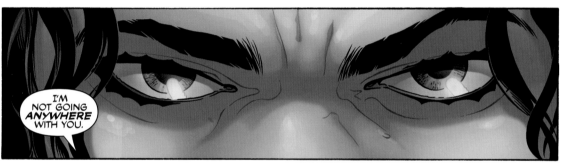

I'M NOT GOING *ANYWHERE* WITH YOU.

NO BLADES, DISCIPLES. I DON'T WANT RIVER TO SUFFER FROM ANY INJURIES THAT WON'T HEAL IN TIME.

PITY. BUT I EXPECTED AS MUCH.

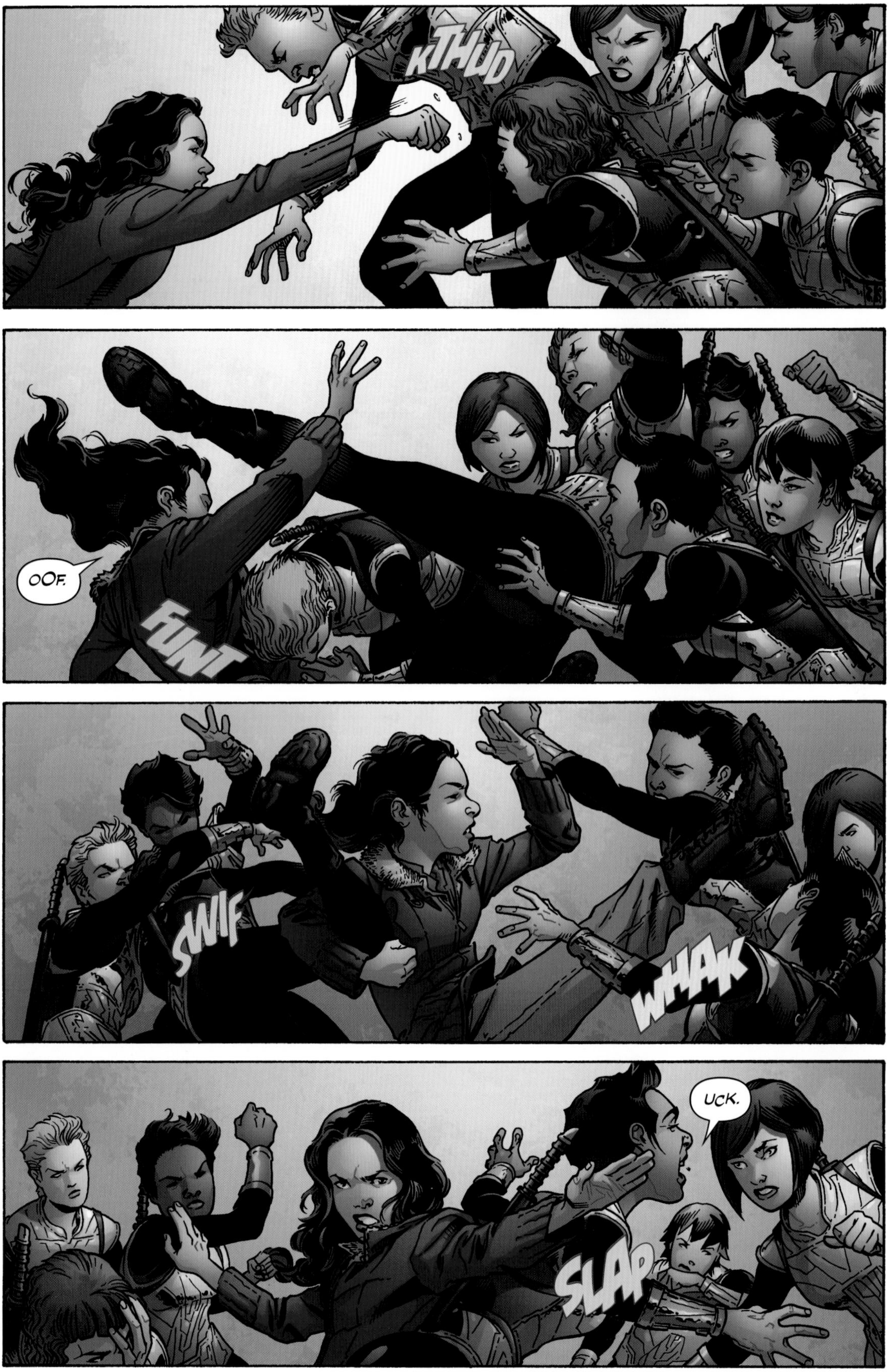
KTHUD
OOF.
FUMT
SWIF
WHAK
UCK.
SLAP

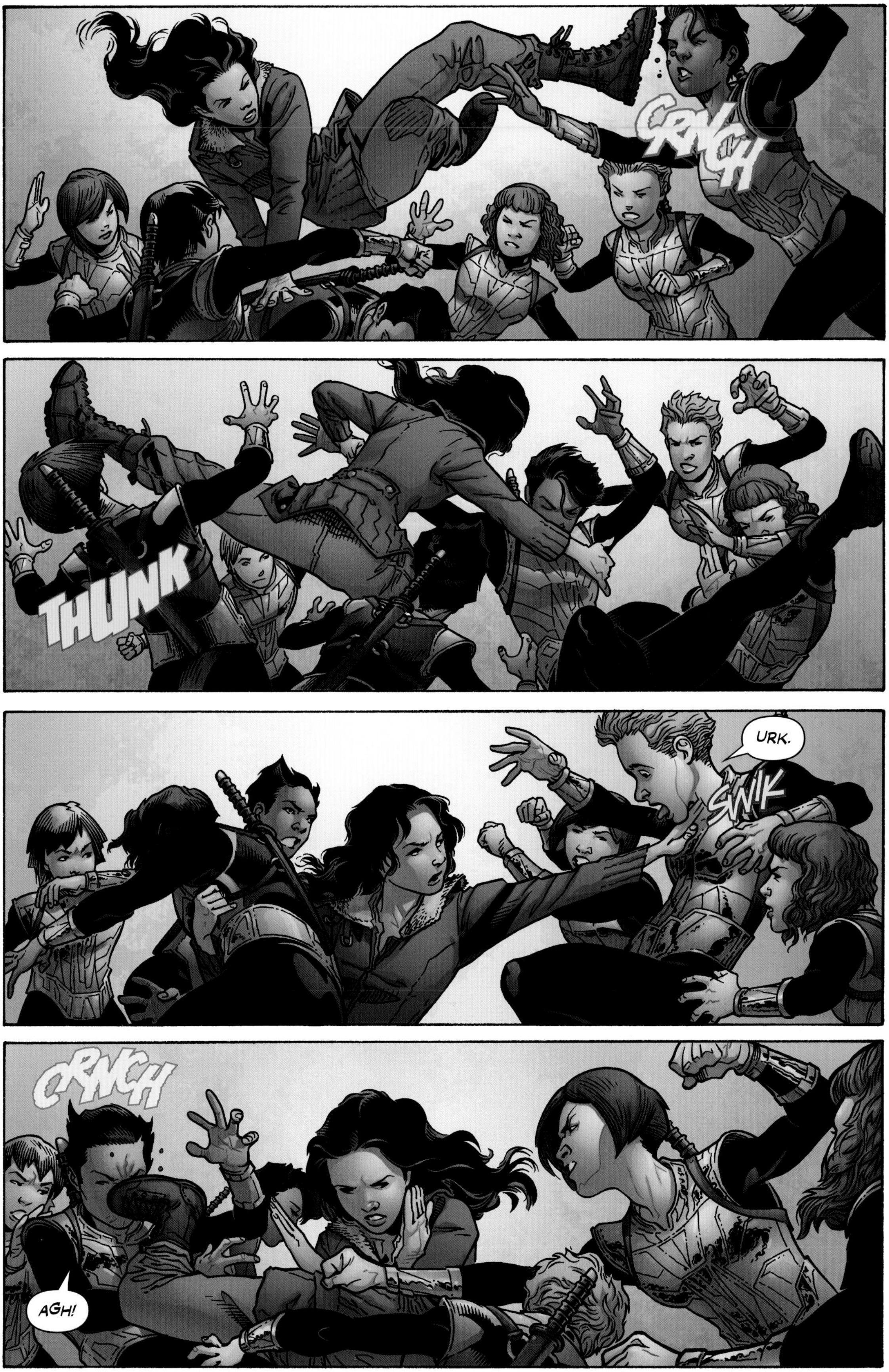
CRNCH
THUNK
URK.
SNIK
CRNCH
AGH!

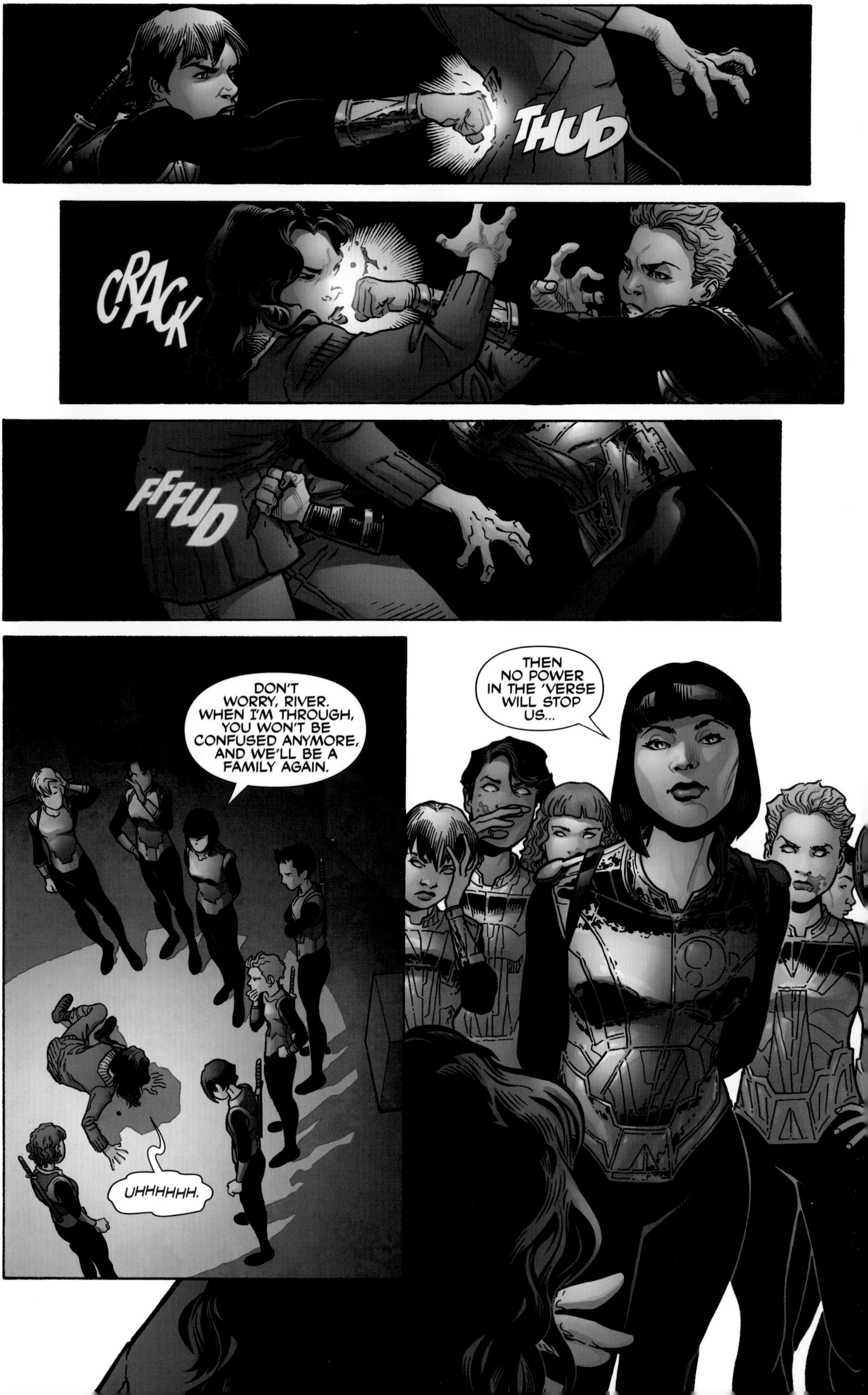
THUD
CRACK
FFFUD
DON'T WORRY, RIVER. WHEN I'M THROUGH, YOU WON'T BE CONFUSED ANYMORE, AND WE'LL BE A FAMILY AGAIN.
UHHHHHH.
THEN NO POWER IN THE 'VERSE WILL STOP US...

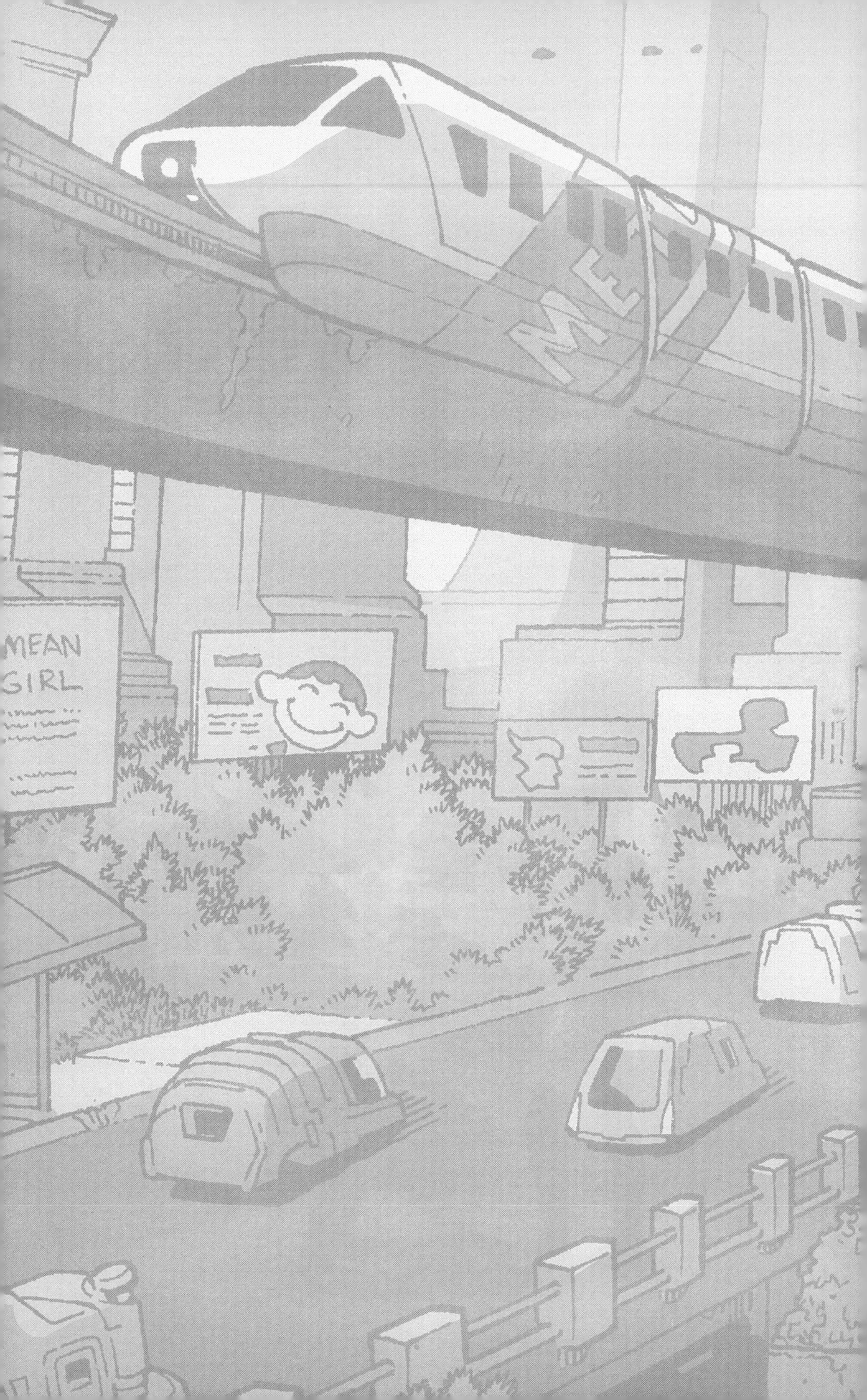
MEAN
GIRL

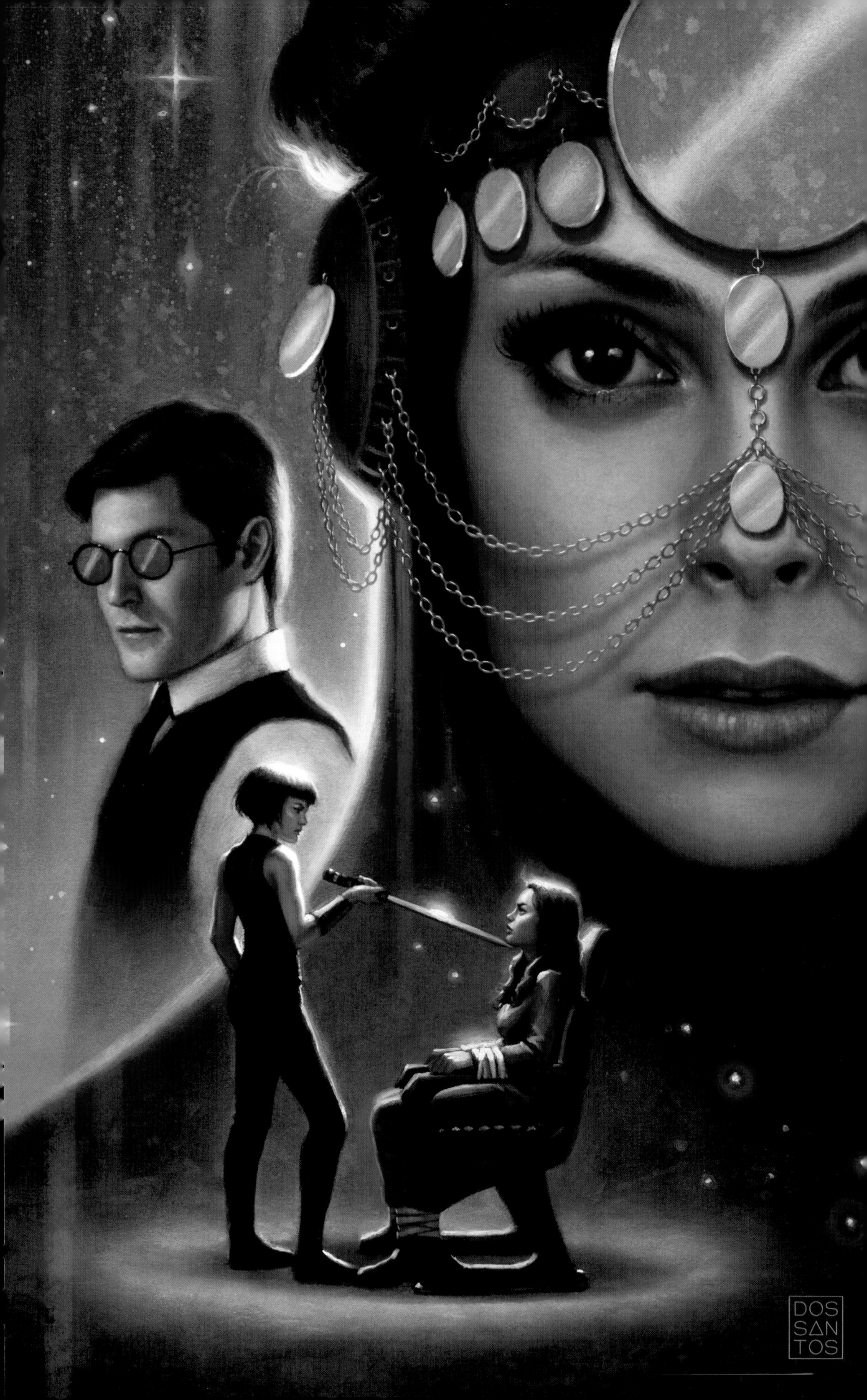
DOS
SAN
TOS

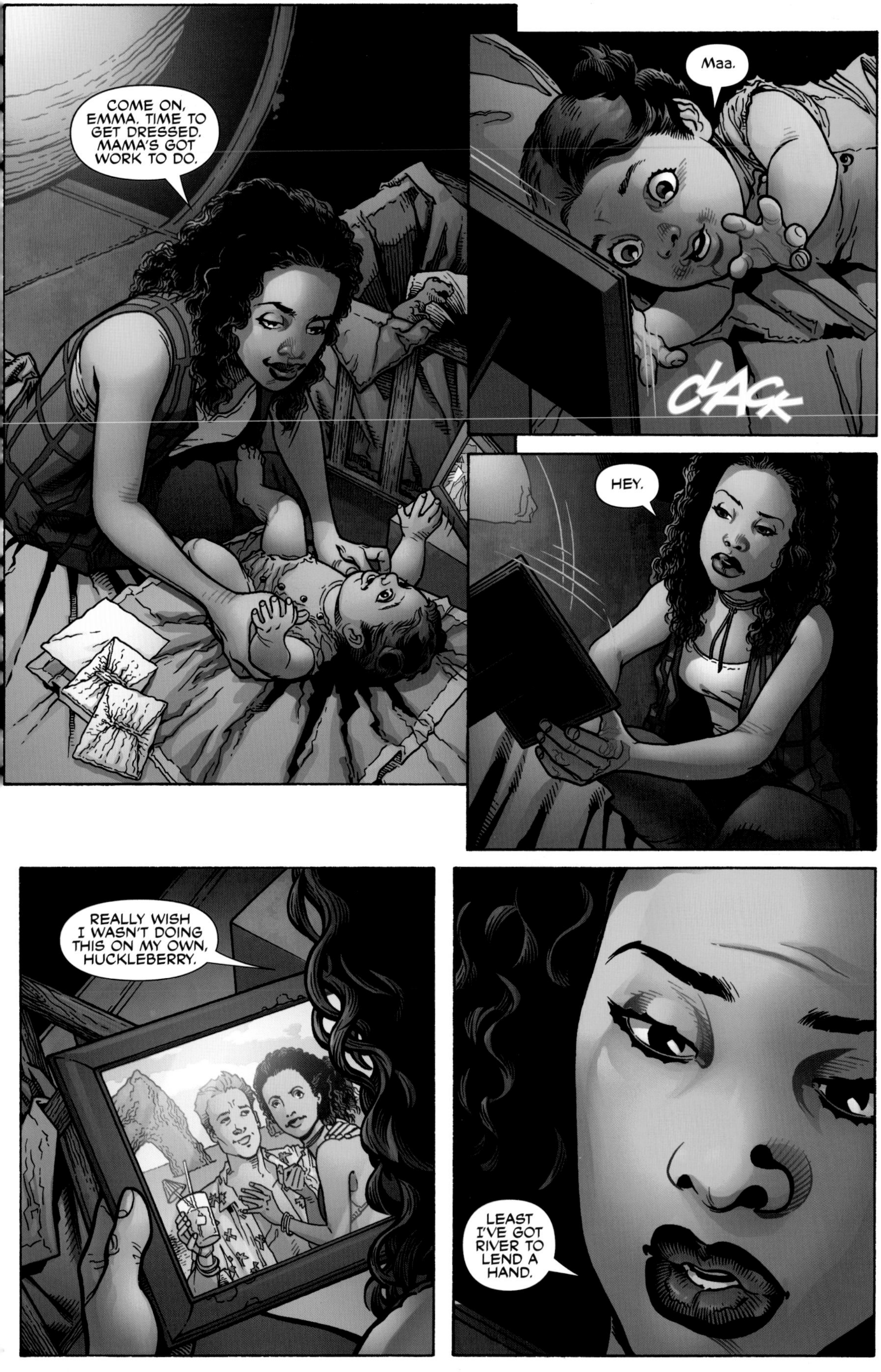

COME ON, EMMA. TIME TO GET DRESSED. MAMA'S GOT WORK TO DO.
Maa.
CLACK
HEY.
REALLY WISH I WASN'T DOING THIS ON MY OWN, HUCKLEBERRY.
LEAST I'VE GOT RIVER TO LEND A HAND.

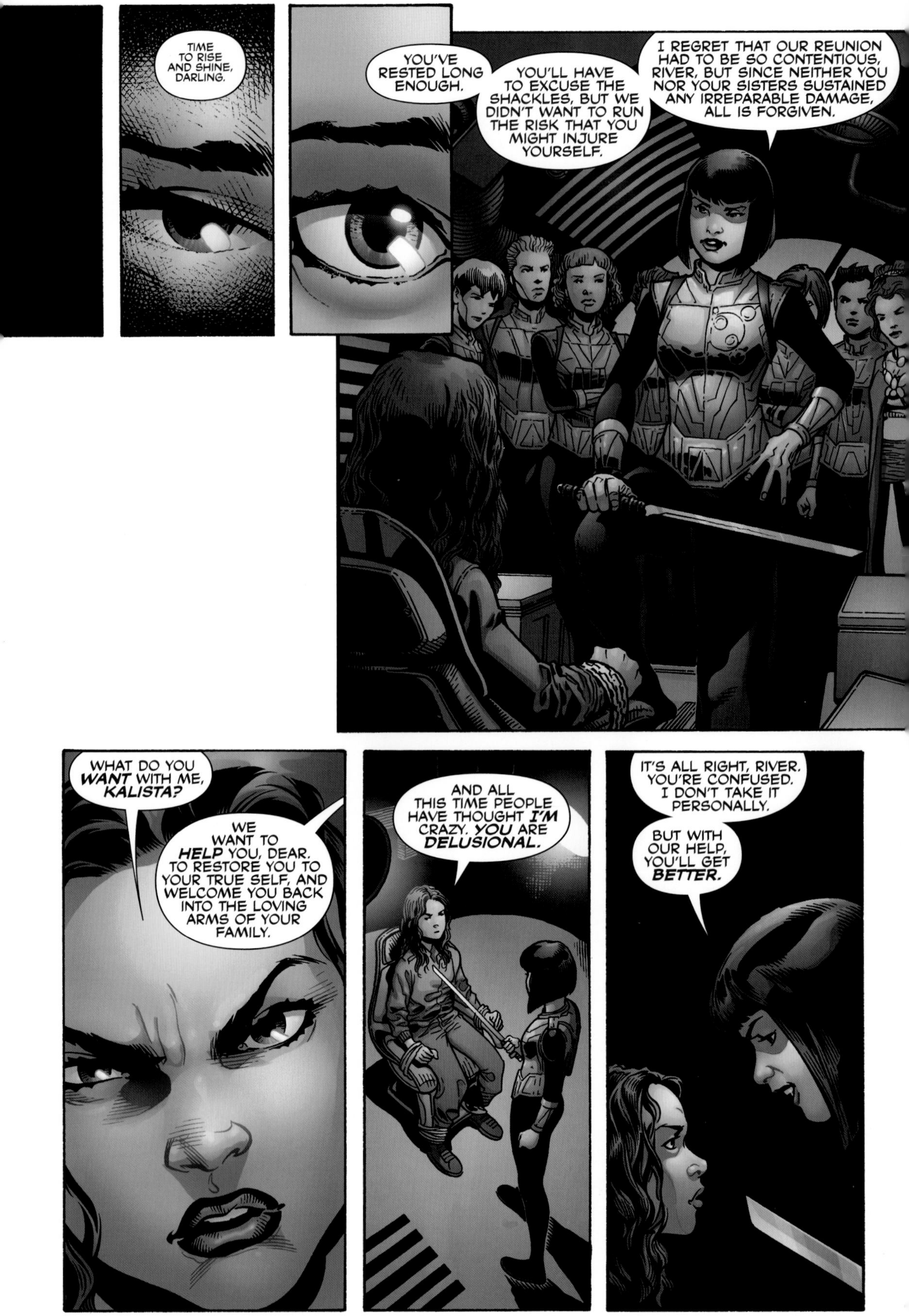
TIME TO RISE AND SHINE, DARLING.
YOU'VE RESTED LONG ENOUGH.
YOU'LL HAVE TO EXCUSE THE SHACKLES, BUT WE DIDN'T WANT TO RUN THE RISK THAT YOU MIGHT INJURE YOURSELF.
I REGRET THAT OUR REUNION HAD TO BE SO CONTENTIOUS, RIVER, BUT SINCE NEITHER YOU NOR YOUR SISTERS SUSTAINED ANY IRREPARABLE DAMAGE, ALL IS FORGIVEN.
WHAT DO YOU WANT WITH ME, KALISTA?
WE WANT TO HELP YOU, DEAR. TO RESTORE YOU TO YOUR TRUE SELF, AND WELCOME YOU BACK INTO THE LOVING ARMS OF YOUR FAMILY.
AND ALL THIS TIME PEOPLE HAVE THOUGHT I'M CRAZY. YOU ARE DELUSIONAL.
IT'S ALL RIGHT, RIVER. YOU'RE CONFUSED. I DON'T TAKE IT PERSONALLY.
BUT WITH OUR HELP, YOU'LL GET BETTER.

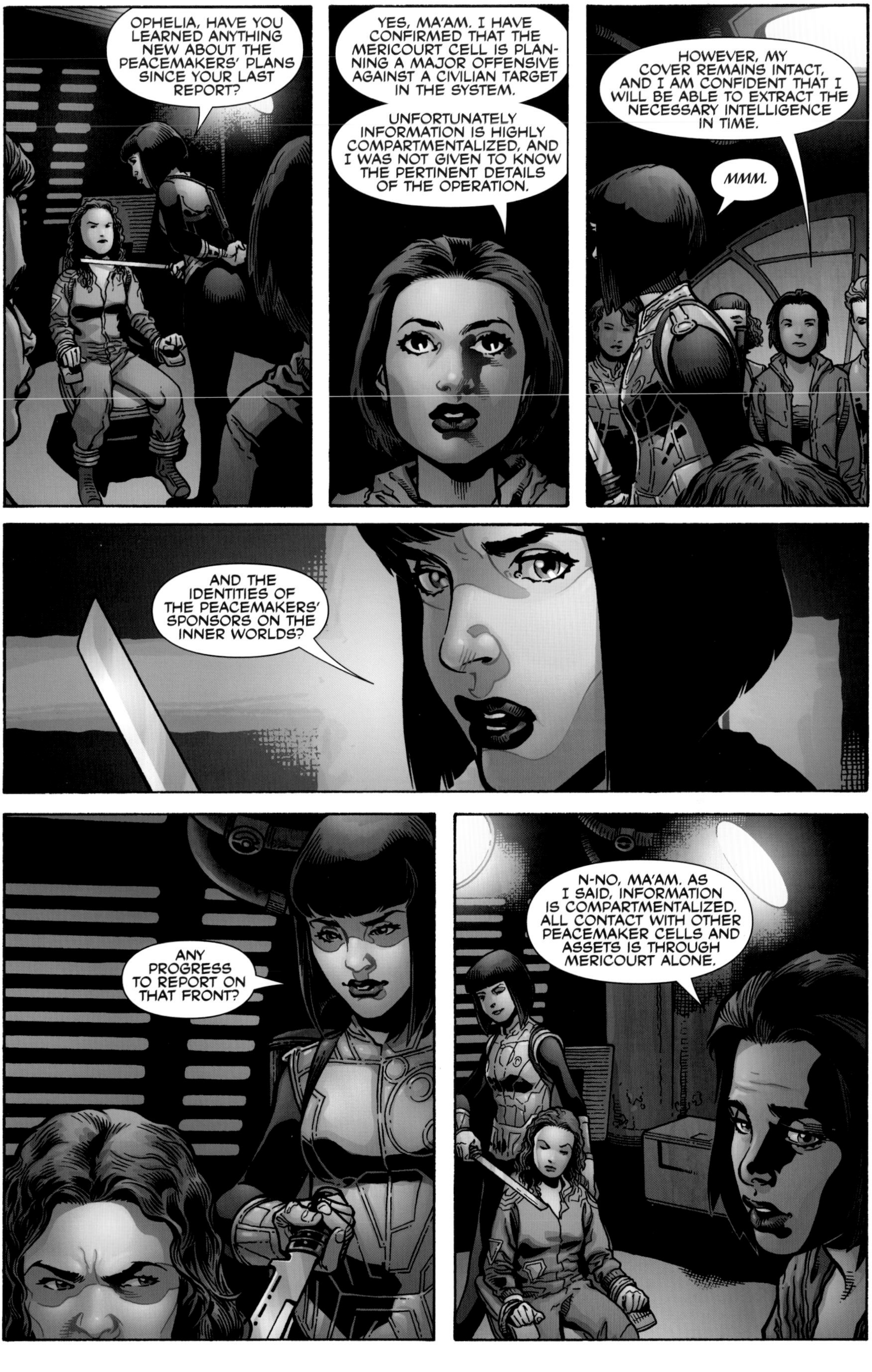
OPHELIA, HAVE YOU LEARNED ANYTHING NEW ABOUT THE PEACEMAKERS' PLANS SINCE YOUR LAST REPORT?
YES, MA'AM. I HAVE CONFIRMED THAT THE MERICOURT CELL IS PLANNING A MAJOR OFFENSIVE AGAINST A CIVILIAN TARGET IN THE SYSTEM.
UNFORTUNATELY INFORMATION IS HIGHLY COMPARTMENTALIZED, AND I WAS NOT GIVEN TO KNOW THE PERTINENT DETAILS OF THE OPERATION.
HOWEVER, MY COVER REMAINS INTACT, AND I AM CONFIDENT THAT I WILL BE ABLE TO EXTRACT THE NECESSARY INTELLIGENCE IN TIME.
MMM.
AND THE IDENTITIES OF THE PEACEMAKERS' SPONSORS ON THE INNER WORLDS?
ANY PROGRESS TO REPORT ON THAT FRONT?
N-NO, MA'AM. AS I SAID, INFORMATION IS COMPARTMENTALIZED. ALL CONTACT WITH OTHER PEACEMAKER CELLS AND ASSETS IS THROUGH MERICOURT ALONE.

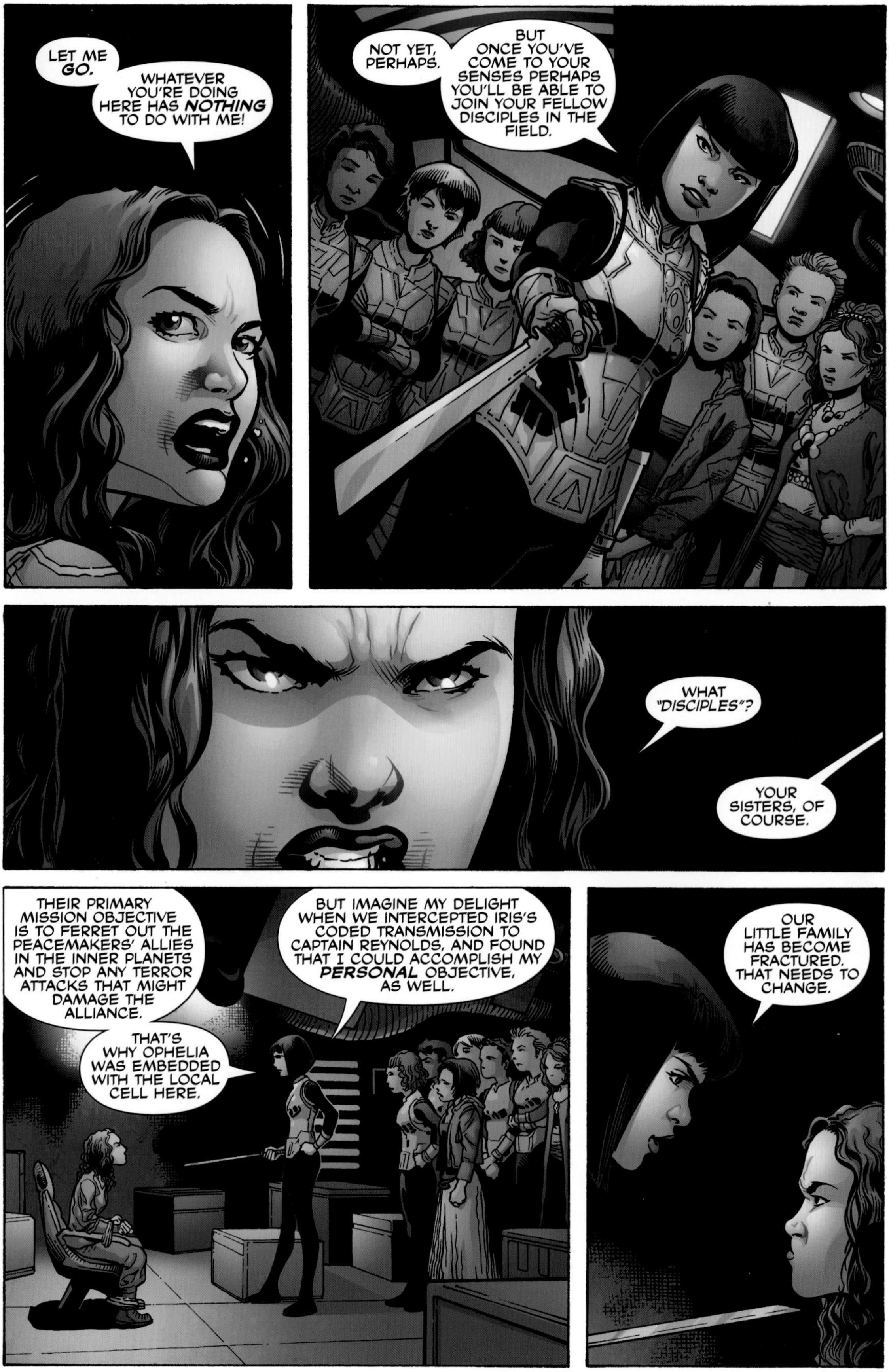
LET ME GO.
WHATEVER YOU'RE DOING HERE HAS NOTHING TO DO WITH ME!
NOT YET, PERHAPS.
BUT ONCE YOU'VE COME TO YOUR SENSES PERHAPS YOU'LL BE ABLE TO JOIN YOUR FELLOW DISCIPLES IN THE FIELD.
WHAT "DISCIPLES"?
YOUR SISTERS, OF COURSE.
THEIR PRIMARY MISSION OBJECTIVE IS TO FERRET OUT THE PEACEMAKERS' ALLIES IN THE INNER PLANETS AND STOP ANY TERROR ATTACKS THAT MIGHT DAMAGE THE ALLIANCE.
THAT'S WHY OPHELIA WAS EMBEDDED WITH THE LOCAL CELL HERE.
BUT IMAGINE MY DELIGHT WHEN WE INTERCEPTED IRIS'S CODED TRANSMISSION TO CAPTAIN REYNOLDS, AND FOUND THAT I COULD ACCOMPLISH MY PERSONAL OBJECTIVE, AS WELL.
OUR LITTLE FAMILY HAS BECOME FRACTURED. THAT NEEDS TO CHANGE.

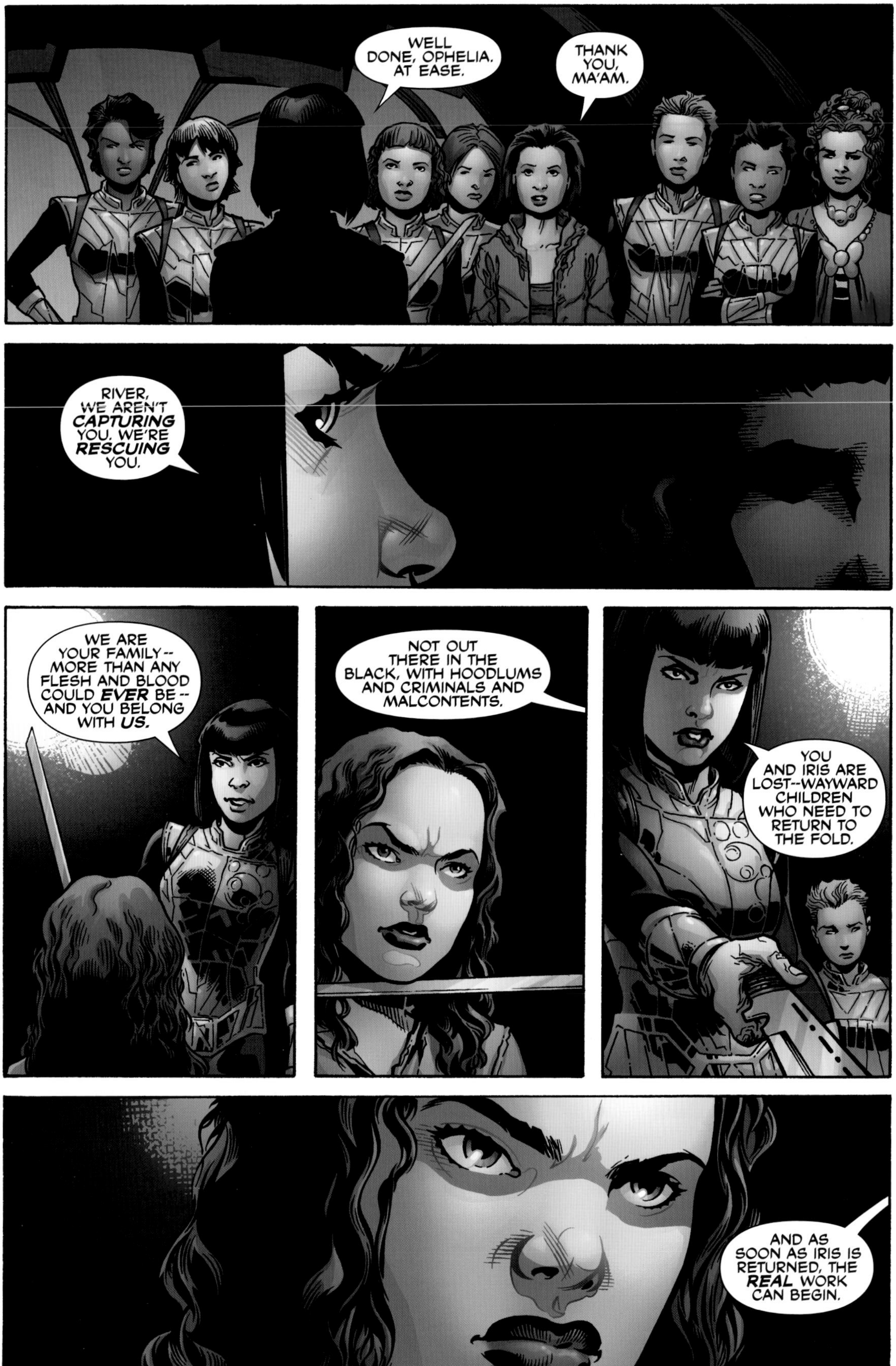
WELL DONE, OPHELIA. AT EASE.
THANK YOU, MA'AM.
RIVER, WE AREN'T CAPTURING YOU. WE'RE RESCUING YOU.
WE ARE YOUR FAMILY--MORE THAN ANY FLESH AND BLOOD COULD EVER BE--AND YOU BELONG WITH US.
NOT OUT THERE IN THE BLACK, WITH HOODLUMS AND CRIMINALS AND MALCONTENTS.
YOU AND IRIS ARE LOST--WAYWARD CHILDREN WHO NEED TO RETURN TO THE FOLD.
AND AS SOON AS IRIS IS RETURNED, THE REAL WORK CAN BEGIN.

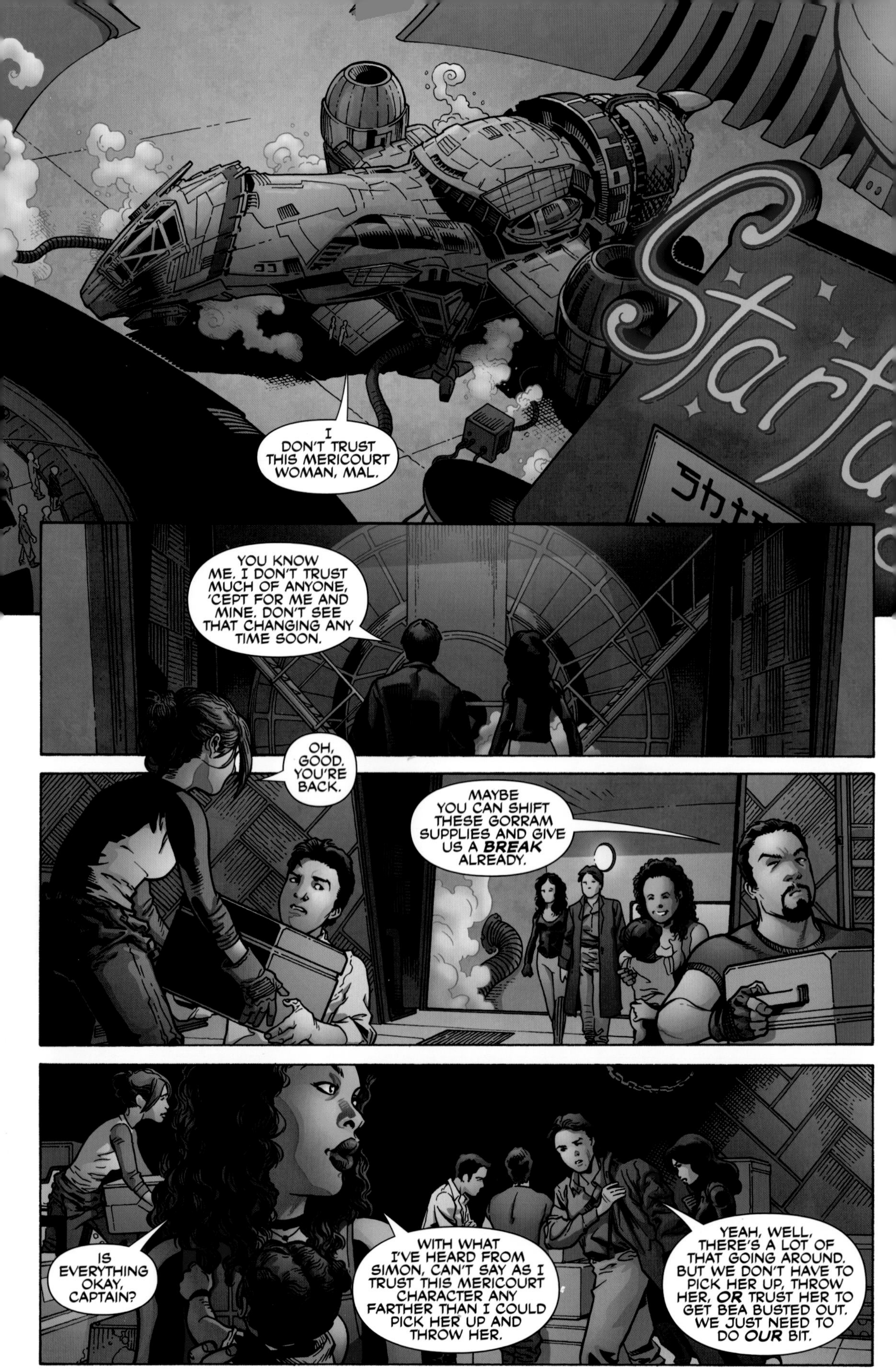
I DON'T TRUST THIS MERICOURT WOMAN, MAL.
YOU KNOW ME. I DON'T TRUST MUCH OF ANYONE, 'CEPT FOR ME AND MINE. DON'T SEE THAT CHANGING ANY TIME SOON.
OH, GOOD. YOU'RE BACK.
MAYBE YOU CAN SHIFT THESE GORRAM SUPPLIES AND GIVE US A ***BREAK*** ALREADY.
IS EVERYTHING OKAY, CAPTAIN?
WITH WHAT I'VE HEARD FROM SIMON, CAN'T SAY AS I TRUST THIS MERICOURT CHARACTER ANY FARTHER THAN I COULD PICK HER UP AND THROW HER.
YEAH, WELL, THERE'S A LOT OF THAT GOING AROUND. BUT WE DON'T HAVE TO PICK HER UP, THROW HER, ***OR*** TRUST HER TO GET BEA BUSTED OUT. WE JUST NEED TO DO ***OUR*** BIT.

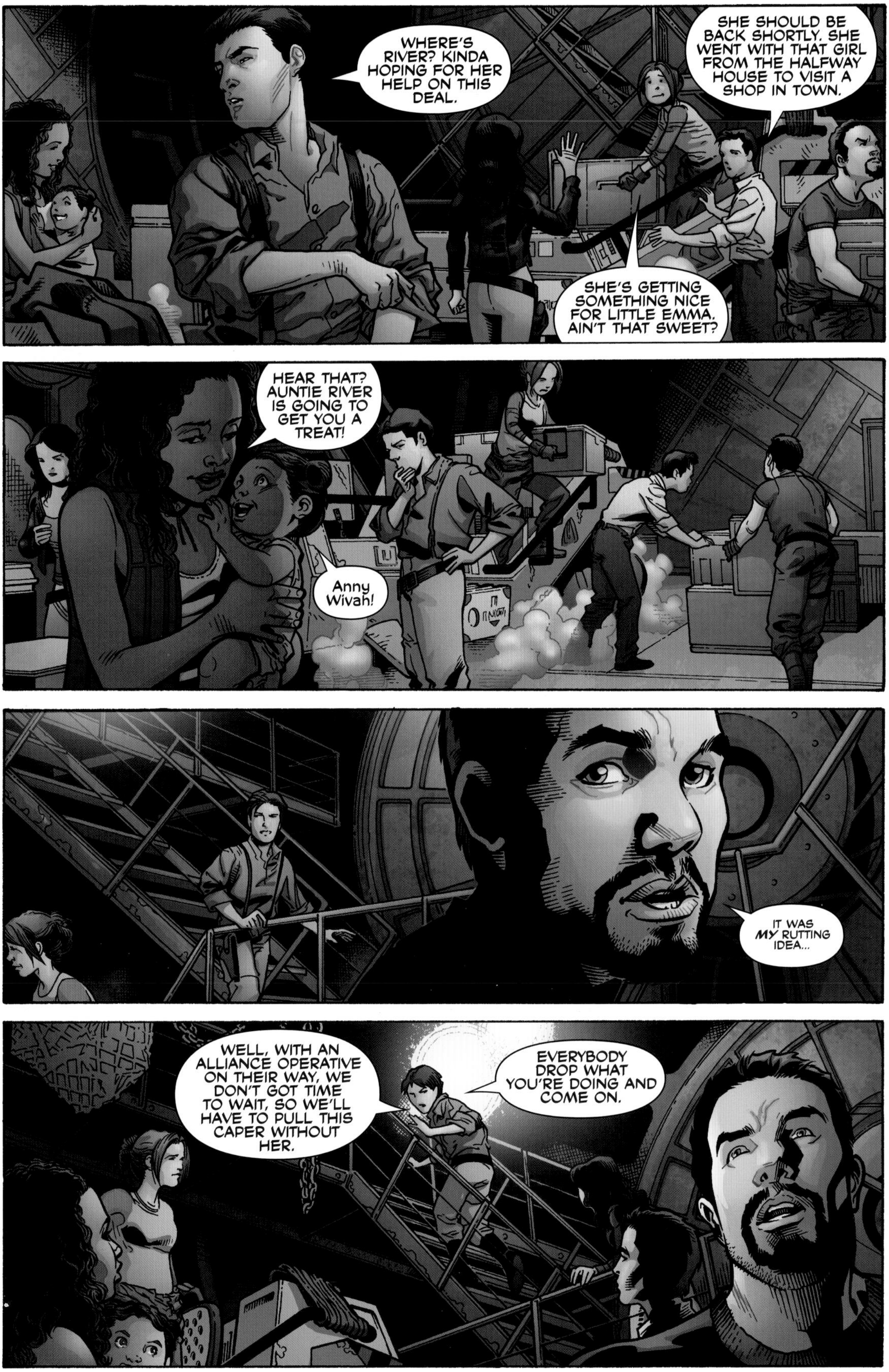
WHERE'S RIVER? KINDA HOPING FOR HER HELP ON THIS DEAL.
SHE SHOULD BE BACK SHORTLY. SHE WENT WITH THAT GIRL FROM THE HALFWAY HOUSE TO VISIT A SHOP IN TOWN.
SHE'S GETTING SOMETHING NICE FOR LITTLE EMMA. AIN'T THAT SWEET?
HEAR THAT? AUNTIE RIVER IS GOING TO GET YOU A TREAT!
Anny Wivah!
IT WAS MY RUTTING IDEA...
WELL, WITH AN ALLIANCE OPERATIVE ON THEIR WAY, WE DON'T GOT TIME TO WAIT, SO WE'LL HAVE TO PULL THIS CAPER WITHOUT HER.
EVERYBODY DROP WHAT YOU'RE DOING AND COME ON.

NOW BEFORE ANYONE ELSE CHIMES IN, *NO*, I DON'T TRUST MERICOURT.

SHE'S HIDING THINGS FROM US, I CAN TELL.

I'M NOT AIMING TO WED HER. WE JUST GOT COMMON CAUSE FOR A SPELL, THAT'S ALL.

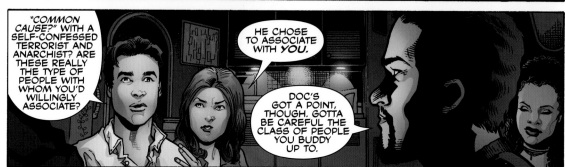

"*COMMON CAUSE?*" WITH A SELF-CONFESSED TERRORIST AND ANARCHIST? ARE THESE REALLY THE TYPE OF PEOPLE WITH WHOM YOU'D WILLINGLY ASSOCIATE?

HE CHOSE TO ASSOCIATE WITH *YOU*.

DOC'S GOT A POINT, THOUGH. GOTTA BE CAREFUL THE CLASS OF PEOPLE YOU BUDDY UP TO.

JAYNE, NOBODY MUCH CARES ABOUT YOUR VIEWS ON WHO WE SHOULD OR SHOULDN'T "BUDDY UP TO."

GOSH, ZOE, I WAS JUST --

ENOUGH ALREADY. THIS AIN'T A DEMOCRACY.

MERICOURT'S RELATIVE MERITS DON'T MAKE A DAMNED BIT OF DIFFERENCE. IT'S *OUR* FRIEND BEA THAT'S LOCKED UP IN ALLIANCE HANDS.

IF IT SUITS MERICOURT'S INTERESTS TO GET BEA BUSTED OUT, THEN WE'LL GLADLY ACCEPT HER HELP.

NOW WE'VE GOT A PLAN, AND WE'RE GONNA STICK TO IT. THAT'S THE END OF DISCUSSION.

INARA, SINCE YOU'RE HAVING TO GET ALL GUSSIED UP, I HOPE YOU STILL GOT SOME OF YOUR FRILLY FINERY SOCKED AWAY SOMEWHERE?

JUST BECAUSE I ADDED A FEW *PRAGMATIC* OPTIONS TO MY WARDROBE DOESN'T MEAN I LOST MY *MIND*, MAL.

AND DOC, ANY CHANCE YOU'VE GOT THOSE FANCY EYEGLASSES OF YOURS CLOSE TO HAND?

OF COURSE, BUT I DON'T SEE WHAT THAT'S GOT TO DO WITH --

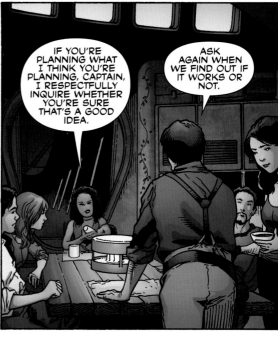

IF YOU'RE PLANNING WHAT I THINK YOU'RE PLANNING, CAPTAIN, I RESPECTFULLY INQUIRE WHETHER YOU'RE SURE THAT'S A GOOD IDEA.

ASK AGAIN WHEN WE FIND OUT IF IT WORKS OR NOT.

SO HERE'S WHAT WE'RE GOING TO DO...

ALLIANCE PLANETARY OFFICES.

NEXT?

NEXT?

IT'S BAD ENOUGH THAT I WAS POSTED TO THIS *MISERABLE* BACKWATER ROCK.

BUT THE UNENDING RIVER OF *NONSENSE* THAT GREETS ME EVERY DAY MERELY ADDS INSULT TO INJURY.

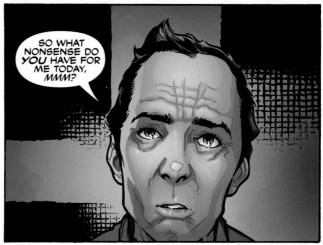

SO WHAT NONSENSE DO *YOU* HAVE FOR ME TODAY, *MMM?*

66

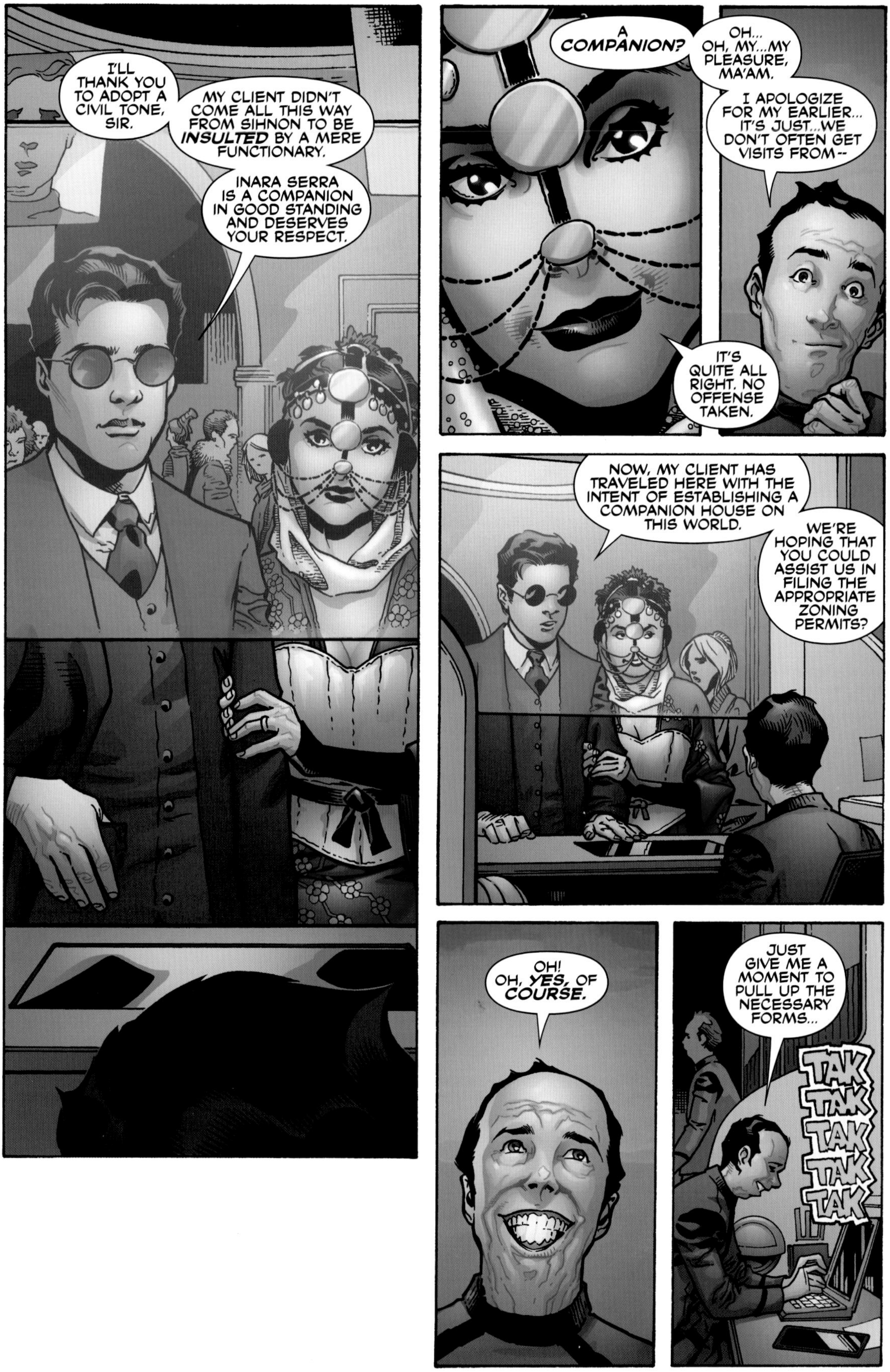

I'LL THANK YOU TO ADOPT A CIVIL TONE, SIR.
MY CLIENT DIDN'T COME ALL THIS WAY FROM SIHNON TO BE *INSULTED* BY A MERE FUNCTIONARY.
INARA SERRA IS A COMPANION IN GOOD STANDING AND DESERVES YOUR RESPECT.
A *COMPANION?*
OH... OH, MY...MY PLEASURE, MA'AM.
I APOLOGIZE FOR MY EARLIER... IT'S JUST...WE DON'T OFTEN GET VISITS FROM--
IT'S QUITE ALL RIGHT. NO OFFENSE TAKEN.
NOW, MY CLIENT HAS TRAVELED HERE WITH THE INTENT OF ESTABLISHING A COMPANION HOUSE ON THIS WORLD.
WE'RE HOPING THAT YOU COULD ASSIST US IN FILING THE APPROPRIATE ZONING PERMITS?
OH! OH, *YES,* OF *COURSE.*
JUST GIVE ME A MOMENT TO PULL UP THE NECESSARY FORMS...
TAK TAK TAK TAK TAK

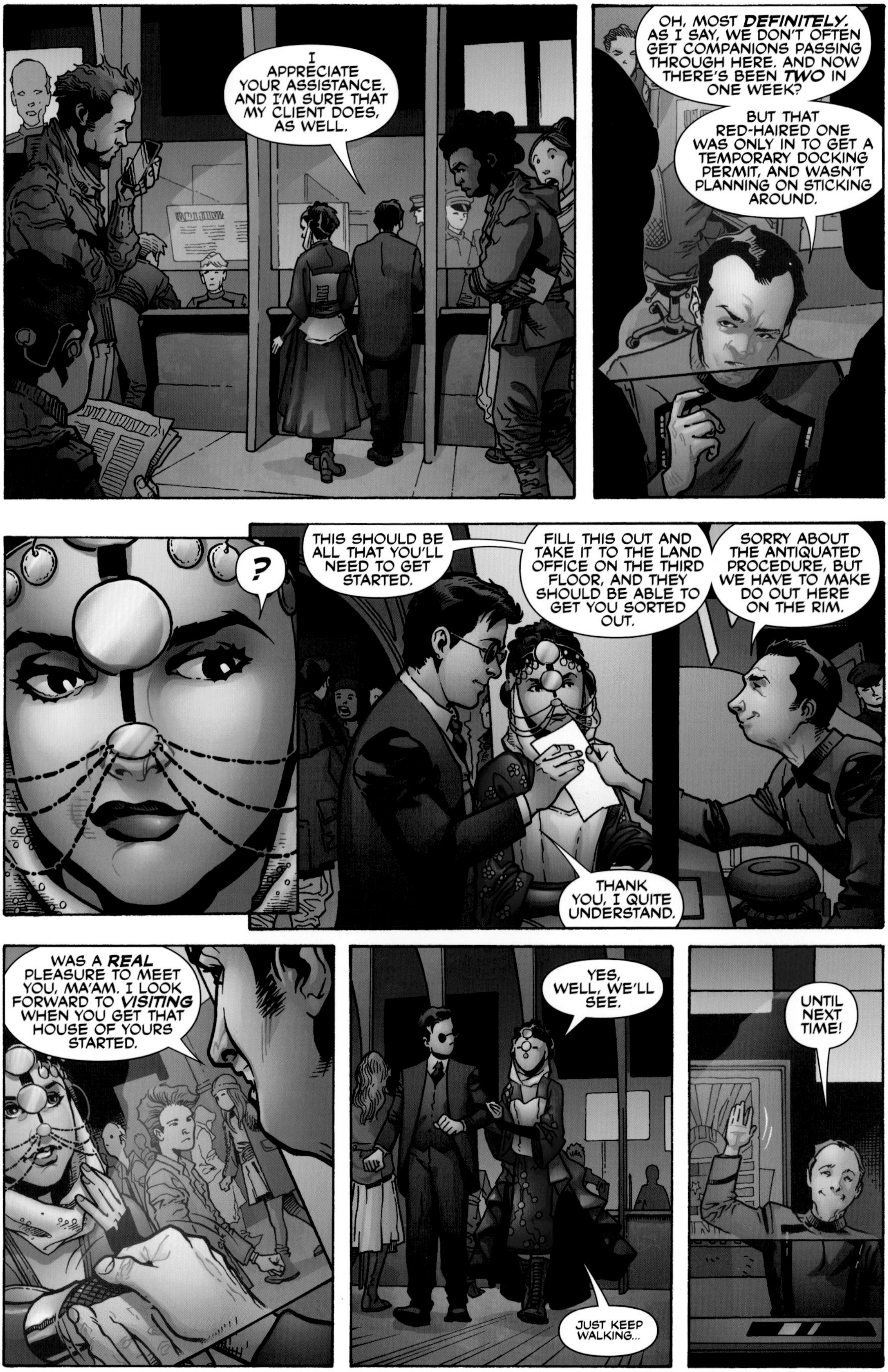
I APPRECIATE YOUR ASSISTANCE. AND I'M SURE THAT MY CLIENT DOES, AS WELL.
OH, MOST DEFINITELY. AS I SAY, WE DON'T OFTEN GET COMPANIONS PASSING THROUGH HERE. AND NOW THERE'S BEEN TWO IN ONE WEEK?
BUT THAT RED-HAIRED ONE WAS ONLY IN TO GET A TEMPORARY DOCKING PERMIT, AND WASN'T PLANNING ON STICKING AROUND.
?
THIS SHOULD BE ALL THAT YOU'LL NEED TO GET STARTED.
FILL THIS OUT AND TAKE IT TO THE LAND OFFICE ON THE THIRD FLOOR, AND THEY SHOULD BE ABLE TO GET YOU SORTED OUT.
SORRY ABOUT THE ANTIQUATED PROCEDURE, BUT WE HAVE TO MAKE DO OUT HERE ON THE RIM.
THANK YOU, I QUITE UNDERSTAND.
WAS A REAL PLEASURE TO MEET YOU, MA'AM. I LOOK FORWARD TO VISITING WHEN YOU GET THAT HOUSE OF YOURS STARTED.
YES, WELL, WE'LL SEE.
JUST KEEP WALKING...
UNTIL NEXT TIME!

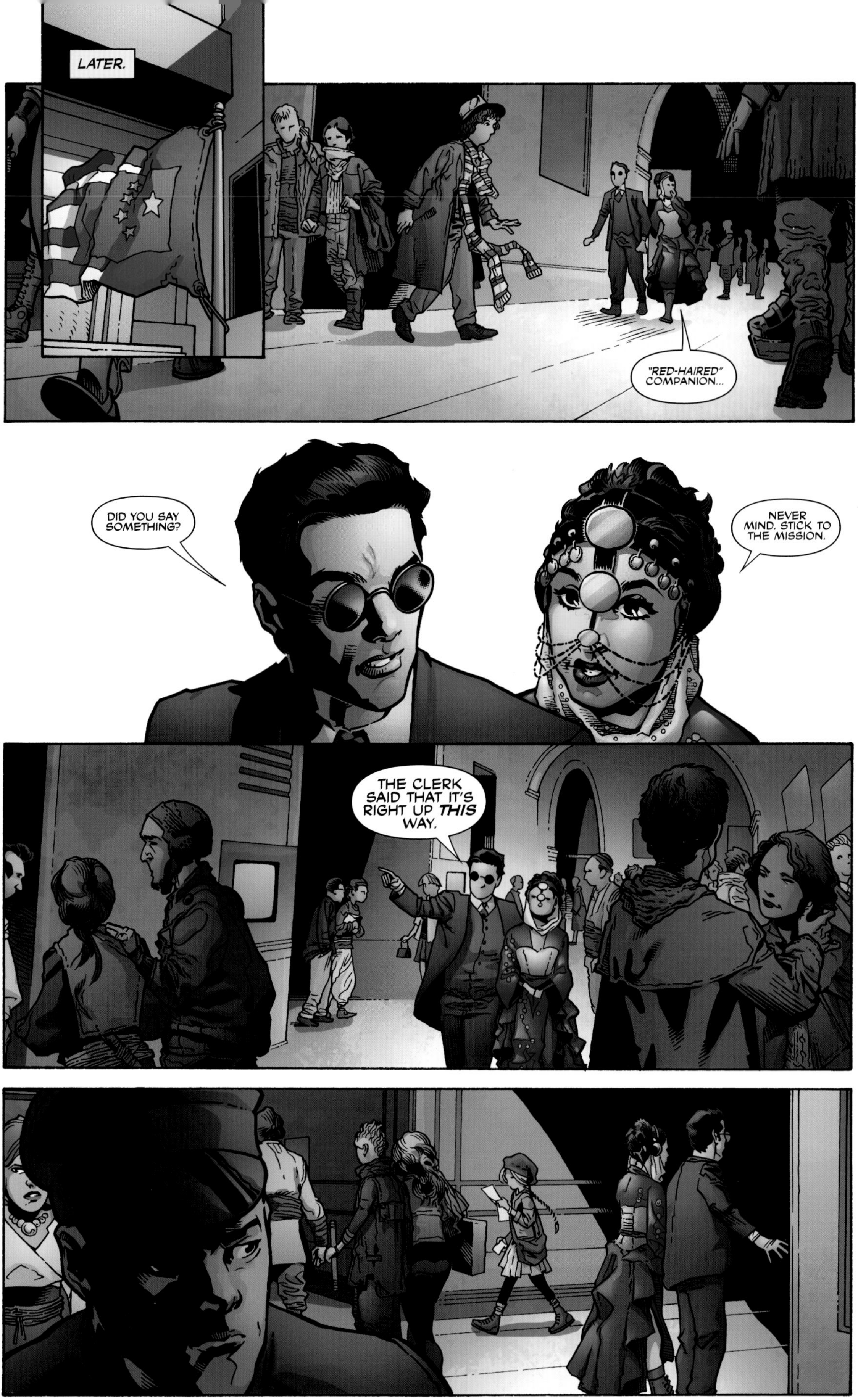
LATER.
"RED-HAIRED" COMPANION...
DID YOU SAY SOMETHING?
NEVER MIND. STICK TO THE MISSION.
THE CLERK SAID THAT IT'S RIGHT UP *THIS* WAY.

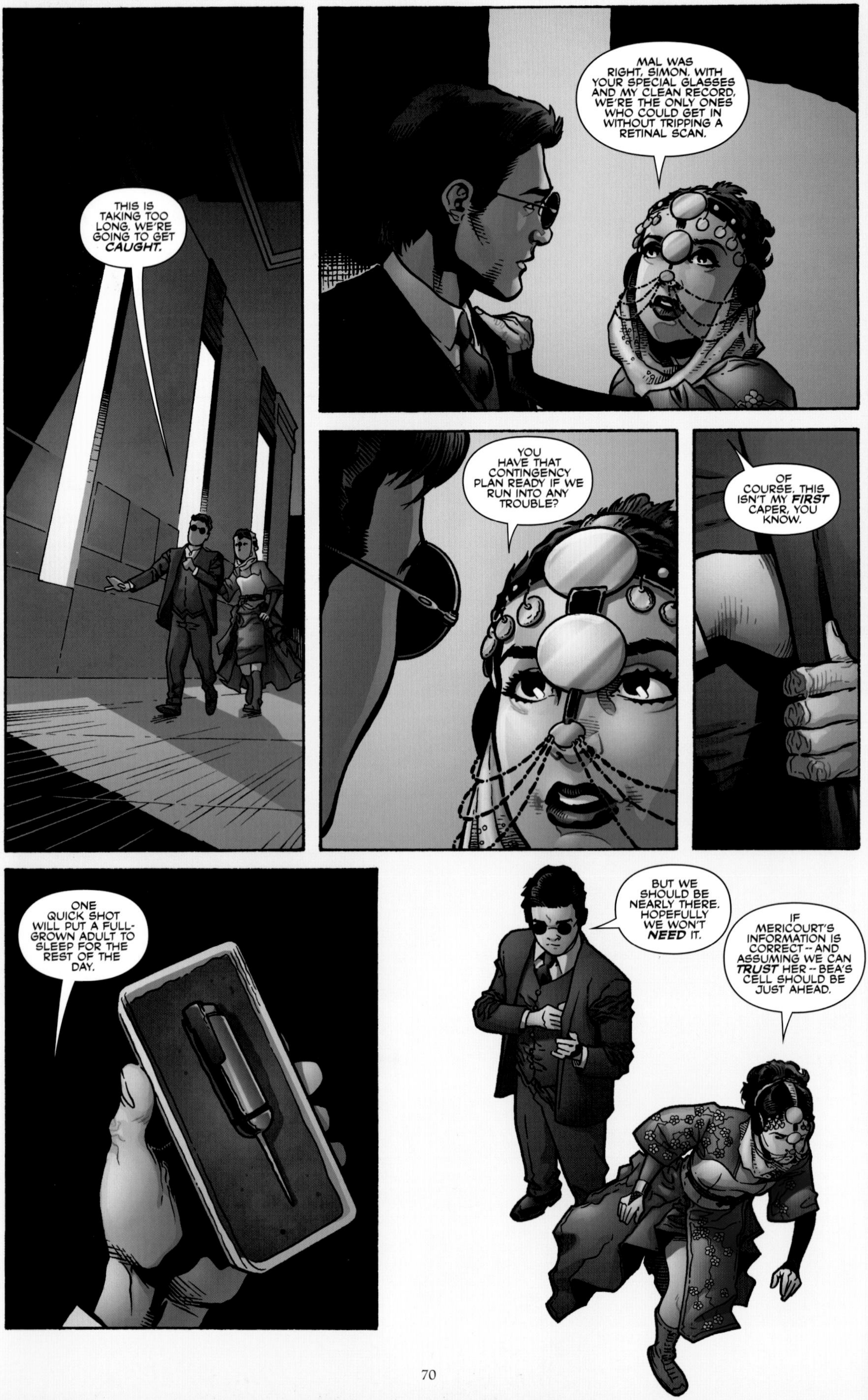
THIS IS TAKING TOO LONG. WE'RE GOING TO GET CAUGHT.
MAL WAS RIGHT, SIMON, WITH YOUR SPECIAL GLASSES AND MY CLEAN RECORD, WE'RE THE ONLY ONES WHO COULD GET IN WITHOUT TRIPPING A RETINAL SCAN.
YOU HAVE THAT CONTINGENCY PLAN READY IF WE RUN INTO ANY TROUBLE?
OF COURSE. THIS ISN'T MY FIRST CAPER, YOU KNOW.
ONE QUICK SHOT WILL PUT A FULL-GROWN ADULT TO SLEEP FOR THE REST OF THE DAY.
BUT WE SHOULD BE NEARLY THERE. HOPEFULLY WE WON'T NEED IT.
IF MERICOURT'S INFORMATION IS CORRECT -- AND ASSUMING WE CAN TRUST HER -- BEA'S CELL SHOULD BE JUST AHEAD.

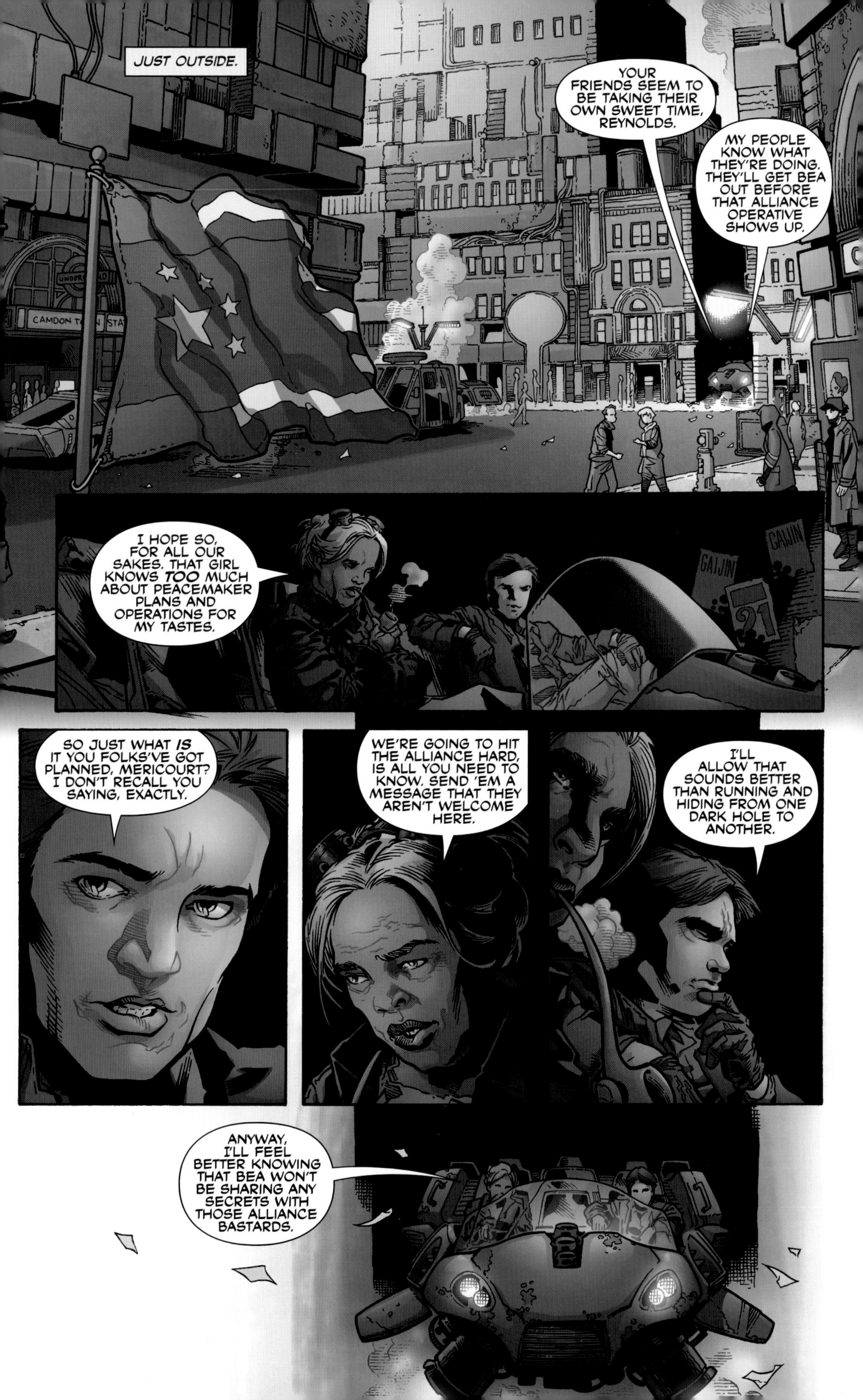
JUST OUTSIDE.
YOUR FRIENDS SEEM TO BE TAKING THEIR OWN SWEET TIME, REYNOLDS.
MY PEOPLE KNOW WHAT THEY'RE DOING. THEY'LL GET BEA OUT BEFORE THAT ALLIANCE OPERATIVE SHOWS UP.
CAMDON T STA
GAIJIN
GAIJIN
21
I HOPE SO, FOR ALL OUR SAKES. THAT GIRL KNOWS TOO MUCH ABOUT PEACEMAKER PLANS AND OPERATIONS FOR MY TASTES.
SO JUST WHAT IS IT YOU FOLKS'VE GOT PLANNED, MERICOURT? I DON'T RECALL YOU SAYING, EXACTLY.
WE'RE GOING TO HIT THE ALLIANCE HARD, IS ALL YOU NEED TO KNOW. SEND 'EM A MESSAGE THAT THEY AREN'T WELCOME HERE.
I'LL ALLOW THAT SOUNDS BETTER THAN RUNNING AND HIDING FROM ONE DARK HOLE TO ANOTHER.
ANYWAY, I'LL FEEL BETTER KNOWING THAT BEA WON'T BE SHARING ANY SECRETS WITH THOSE ALLIANCE BASTARDS.

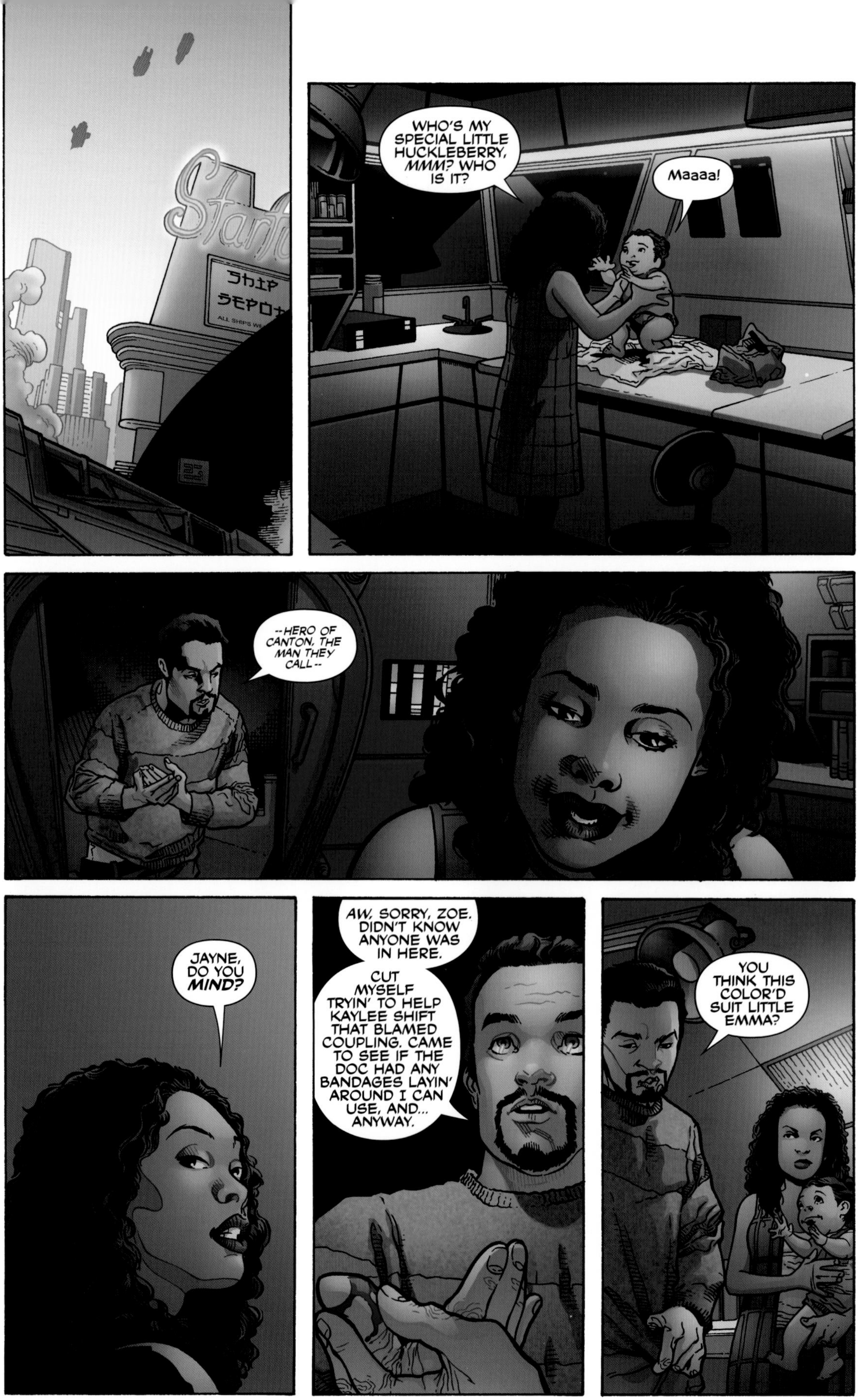
Starf
SHIP
DEPOT
ALL SHIPS WE
WHO'S MY SPECIAL LITTLE HUCKLEBERRY, *MMM?* WHO IS IT?
Maaaa!
--HERO OF CANTON, THE MAN THEY CALL--
JAYNE, DO YOU *MIND?*
AW, SORRY, ZOE. DIDN'T KNOW ANYONE WAS IN HERE.
CUT MYSELF TRYIN' TO HELP KAYLEE SHIFT THAT BLAMED COUPLING. CAME TO SEE IF THE DOC HAD ANY BANDAGES LAYIN' AROUND I CAN USE, AND... ANYWAY.
YOU THINK THIS COLOR'D SUIT LITTLE EMMA?

CLANG CLANG

LOT OF HELP *HE* IS. "I *CUT* MYSELF, KAYLEE. I'M *BLEEDIN'*, KAYLEE."

JAYNE WOULDN'T LAST FIVE MINUTES, HE HAD TO DO *MY* JOB.

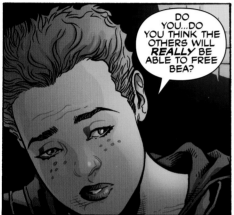

DO YOU...DO YOU THINK THE OTHERS WILL *REALLY* BE ABLE TO FREE BEA?

AW, YOU'RE WORRIED ABOUT YOUR FRIEND, AIN'T YA? POOR THING.

NOW DON'T YOU WORRY FOR A SEC, IRIS. SIMON AND INARA WILL HAVE HER OUT IN *NO* TIME.

AND SOON AS THEY DO, YOU TWO WILL BE FREE TO ROAM THE 'VERSE AGAIN, HAVING ADVENTURES AND THE LIKE.

I HOPE SO. BUT MAYBE NEXT TIME --

BREEP

SIMMER DOWN, GIRL, IT'S JUST THE DOORBELL. YOU STAY HERE AND I'LL CHECK IT OUT.

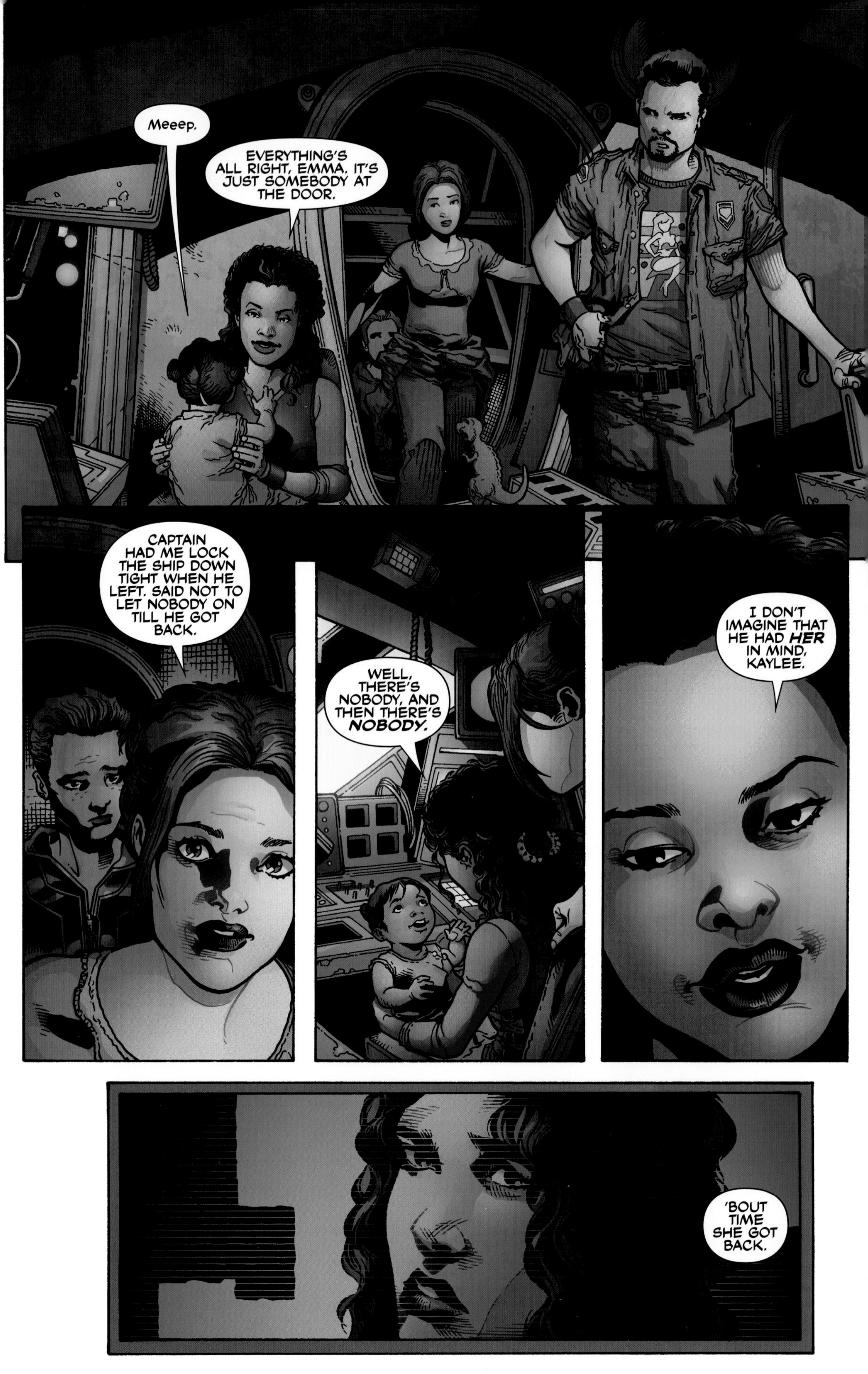
Meeep.
EVERYTHING'S ALL RIGHT, EMMA. IT'S JUST SOMEBODY AT THE DOOR.
CAPTAIN HAD ME LOCK THE SHIP DOWN TIGHT WHEN HE LEFT. SAID NOT TO LET NOBODY ON TILL HE GOT BACK.
WELL, THERE'S NOBODY, AND THEN THERE'S NOBODY.
I DON'T IMAGINE THAT HE HAD HER IN MIND, KAYLEE.
'BOUT TIME SHE GOT BACK.

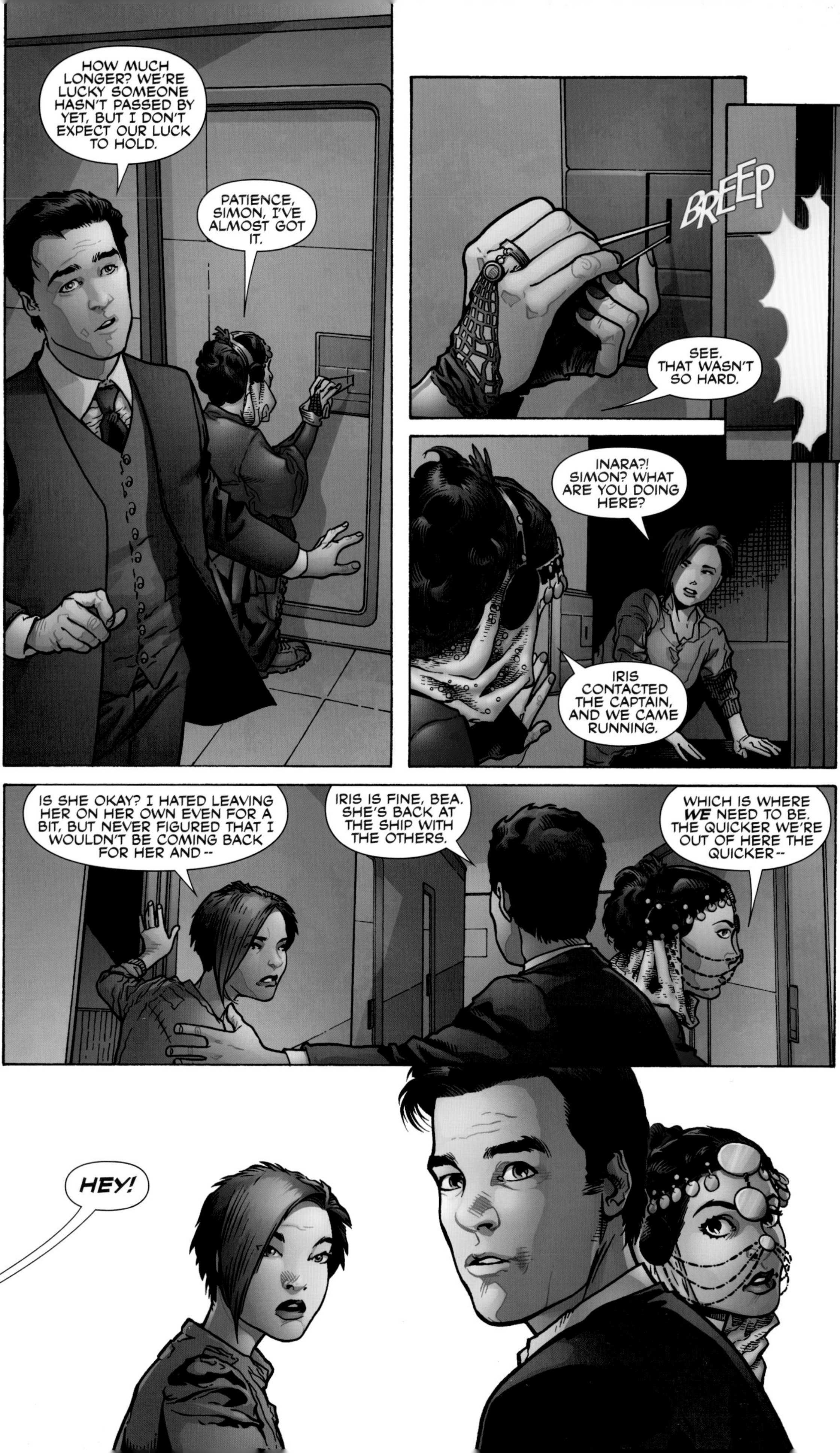
HOW MUCH LONGER? WE'RE LUCKY SOMEONE HASN'T PASSED BY YET, BUT I DON'T EXPECT OUR LUCK TO HOLD.
PATIENCE, SIMON, I'VE ALMOST GOT IT.
BREEP
SEE. THAT WASN'T SO HARD.
INARA?! SIMON? WHAT ARE YOU DOING HERE?
IRIS CONTACTED THE CAPTAIN, AND WE CAME RUNNING.
IS SHE OKAY? I HATED LEAVING HER ON HER OWN EVEN FOR A BIT, BUT NEVER FIGURED THAT I WOULDN'T BE COMING BACK FOR HER AND --
IRIS IS FINE, BEA. SHE'S BACK AT THE SHIP WITH THE OTHERS.
WHICH IS WHERE *WE* NEED TO BE. THE QUICKER WE'RE OUT OF HERE THE QUICKER --
HEY!

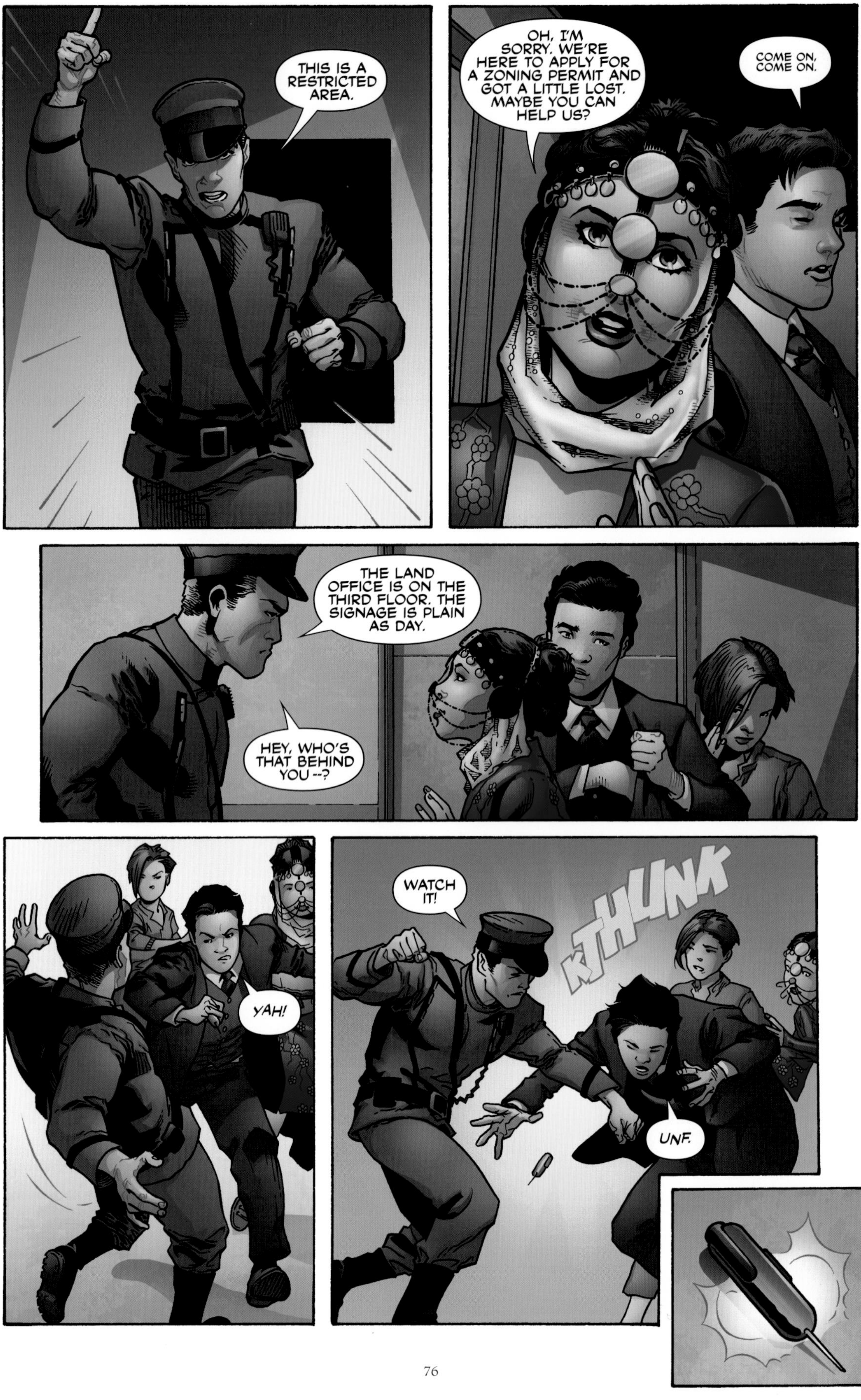
THIS IS A RESTRICTED AREA.
OH, I'M SORRY. WE'RE HERE TO APPLY FOR A ZONING PERMIT AND GOT A LITTLE LOST. MAYBE YOU CAN HELP US?
COME ON, COME ON.
THE LAND OFFICE IS ON THE THIRD FLOOR. THE SIGNAGE IS PLAIN AS DAY.
HEY, WHO'S THAT BEHIND YOU --?
YAH!
WATCH IT!
KTHUNK
UNF.

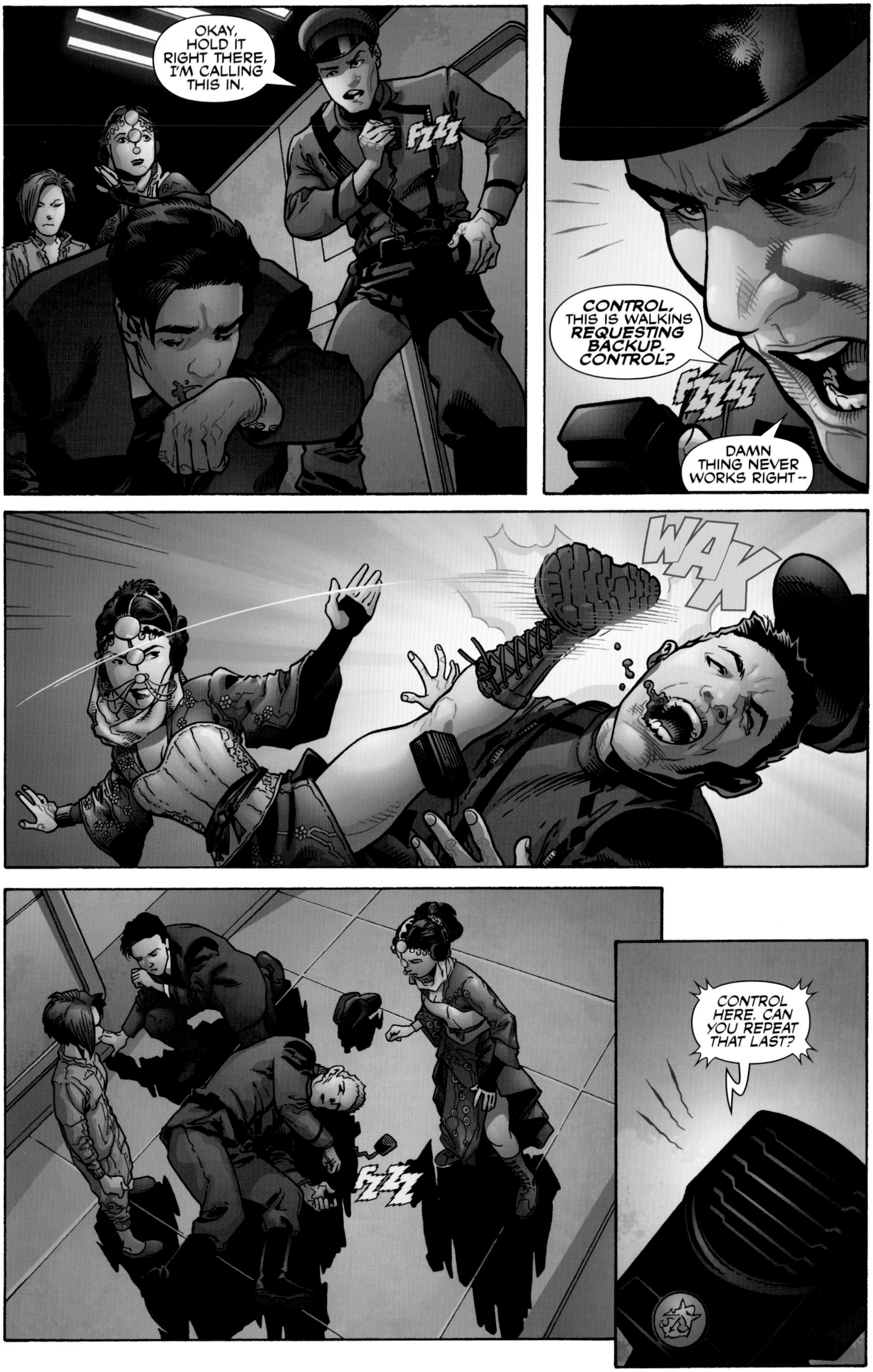
OKAY, HOLD IT RIGHT THERE, I'M CALLING THIS IN.
FZZZ
CONTROL, THIS IS WALKINS REQUESTING BACKUP. CONTROL?
FZZZZ
DAMN THING NEVER WORKS RIGHT--
WAK
CONTROL HERE. CAN YOU REPEAT THAT LAST?
FZZZ

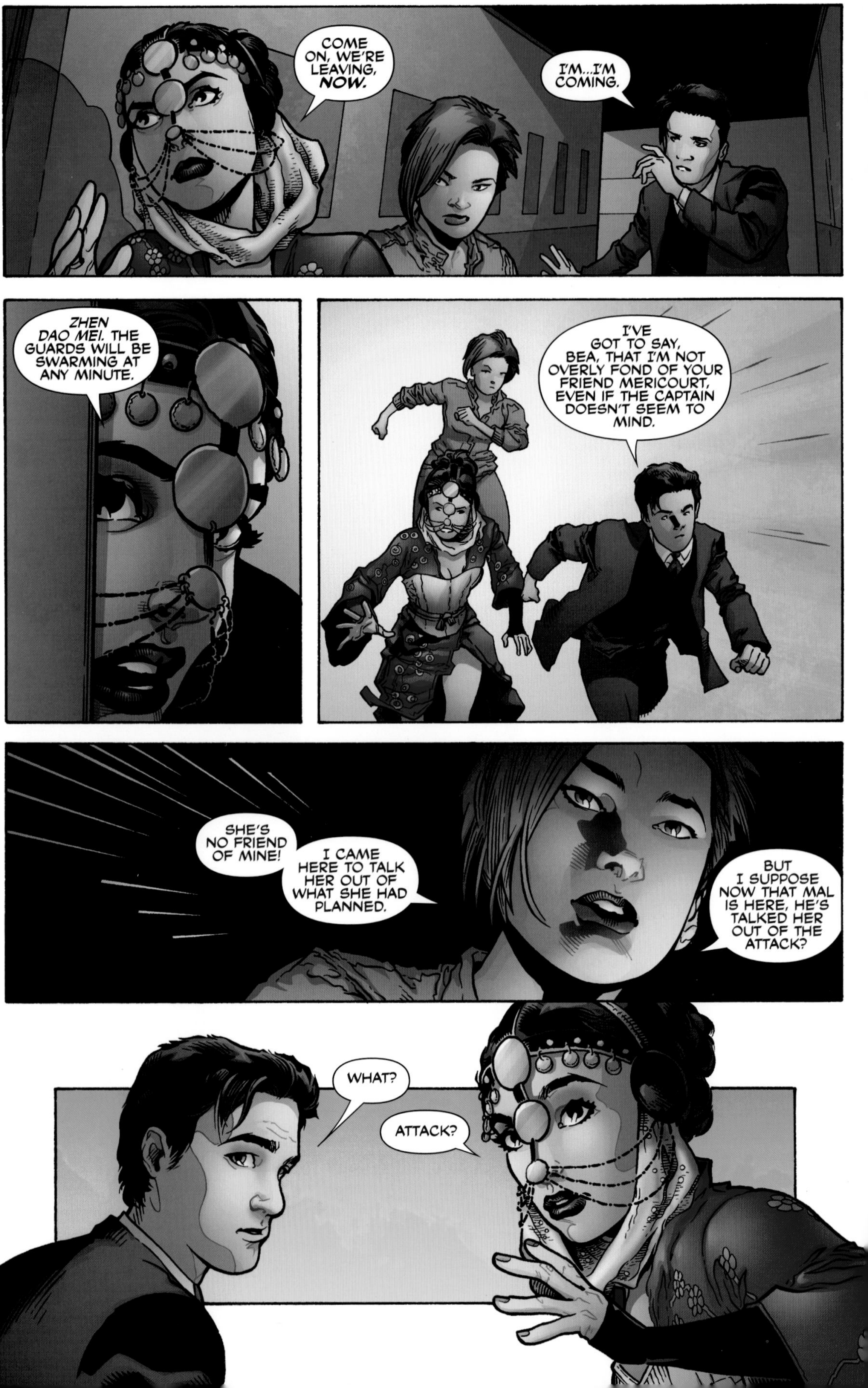
COME ON, WE'RE LEAVING, NOW.
I'M...I'M COMING.
ZHEN DAO MEI. THE GUARDS WILL BE SWARMING AT ANY MINUTE.
I'VE GOT TO SAY, BEA, THAT I'M NOT OVERLY FOND OF YOUR FRIEND MERICOURT, EVEN IF THE CAPTAIN DOESN'T SEEM TO MIND.
SHE'S NO FRIEND OF MINE!
I CAME HERE TO TALK HER OUT OF WHAT SHE HAD PLANNED.
BUT I SUPPOSE NOW THAT MAL IS HERE, HE'S TALKED HER OUT OF THE ATTACK?
WHAT?
ATTACK?

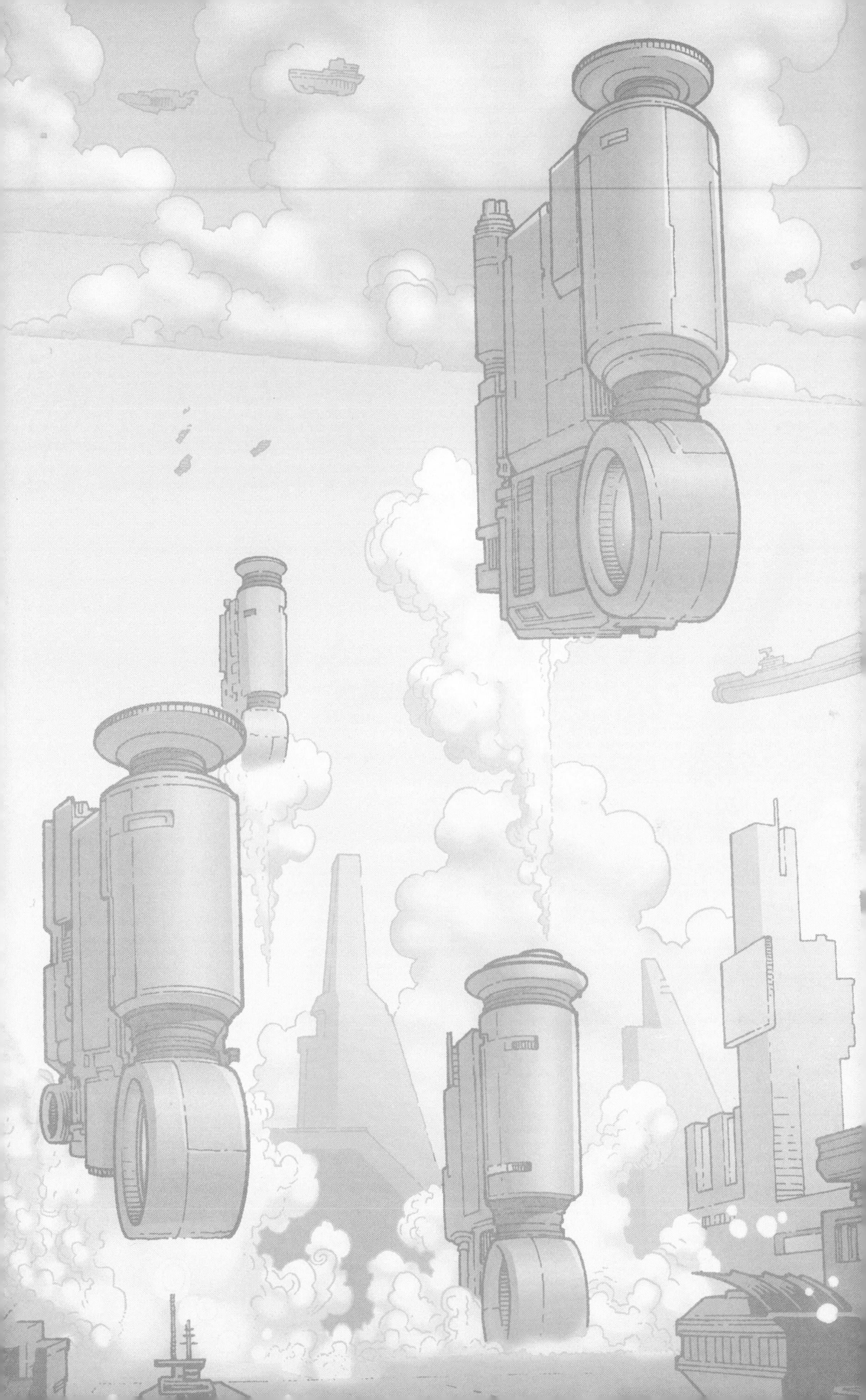

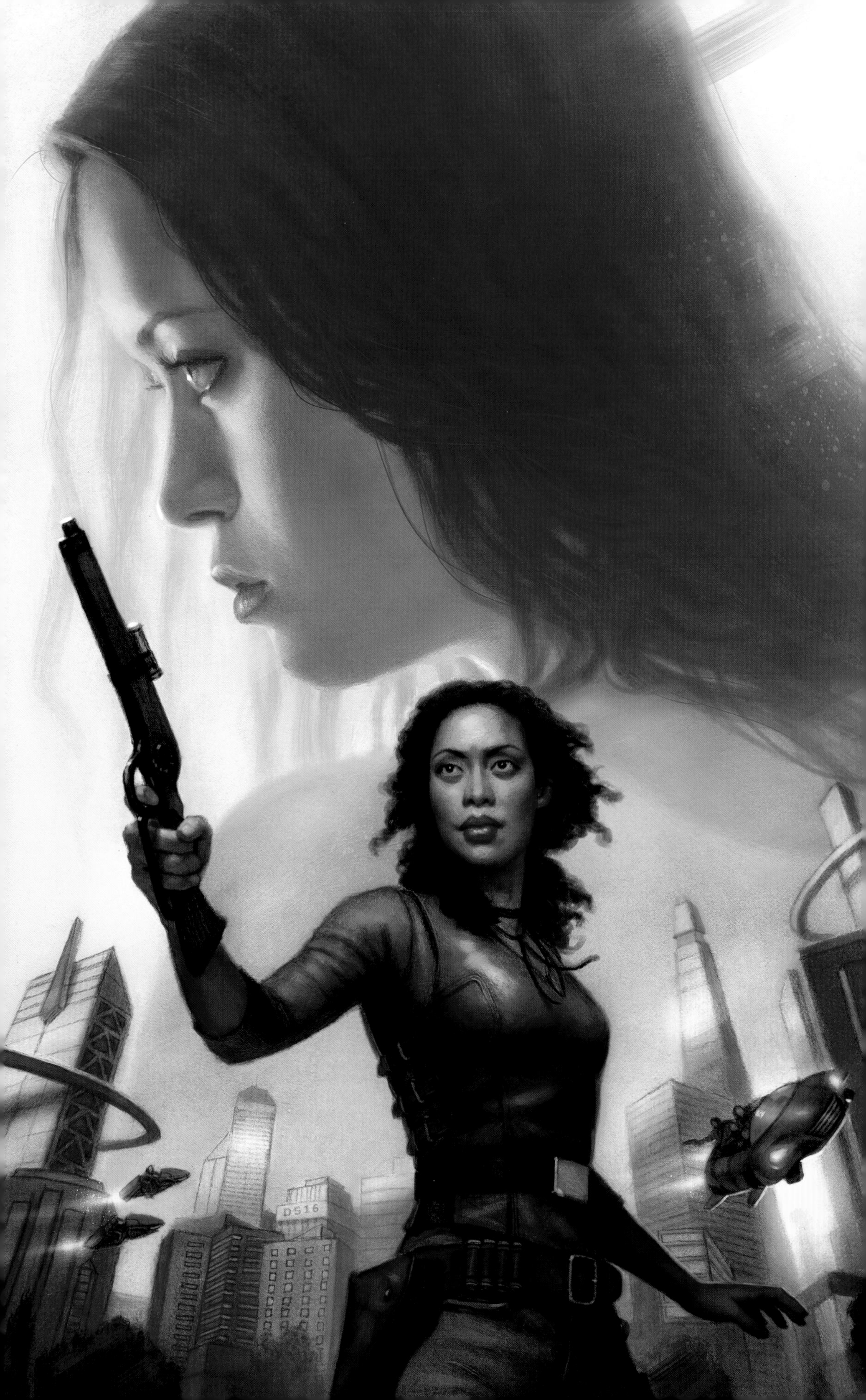
D516

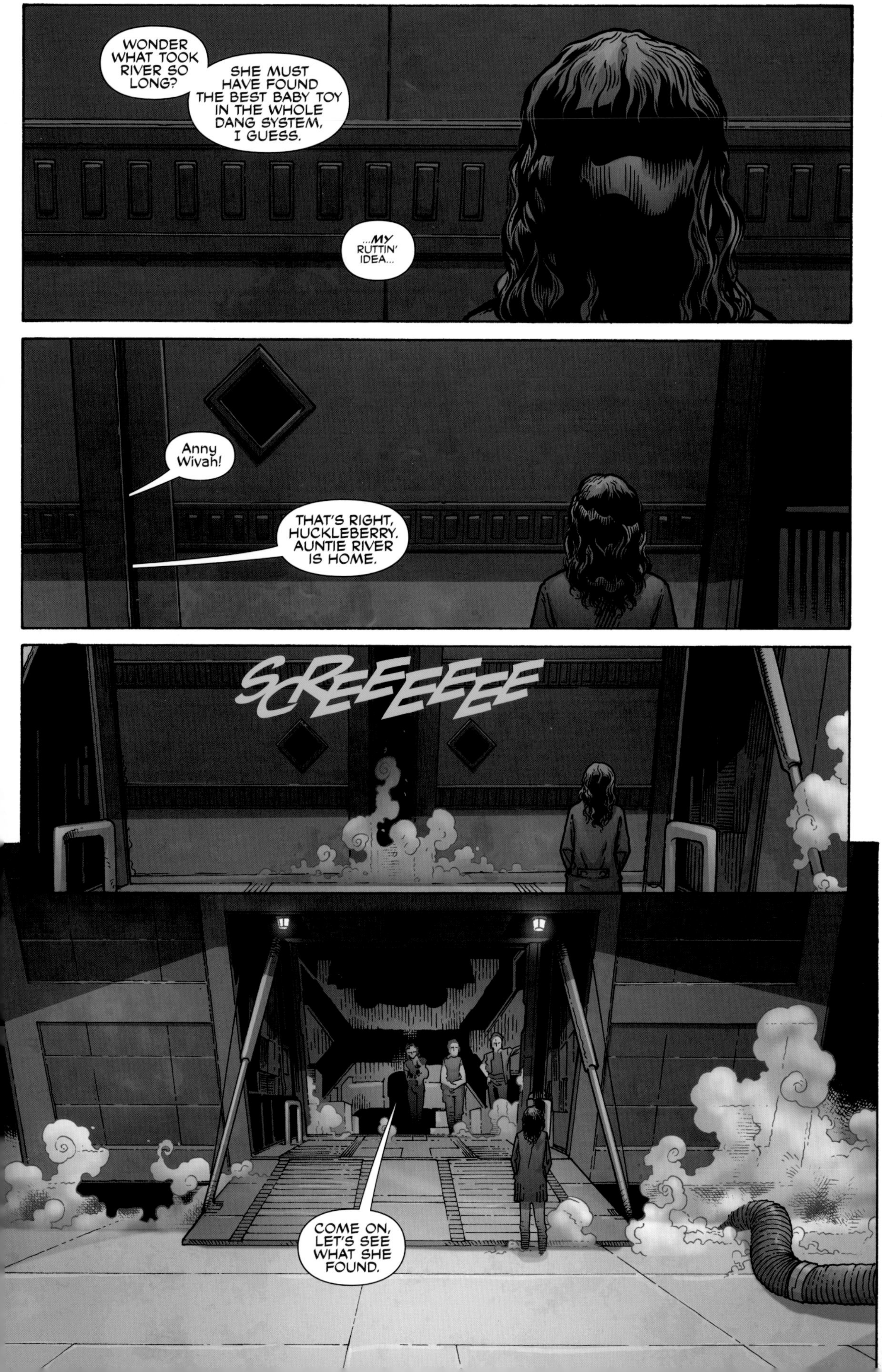
WONDER WHAT TOOK RIVER SO LONG?
SHE MUST HAVE FOUND THE BEST BABY TOY IN THE WHOLE DANG SYSTEM, I GUESS.
...MY RUTTIN' IDEA...
Anny Wivah!
THAT'S RIGHT, HUCKLEBERRY. AUNTIE RIVER IS HOME.
SCREEEEEEE
COME ON, LET'S SEE WHAT SHE FOUND.

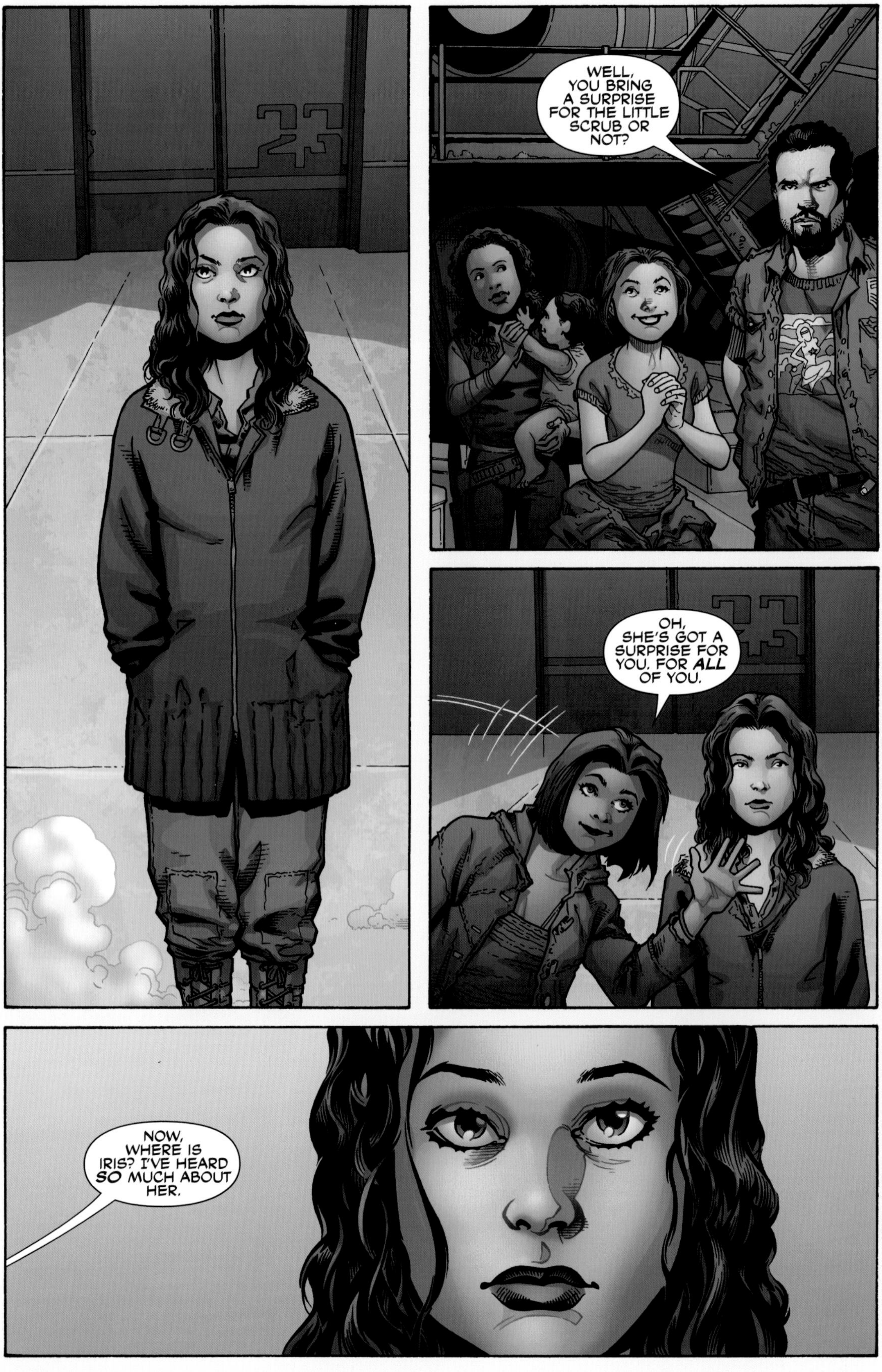
WELL, YOU BRING A SURPRISE FOR THE LITTLE SCRUB OR NOT?
OH, SHE'S GOT A SURPRISE FOR YOU. FOR **ALL** OF YOU.
NOW, WHERE IS IRIS? I'VE HEARD **SO** MUCH ABOUT HER.

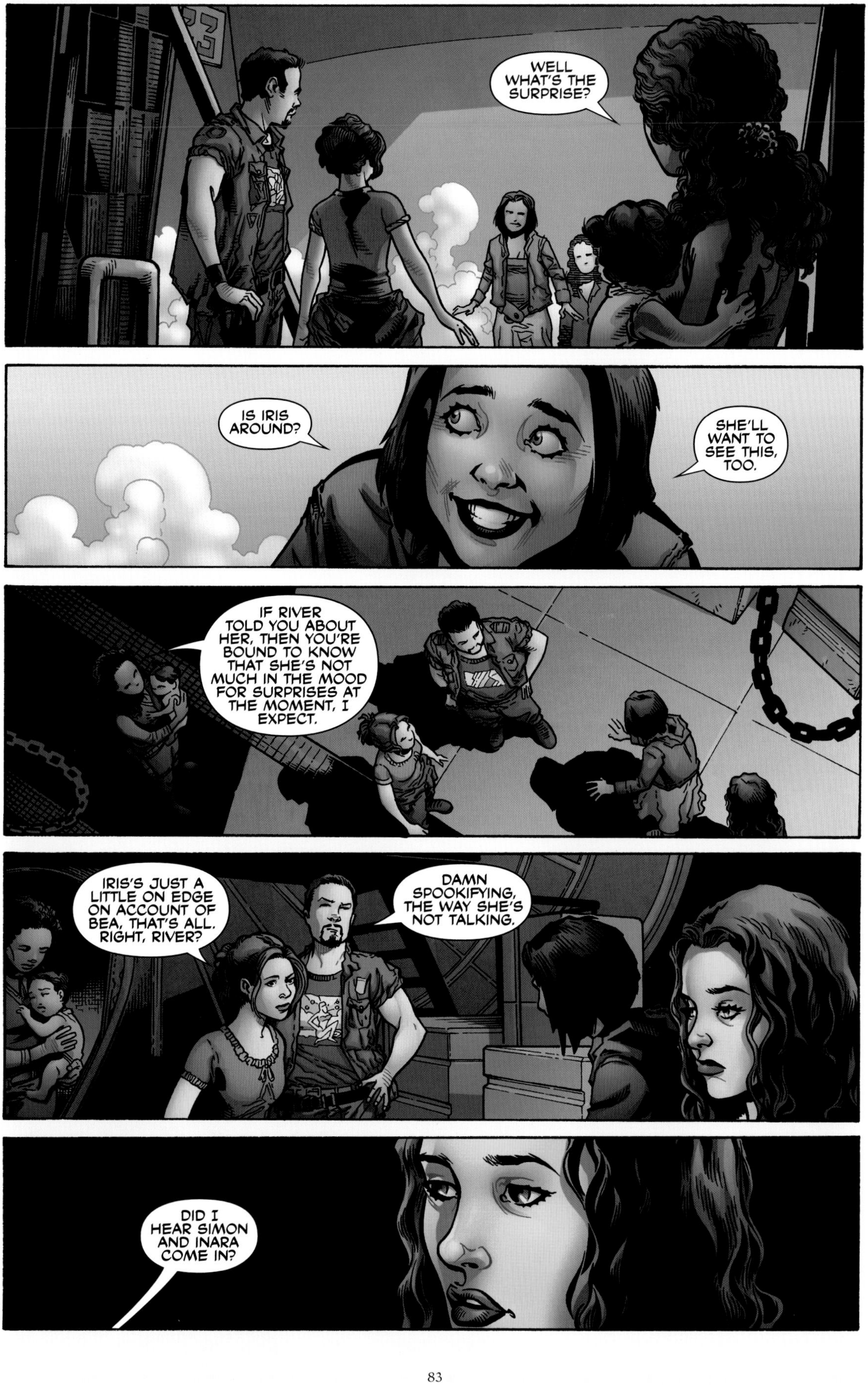
WELL WHAT'S THE SURPRISE?
IS IRIS AROUND?
SHE'LL WANT TO SEE THIS, TOO.
IF RIVER TOLD YOU ABOUT HER, THEN YOU'RE BOUND TO KNOW THAT SHE'S NOT MUCH IN THE MOOD FOR SURPRISES AT THE MOMENT, I EXPECT.
IRIS'S JUST A LITTLE ON EDGE ON ACCOUNT OF BEA, THAT'S ALL. RIGHT, RIVER?
DAMN SPOOKIFYING, THE WAY SHE'S NOT TALKING.
DID I HEAR SIMON AND INARA COME IN?

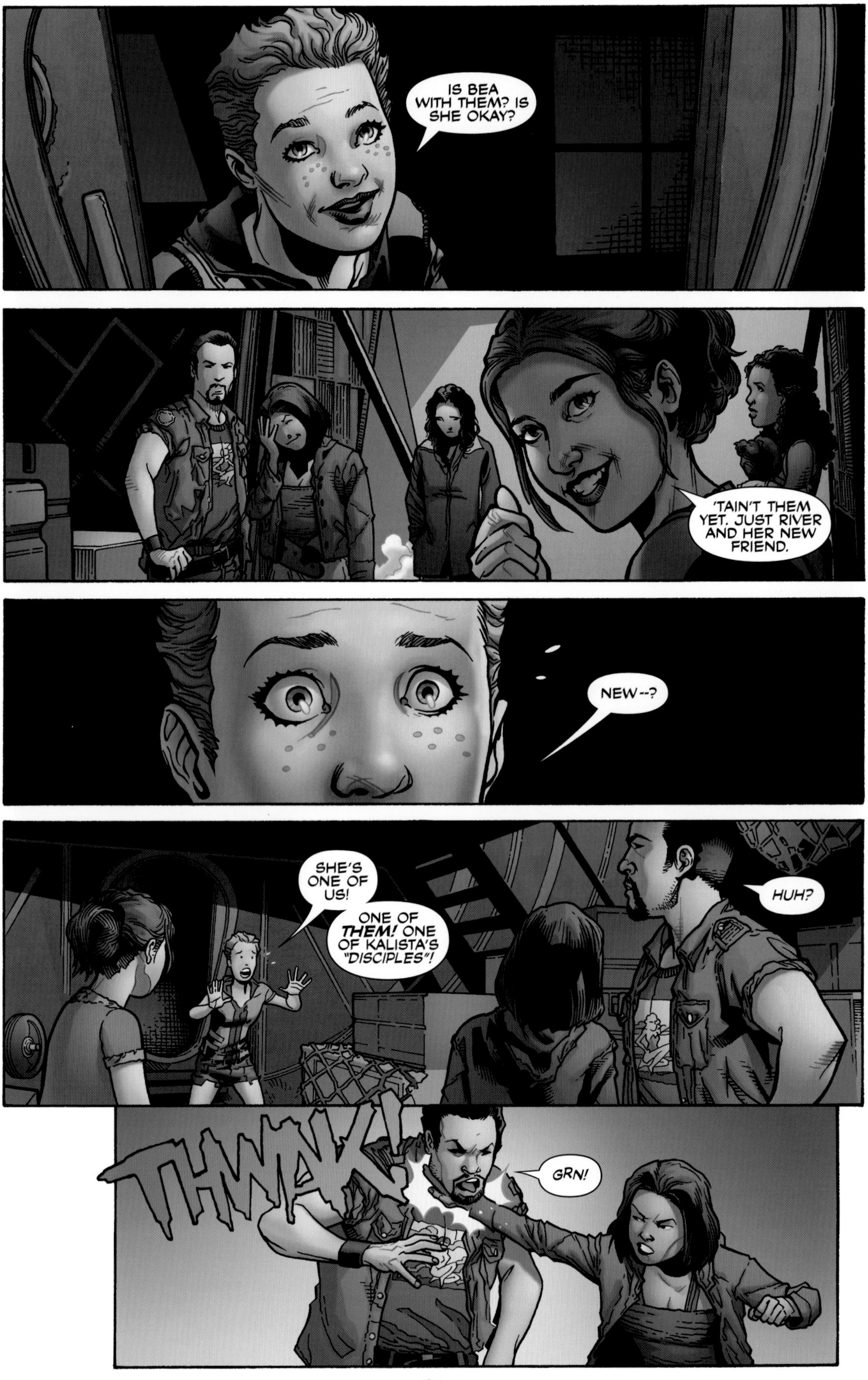
IS BEA WITH THEM? IS SHE OKAY?
'TAIN'T THEM YET. JUST RIVER AND HER NEW FRIEND.
NEW--?
SHE'S ONE OF US!
ONE OF *THEM!* ONE OF KALISTA'S "DISCIPLES"!
HUH?
THWAK!
GRN!

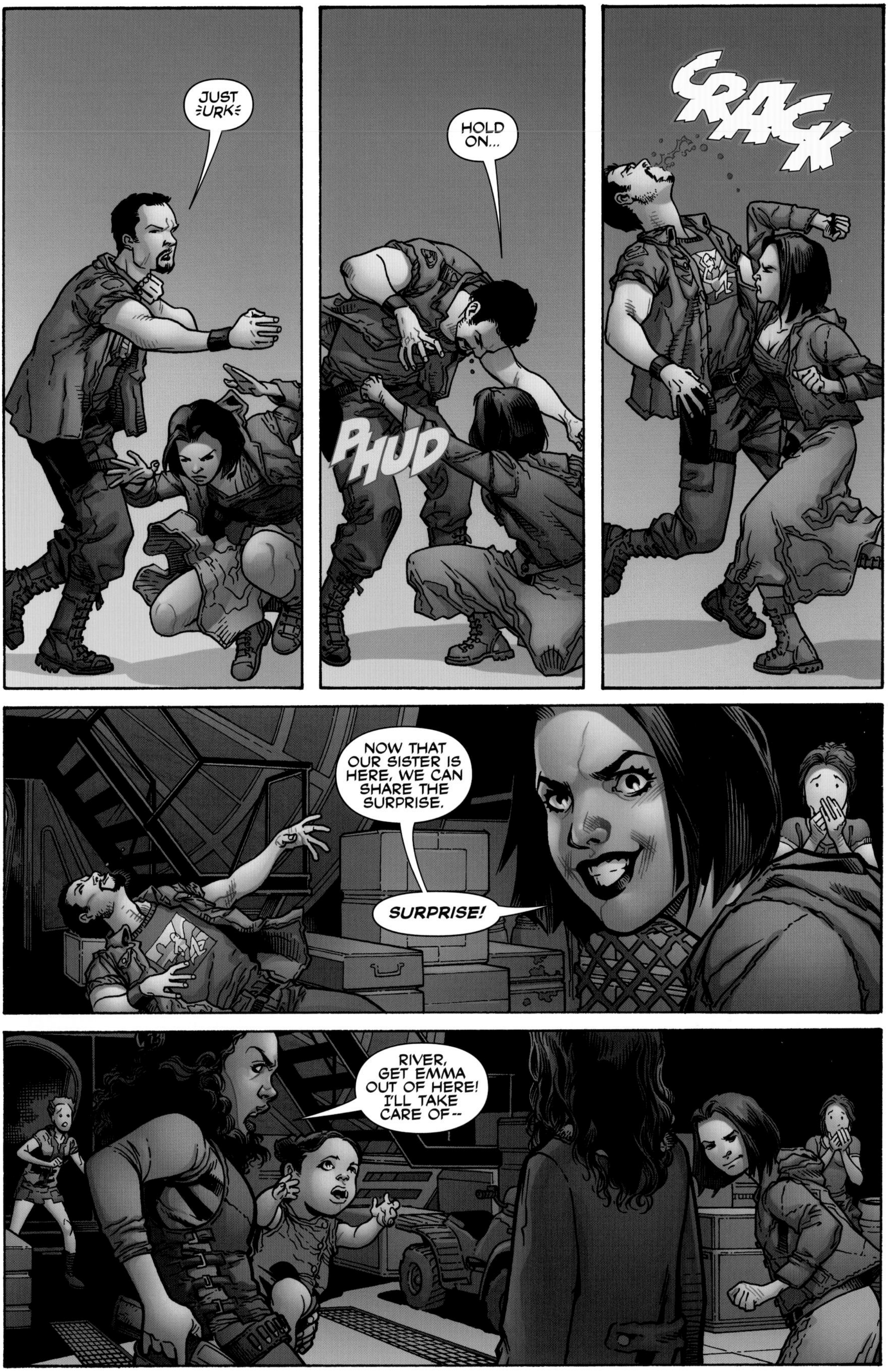
JUST URK
HOLD ON...
PHUD
CRACK
NOW THAT OUR SISTER IS HERE, WE CAN SHARE THE SURPRISE.
SURPRISE!
RIVER, GET EMMA OUT OF HERE! I'LL TAKE CARE OF--

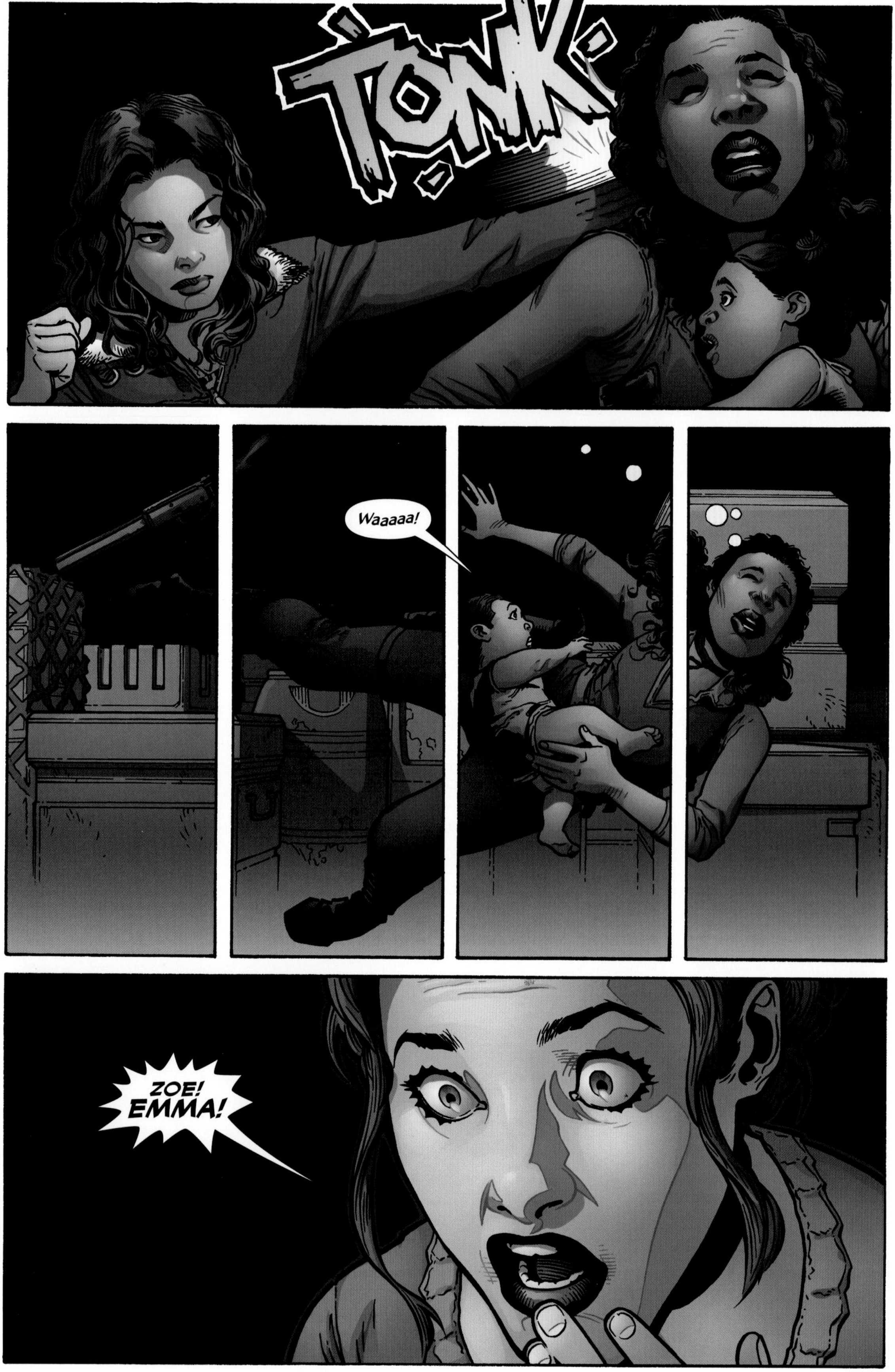
TONK
Waaaaa!
ZOE! EMMA!

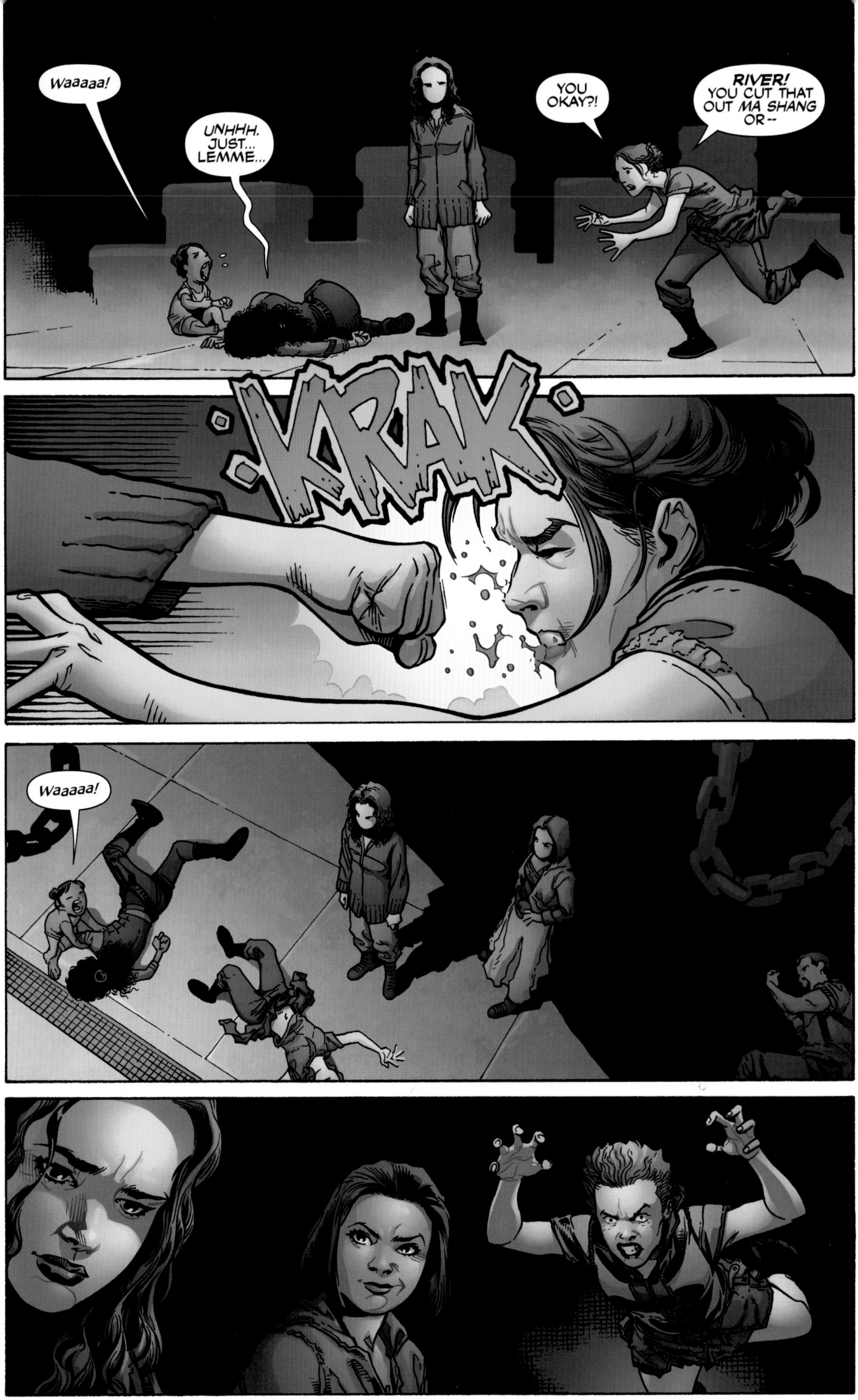
Waaaaa!
UNHHH. JUST... LEMME...
YOU OKAY?!
RIVER! YOU CUT THAT OUT MA SHANG OR--
KRAK
Waaaaa!

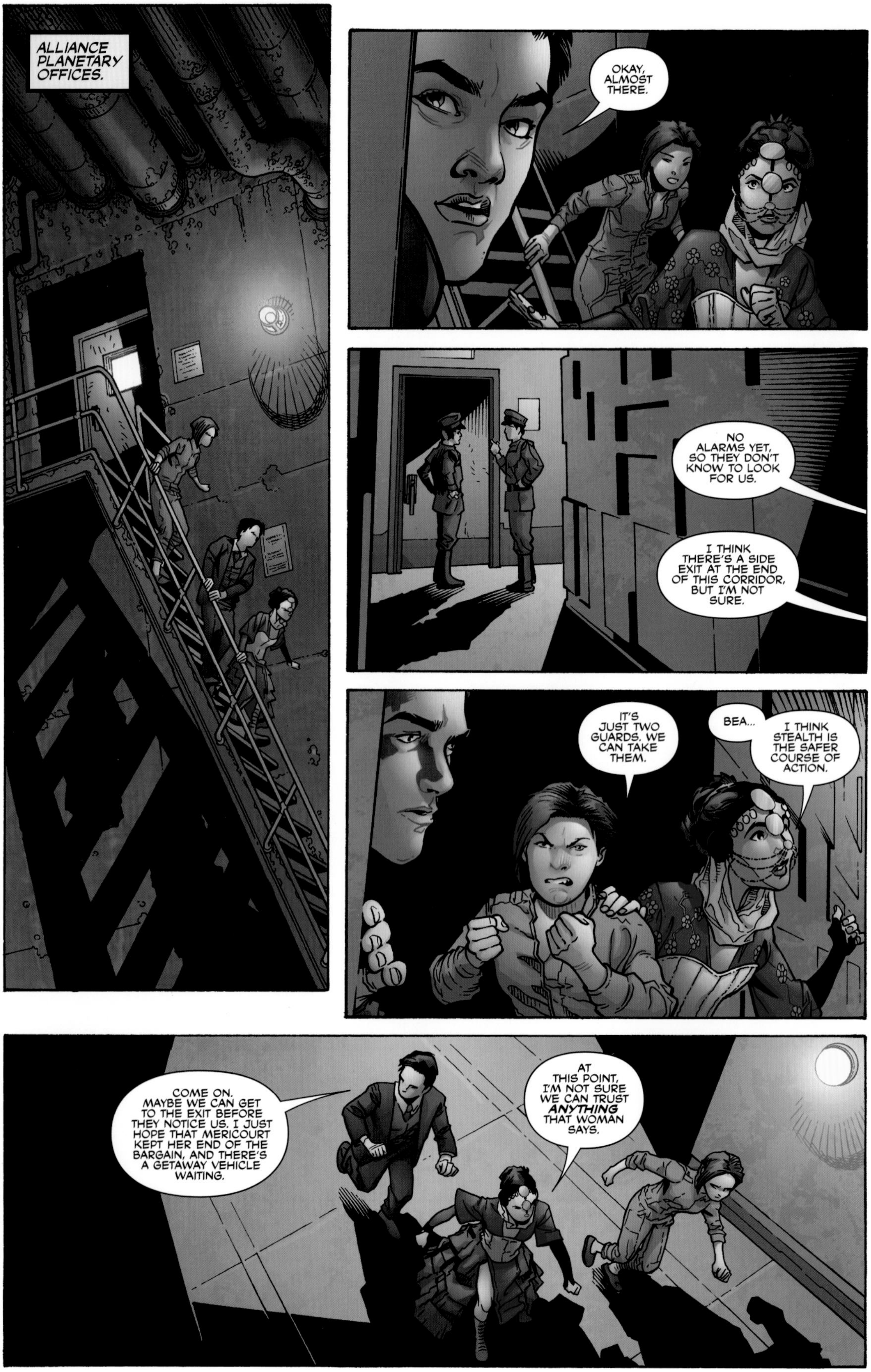
ALLIANCE PLANETARY OFFICES.
OKAY, ALMOST THERE.
NO ALARMS YET, SO THEY DON'T KNOW TO LOOK FOR US.
I THINK THERE'S A SIDE EXIT AT THE END OF THIS CORRIDOR, BUT I'M NOT SURE.
IT'S JUST TWO GUARDS. WE CAN TAKE THEM.
BEA...
I THINK STEALTH IS THE SAFER COURSE OF ACTION.
COME ON. MAYBE WE CAN GET TO THE EXIT BEFORE THEY NOTICE US. I JUST HOPE THAT MERICOURT KEPT HER END OF THE BARGAIN, AND THERE'S A GETAWAY VEHICLE WAITING.
AT THIS POINT, I'M NOT SURE WE CAN TRUST *ANYTHING* THAT WOMAN SAYS.

WELL, SO MUCH FOR *"STEALTH."*

THEY MUST HAVE FOUND THAT GUARD YOU KNOCKED OUT. BUT IF THE ALARM IS SOUNDING THEN...

HEY!

HOLD IT RIGHT THERE!

I'M NOT LETTING THESE BASTARDS PUT ME--

WE CAN STILL MAKE IT--

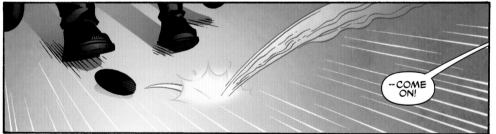

--COME ON!

POOF

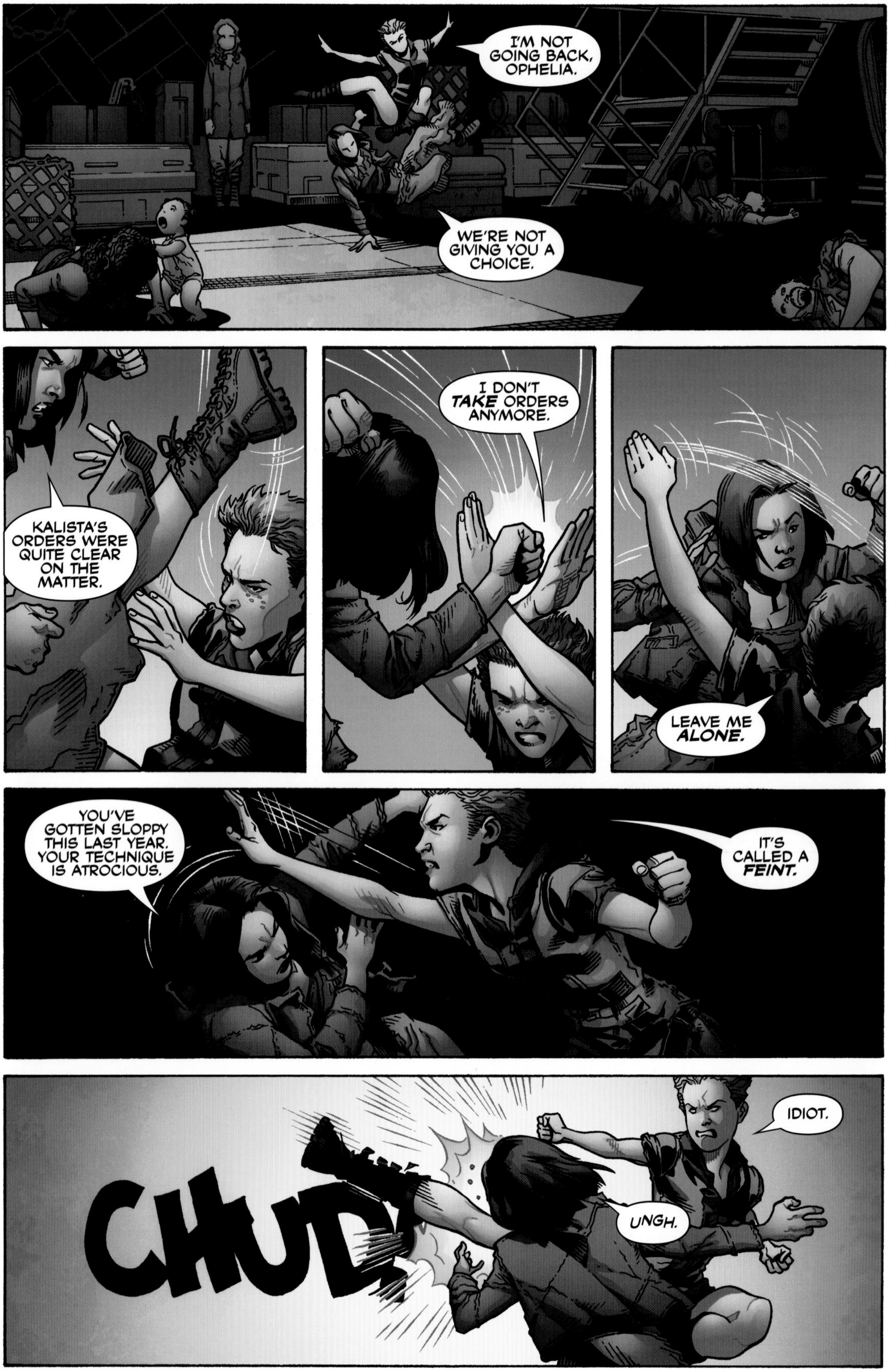
I'M NOT GOING BACK, OPHELIA.
WE'RE NOT GIVING YOU A CHOICE.
KALISTA'S ORDERS WERE QUITE CLEAR ON THE MATTER.
I DON'T TAKE ORDERS ANYMORE.
LEAVE ME ALONE.
YOU'VE GOTTEN SLOPPY THIS LAST YEAR. YOUR TECHNIQUE IS ATROCIOUS.
IT'S CALLED A FEINT.
IDIOT.
CHUD
UNGH.

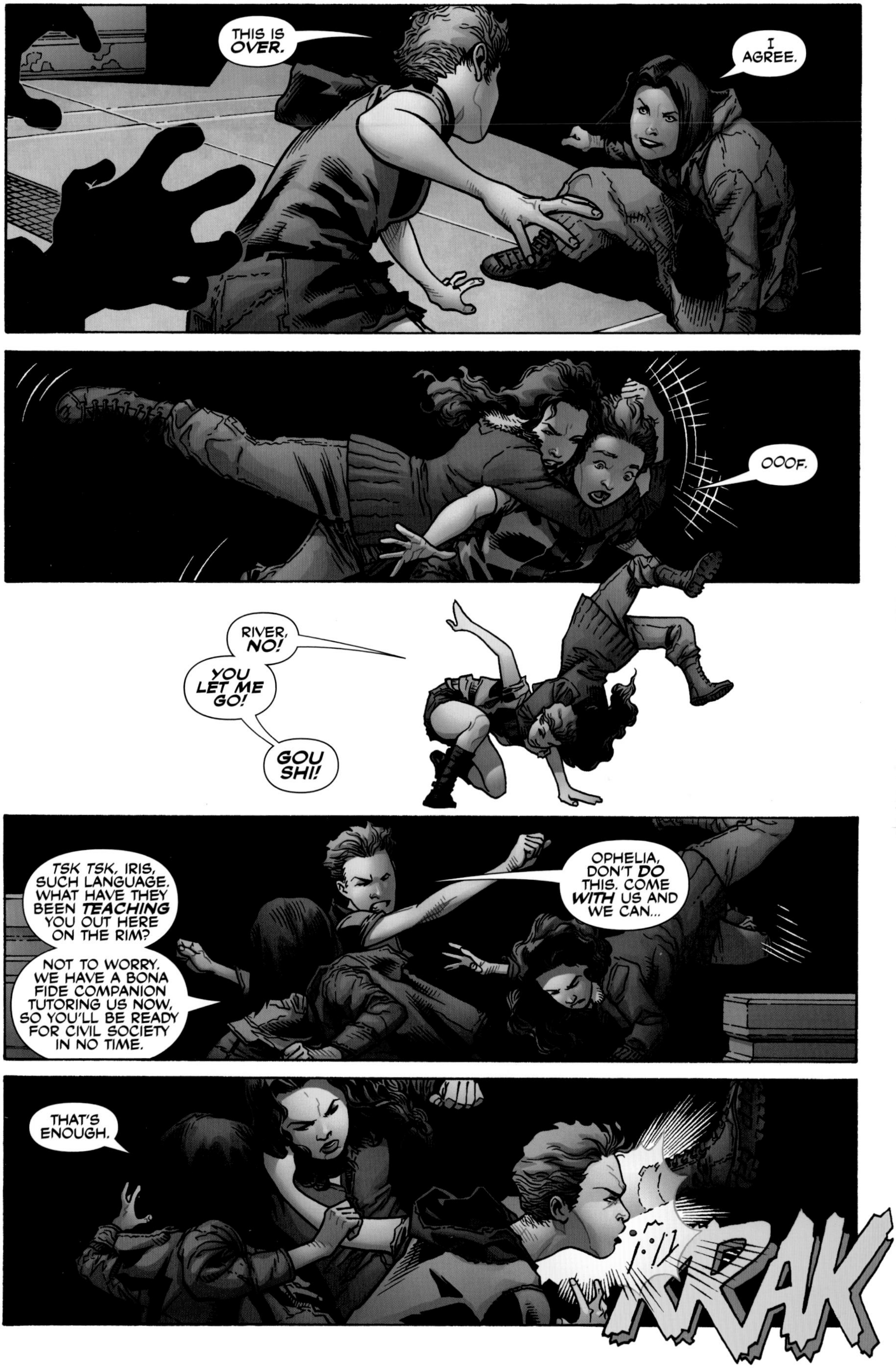
THIS IS OVER.
I AGREE.
OOOF.
RIVER, NO!
YOU LET ME GO!
GOU SHI!
TSK TSK, IRIS, SUCH LANGUAGE. WHAT HAVE THEY BEEN TEACHING YOU OUT HERE ON THE RIM?
NOT TO WORRY. WE HAVE A BONA FIDE COMPANION TUTORING US NOW, SO YOU'LL BE READY FOR CIVIL SOCIETY IN NO TIME.
OPHELIA, DON'T DO THIS. COME WITH US AND WE CAN...
THAT'S ENOUGH.
KRAK

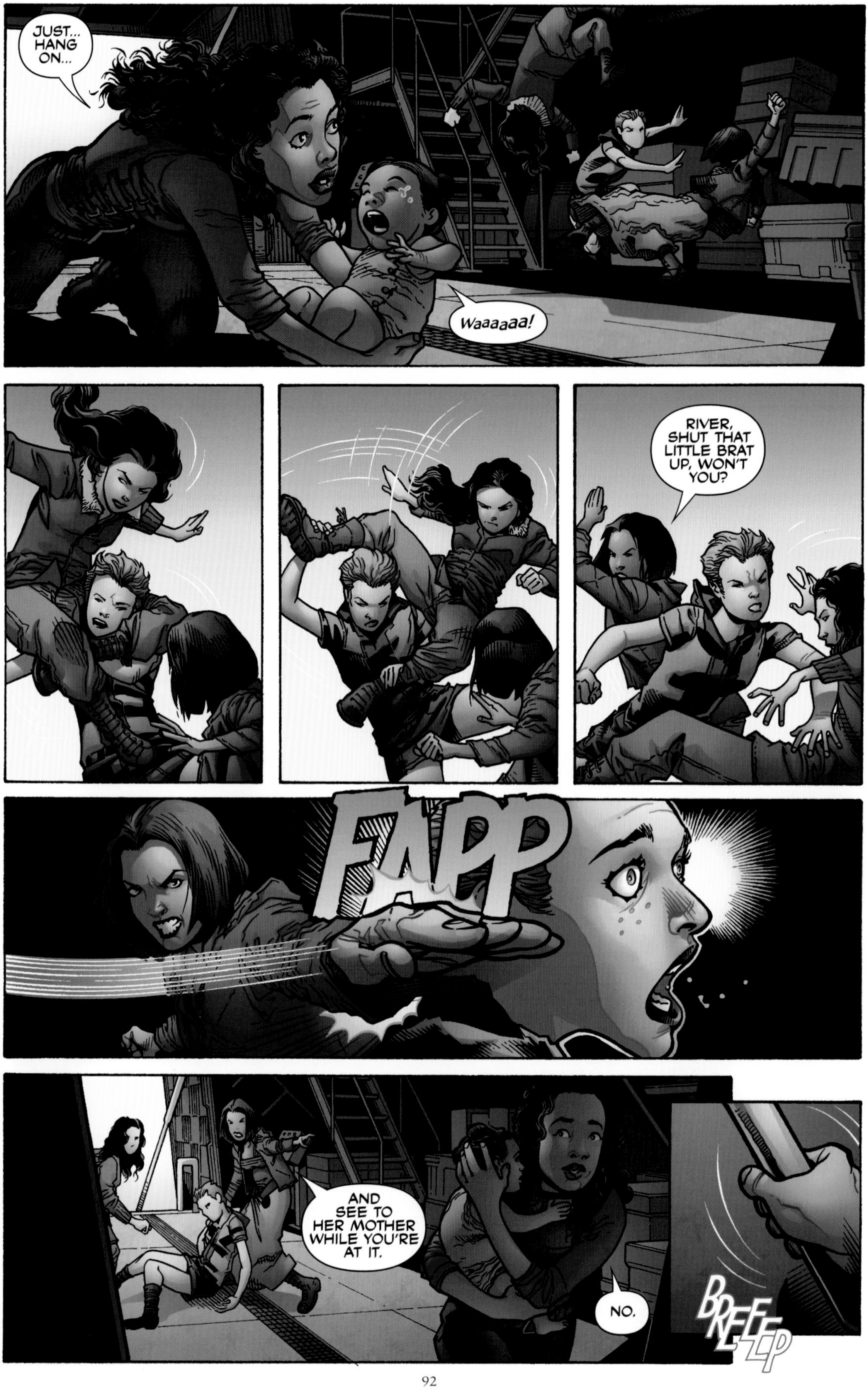
JUST... HANG ON...
Waaaaaa!
RIVER, SHUT THAT LITTLE BRAT UP, WON'T YOU?
FAPP
AND SEE TO HER MOTHER WHILE YOU'RE AT IT.
NO.
BREEEP

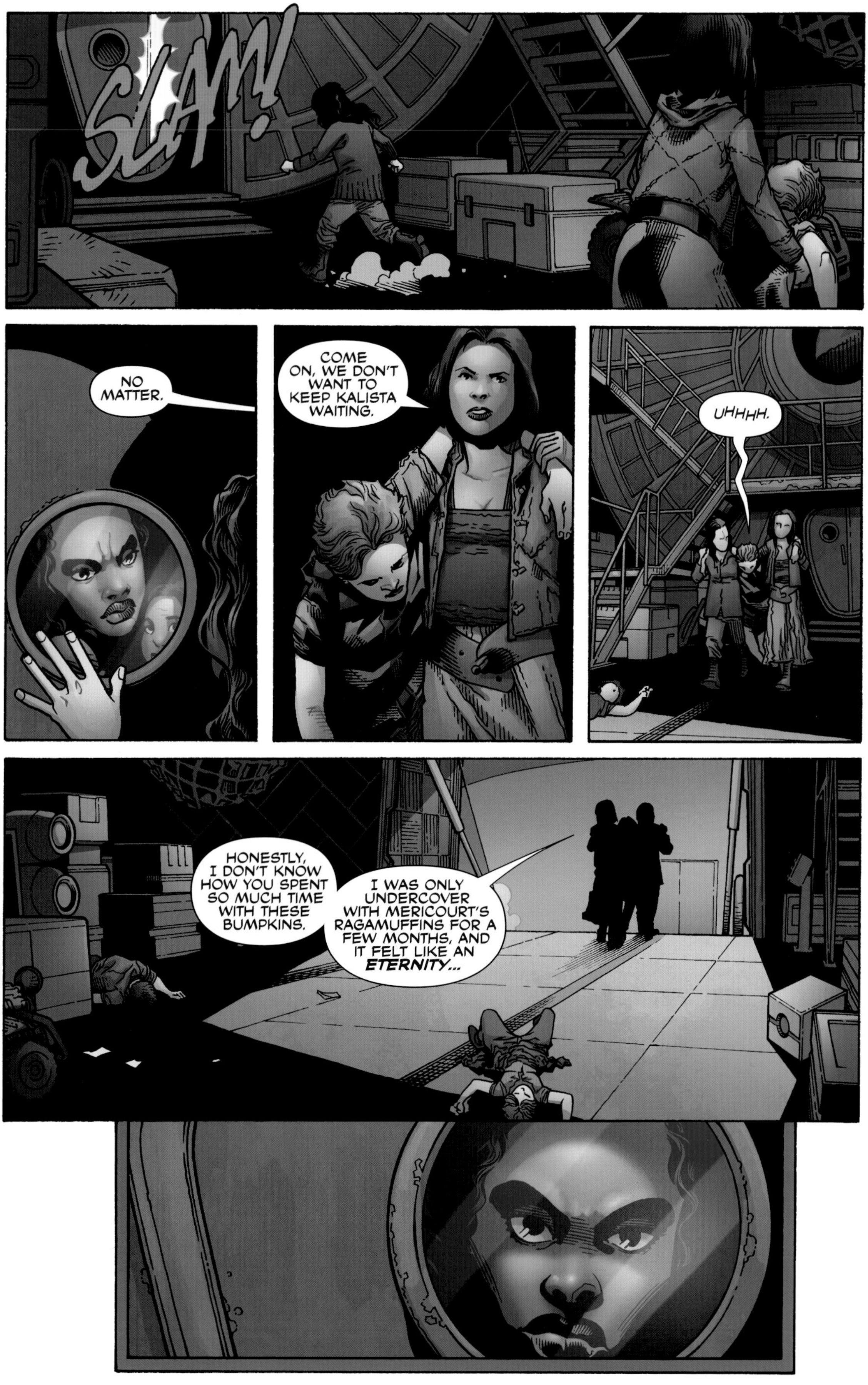
SLAM!
NO MATTER.
COME ON, WE DON'T WANT TO KEEP KALISTA WAITING.
UHHHH.
HONESTLY, I DON'T KNOW HOW YOU SPENT SO MUCH TIME WITH THESE BUMPKINS.
I WAS ONLY UNDERCOVER WITH MERICOURT'S RAGAMUFFINS FOR A FEW MONTHS, AND IT FELT LIKE AN *ETERNITY*...

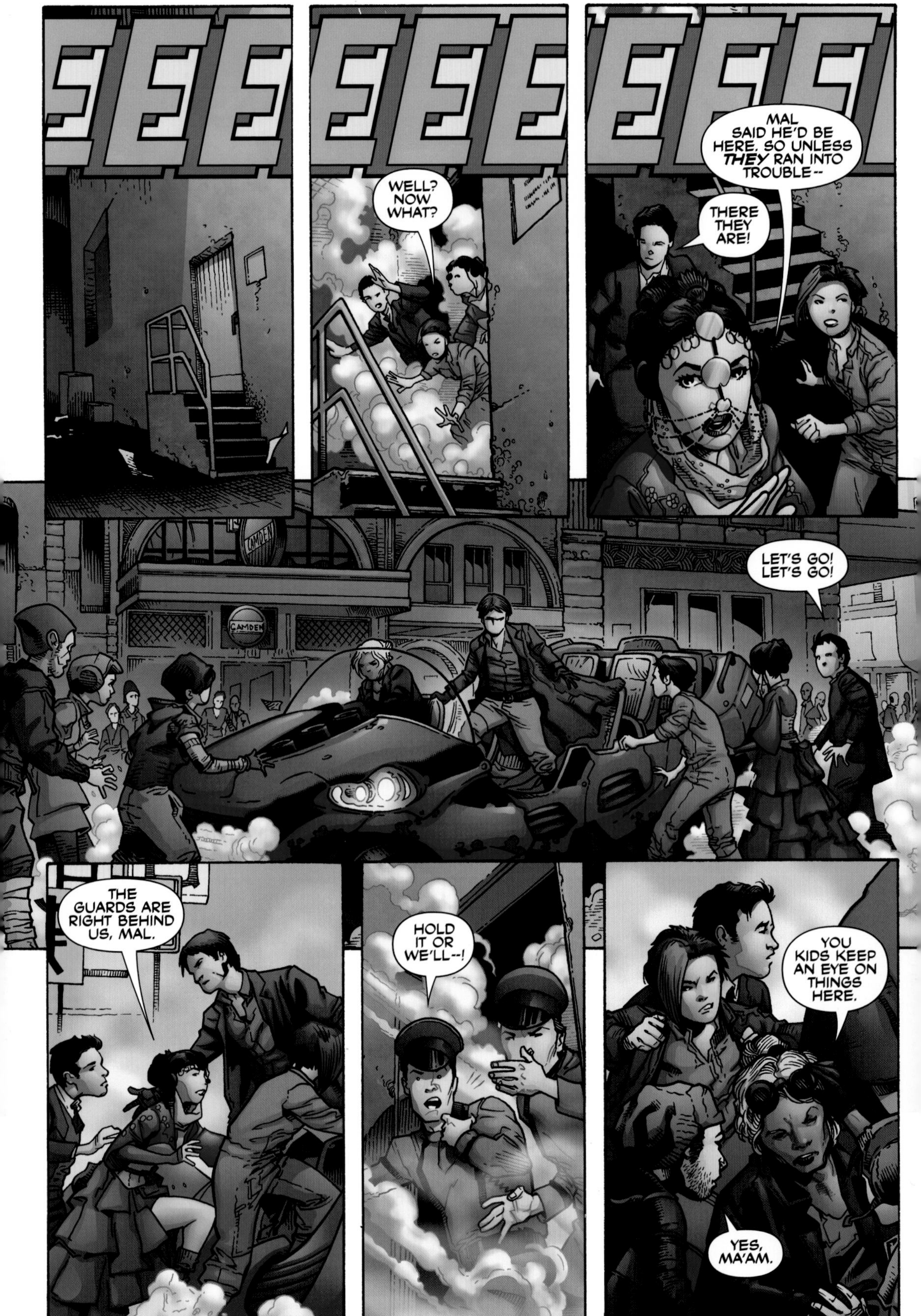
EEEEEEEE
WELL? NOW WHAT?
MAL SAID HE'D BE HERE. SO UNLESS THEY RAN INTO TROUBLE--
THERE THEY ARE!
CAMDEN
CAMDEN
LET'S GO! LET'S GO!
THE GUARDS ARE RIGHT BEHIND US, MAL.
HOLD IT OR WE'LL--!
YOU KIDS KEEP AN EYE ON THINGS HERE.
YES, MA'AM.

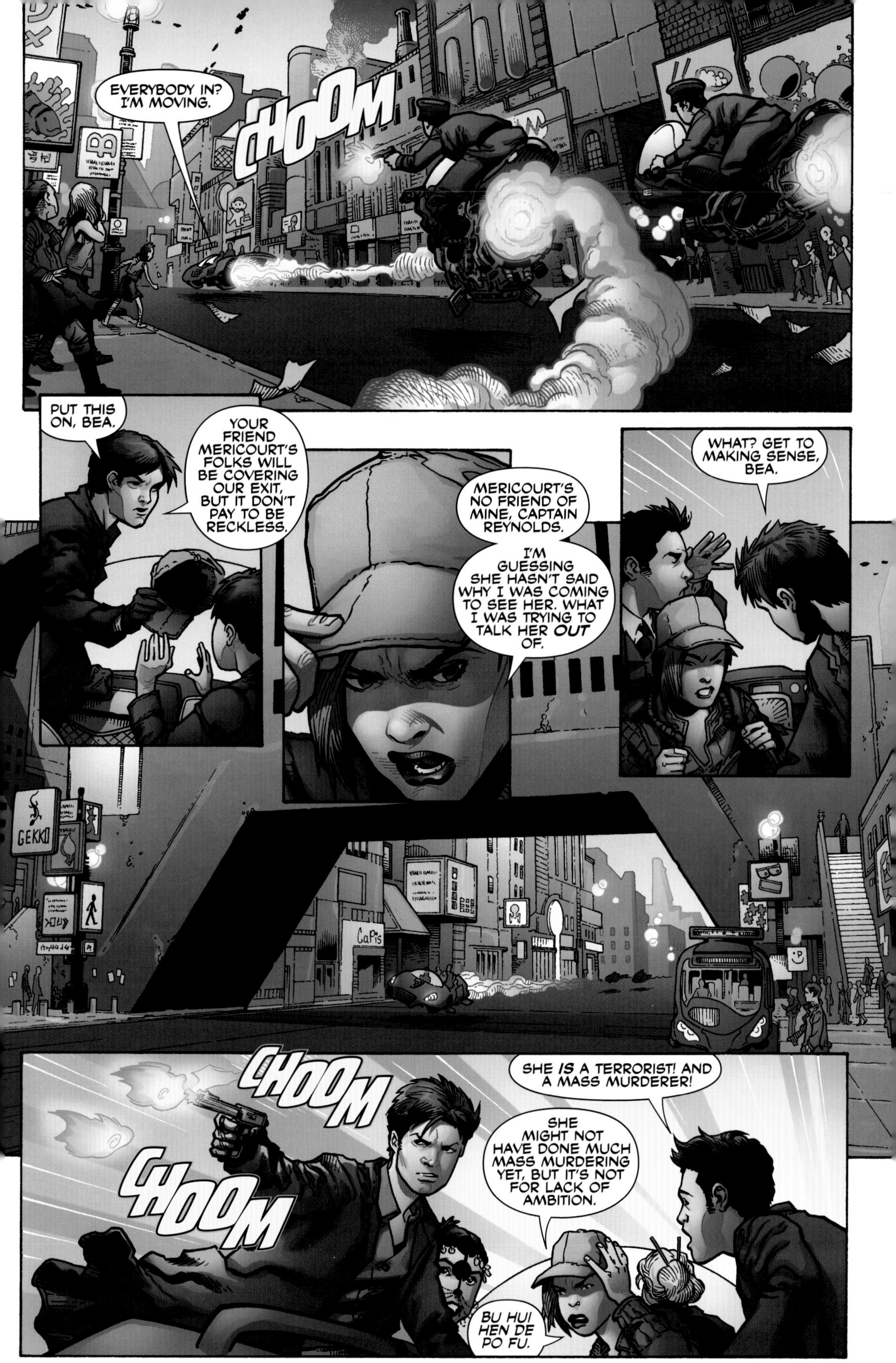
EVERYBODY IN? I'M MOVING.
CHOOM
PUT THIS ON, BEA.
YOUR FRIEND MERICOURT'S FOLKS WILL BE COVERING OUR EXIT, BUT IT DON'T PAY TO BE RECKLESS.
MERICOURT'S NO FRIEND OF MINE, CAPTAIN REYNOLDS.
I'M GUESSING SHE HASN'T SAID WHY I WAS COMING TO SEE HER. WHAT I WAS TRYING TO TALK HER *OUT* OF.
WHAT? GET TO MAKING SENSE, BEA.
GEKKO
CaPis
CHOOM
CHOOM
SHE *IS* A TERRORIST! AND A MASS MURDERER!
SHE MIGHT NOT HAVE DONE MUCH MASS MURDERING YET, BUT IT'S NOT FOR LACK OF AMBITION.
BU HUI HEN DE PO FU.

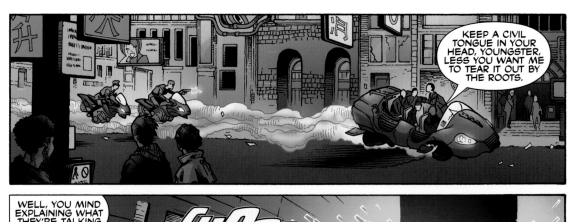

KEEP A CIVIL TONGUE IN YOUR HEAD, YOUNGSTER, LESS YOU WANT ME TO TEAR IT OUT BY THE ROOTS.

WELL, YOU MIND EXPLAINING WHAT THEY'RE TALKING ABOUT?

WHOOM

I TOLD YOU, REYNOLDS. SECESSION JUST AIN'T GONNA CUT IT. WE NEED TO PUSH THE PURPLEBELLIES *OUT*.

MOST FOLKS HERE MAKE THEIR LIVING PROSPECTING FOR IRIDIUM, OR BY SELLING GOODS AND SERVICES TO THEM THAT DO.

KRRSH

BOOM

IT'S A HARD LIFE, WITH LOW RETURN FOR LONG HOURS, BUT THEY GET BY. AND THEN THEY'VE GOT TO DEAL WITH THE LIKES OF *THEM*.

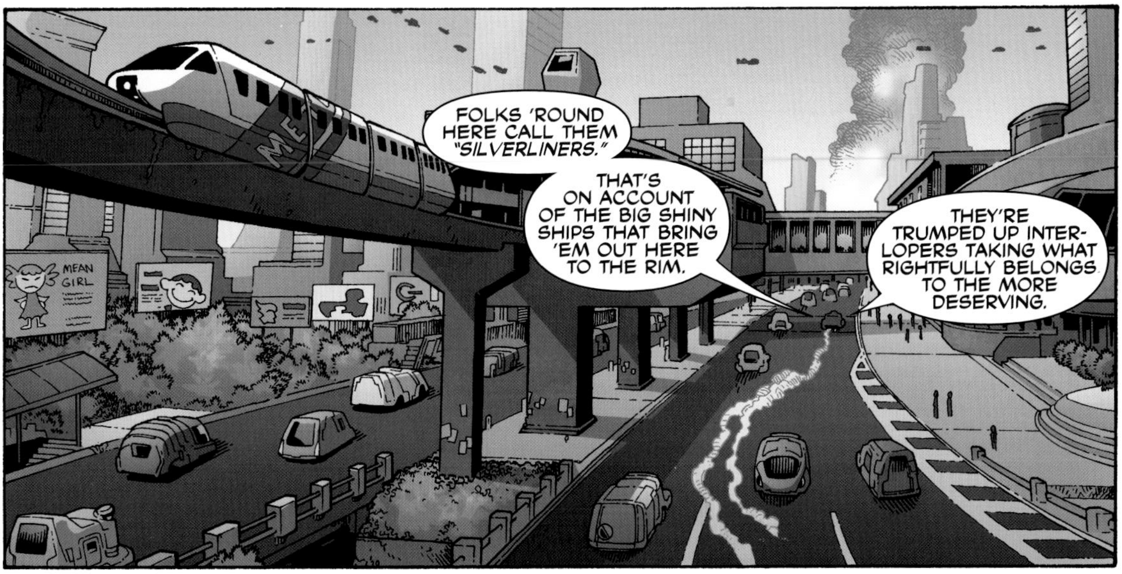
MEAN GIRL
FOLKS 'ROUND HERE CALL THEM *"SILVERLINERS."*
THAT'S ON ACCOUNT OF THE BIG SHINY SHIPS THAT BRING 'EM OUT HERE TO THE RIM.
THEY'RE TRUMPED UP INTER-LOPERS TAKING WHAT RIGHTFULLY BELONGS TO THE MORE DESERVING.

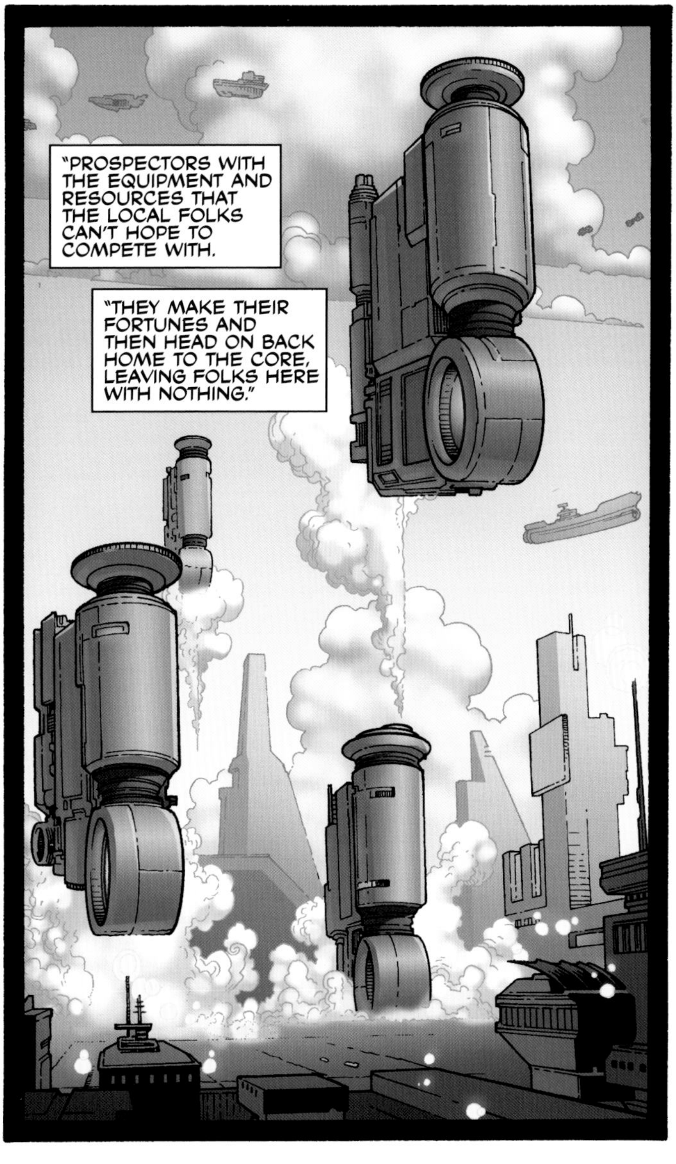
"PROSPECTORS WITH THE EQUIPMENT AND RESOURCES THAT THE LOCAL FOLKS CAN'T HOPE TO COMPETE WITH.
"THEY MAKE THEIR FORTUNES AND THEN HEAD ON BACK HOME TO THE CORE, LEAVING FOLKS HERE WITH NOTHING."

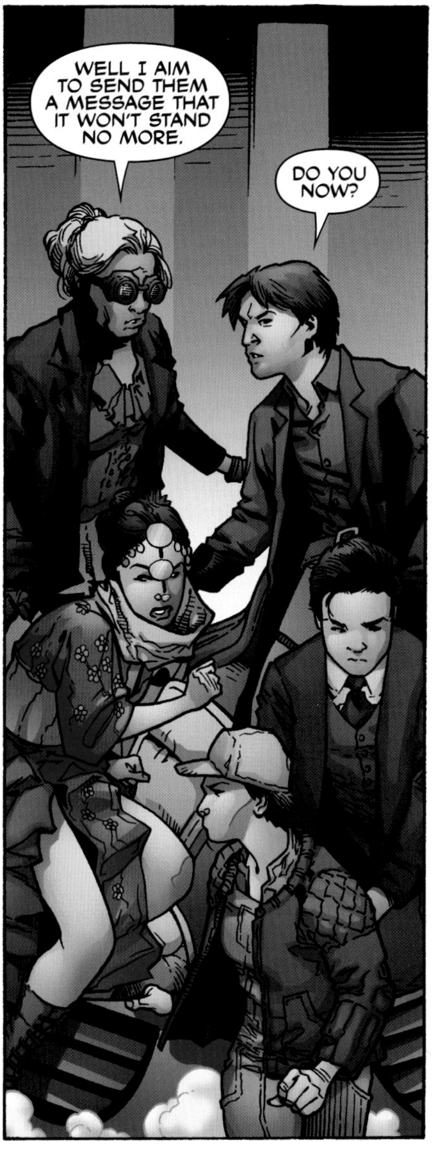
WELL I AIM TO SEND THEM A MESSAGE THAT IT WON'T STAND NO MORE.
DO YOU NOW?

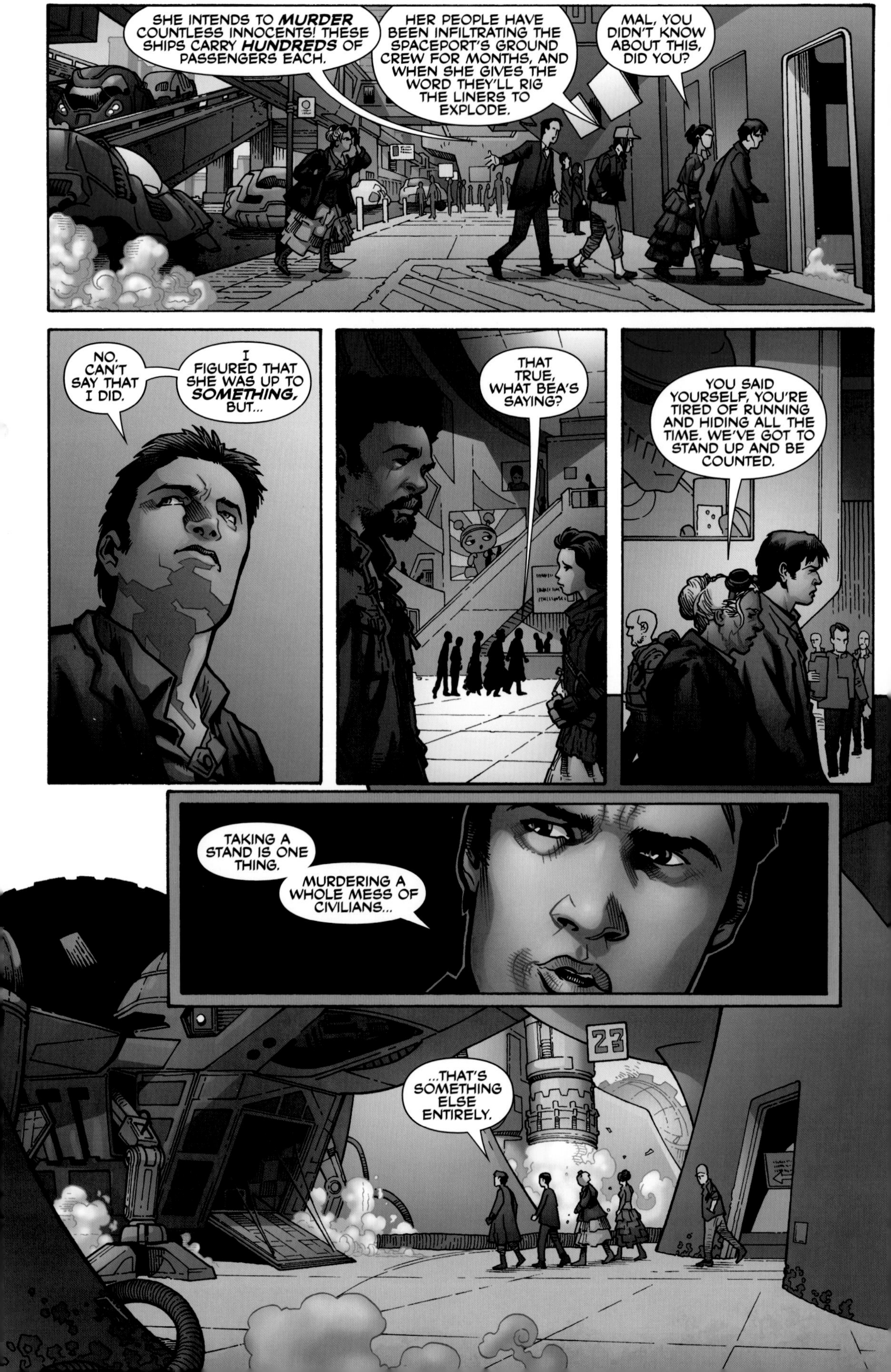
SHE INTENDS TO MURDER COUNTLESS INNOCENTS! THESE SHIPS CARRY HUNDREDS OF PASSENGERS EACH.
HER PEOPLE HAVE BEEN INFILTRATING THE SPACEPORT'S GROUND CREW FOR MONTHS, AND WHEN SHE GIVES THE WORD THEY'LL RIG THE LINERS TO EXPLODE.
MAL, YOU DIDN'T KNOW ABOUT THIS, DID YOU?
NO. CAN'T SAY THAT I DID.
I FIGURED THAT SHE WAS UP TO SOMETHING, BUT...
THAT TRUE, WHAT BEA'S SAYING?
YOU SAID YOURSELF, YOU'RE TIRED OF RUNNING AND HIDING ALL THE TIME. WE'VE GOT TO STAND UP AND BE COUNTED.
TAKING A STAND IS ONE THING.
MURDERING A WHOLE MESS OF CIVILIANS...
23
...THAT'S SOMETHING ELSE ENTIRELY.

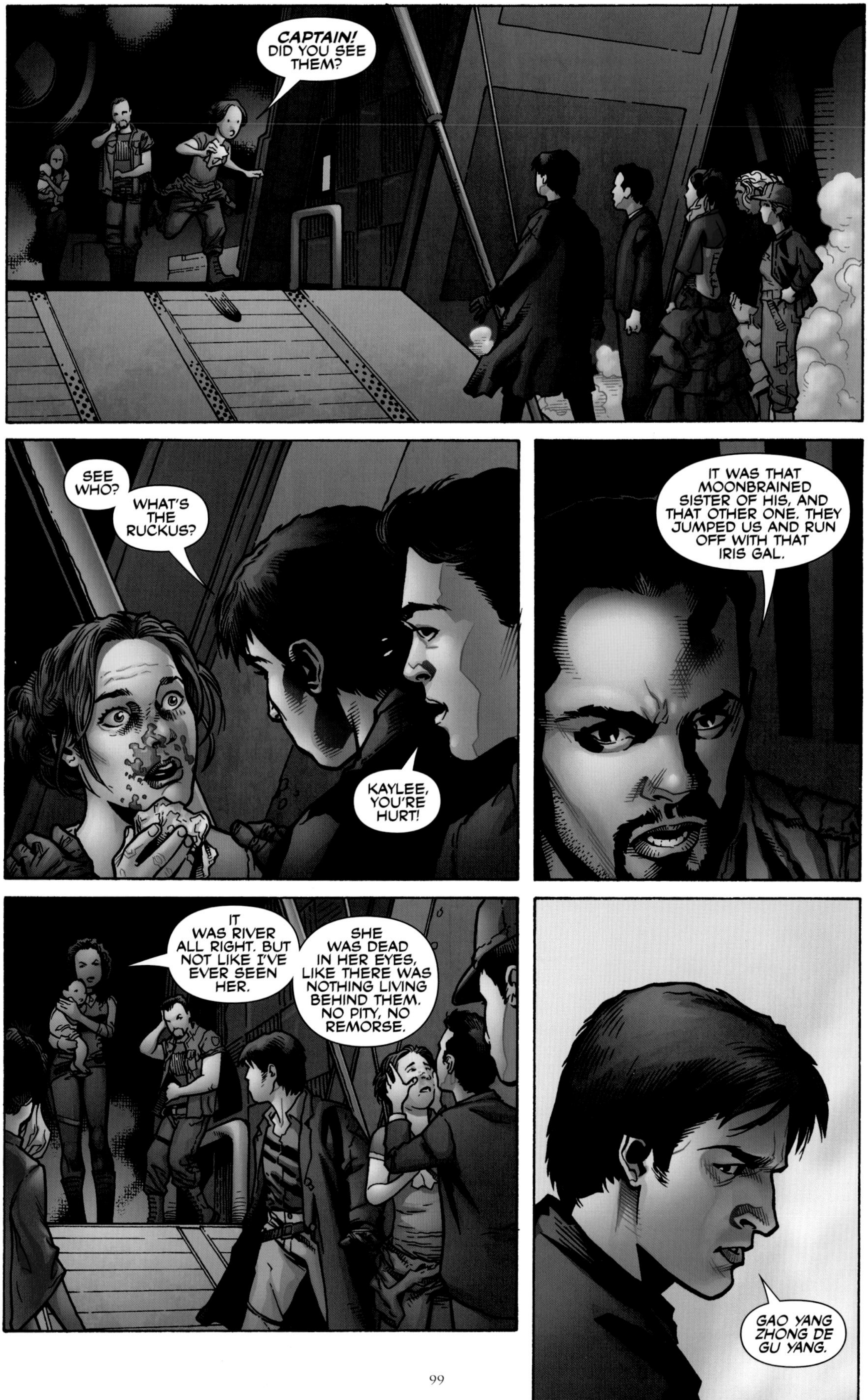
CAPTAIN! DID YOU SEE THEM?
SEE WHO?
WHAT'S THE RUCKUS?
KAYLEE, YOU'RE HURT!
IT WAS THAT MOONBRAINED SISTER OF HIS, AND THAT OTHER ONE. THEY JUMPED US AND RUN OFF WITH THAT IRIS GAL.
IT WAS RIVER ALL RIGHT. BUT NOT LIKE I'VE EVER SEEN HER.
SHE WAS DEAD IN HER EYES, LIKE THERE WAS NOTHING LIVING BEHIND THEM. NO PITY, NO REMORSE.
GAO YANG ZHONG DE GU YANG.

OKAY, SO WE KNOW THAT KALISTA IS HERE, AND HER PEOPLE HAVE GOT RIVER AND IRIS.

WE CAME HERE TO BUST LOOSE ONE OF OUR FRIENDS.

BUT NOW WE'VE GOT TWO MORE TO DEAL WITH.

ONE FRIEND, MORE LIKE. YOU ASK ME, RIVER'S ALREADY LOST TO US. WE SHOULD JUST LEAVE HER TO ROT.

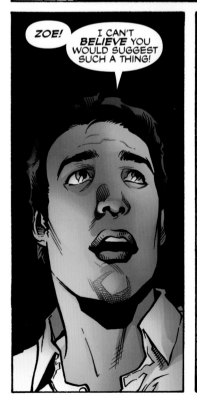

ZOE!

I CAN'T *BELIEVE* YOU WOULD SUGGEST SUCH A THING!

I EXPECT THAT KIND OF CASUAL CRUELTY FROM *JAYNE,* BUT NOT FROM *YOU.*

HEY, NOW, WHY YOU GOTTA DRAG *ME* INTO THIS.

I'M JUST GLAD THAT NOTHING BAD HAPPENED TO LITTLE EMMA.

SAVE IT, JAYNE. I'M NOT BUYING THE ACT.

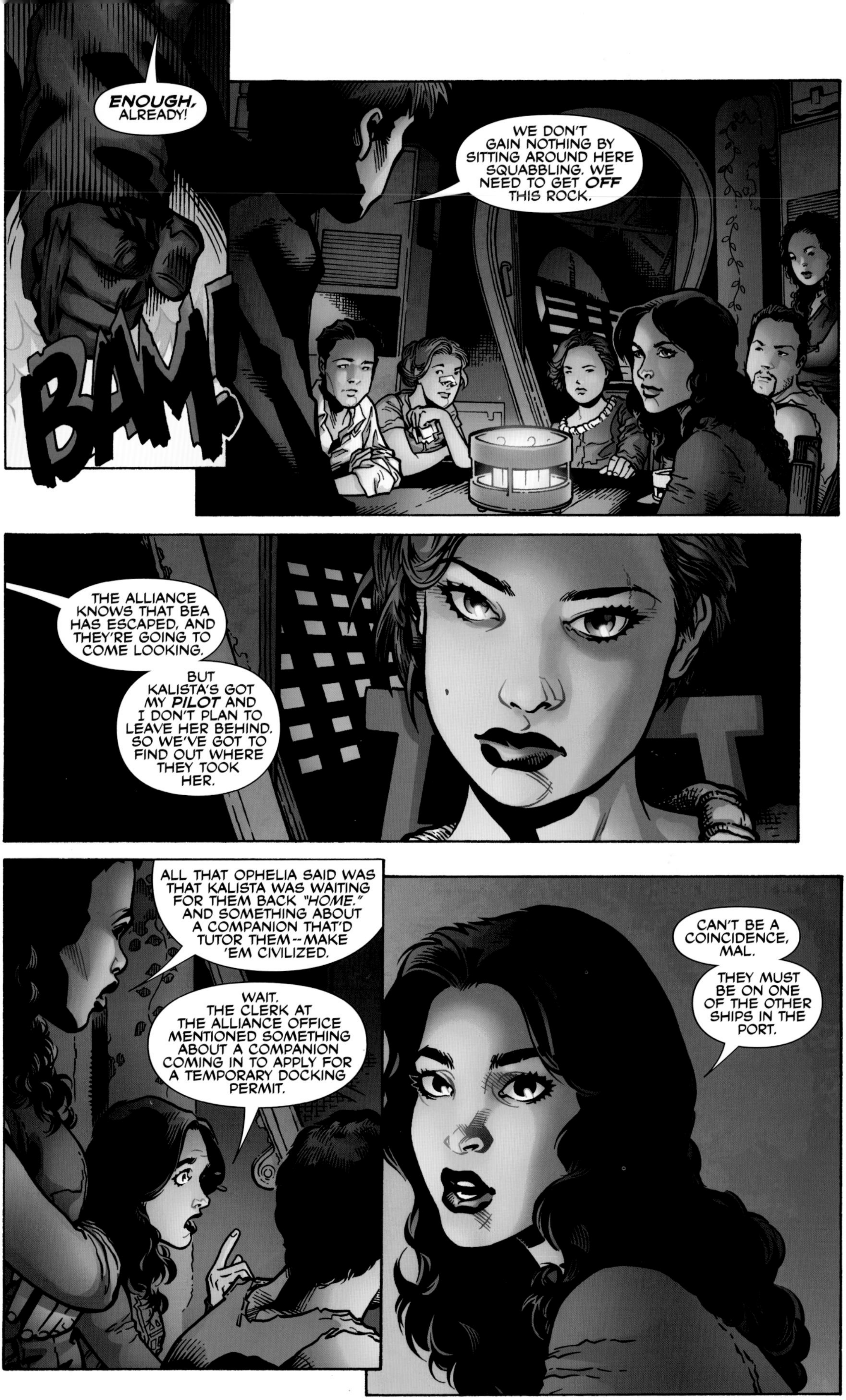
ENOUGH, ALREADY!
BAM!
WE DON'T GAIN NOTHING BY SITTING AROUND HERE SQUABBLING. WE NEED TO GET OFF THIS ROCK.
THE ALLIANCE KNOWS THAT BEA HAS ESCAPED, AND THEY'RE GOING TO COME LOOKING.
BUT KALISTA'S GOT MY PILOT AND I DON'T PLAN TO LEAVE HER BEHIND. SO WE'VE GOT TO FIND OUT WHERE THEY TOOK HER.
ALL THAT OPHELIA SAID WAS THAT KALISTA WAS WAITING FOR THEM BACK "HOME." AND SOMETHING ABOUT A COMPANION THAT'D TUTOR THEM--MAKE 'EM CIVILIZED.
WAIT. THE CLERK AT THE ALLIANCE OFFICE MENTIONED SOMETHING ABOUT A COMPANION COMING IN TO APPLY FOR A TEMPORARY DOCKING PERMIT.
CAN'T BE A COINCIDENCE, MAL.
THEY MUST BE ON ONE OF THE OTHER SHIPS IN THE PORT.

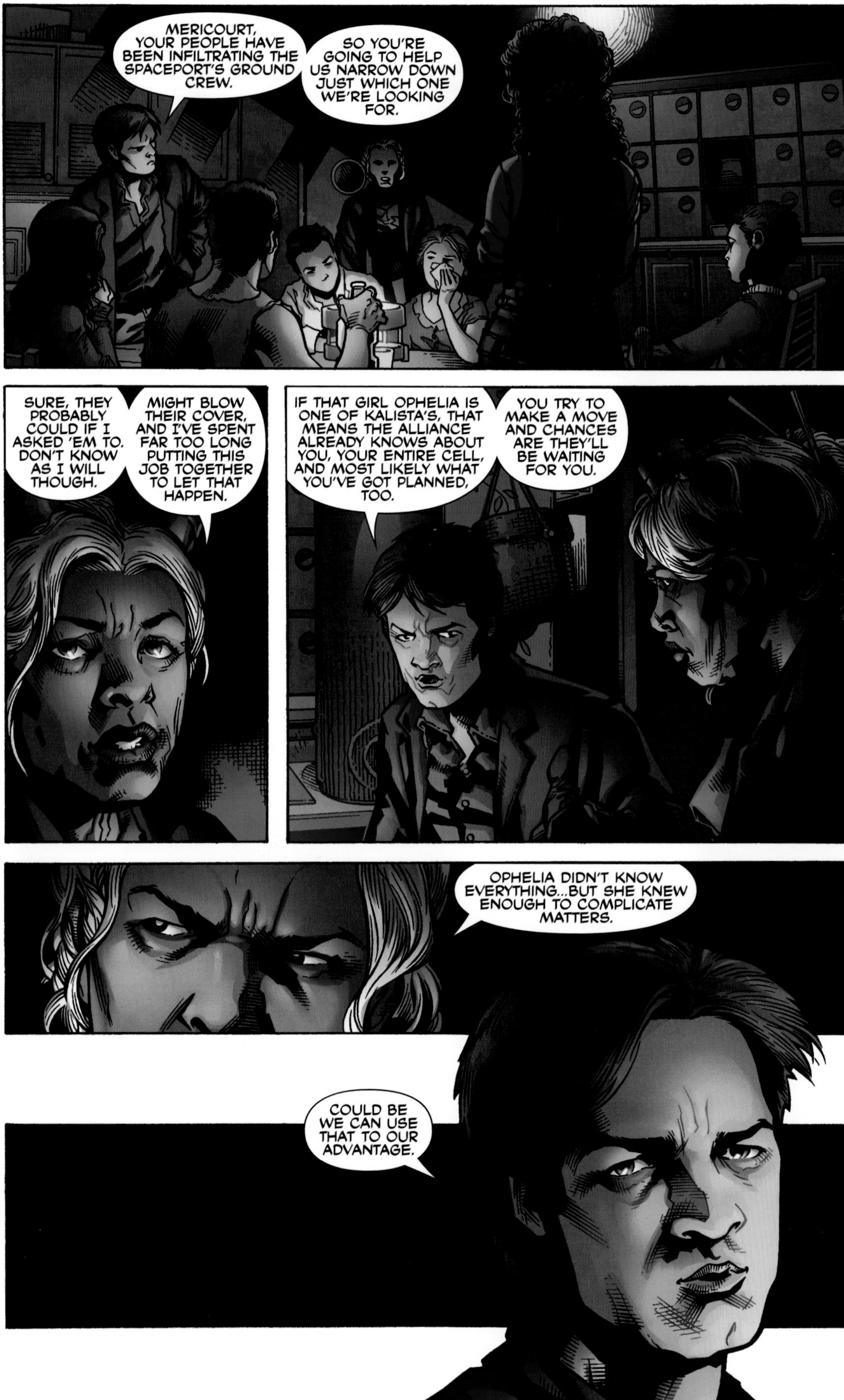
MERICOURT, YOUR PEOPLE HAVE BEEN INFILTRATING THE SPACEPORT'S GROUND CREW.
SO YOU'RE GOING TO HELP US NARROW DOWN JUST WHICH ONE WE'RE LOOKING FOR.
SURE, THEY PROBABLY COULD IF I ASKED 'EM TO. DON'T KNOW AS I WILL THOUGH.
MIGHT BLOW THEIR COVER, AND I'VE SPENT FAR TOO LONG PUTTING THIS JOB TOGETHER TO LET THAT HAPPEN.
IF THAT GIRL OPHELIA IS ONE OF KALISTA'S, THAT MEANS THE ALLIANCE ALREADY KNOWS ABOUT YOU, YOUR ENTIRE CELL, AND MOST LIKELY WHAT YOU'VE GOT PLANNED, TOO.
YOU TRY TO MAKE A MOVE AND CHANCES ARE THEY'LL BE WAITING FOR YOU.
OPHELIA DIDN'T KNOW EVERYTHING...BUT SHE KNEW ENOUGH TO COMPLICATE MATTERS.
COULD BE WE CAN USE THAT TO OUR ADVANTAGE.

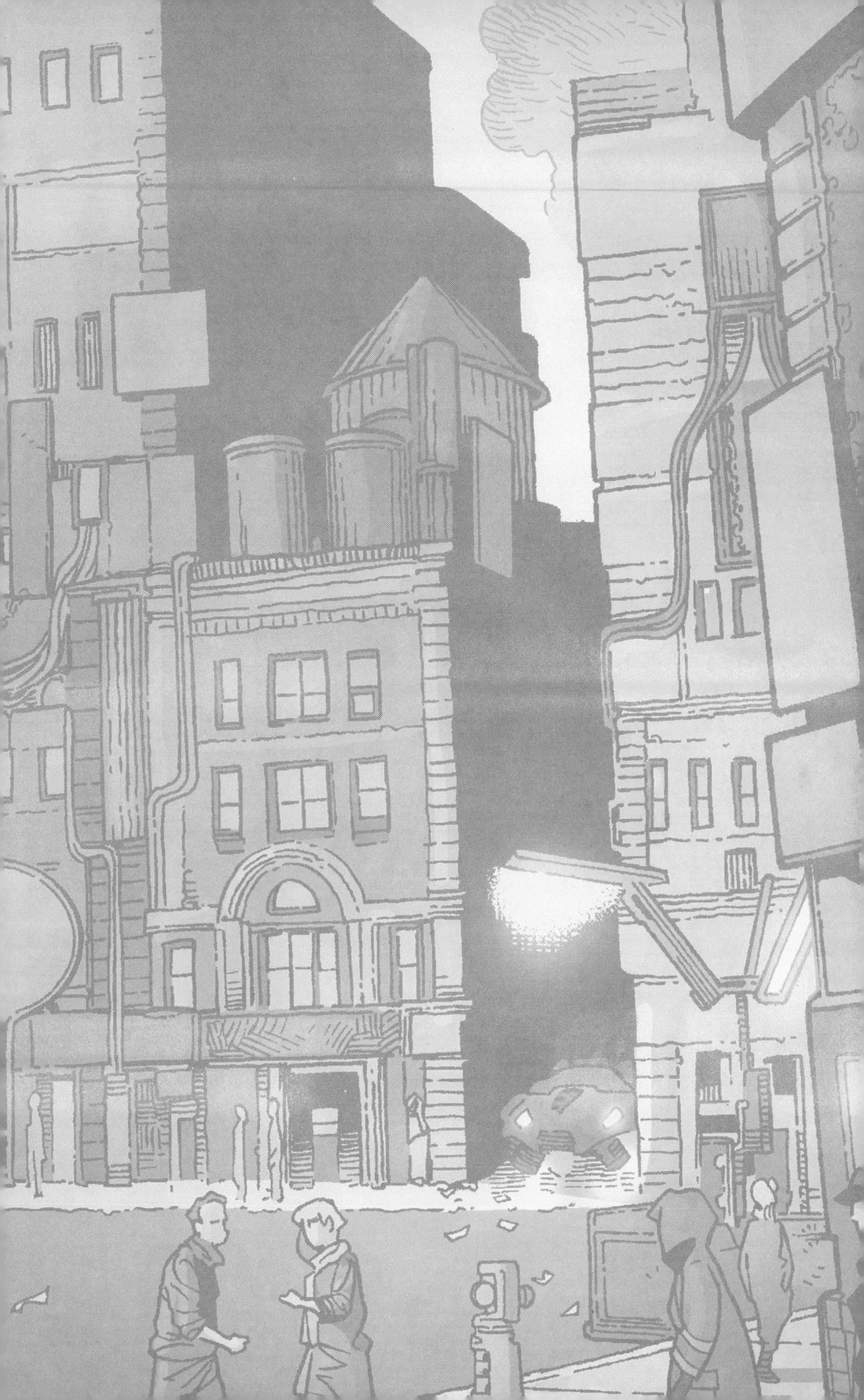

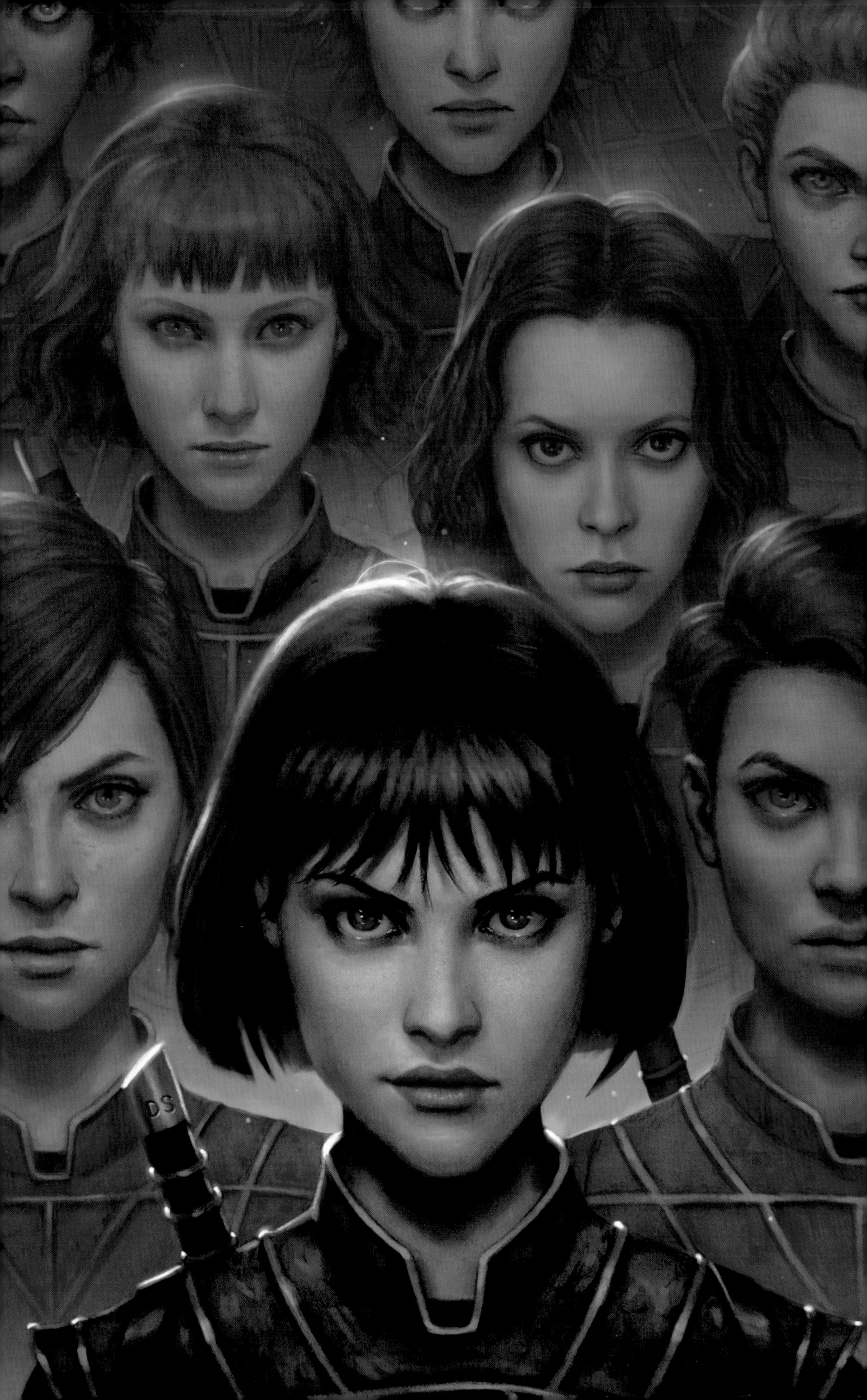
DS

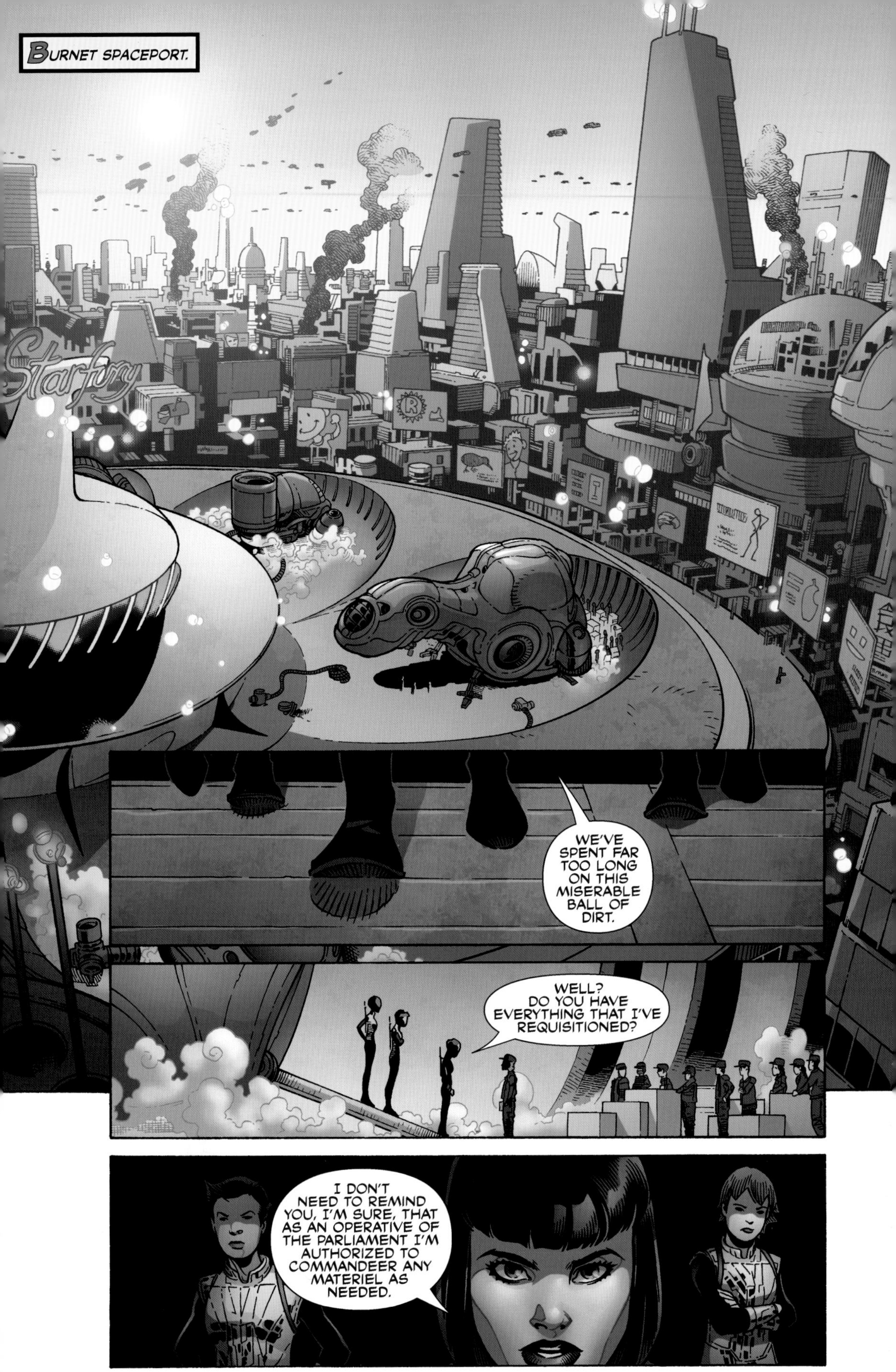
BURNET SPACEPORT.
Starfury
WE'VE SPENT FAR TOO LONG ON THIS MISERABLE BALL OF DIRT.
WELL? DO YOU HAVE EVERYTHING THAT I'VE REQUISITIONED?
I DON'T NEED TO REMIND YOU, I'M SURE, THAT AS AN OPERATIVE OF THE PARLIAMENT I'M AUTHORIZED TO COMMANDEER ANY MATERIEL AS NEEDED.

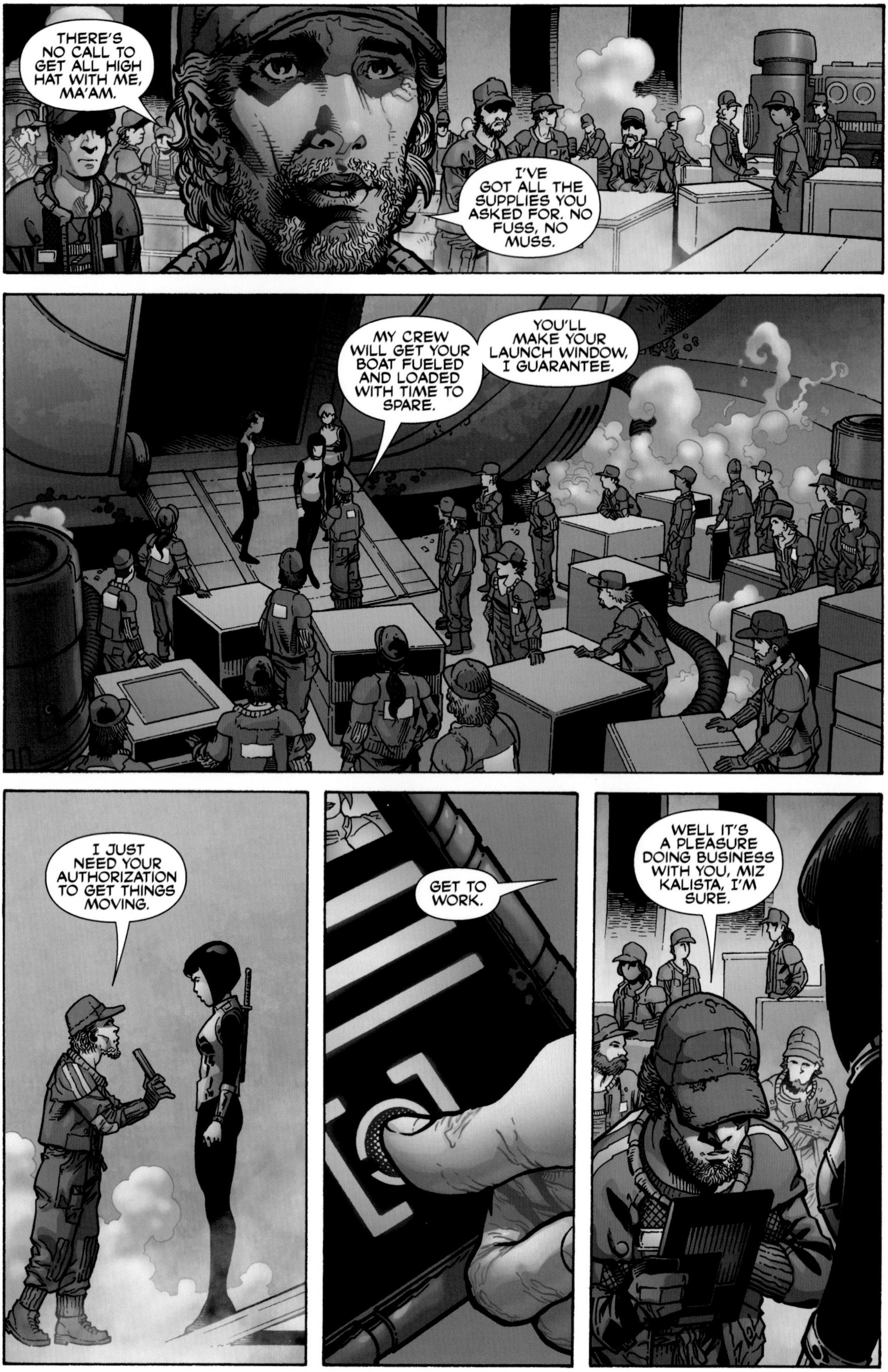
THERE'S NO CALL TO GET ALL HIGH HAT WITH ME, MA'AM.
I'VE GOT ALL THE SUPPLIES YOU ASKED FOR. NO FUSS, NO MUSS.
MY CREW WILL GET YOUR BOAT FUELED AND LOADED WITH TIME TO SPARE.
YOU'LL MAKE YOUR LAUNCH WINDOW, I GUARANTEE.
I JUST NEED YOUR AUTHORIZATION TO GET THINGS MOVING.
GET TO WORK.
WELL IT'S A PLEASURE DOING BUSINESS WITH YOU, MIZ KALISTA, I'M SURE.

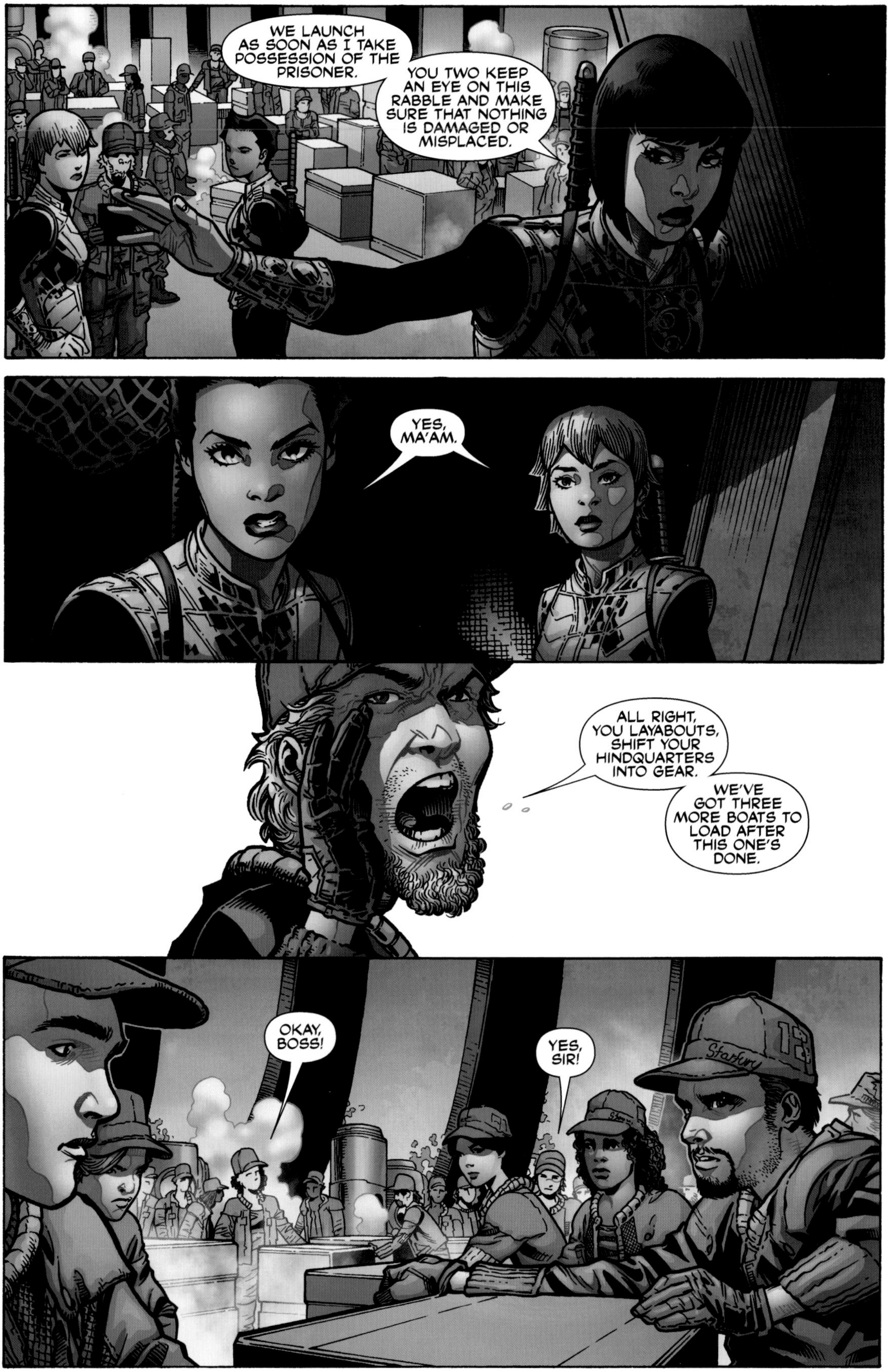
WE LAUNCH AS SOON AS I TAKE POSSESSION OF THE PRISONER.
YOU TWO KEEP AN EYE ON THIS RABBLE AND MAKE SURE THAT NOTHING IS DAMAGED OR MISPLACED.
YES, MA'AM.
ALL RIGHT, YOU LAYABOUTS, SHIFT YOUR HINDQUARTERS INTO GEAR.
WE'VE GOT THREE MORE BOATS TO LOAD AFTER THIS ONE'S DONE.
OKAY, BOSS!
YES, SIR!
Starfury

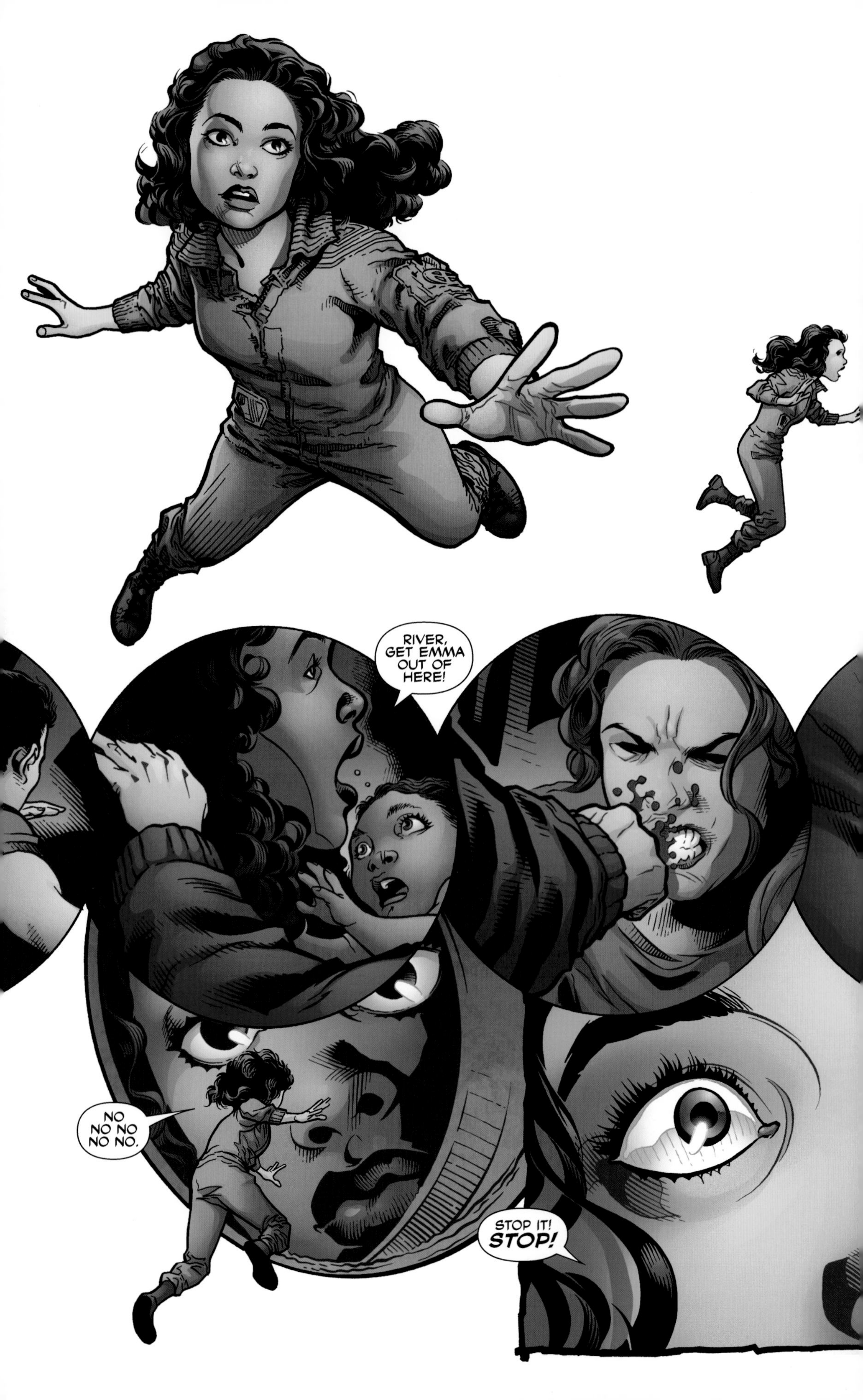
RIVER, GET EMMA OUT OF HERE!
NO NO NO NO NO.
STOP IT! STOP!

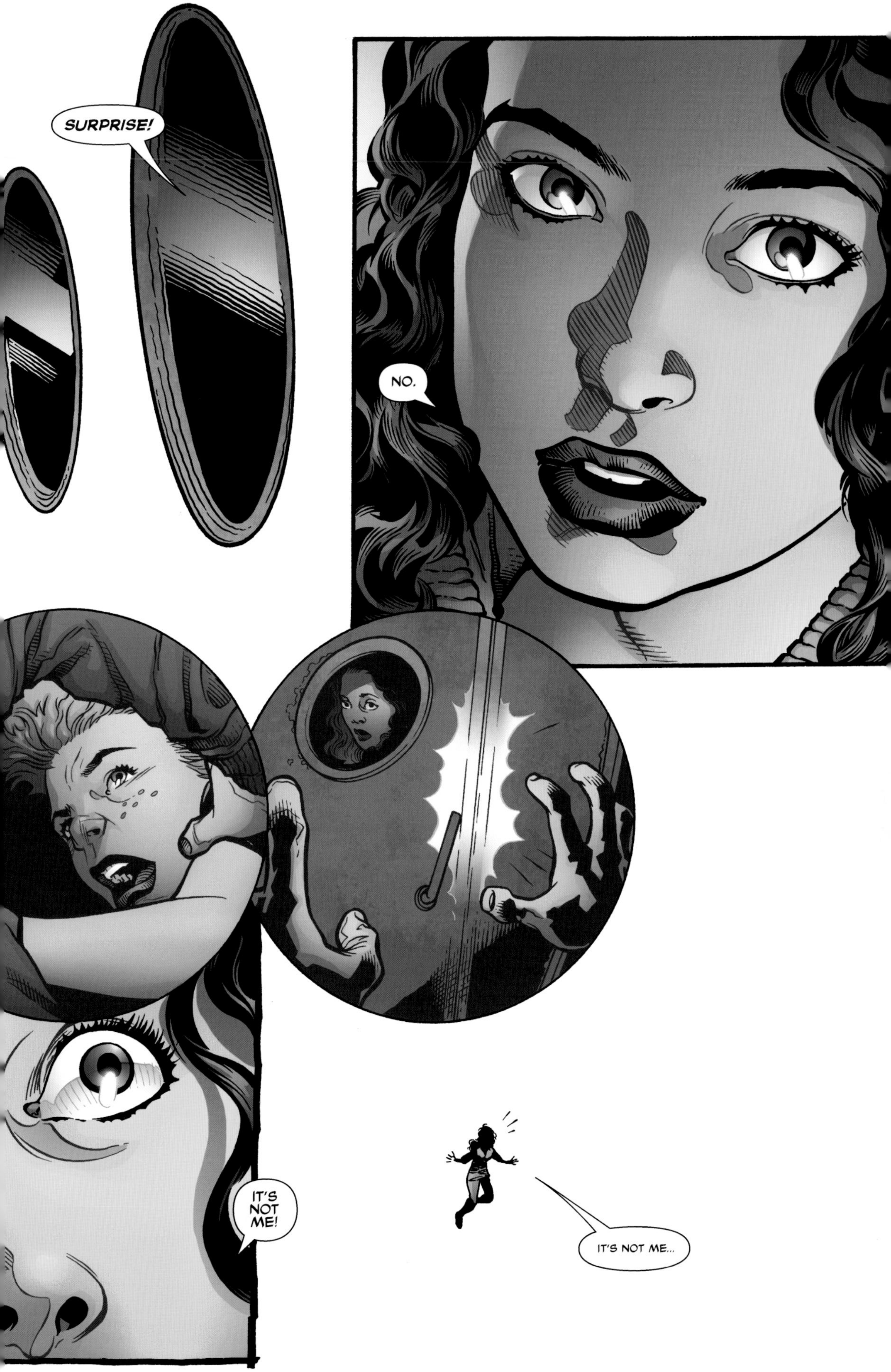
SURPRISE!
NO.
IT'S NOT ME!
IT'S NOT ME...

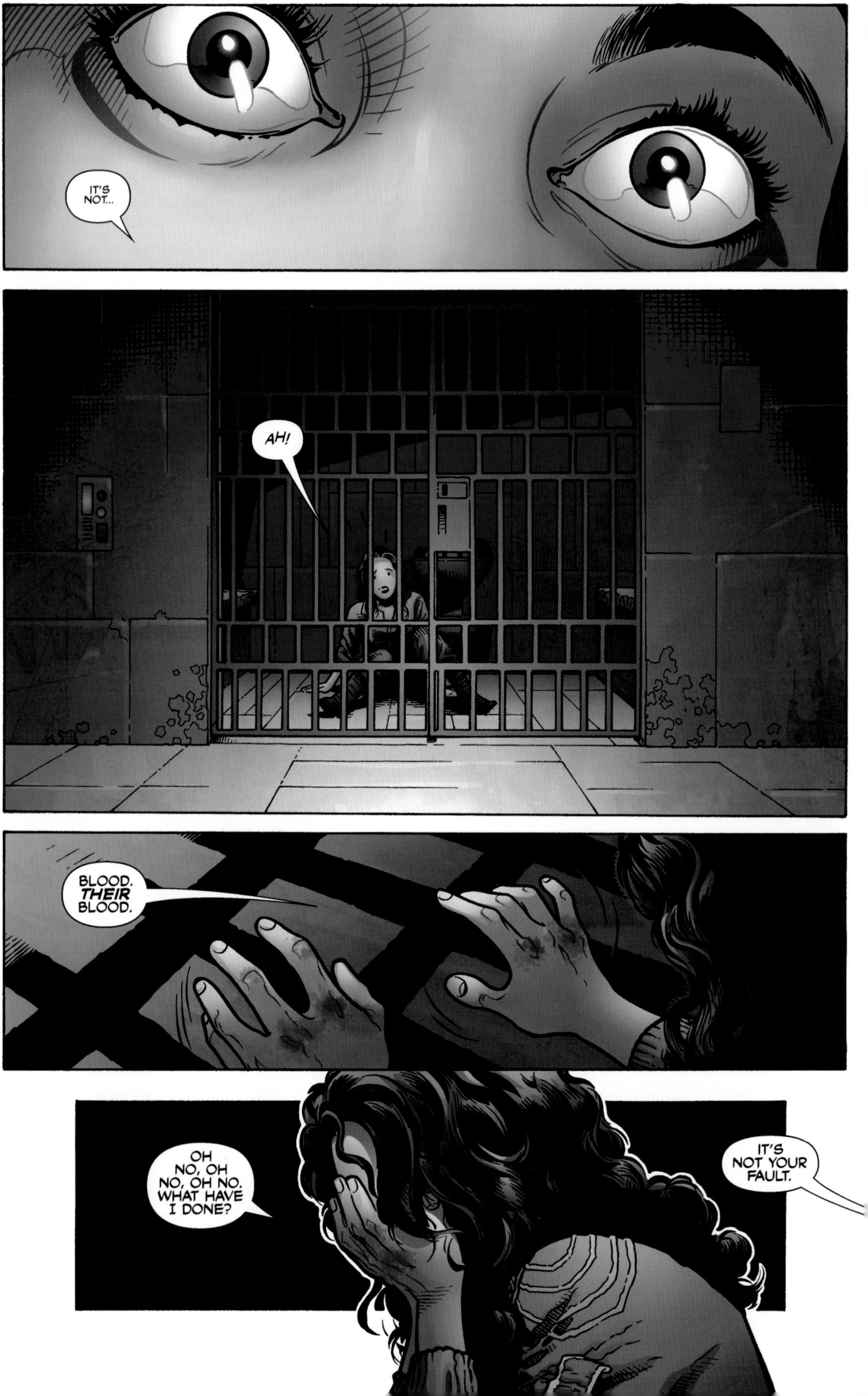
IT'S NOT...
AH!
BLOOD. THEIR BLOOD.
OH NO, OH NO, OH NO. WHAT HAVE I DONE?
IT'S NOT YOUR FAULT.

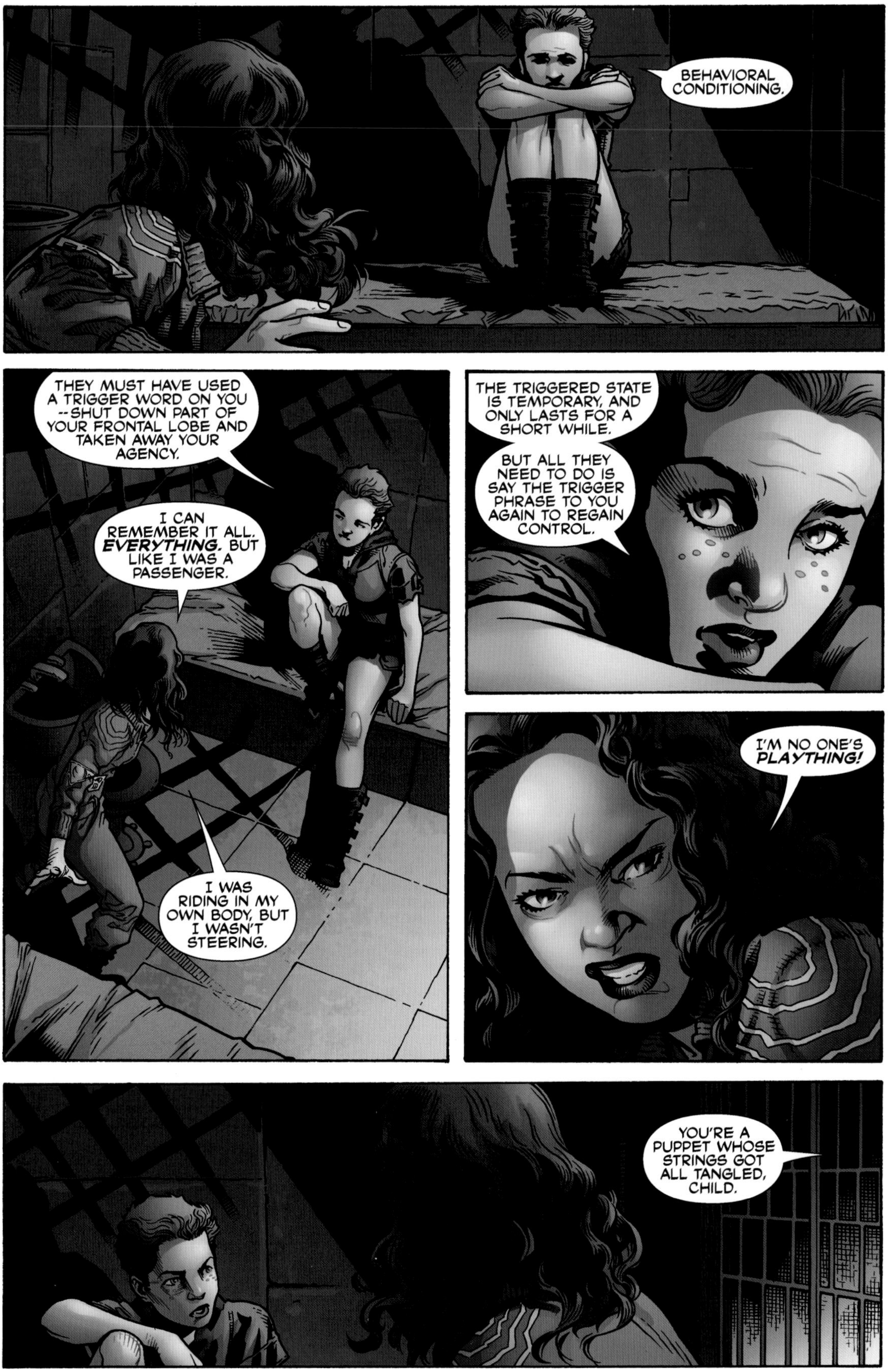
BEHAVIORAL CONDITIONING.
THEY MUST HAVE USED A TRIGGER WORD ON YOU --SHUT DOWN PART OF YOUR FRONTAL LOBE AND TAKEN AWAY YOUR AGENCY.
I CAN REMEMBER IT ALL. *EVERYTHING.* BUT LIKE I WAS A PASSENGER.
I WAS RIDING IN MY OWN BODY, BUT I WASN'T STEERING.
THE TRIGGERED STATE IS TEMPORARY, AND ONLY LASTS FOR A SHORT WHILE.
BUT ALL THEY NEED TO DO IS SAY THE TRIGGER PHRASE TO YOU AGAIN TO REGAIN CONTROL.
I'M NO ONE'S *PLAYTHING!*
YOU'RE A PUPPET WHOSE STRINGS GOT ALL TANGLED, CHILD.

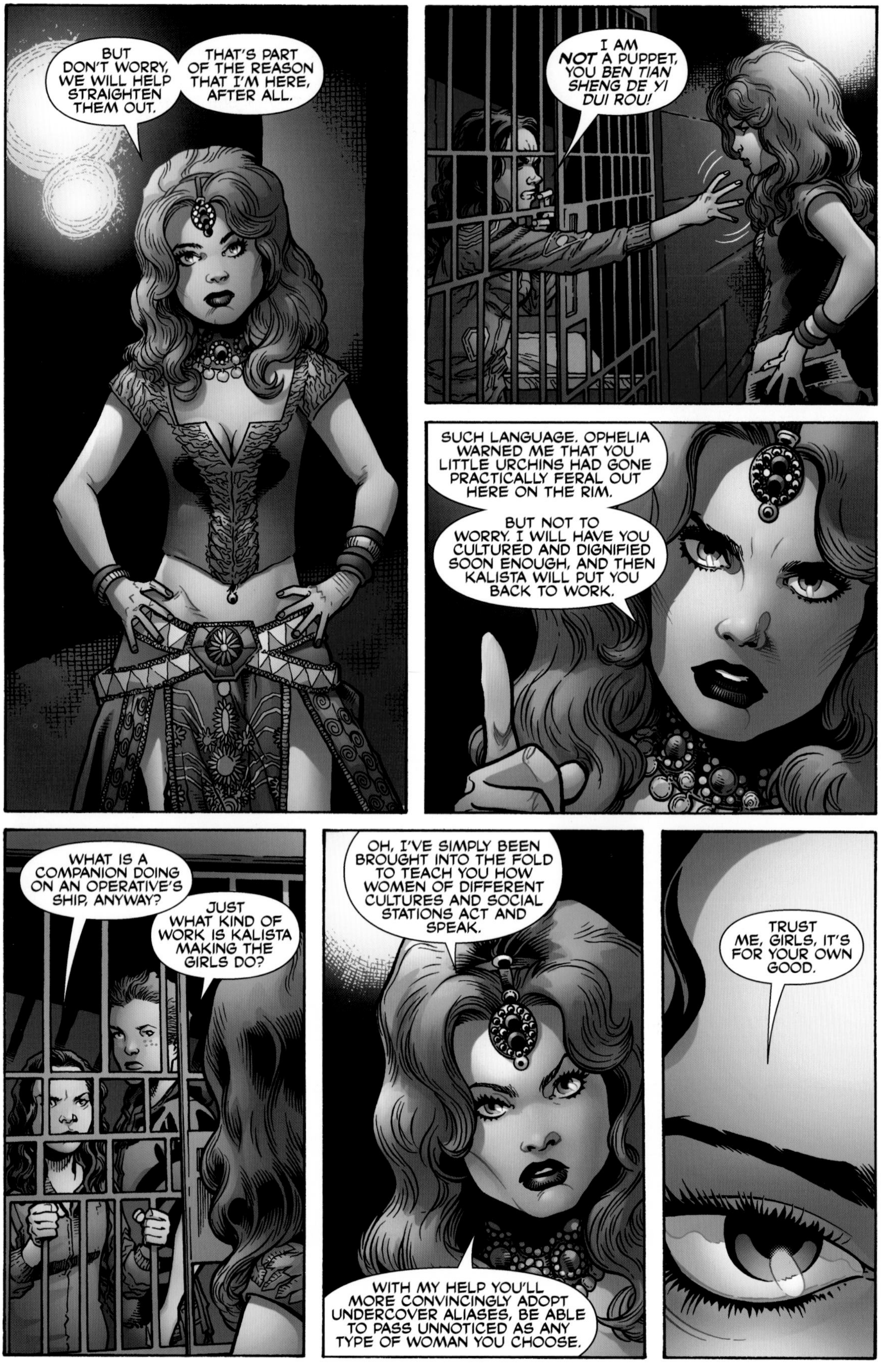
BUT DON'T WORRY, WE WILL HELP STRAIGHTEN THEM OUT.
THAT'S PART OF THE REASON THAT I'M HERE, AFTER ALL.
I AM *NOT* A PUPPET, YOU *BEN TIAN SHENG DE YI DUI ROU!*
SUCH LANGUAGE. OPHELIA WARNED ME THAT YOU LITTLE URCHINS HAD GONE PRACTICALLY FERAL OUT HERE ON THE RIM.
BUT NOT TO WORRY. I WILL HAVE YOU CULTURED AND DIGNIFIED SOON ENOUGH, AND THEN KALISTA WILL PUT YOU BACK TO WORK.
WHAT IS A COMPANION DOING ON AN OPERATIVE'S SHIP, ANYWAY?
JUST WHAT KIND OF WORK IS KALISTA MAKING THE GIRLS DO?
OH, I'VE SIMPLY BEEN BROUGHT INTO THE FOLD TO TEACH YOU HOW WOMEN OF DIFFERENT CULTURES AND SOCIAL STATIONS ACT AND SPEAK.
WITH MY HELP YOU'LL MORE CONVINCINGLY ADOPT UNDERCOVER ALIASES, BE ABLE TO PASS UNNOTICED AS ANY TYPE OF WOMAN YOU CHOOSE.
TRUST ME, GIRLS, IT'S FOR YOUR OWN GOOD.

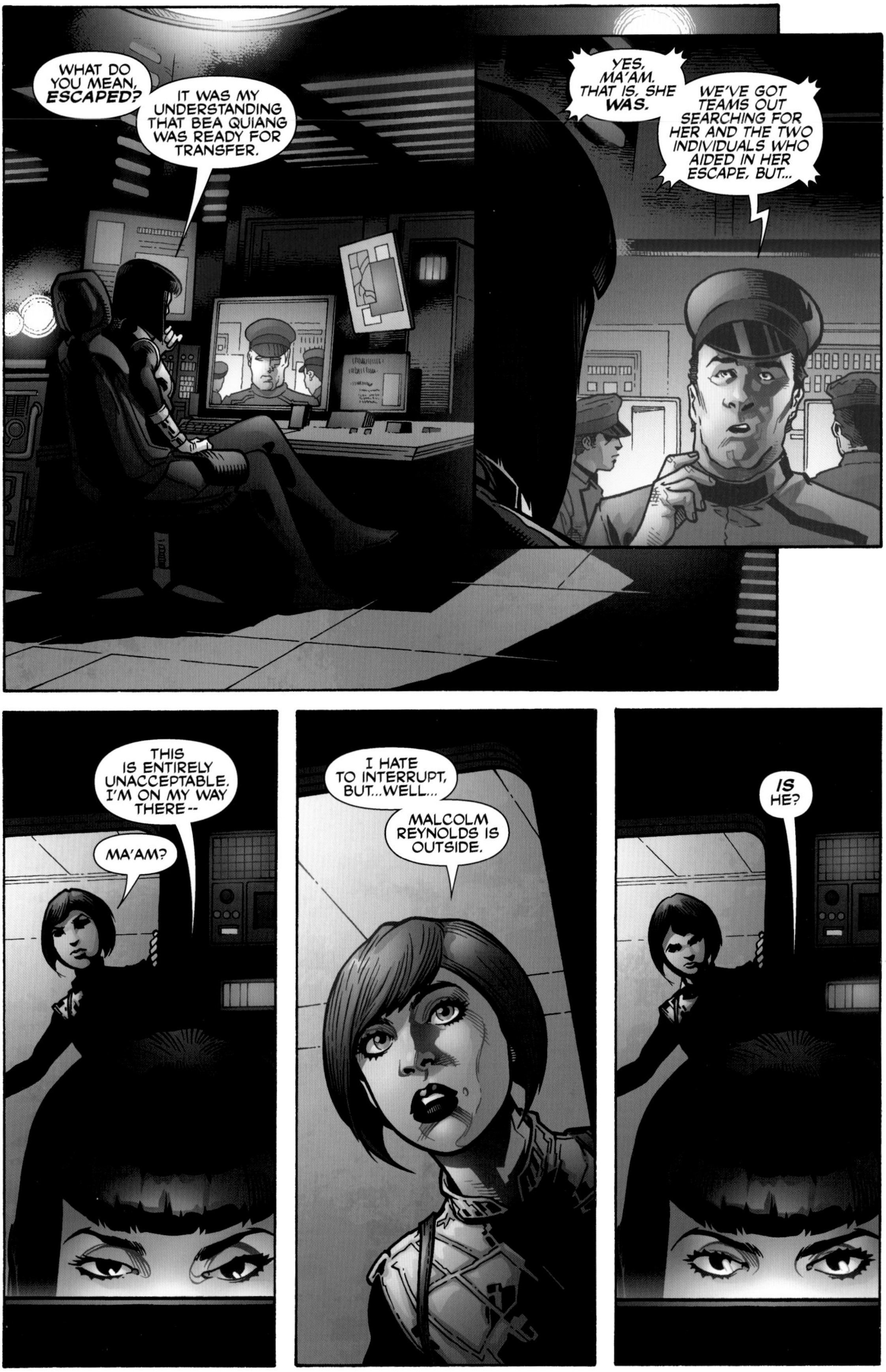
WHAT DO YOU MEAN, ESCAPED?
IT WAS MY UNDERSTANDING THAT BEA QUIANG WAS READY FOR TRANSFER.
YES, MA'AM. THAT IS, SHE WAS.
WE'VE GOT TEAMS OUT SEARCHING FOR HER AND THE TWO INDIVIDUALS WHO AIDED IN HER ESCAPE, BUT...
THIS IS ENTIRELY UNACCEPTABLE. I'M ON MY WAY THERE--
MA'AM?
I HATE TO INTERRUPT, BUT...WELL...
MALCOLM REYNOLDS IS OUTSIDE.
IS HE?

DON'T SEEM EXACTLY NEIGHBORLY, THEM MAKING ME WAIT LIKE THIS.

MAL, I'M STILL NOT CONVINCED THIS IS THE BEST IDEA.

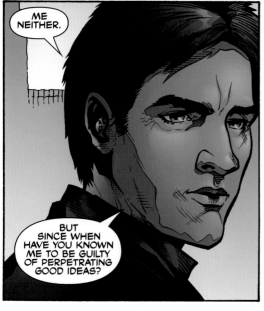

ME NEITHER.

BUT SINCE WHEN HAVE YOU KNOWN ME TO BE GUILTY OF PERPETRATING GOOD IDEAS?

HSSSS

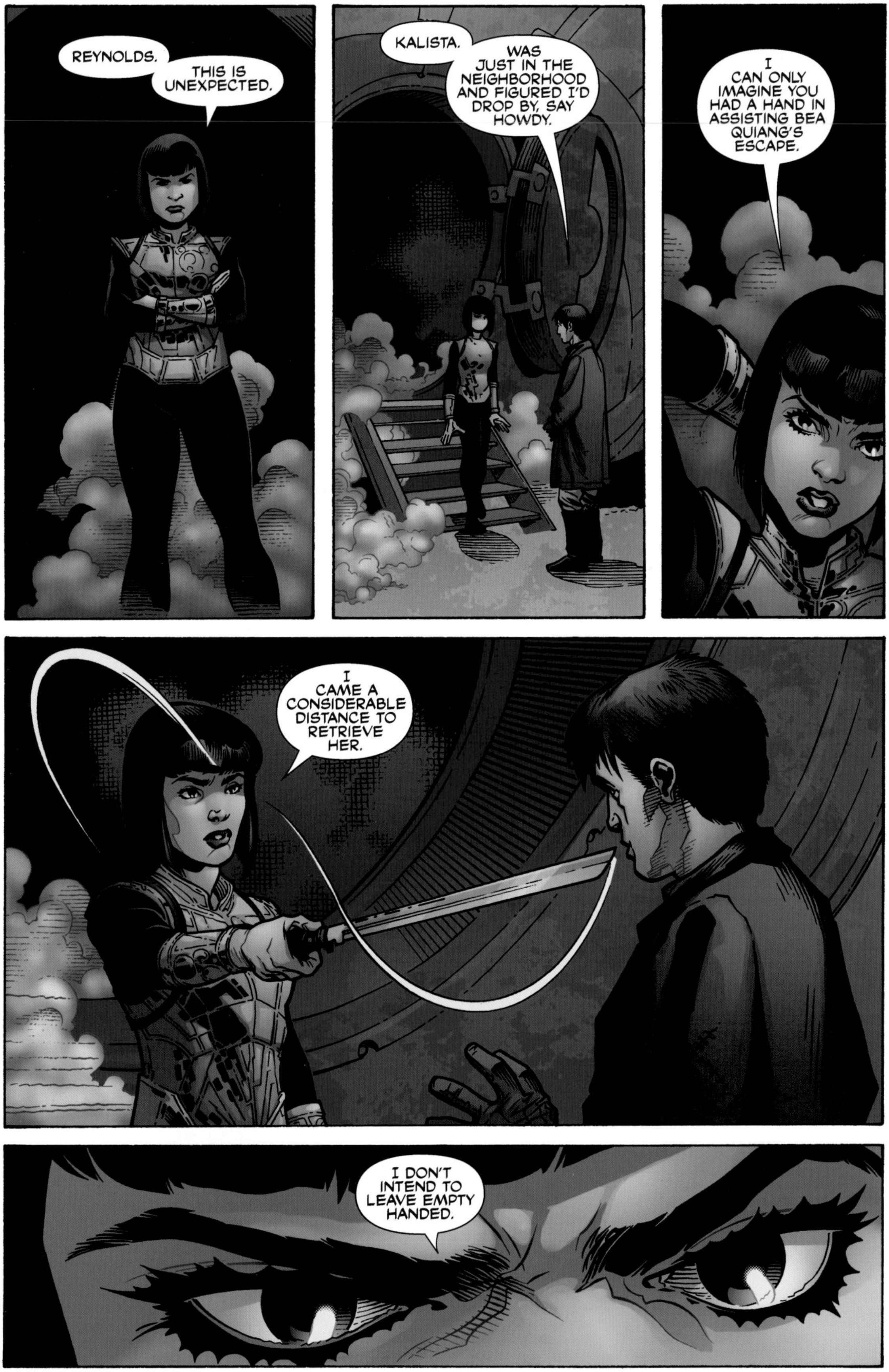
REYNOLDS.
THIS IS UNEXPECTED.
KALISTA.
WAS JUST IN THE NEIGHBORHOOD AND FIGURED I'D DROP BY, SAY HOWDY.
I CAN ONLY IMAGINE YOU HAD A HAND IN ASSISTING BEA QUIANG'S ESCAPE.
I CAME A CONSIDERABLE DISTANCE TO RETRIEVE HER.
I DON'T INTEND TO LEAVE EMPTY HANDED.

CAREFUL WITH THOSE CRATES.

KALISTA WILL HAVE YOUR HIDE IF YOU DAMAGE ANY OF THAT EQUIPMENT.

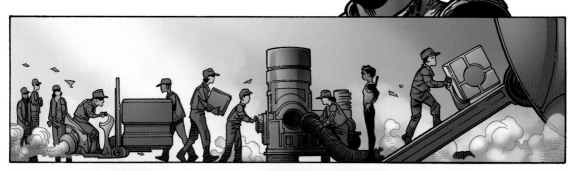

I HOPE SO, BEA.

DO YOU THINK IRIS AND YOUR SISTER ARE OKAY?

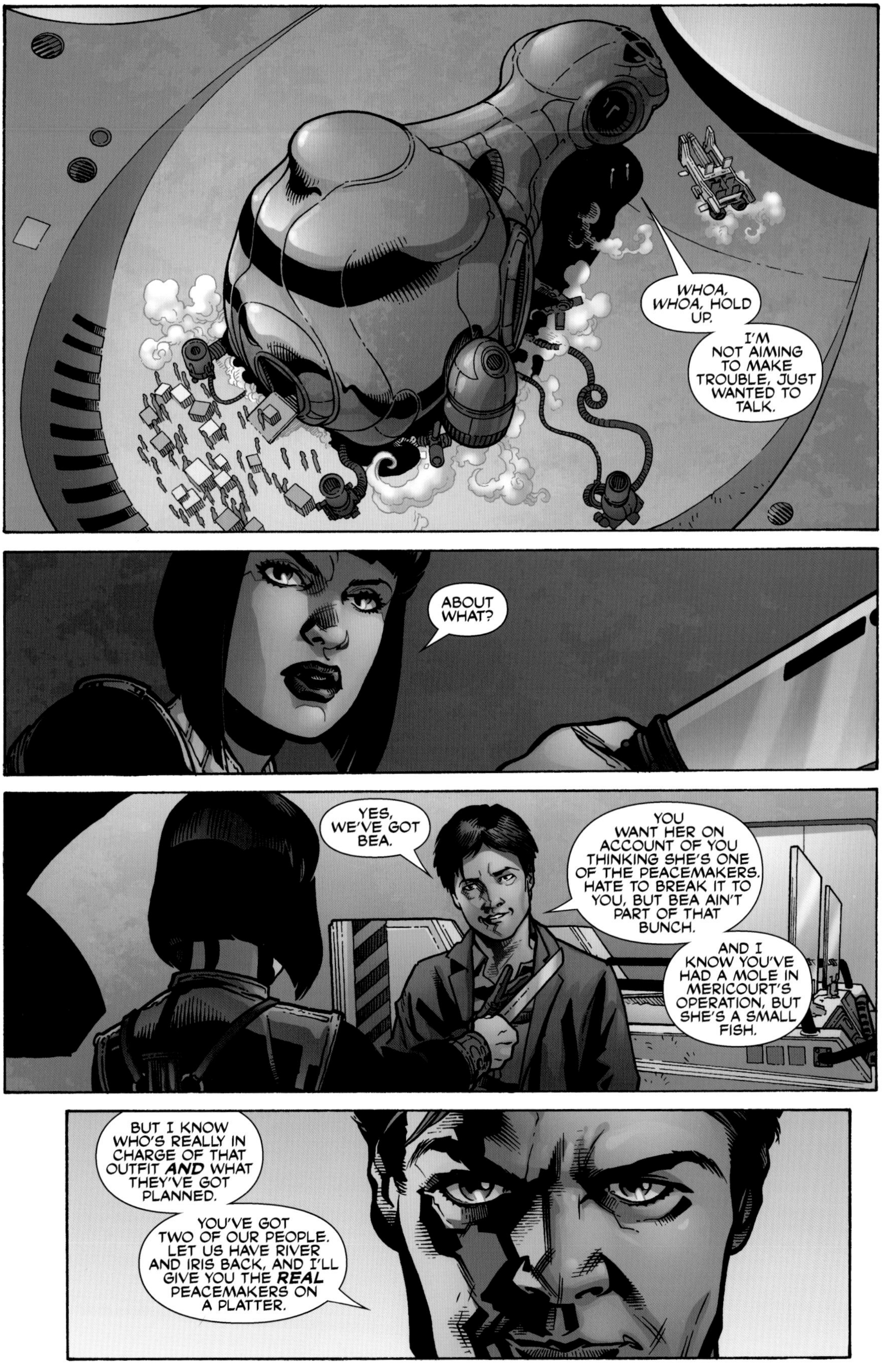
WHOA, WHOA, HOLD UP.
I'M NOT AIMING TO MAKE TROUBLE, JUST WANTED TO TALK.
ABOUT WHAT?
YES, WE'VE GOT BEA.
YOU WANT HER ON ACCOUNT OF YOU THINKING SHE'S ONE OF THE PEACEMAKERS. HATE TO BREAK IT TO YOU, BUT BEA AIN'T PART OF THAT BUNCH.
AND I KNOW YOU'VE HAD A MOLE IN MERICOURT'S OPERATION, BUT SHE'S A SMALL FISH.
BUT I KNOW WHO'S REALLY IN CHARGE OF THAT OUTFIT **AND** WHAT THEY'VE GOT PLANNED.
YOU'VE GOT TWO OF OUR PEOPLE. LET US HAVE RIVER AND IRIS BACK, AND I'LL GIVE YOU THE ***REAL*** PEACEMAKERS ON A PLATTER.

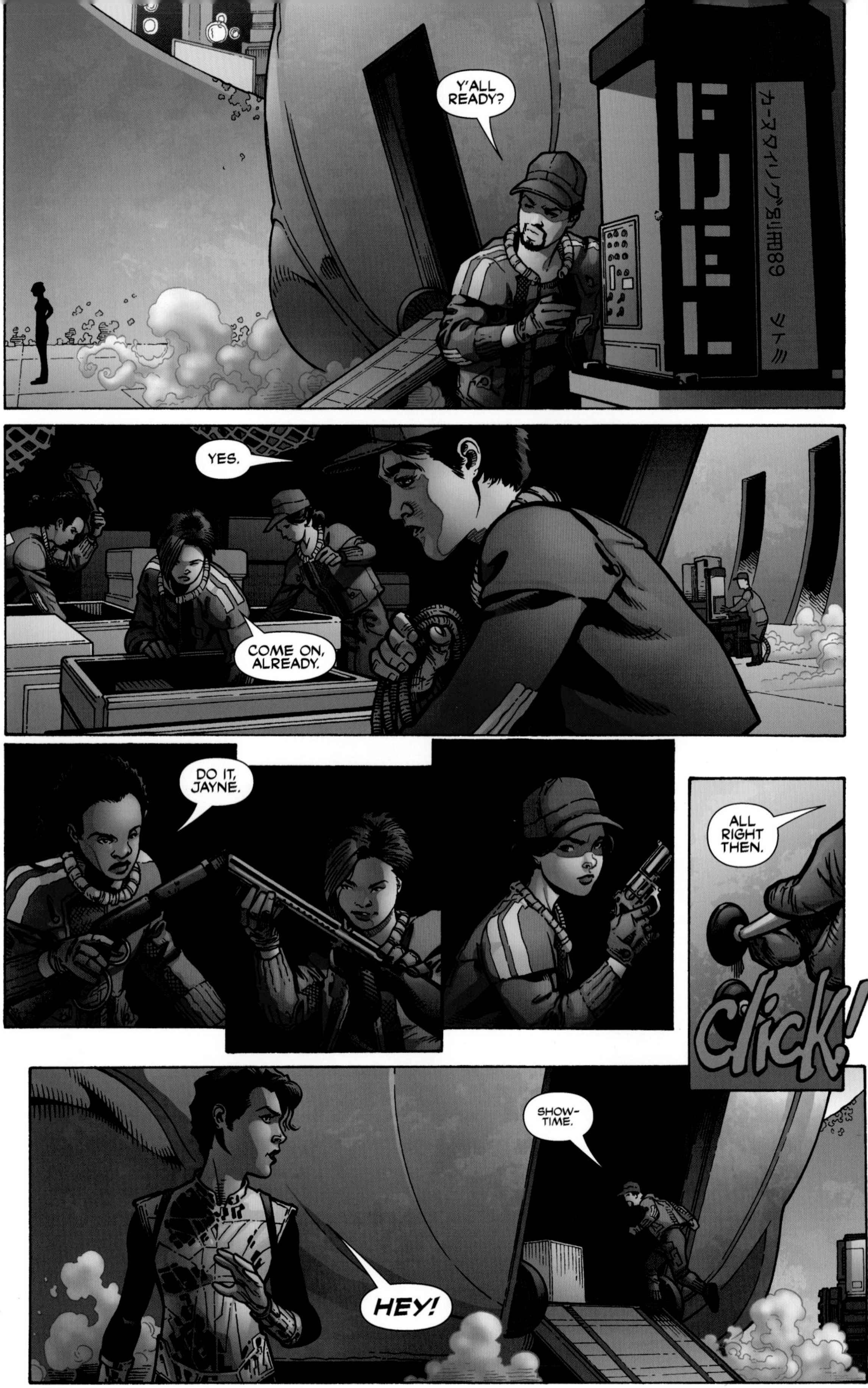

Y'ALL READY?
YES.
COME ON, ALREADY.
DO IT, JAYNE.
ALL RIGHT THEN.
click!
SHOW-TIME.
HEY!

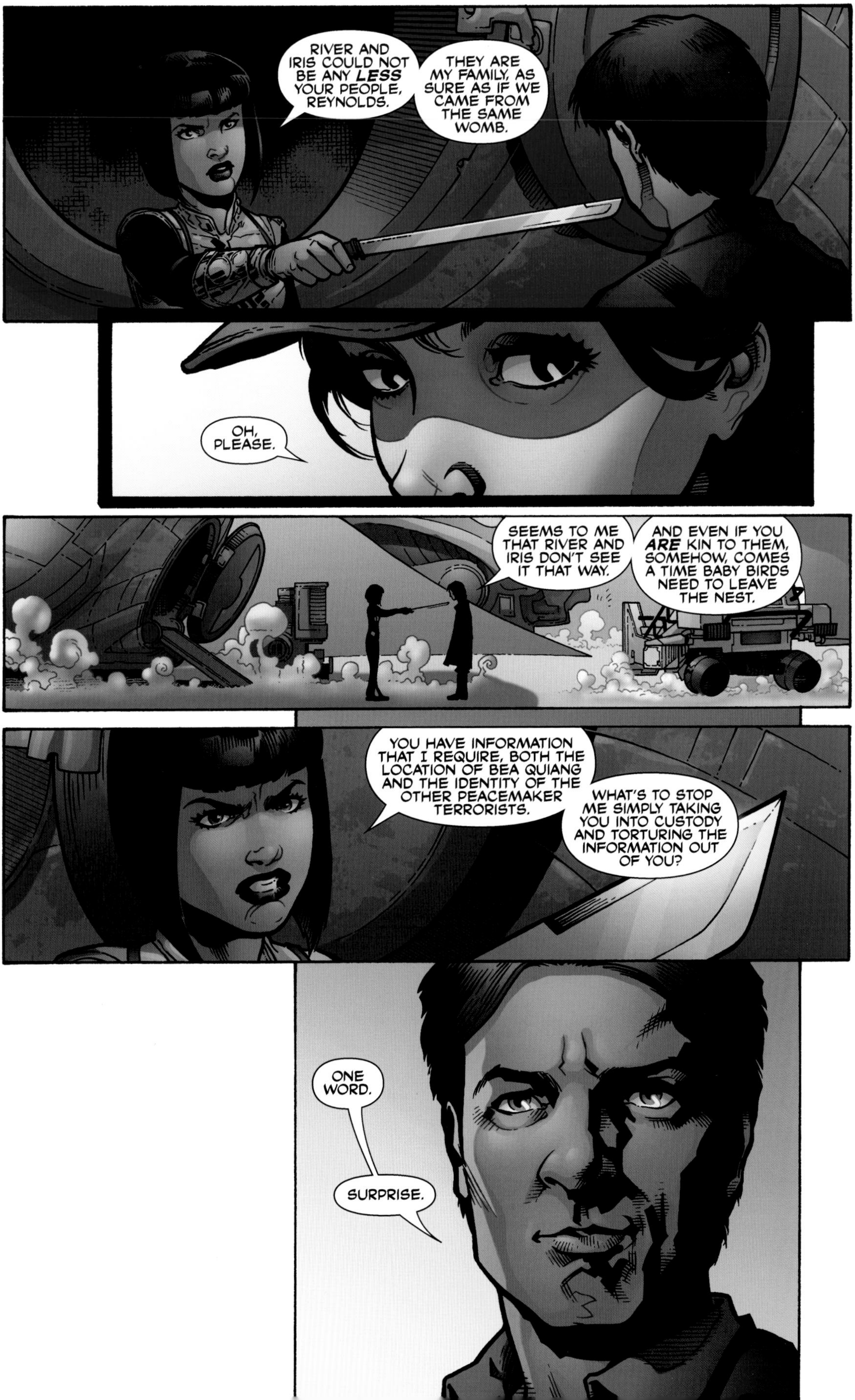
RIVER AND IRIS COULD NOT BE ANY LESS YOUR PEOPLE, REYNOLDS.
THEY ARE MY FAMILY, AS SURE AS IF WE CAME FROM THE SAME WOMB.
OH, PLEASE.
SEEMS TO ME THAT RIVER AND IRIS DON'T SEE IT THAT WAY.
AND EVEN IF YOU ARE KIN TO THEM, SOMEHOW, COMES A TIME BABY BIRDS NEED TO LEAVE THE NEST.
YOU HAVE INFORMATION THAT I REQUIRE, BOTH THE LOCATION OF BEA QUIANG AND THE IDENTITY OF THE OTHER PEACEMAKER TERRORISTS.
WHAT'S TO STOP ME SIMPLY TAKING YOU INTO CUSTODY AND TORTURING THE INFORMATION OUT OF YOU?
ONE WORD.
SURPRISE.

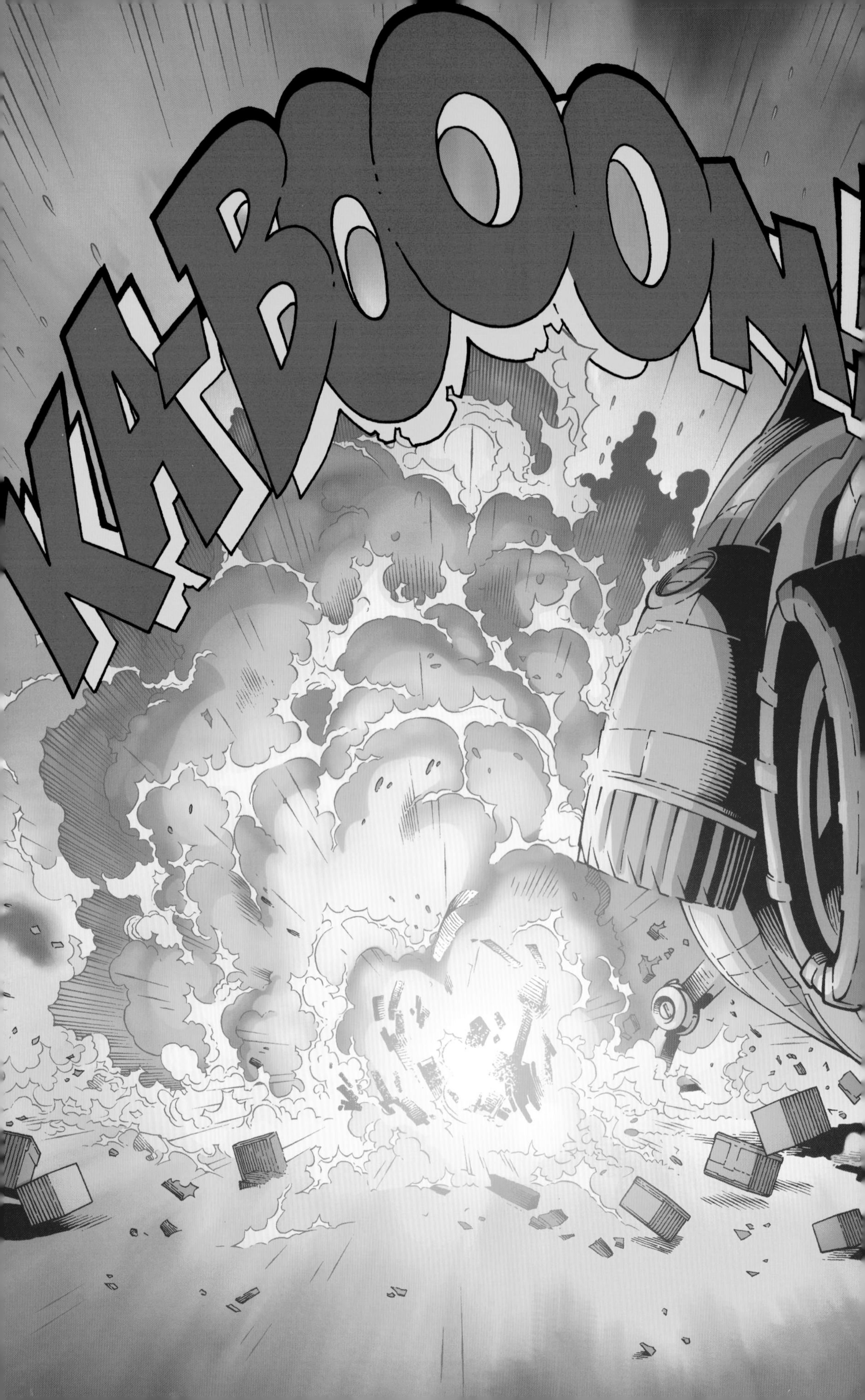
KA-BOOOM!

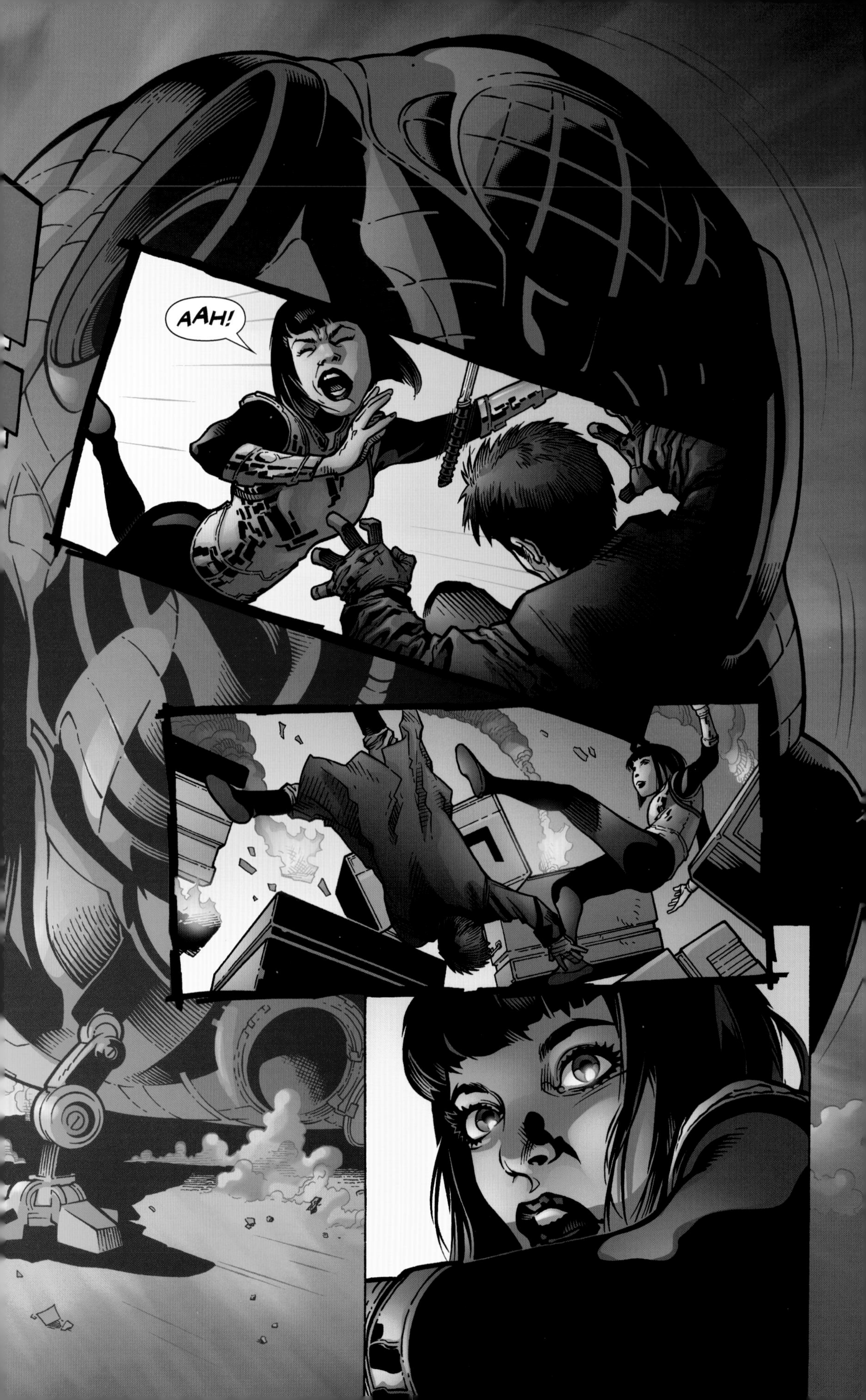
AAH!

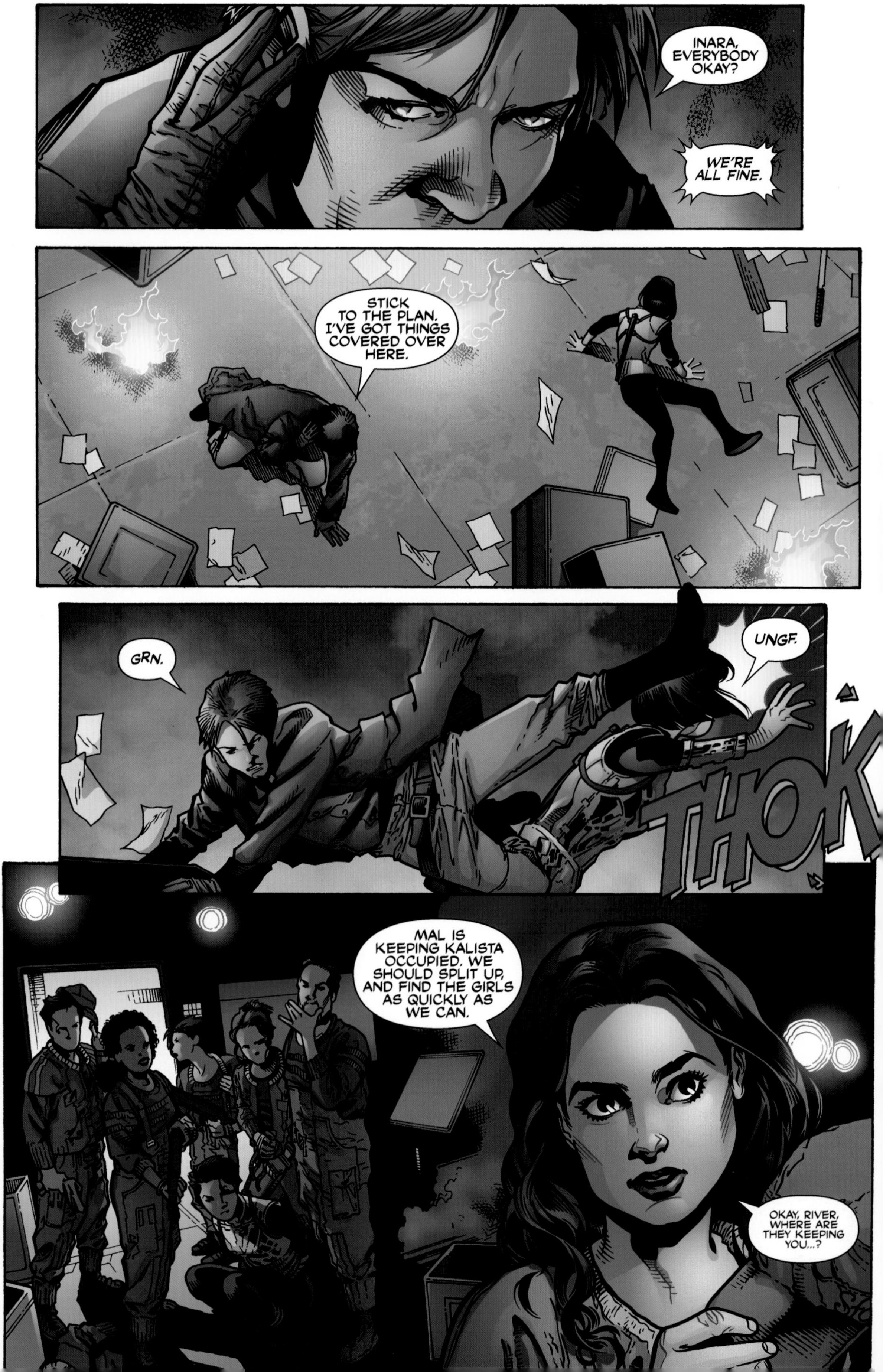
INARA, EVERYBODY OKAY?
WE'RE ALL FINE.
STICK TO THE PLAN. I'VE GOT THINGS COVERED OVER HERE.
GRN.
UNGF.
THOK
MAL IS KEEPING KALISTA OCCUPIED. WE SHOULD SPLIT UP, AND FIND THE GIRLS AS QUICKLY AS WE CAN.
OKAY, RIVER, WHERE ARE THEY KEEPING YOU...?

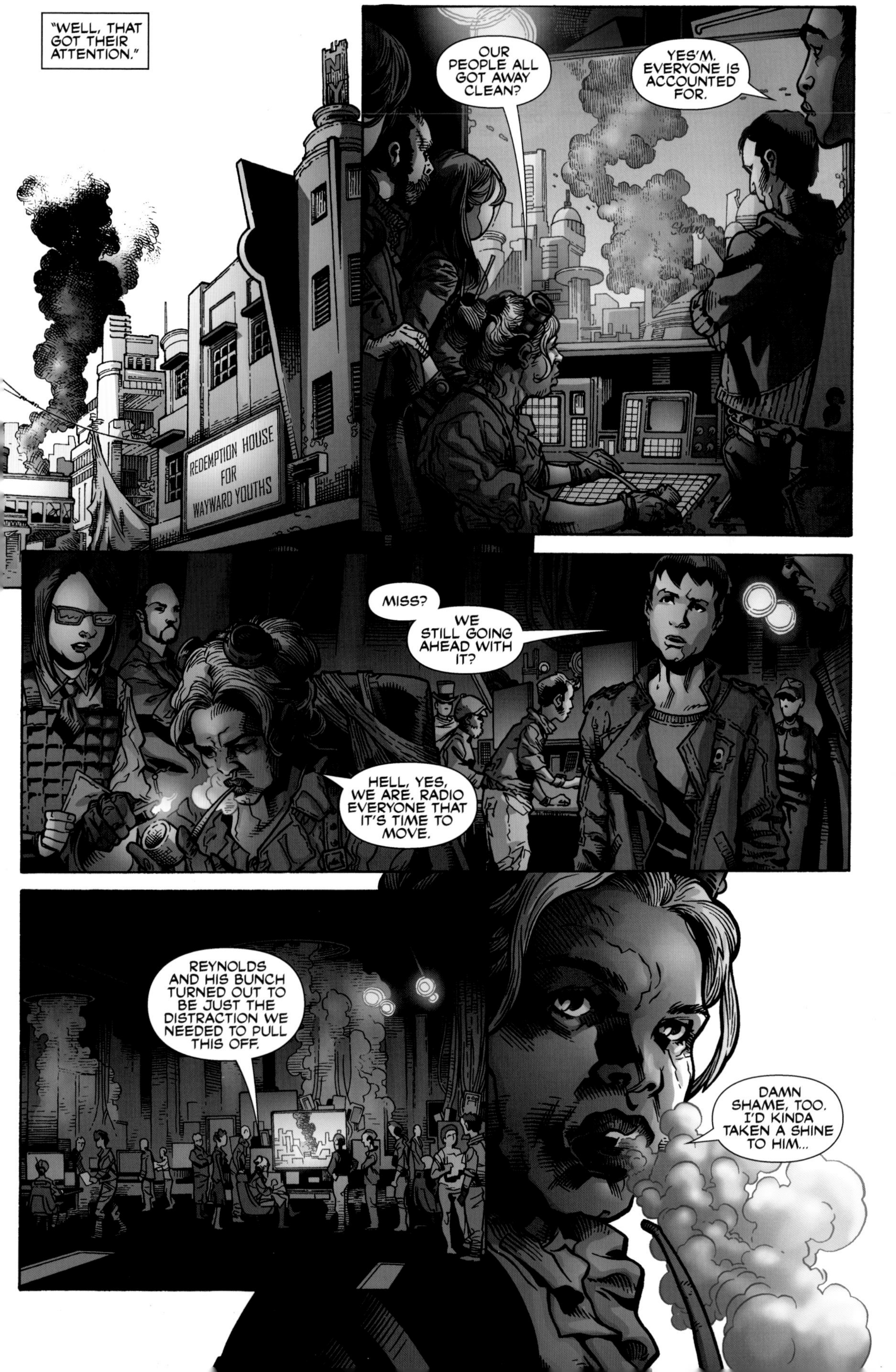
"WELL, THAT GOT THEIR ATTENTION."
REDEMPTION HOUSE FOR WAYWARD YOUTHS
OUR PEOPLE ALL GOT AWAY CLEAN?
YES'M. EVERYONE IS ACCOUNTED FOR.
MISS?
WE STILL GOING AHEAD WITH IT?
HELL, YES, WE ARE. RADIO EVERYONE THAT IT'S TIME TO MOVE.
REYNOLDS AND HIS BUNCH TURNED OUT TO BE JUST THE DISTRACTION WE NEEDED TO PULL THIS OFF.
DAMN SHAME, TOO. I'D KINDA TAKEN A SHINE TO HIM...

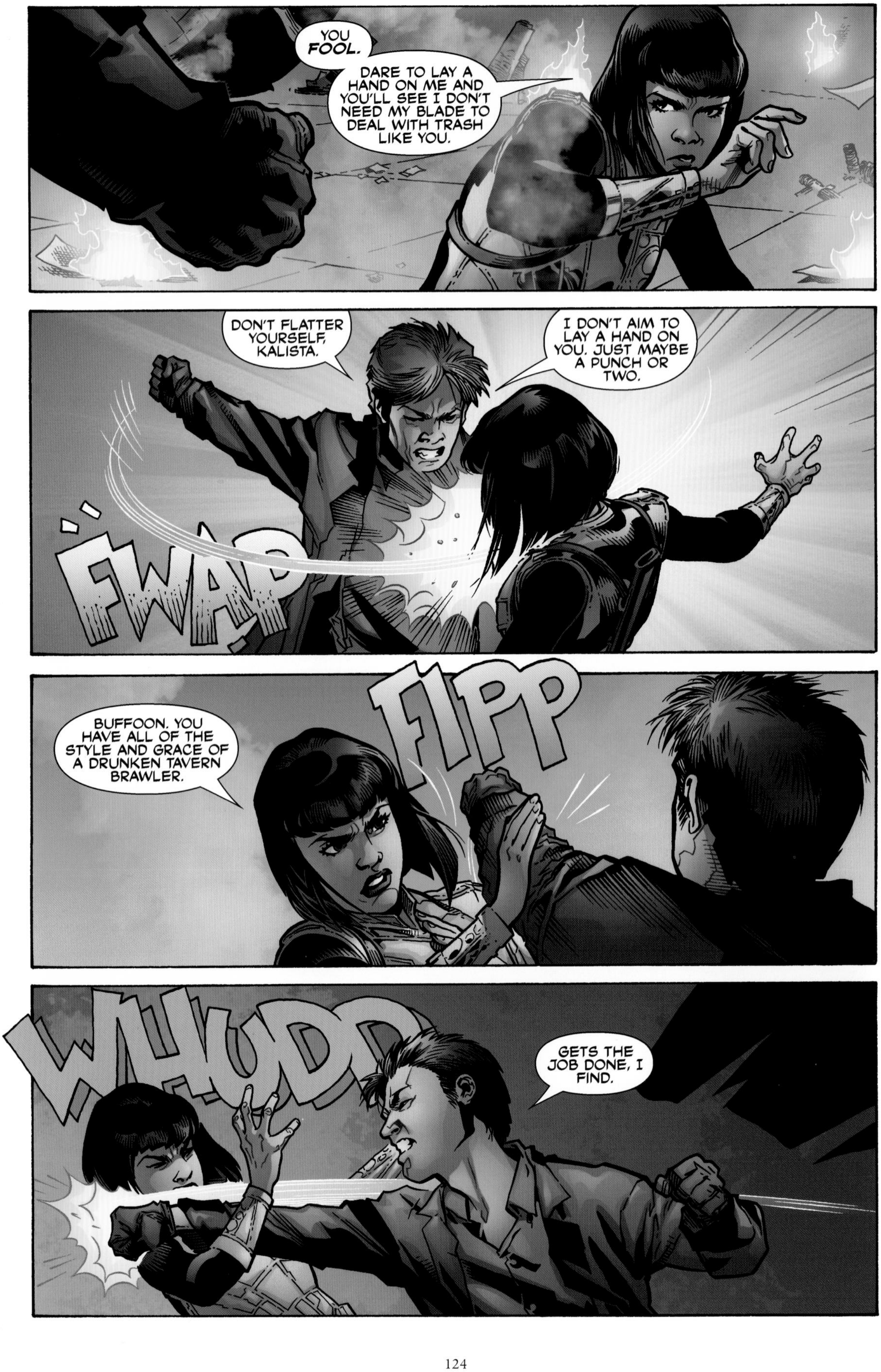
YOU FOOL.
DARE TO LAY A HAND ON ME AND YOU'LL SEE I DON'T NEED MY BLADE TO DEAL WITH TRASH LIKE YOU.
DON'T FLATTER YOURSELF, KALISTA.
I DON'T AIM TO LAY A HAND ON YOU. JUST MAYBE A PUNCH OR TWO.
FWAP
FIPP
BUFFOON. YOU HAVE ALL OF THE STYLE AND GRACE OF A DRUNKEN TAVERN BRAWLER.
WHUDD
GETS THE JOB DONE, I FIND.

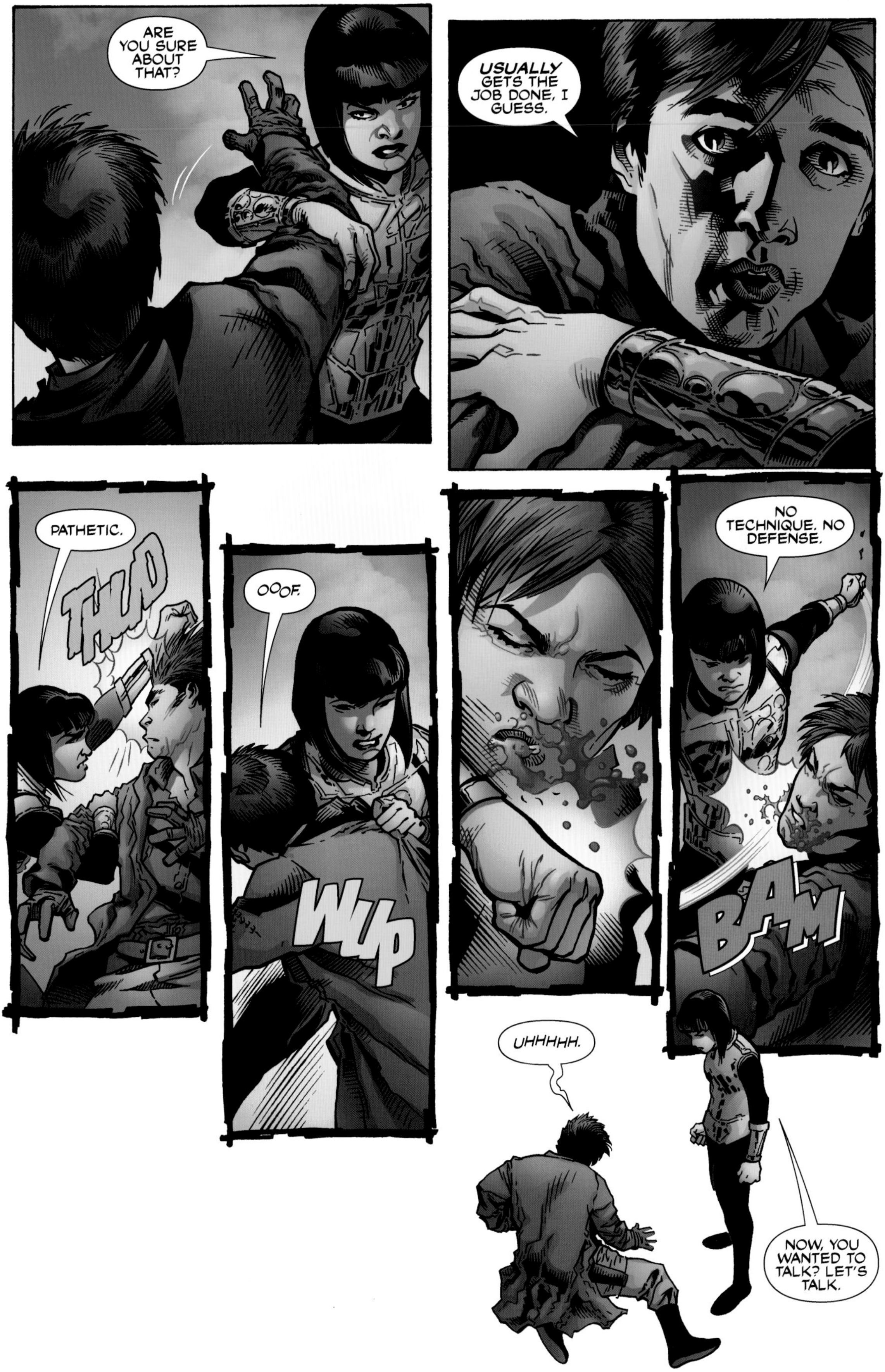
ARE YOU SURE ABOUT THAT?
USUALLY GETS THE JOB DONE, I GUESS.
PATHETIC.
THUD
OOOF.
WUP
NO TECHNIQUE. NO DEFENSE.
BAM
UHHHHH.
NOW, YOU WANTED TO TALK? LET'S TALK.

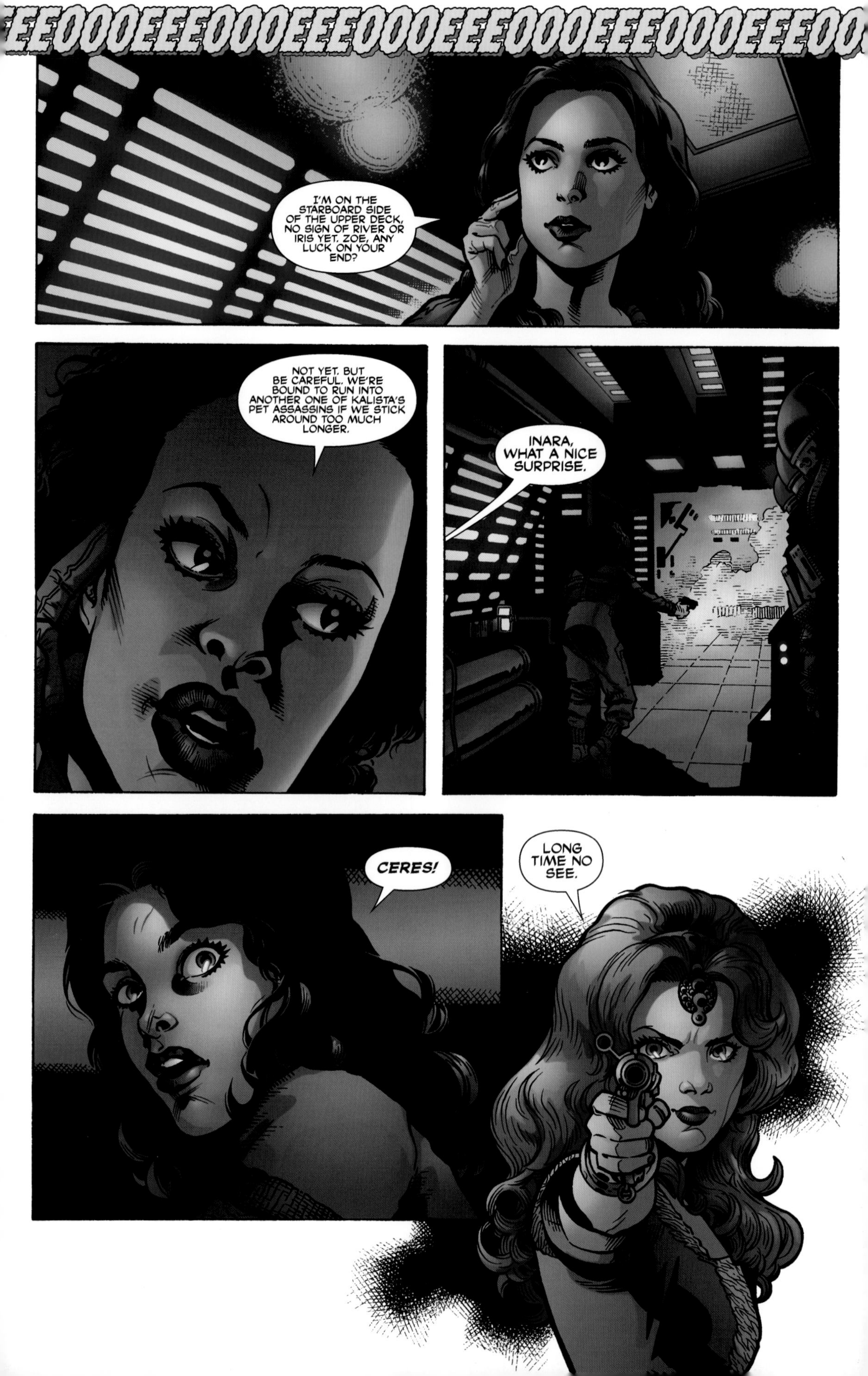
EEOOOEEEOOOEEEOOOEEEOOOEEEOOOEEEOO
I'M ON THE STARBOARD SIDE OF THE UPPER DECK, NO SIGN OF RIVER OR IRIS YET. ZOE, ANY LUCK ON YOUR END?
NOT YET. BUT BE CAREFUL. WE'RE BOUND TO RUN INTO ANOTHER ONE OF KALISTA'S PET ASSASSINS IF WE STICK AROUND TOO MUCH LONGER.
INARA, WHAT A NICE SURPRISE.
CERES!
LONG TIME NO SEE.

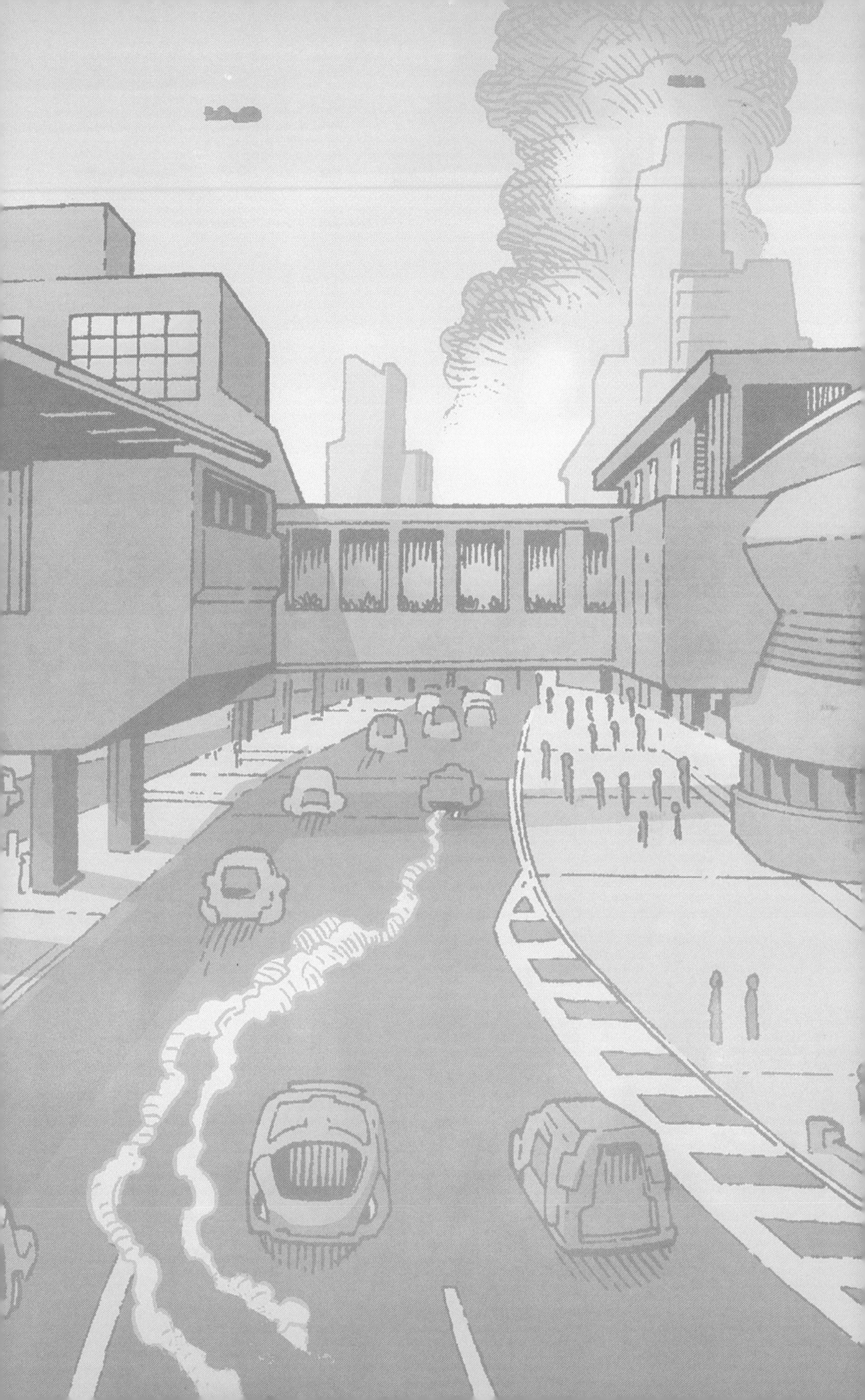

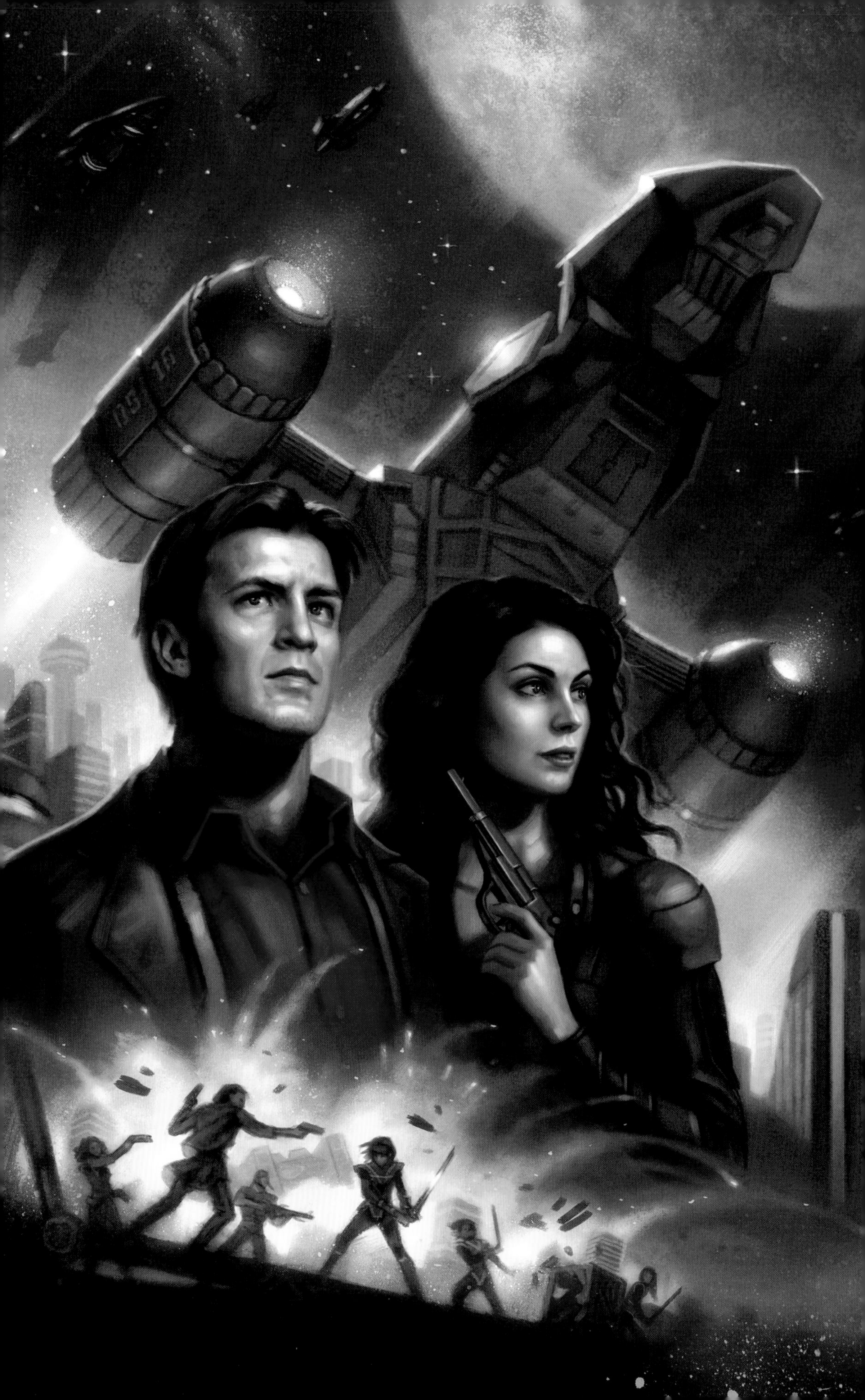

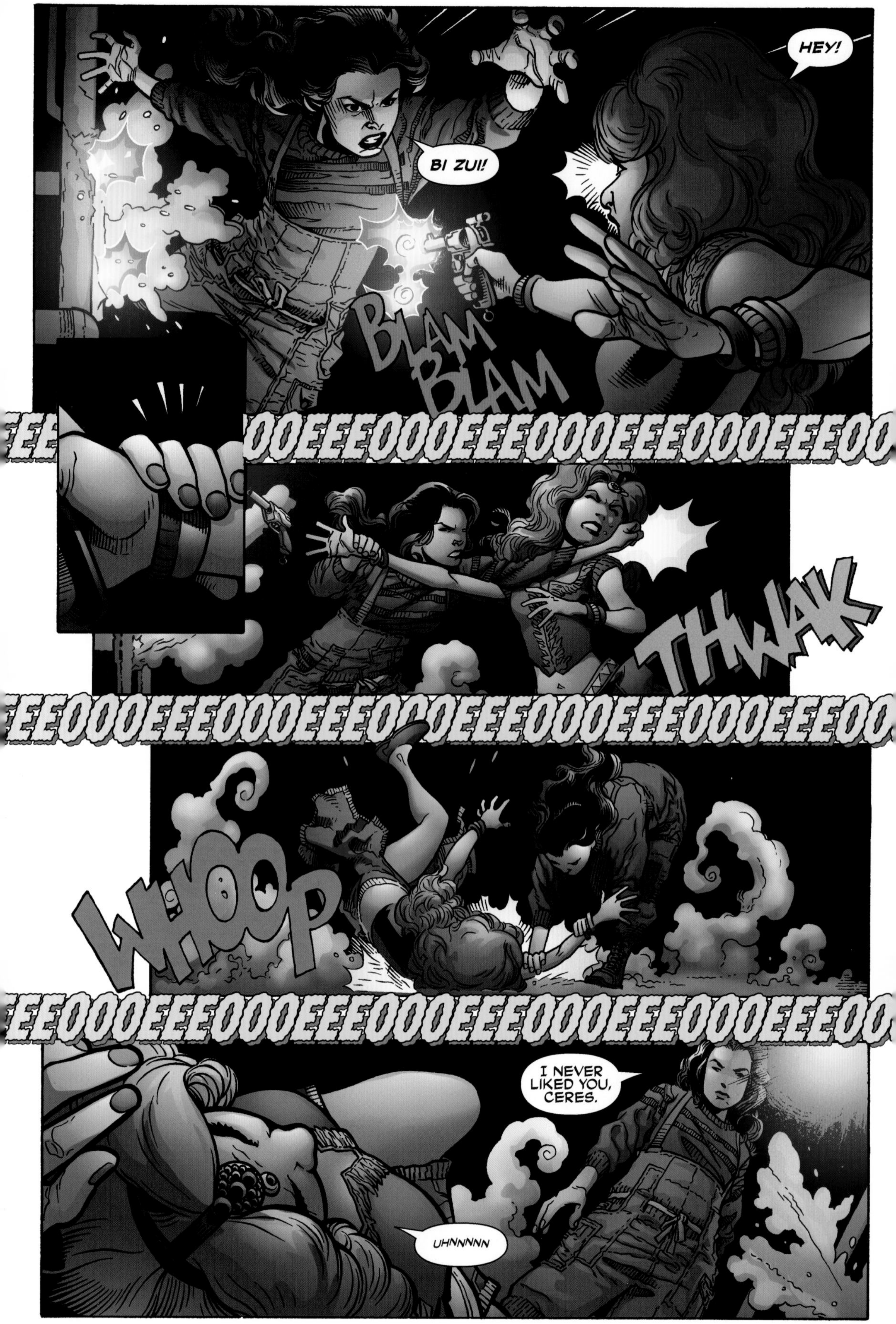
BI ZUI!
BLAM BLAM
HEY!
EEOOOEEEOOOEEEOOOEEEOOOEEEOO
THWAK
EEOOOEEEOOOEEEOOOEEEOOOEEEOOOEEEOO
WHOOP
EEOOOEEEOOOEEEOOOEEEOOOEEEOOOEEEOO
I NEVER LIKED YOU, CERES.
UHNNNNN

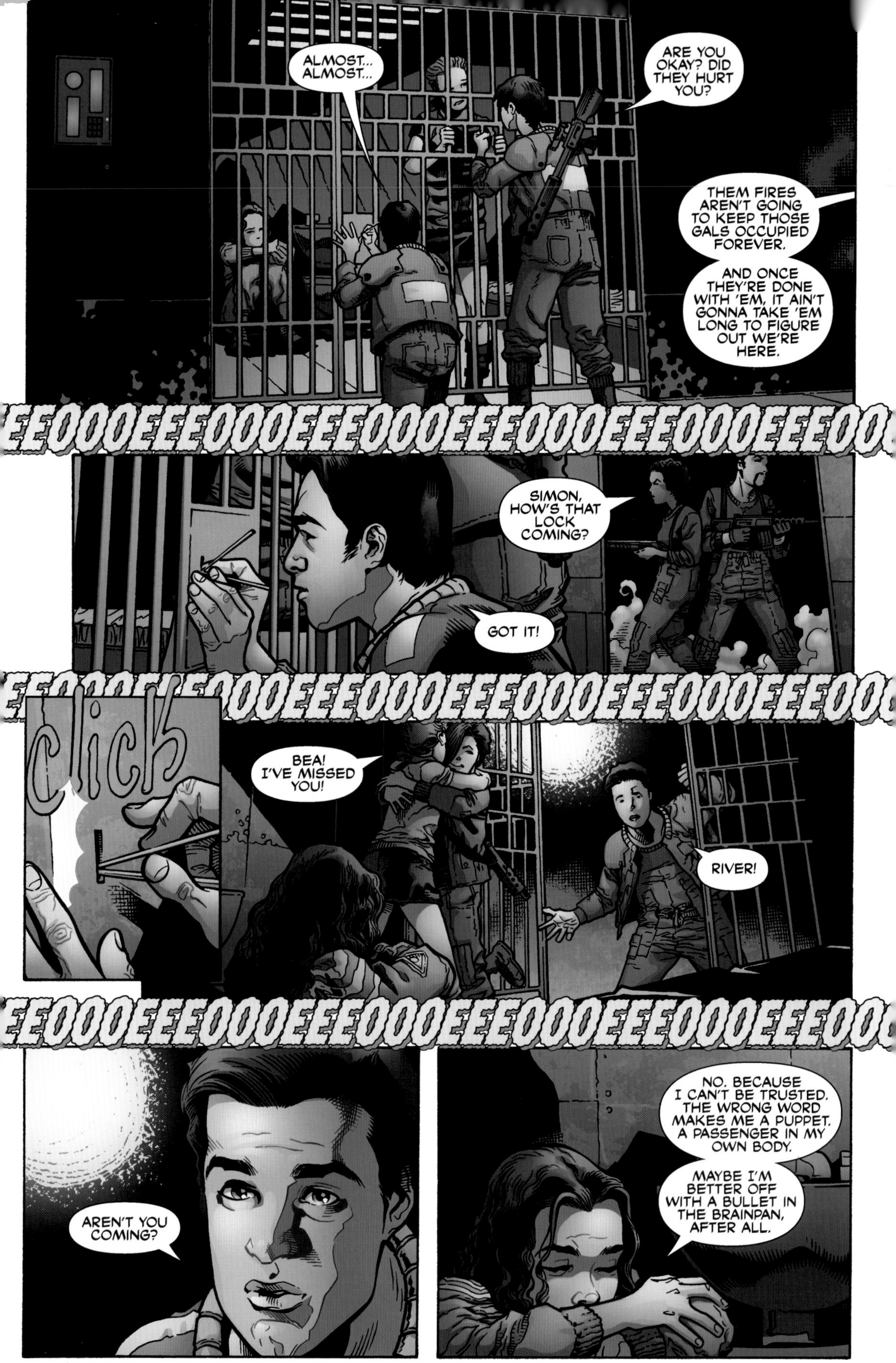
ALMOST... ALMOST...
ARE YOU OKAY? DID THEY HURT YOU?
THEM FIRES AREN'T GOING TO KEEP THOSE GALS OCCUPIED FOREVER.
AND ONCE THEY'RE DONE WITH 'EM, IT AIN'T GONNA TAKE 'EM LONG TO FIGURE OUT WE'RE HERE.
EEOOOEEEOOOEEEOOOEEEOOOEEEOOOEEEOO
SIMON, HOW'S THAT LOCK COMING?
GOT IT!
EEOOOEEEOOOEEEOOOEEEOOOEEEOOOEEEOO
click
BEA! I'VE MISSED YOU!
RIVER!
EEOOOEEEOOOEEEOOOEEEOOOEEEOOOEEEOO
AREN'T YOU COMING?
NO. BECAUSE I CAN'T BE TRUSTED. THE WRONG WORD MAKES ME A PUPPET. A PASSENGER IN MY OWN BODY.
MAYBE I'M BETTER OFF WITH A BULLET IN THE BRAINPAN, AFTER ALL.

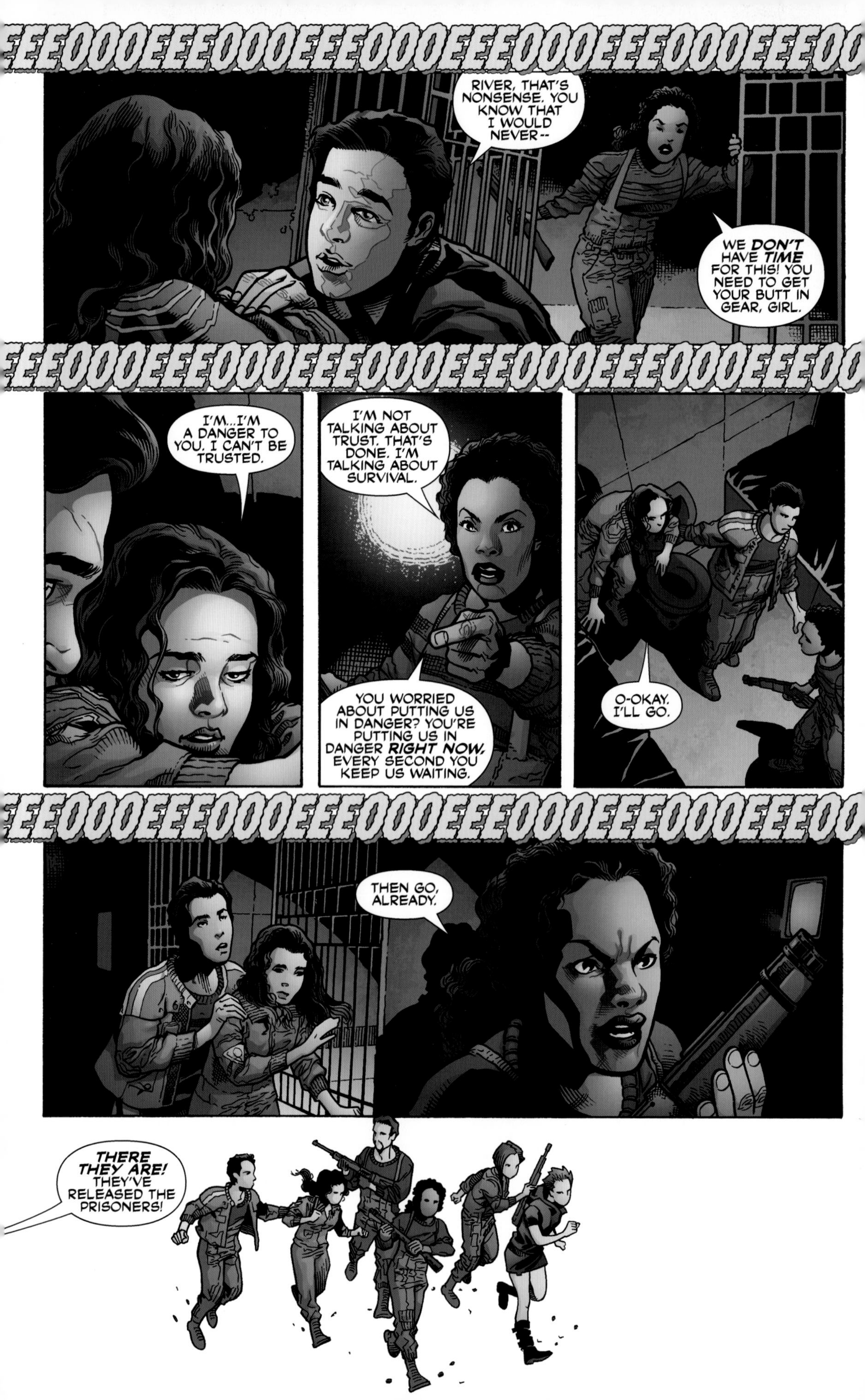
EEEOOOEEEOOOEEEOOOEEEOOOEEEOOOEEEOO
RIVER, THAT'S NONSENSE. YOU KNOW THAT I WOULD NEVER--
WE DON'T HAVE TIME FOR THIS! YOU NEED TO GET YOUR BUTT IN GEAR, GIRL.
EEEOOOEEEOOOEEEOOOEEEOOOEEEOOOEEEOO
I'M...I'M A DANGER TO YOU. I CAN'T BE TRUSTED.
I'M NOT TALKING ABOUT TRUST. THAT'S DONE. I'M TALKING ABOUT SURVIVAL.
YOU WORRIED ABOUT PUTTING US IN DANGER? YOU'RE PUTTING US IN DANGER RIGHT NOW. EVERY SECOND YOU KEEP US WAITING.
O-OKAY. I'LL GO.
EEEOOOEEEOOOEEEOOOEEEOOOEEEOOOEEEOO
THEN GO, ALREADY.
THERE THEY ARE! THEY'VE RELEASED THE PRISONERS!

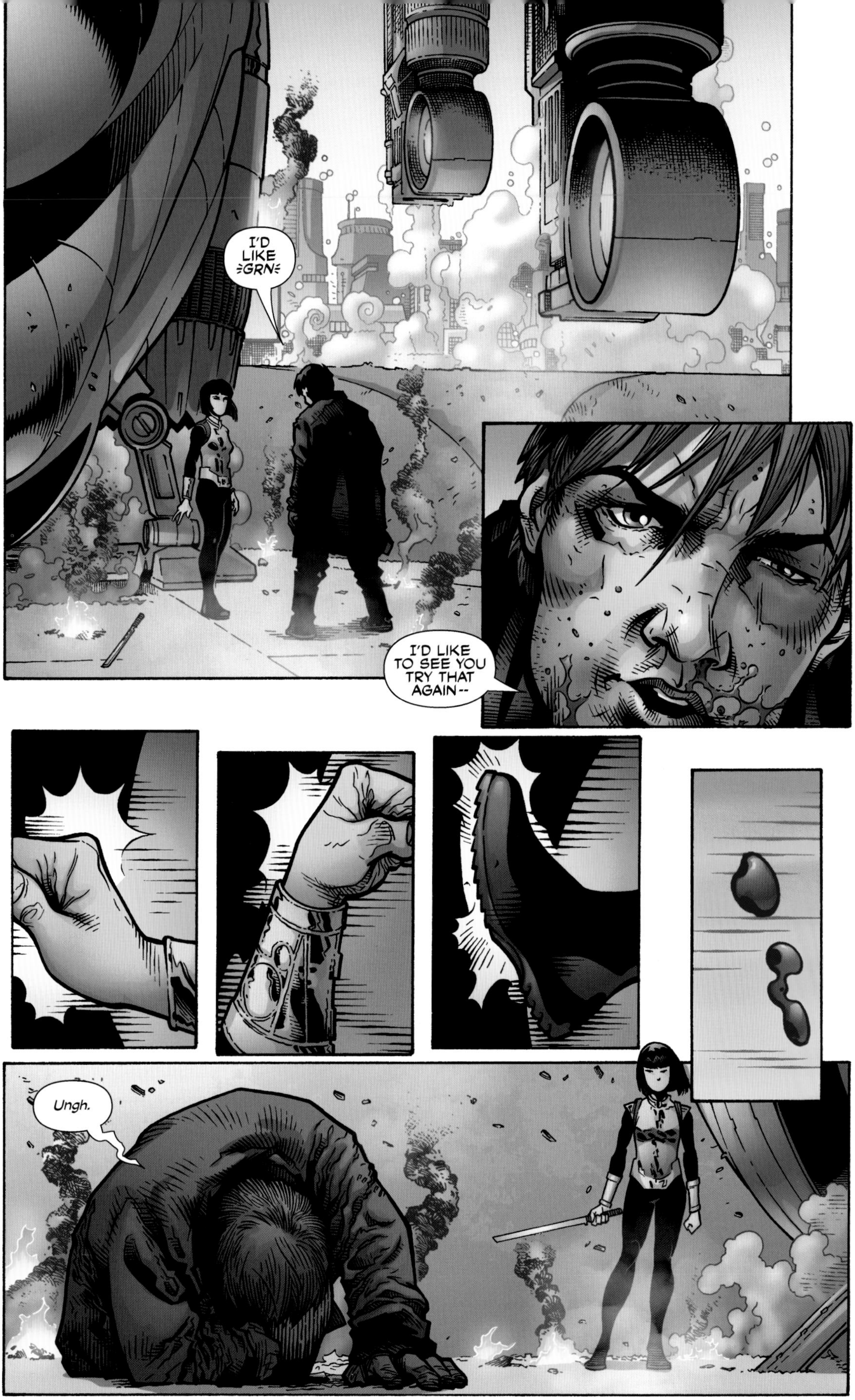
I'D LIKE GRN
I'D LIKE TO SEE YOU TRY THAT AGAIN--
Ungh.

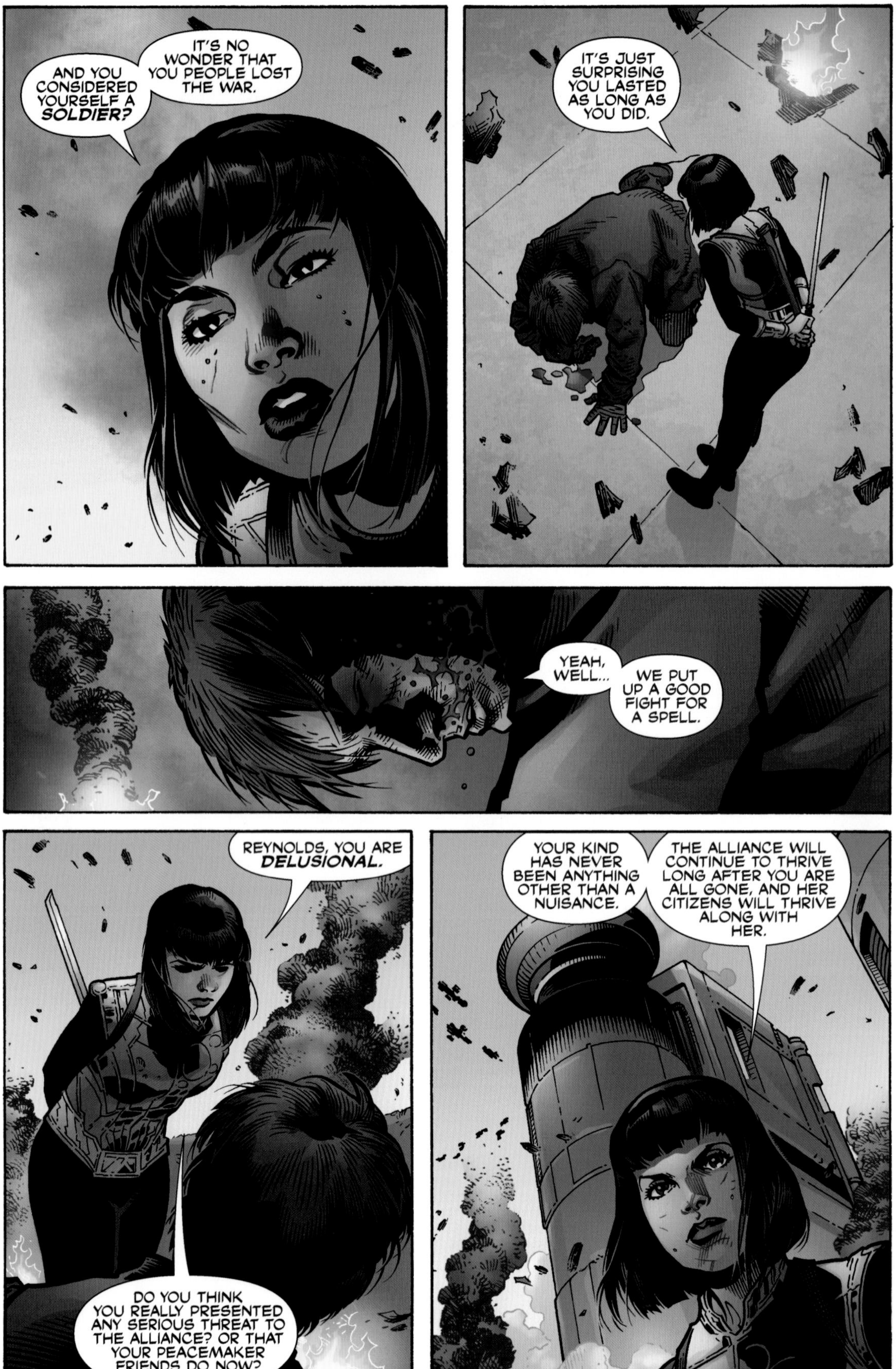
AND YOU CONSIDERED YOURSELF A SOLDIER?
IT'S NO WONDER THAT YOU PEOPLE LOST THE WAR.
IT'S JUST SURPRISING YOU LASTED AS LONG AS YOU DID.
YEAH, WELL...
WE PUT UP A GOOD FIGHT FOR A SPELL.
REYNOLDS, YOU ARE DELUSIONAL.
DO YOU THINK YOU REALLY PRESENTED ANY SERIOUS THREAT TO THE ALLIANCE? OR THAT YOUR PEACEMAKER FRIENDS DO NOW?
YOUR KIND HAS NEVER BEEN ANYTHING OTHER THAN A NUISANCE.
THE ALLIANCE WILL CONTINUE TO THRIVE LONG AFTER YOU ARE ALL GONE, AND HER CITIZENS WILL THRIVE ALONG WITH HER.

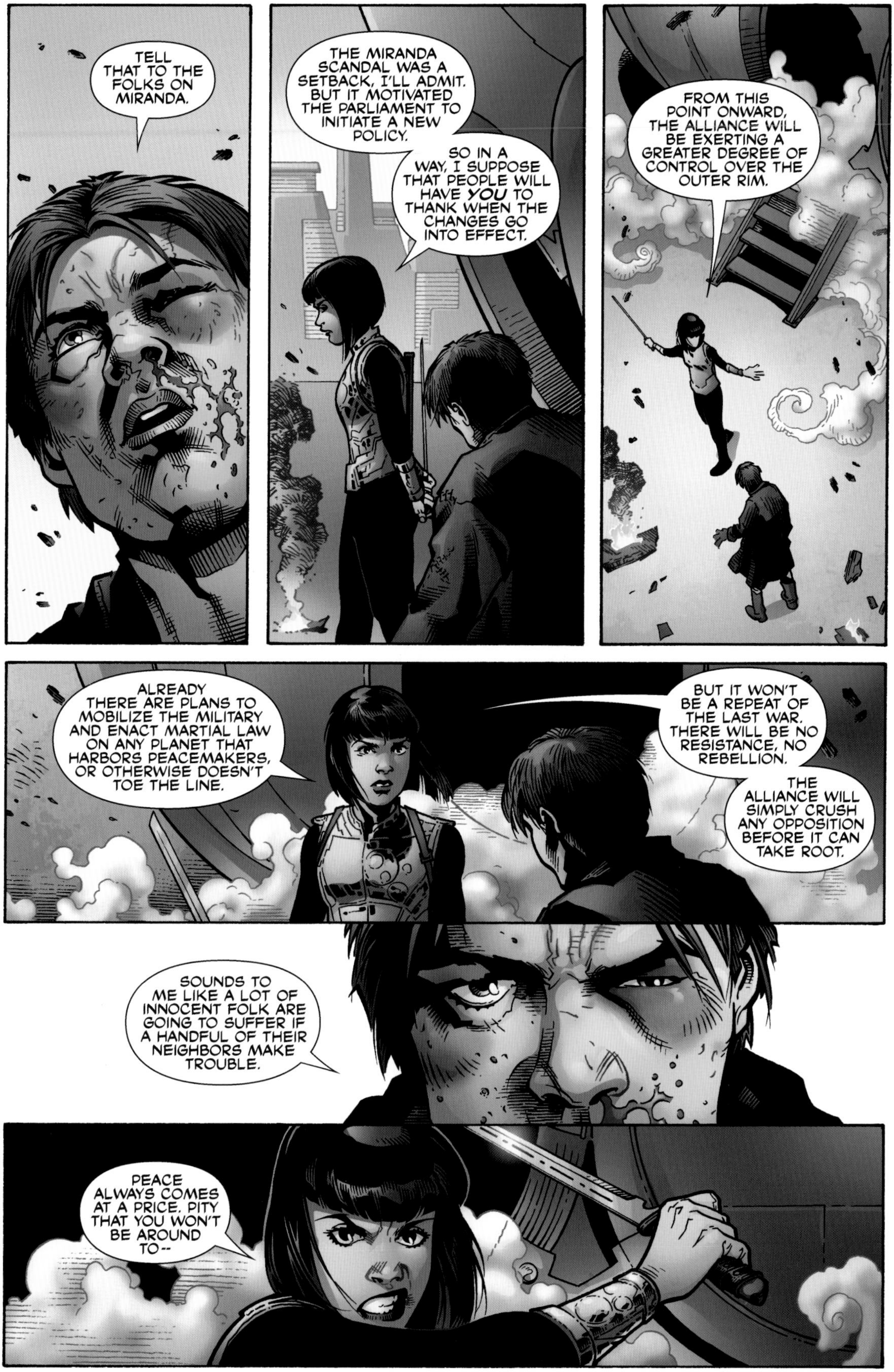
TELL THAT TO THE FOLKS ON MIRANDA.
THE MIRANDA SCANDAL WAS A SETBACK, I'LL ADMIT. BUT IT MOTIVATED THE PARLIAMENT TO INITIATE A NEW POLICY.
SO IN A WAY, I SUPPOSE THAT PEOPLE WILL HAVE *YOU* TO THANK WHEN THE CHANGES GO INTO EFFECT.
FROM THIS POINT ONWARD, THE ALLIANCE WILL BE EXERTING A GREATER DEGREE OF CONTROL OVER THE OUTER RIM.
ALREADY THERE ARE PLANS TO MOBILIZE THE MILITARY AND ENACT MARTIAL LAW ON ANY PLANET THAT HARBORS PEACEMAKERS, OR OTHERWISE DOESN'T TOE THE LINE.
BUT IT WON'T BE A REPEAT OF THE LAST WAR. THERE WILL BE NO RESISTANCE, NO REBELLION.
THE ALLIANCE WILL SIMPLY CRUSH ANY OPPOSITION BEFORE IT CAN TAKE ROOT.
SOUNDS TO ME LIKE A LOT OF INNOCENT FOLK ARE GOING TO SUFFER IF A HANDFUL OF THEIR NEIGHBORS MAKE TROUBLE.
PEACE ALWAYS COMES AT A PRICE. PITY THAT YOU WON'T BE AROUND TO--

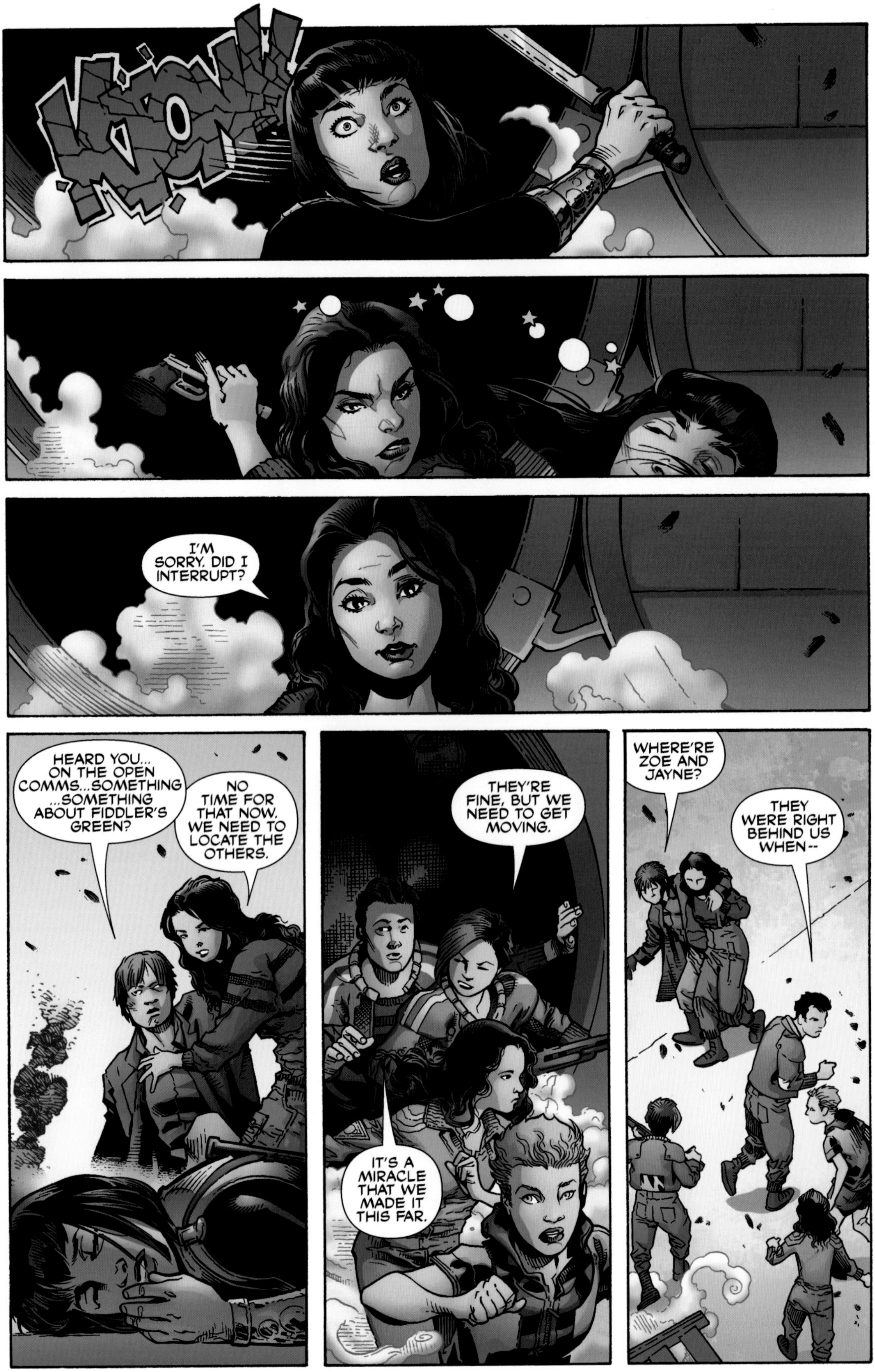
WHOOM!!
I'M SORRY. DID I INTERRUPT?
HEARD YOU... ON THE OPEN COMMS...SOMETHING ...SOMETHING ABOUT FIDDLER'S GREEN?
NO TIME FOR THAT NOW. WE NEED TO LOCATE THE OTHERS.
THEY'RE FINE, BUT WE NEED TO GET MOVING.
IT'S A MIRACLE THAT WE MADE IT THIS FAR.
WHERE'RE ZOE AND JAYNE?
THEY WERE RIGHT BEHIND US WHEN--

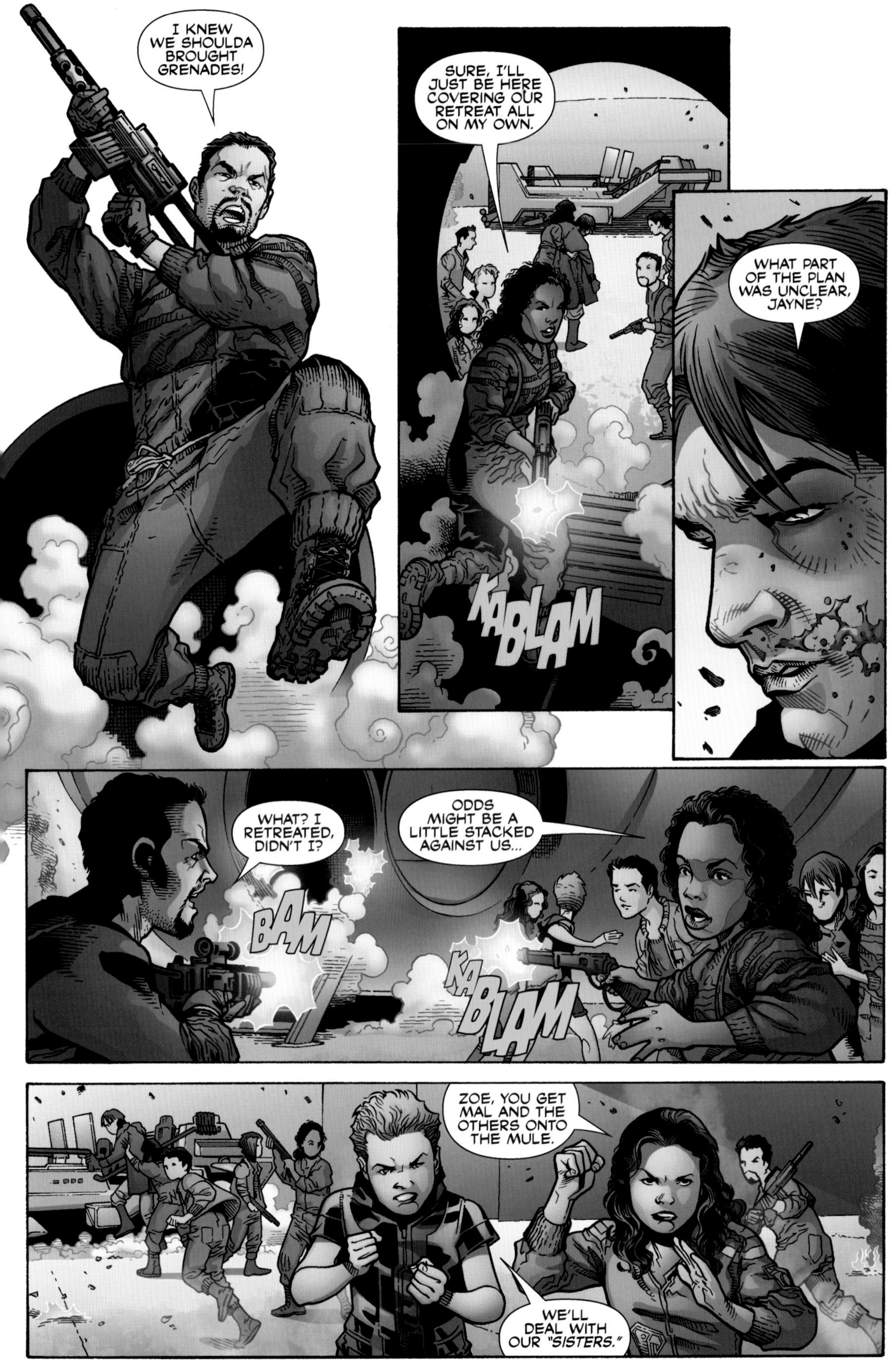
I KNEW WE SHOULDA BROUGHT GRENADES!
SURE, I'LL JUST BE HERE COVERING OUR RETREAT ALL ON MY OWN.
KABLAM
WHAT PART OF THE PLAN WAS UNCLEAR, JAYNE?
WHAT? I RETREATED, DIDN'T I?
ODDS MIGHT BE A LITTLE STACKED AGAINST US...
BAM
KABLAM
ZOE, YOU GET MAL AND THE OTHERS ONTO THE MULE.
WE'LL DEAL WITH OUR "SISTERS."

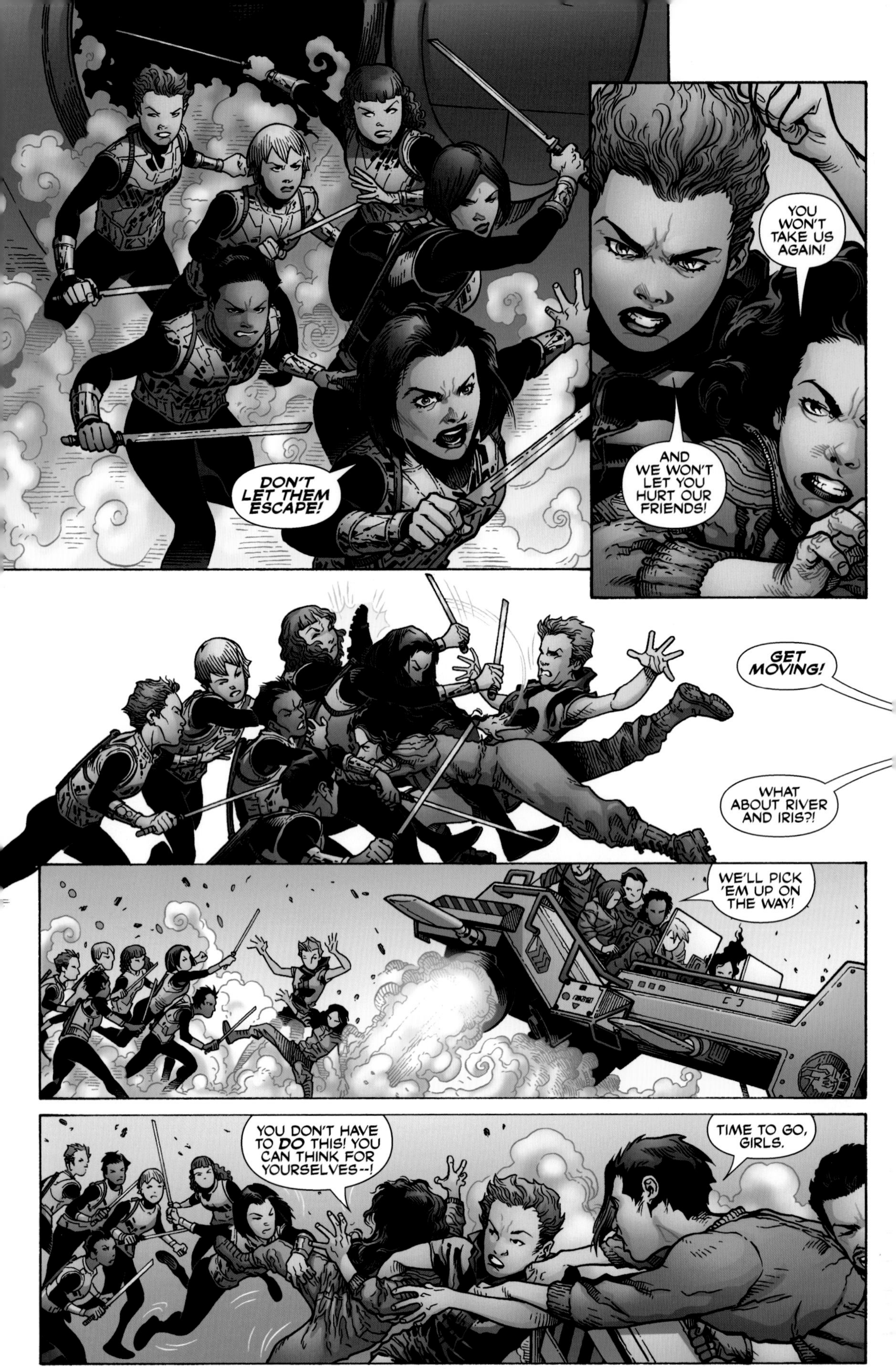
DON'T LET THEM ESCAPE!
YOU WON'T TAKE US AGAIN!
AND WE WON'T LET YOU HURT OUR FRIENDS!
GET MOVING!
WHAT ABOUT RIVER AND IRIS?!
WE'LL PICK 'EM UP ON THE WAY!
YOU DON'T HAVE TO DO THIS! YOU CAN THINK FOR YOURSELVES--!
TIME TO GO, GIRLS.

WHAP

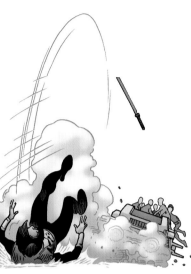

WAIT...?

AIN'T THAT SOME OF MERICOURT'S KIDS...?

THEY GOT NO BUSINESS BEING BY THAT SILVERLINER...

OH, NO.

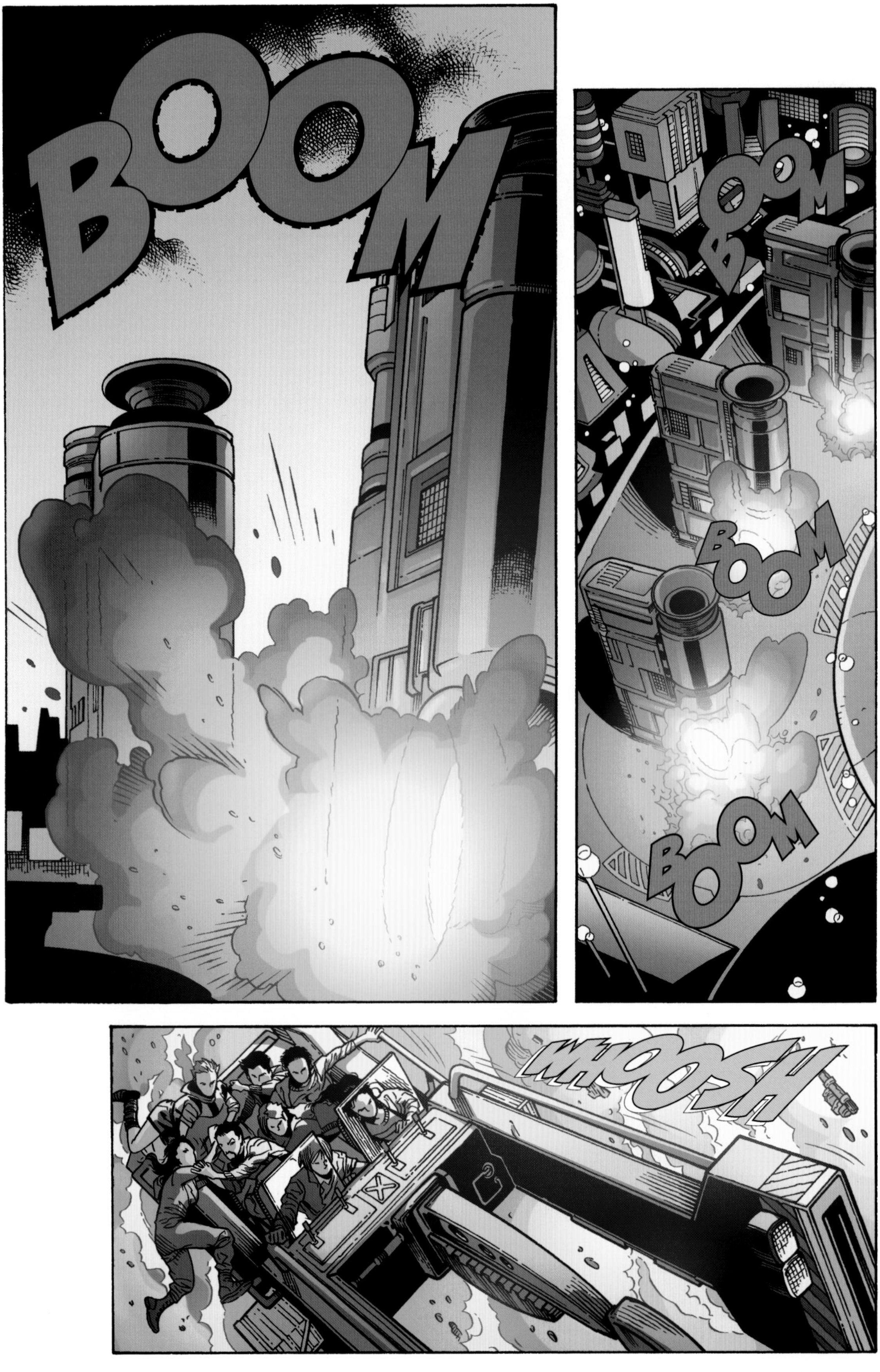
BOOM
BOOM
BOOM
BOOM
WHOOOSH

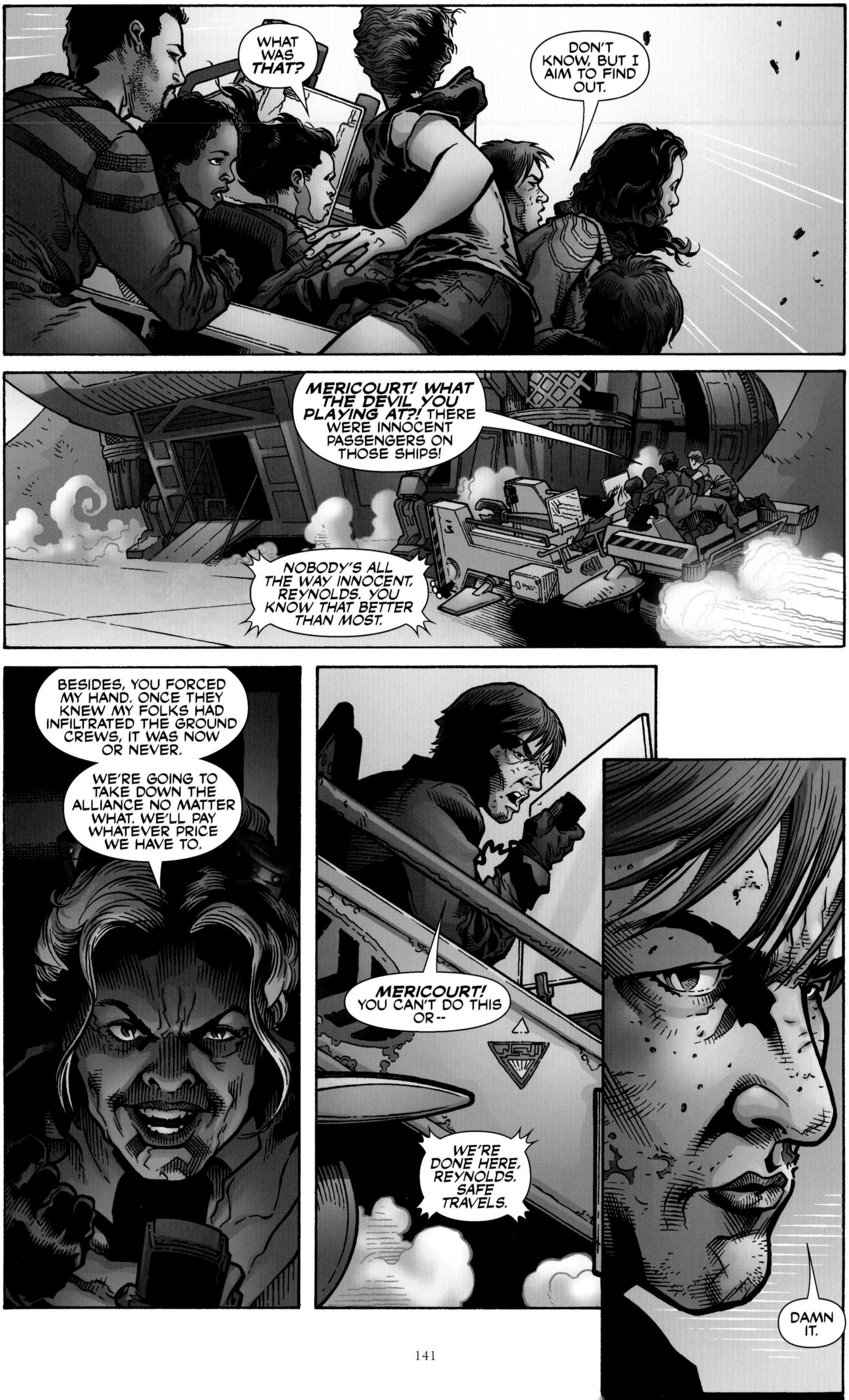
WHAT WAS THAT?
DON'T KNOW, BUT I AIM TO FIND OUT.
MERICOURT! WHAT THE DEVIL YOU PLAYING AT?! THERE WERE INNOCENT PASSENGERS ON THOSE SHIPS!
NOBODY'S ALL THE WAY INNOCENT, REYNOLDS. YOU KNOW THAT BETTER THAN MOST.
BESIDES, YOU FORCED MY HAND. ONCE THEY KNEW MY FOLKS HAD INFILTRATED THE GROUND CREWS, IT WAS NOW OR NEVER.
WE'RE GOING TO TAKE DOWN THE ALLIANCE NO MATTER WHAT. WE'LL PAY WHATEVER PRICE WE HAVE TO.
MERICOURT! YOU CAN'T DO THIS OR--
WE'RE DONE HERE, REYNOLDS. SAFE TRAVELS.
DAMN IT.

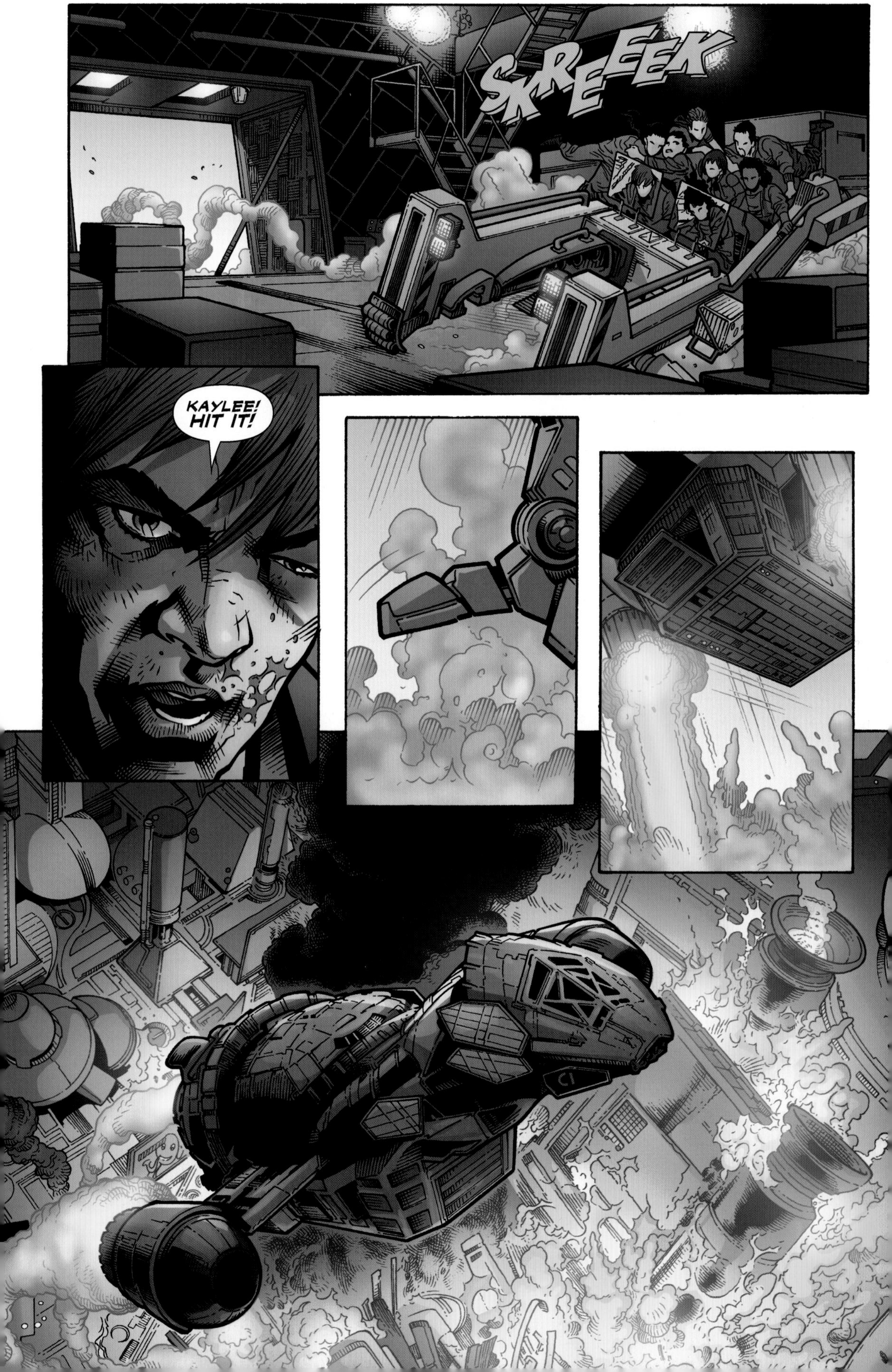
SKREEEEK
KAYLEE! HIT IT!

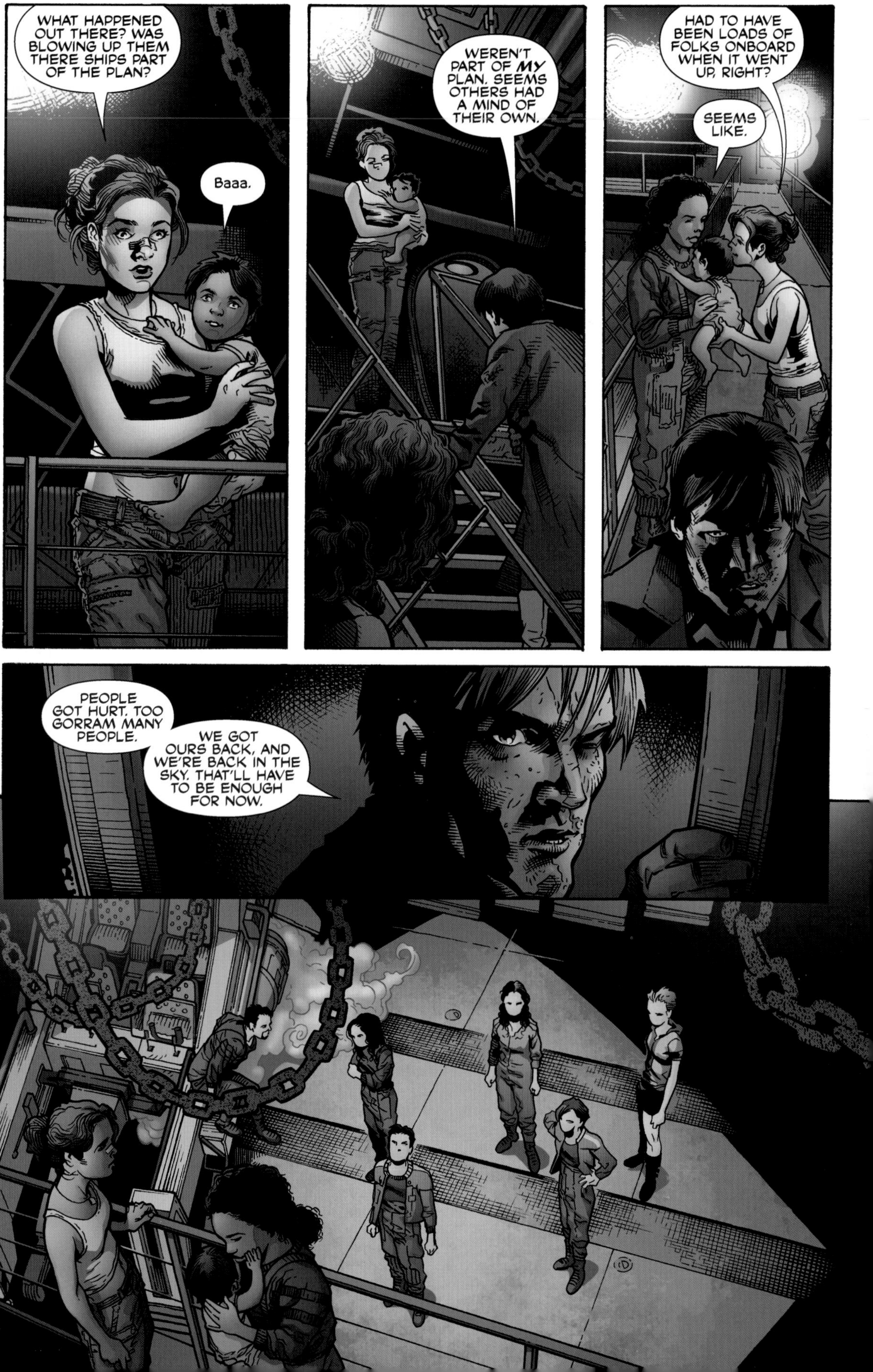
WHAT HAPPENED OUT THERE? WAS BLOWING UP THEM THERE SHIPS PART OF THE PLAN?
Baaa.
WEREN'T PART OF MY PLAN. SEEMS OTHERS HAD A MIND OF THEIR OWN.
HAD TO HAVE BEEN LOADS OF FOLKS ONBOARD WHEN IT WENT UP, RIGHT?
SEEMS LIKE.
PEOPLE GOT HURT. TOO GORRAM MANY PEOPLE.
WE GOT OURS BACK, AND WE'RE BACK IN THE SKY. THAT'LL HAVE TO BE ENOUGH FOR NOW.

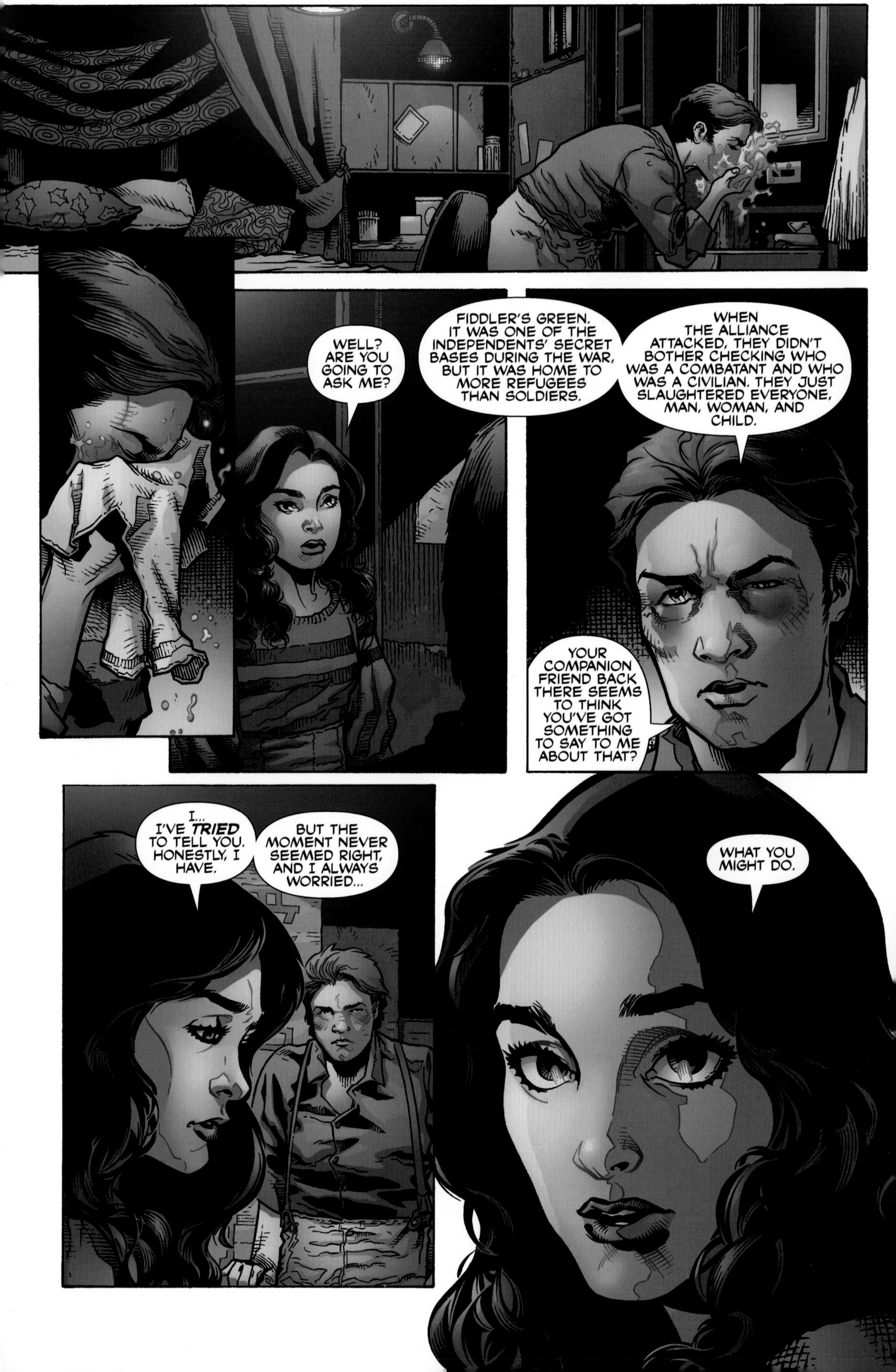
WELL? ARE YOU GOING TO ASK ME?
FIDDLER'S GREEN. IT WAS ONE OF THE INDEPENDENTS' SECRET BASES DURING THE WAR, BUT IT WAS HOME TO MORE REFUGEES THAN SOLDIERS.
WHEN THE ALLIANCE ATTACKED, THEY DIDN'T BOTHER CHECKING WHO WAS A COMBATANT AND WHO WAS A CIVILIAN. THEY JUST SLAUGHTERED EVERYONE, MAN, WOMAN, AND CHILD.
YOUR COMPANION FRIEND BACK THERE SEEMS TO THINK YOU'VE GOT SOMETHING TO SAY TO ME ABOUT THAT?
I... I'VE ***TRIED*** TO TELL YOU. HONESTLY, I HAVE.
BUT THE MOMENT NEVER SEEMED RIGHT, AND I ALWAYS WORRIED...
WHAT YOU MIGHT DO.

THE REASON I LEFT SIHNON IS THAT I BROKE THE CONFIDENTIALITY RULES OF HOUSE MADRASSA. COMPANIONS ARE SWORN NEVER TO REVEAL THINGS SPOKEN TO THEM IN CONFIDENCE.

ONE OF MY CLIENTS WAS A SECRET SUPPLIER TO THE INDEPENDENTS, AND DURING ONE OF OUR SESSIONS HE LET SLIP SOME DETAILS ABOUT A MAJOR OFFENSIVE THEY HAD PLANNED.

I...I ALERTED THE AUTHORITIES, AND LET THEM KNOW THE LOCATION OF THE BASE THAT HE WAS SUPPLYING.

YOU'VE GOT TO UNDERSTAND THAT MY HOPE WAS TO PREVENT NEEDLESS DEATHS, ON *BOTH* SIDES. BUT...

HONESTLY, MAL, IF I'D EVEN SUSPECTED...

IT WAS A HUGE SCANDAL IN HOUSE MADRASSA.

NOT BECAUSE THEY WERE SYMPATHETIC TO THE INDEPENDENTS, BUT BECAUSE THE CONFIDENTIALITY VOWS ARE SACROSANCT.

I WAS ASKED TO LEAVE AND NEVER RETURN. I WOULD REMAIN A COMPANION, BUT I COULD NEVER GO HOME.

I CAN'T BEGIN TO EXPRESS THE GUILT THAT I'VE FELT OVER THOSE DEATHS ALL THESE YEARS.

I JUST HOPED THAT SOMEHOW... WELL...

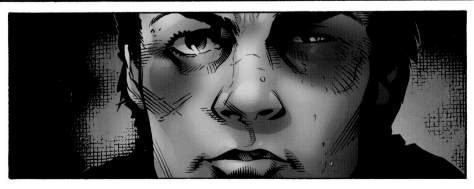

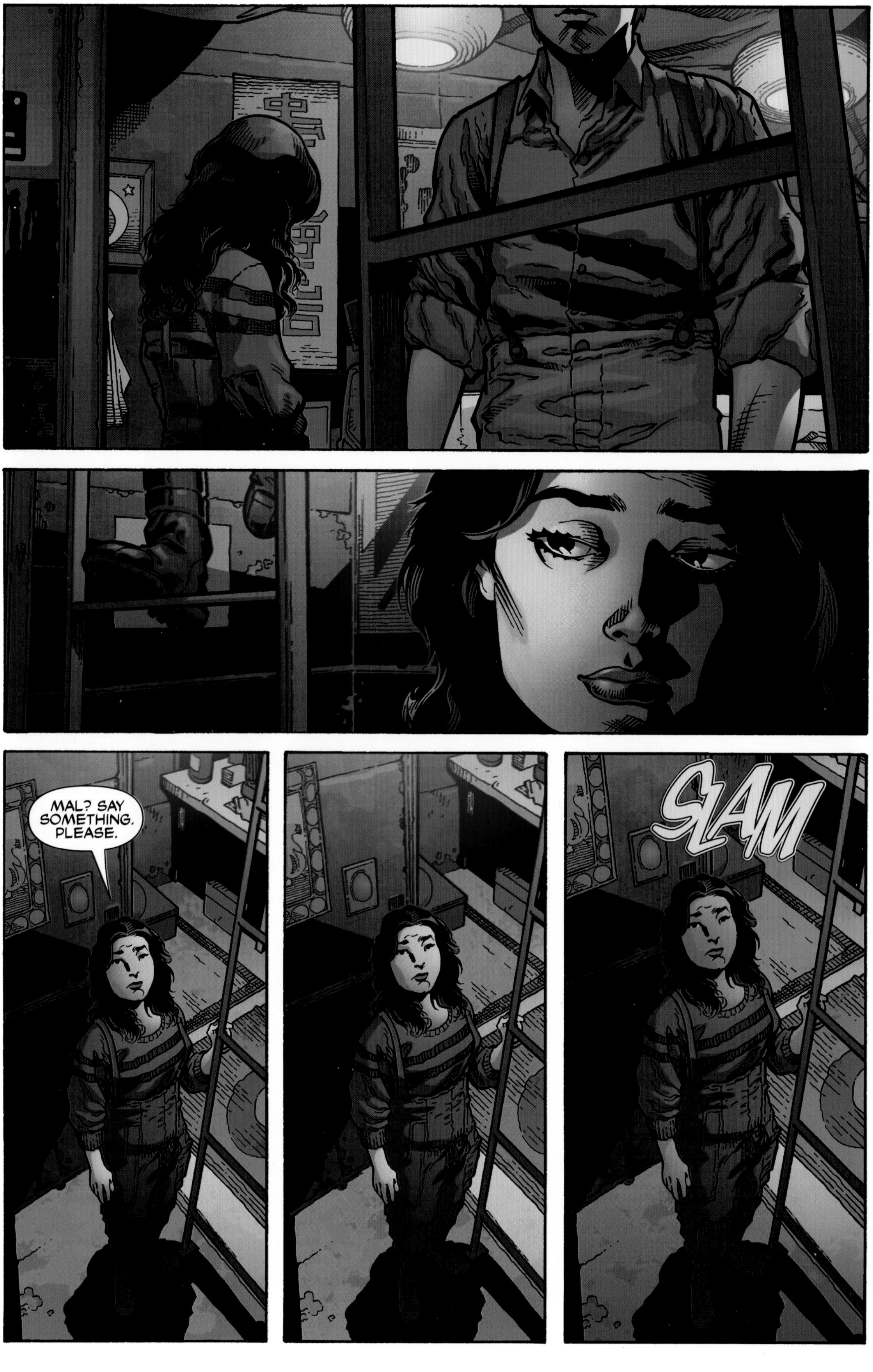
MAL? SAY SOMETHING. PLEASE.
SLAM

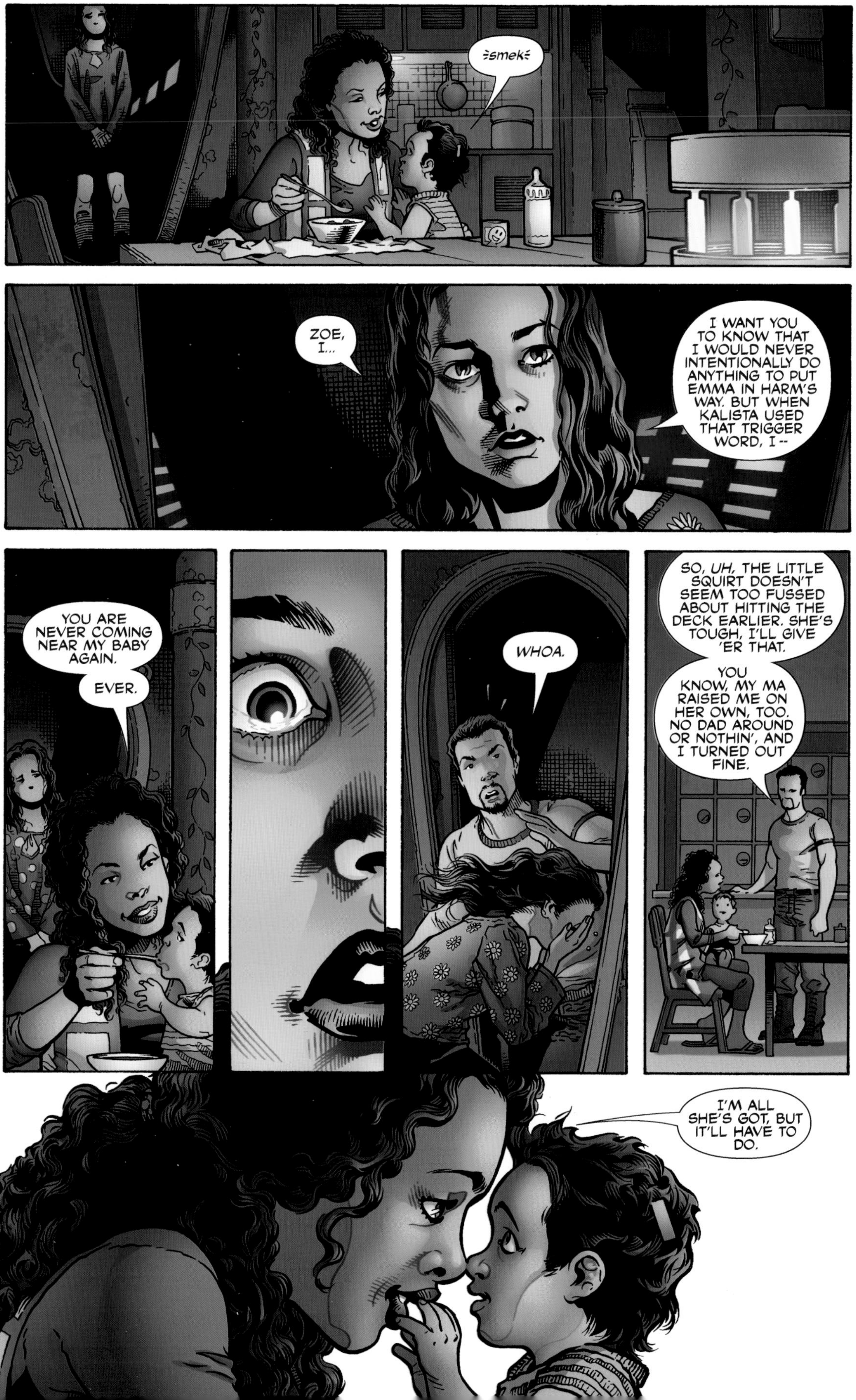
smek
ZOE, I...
I WANT YOU TO KNOW THAT I WOULD NEVER INTENTIONALLY DO ANYTHING TO PUT EMMA IN HARM'S WAY. BUT WHEN KALISTA USED THAT TRIGGER WORD, I --
YOU ARE NEVER COMING NEAR MY BABY AGAIN.
EVER.
WHOA.
SO, UH, THE LITTLE SQUIRT DOESN'T SEEM TOO FUSSED ABOUT HITTING THE DECK EARLIER. SHE'S TOUGH, I'LL GIVE 'ER THAT.
YOU KNOW, MY MA RAISED ME ON HER OWN, TOO. NO DAD AROUND OR NOTHIN', AND I TURNED OUT FINE.
I'M ALL SHE'S GOT, BUT IT'LL HAVE TO DO.

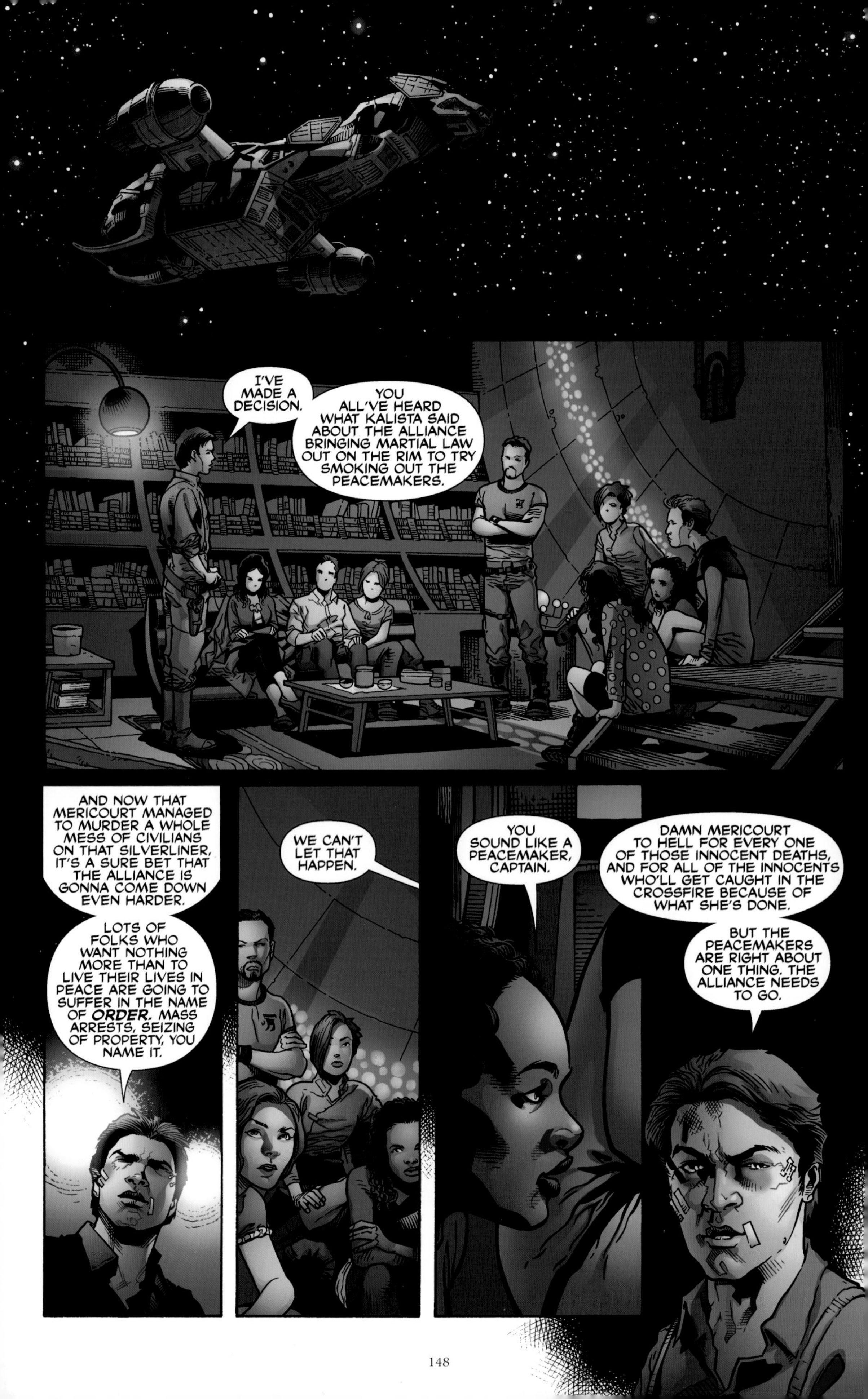
I'VE MADE A DECISION.
YOU ALL'VE HEARD WHAT KALISTA SAID ABOUT THE ALLIANCE BRINGING MARTIAL LAW OUT ON THE RIM TO TRY SMOKING OUT THE PEACEMAKERS.
AND NOW THAT MERICOURT MANAGED TO MURDER A WHOLE MESS OF CIVILIANS ON THAT SILVERLINER, IT'S A SURE BET THAT THE ALLIANCE IS GONNA COME DOWN EVEN HARDER.
LOTS OF FOLKS WHO WANT NOTHING MORE THAN TO LIVE THEIR LIVES IN PEACE ARE GOING TO SUFFER IN THE NAME OF ***ORDER.*** MASS ARRESTS, SEIZING OF PROPERTY, YOU NAME IT.
WE CAN'T LET THAT HAPPEN.
YOU SOUND LIKE A PEACEMAKER, CAPTAIN.
DAMN MERICOURT TO HELL FOR EVERY ONE OF THOSE INNOCENT DEATHS, AND FOR ALL OF THE INNOCENTS WHO'LL GET CAUGHT IN THE CROSSFIRE BECAUSE OF WHAT SHE'S DONE.
BUT THE PEACEMAKERS ARE RIGHT ABOUT ONE THING. THE ALLIANCE NEEDS TO GO.

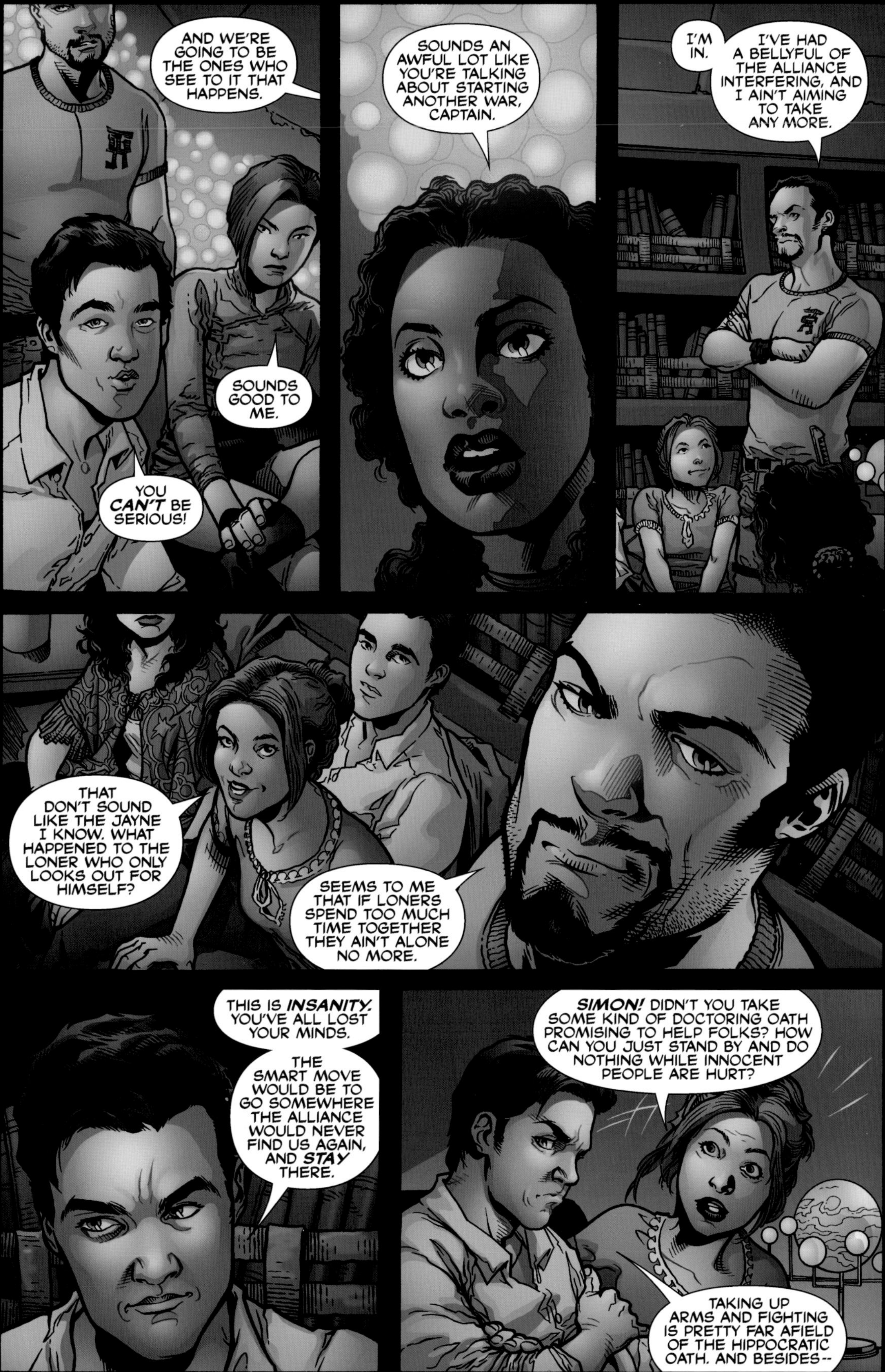
AND WE'RE GOING TO BE THE ONES WHO SEE TO IT THAT HAPPENS.
SOUNDS GOOD TO ME.
YOU CAN'T BE SERIOUS!
SOUNDS AN AWFUL LOT LIKE YOU'RE TALKING ABOUT STARTING ANOTHER WAR, CAPTAIN.
I'M IN.
I'VE HAD A BELLYFUL OF THE ALLIANCE INTERFERING, AND I AIN'T AIMING TO TAKE ANY MORE.
THAT DON'T SOUND LIKE THE JAYNE I KNOW. WHAT HAPPENED TO THE LONER WHO ONLY LOOKS OUT FOR HIMSELF?
SEEMS TO ME THAT IF LONERS SPEND TOO MUCH TIME TOGETHER THEY AIN'T ALONE NO MORE.
THIS IS INSANITY. YOU'VE ALL LOST YOUR MINDS.
THE SMART MOVE WOULD BE TO GO SOMEWHERE THE ALLIANCE WOULD NEVER FIND US AGAIN, AND STAY THERE.
SIMON! DIDN'T YOU TAKE SOME KIND OF DOCTORING OATH PROMISING TO HELP FOLKS? HOW CAN YOU JUST STAND BY AND DO NOTHING WHILE INNOCENT PEOPLE ARE HURT?
TAKING UP ARMS AND FIGHTING IS PRETTY FAR AFIELD OF THE HIPPOCRATIC OATH. AND BESIDES--

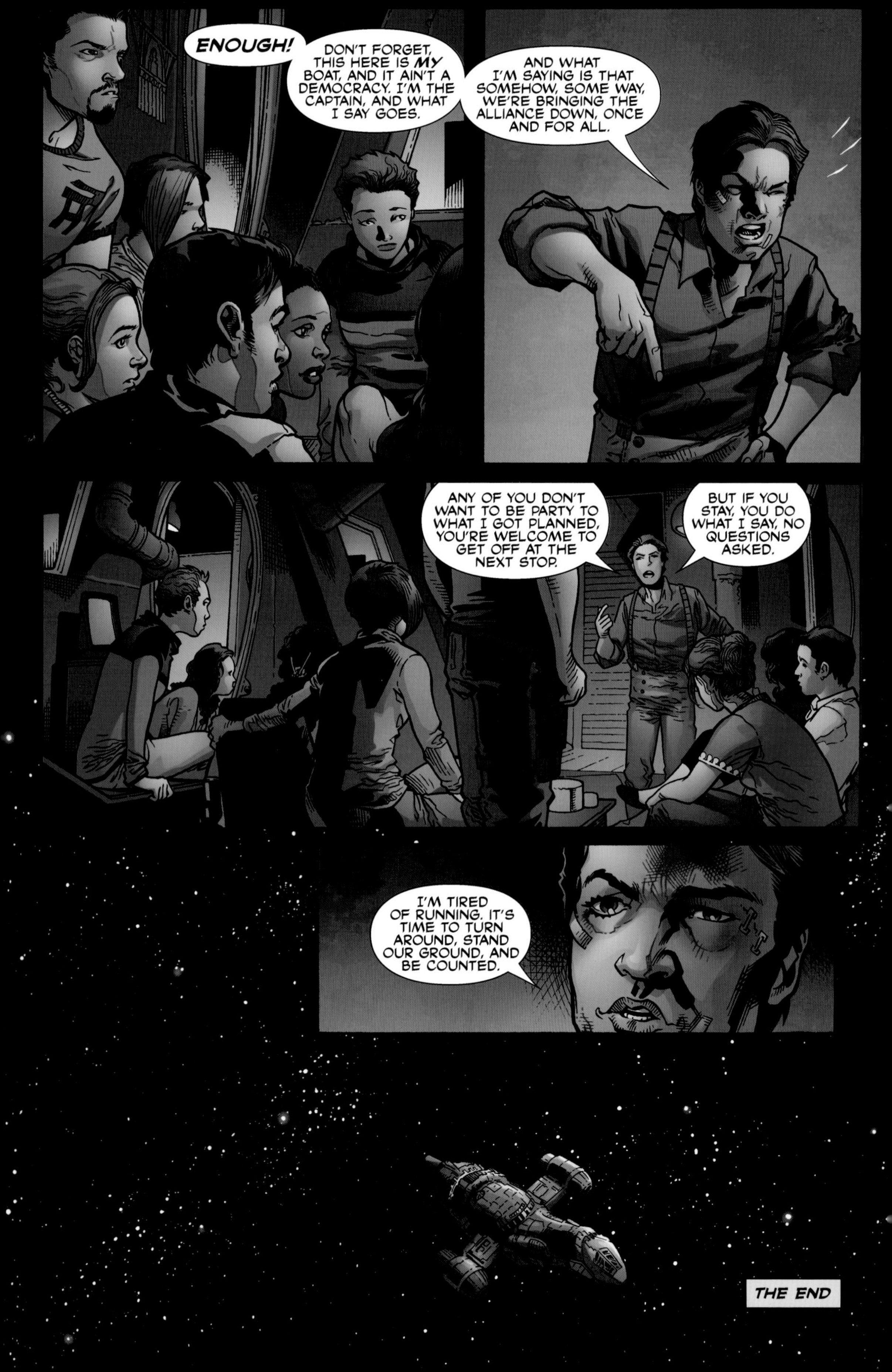
ENOUGH!
DON'T FORGET, THIS HERE IS MY BOAT, AND IT AIN'T A DEMOCRACY. I'M THE CAPTAIN, AND WHAT I SAY GOES.
AND WHAT I'M SAYING IS THAT SOMEHOW, SOME WAY, WE'RE BRINGING THE ALLIANCE DOWN, ONCE AND FOR ALL.
ANY OF YOU DON'T WANT TO BE PARTY TO WHAT I GOT PLANNED, YOU'RE WELCOME TO GET OFF AT THE NEXT STOP.
BUT IF YOU STAY, YOU DO WHAT I SAY, NO QUESTIONS ASKED.
I'M TIRED OF RUNNING. IT'S TIME TO TURN AROUND, STAND OUR GROUND, AND BE COUNTED.
THE END

THE WARRIOR AND THE WIND

SCRIPT
CHRIS ROBERSON

ART
STEPHEN BYRNE

LETTERS
MICHAEL HEISLER

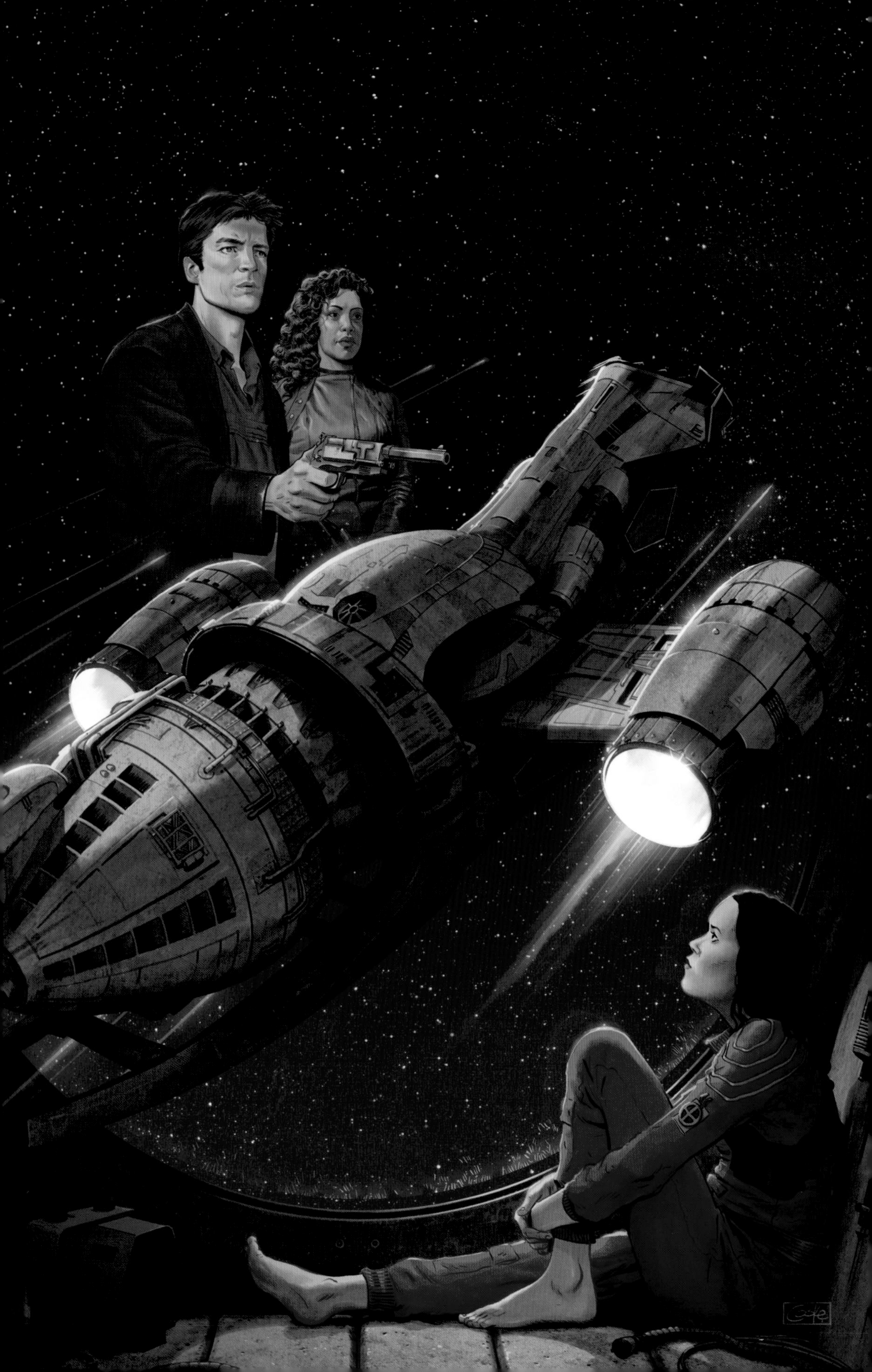

Illustration by Sean Cooke

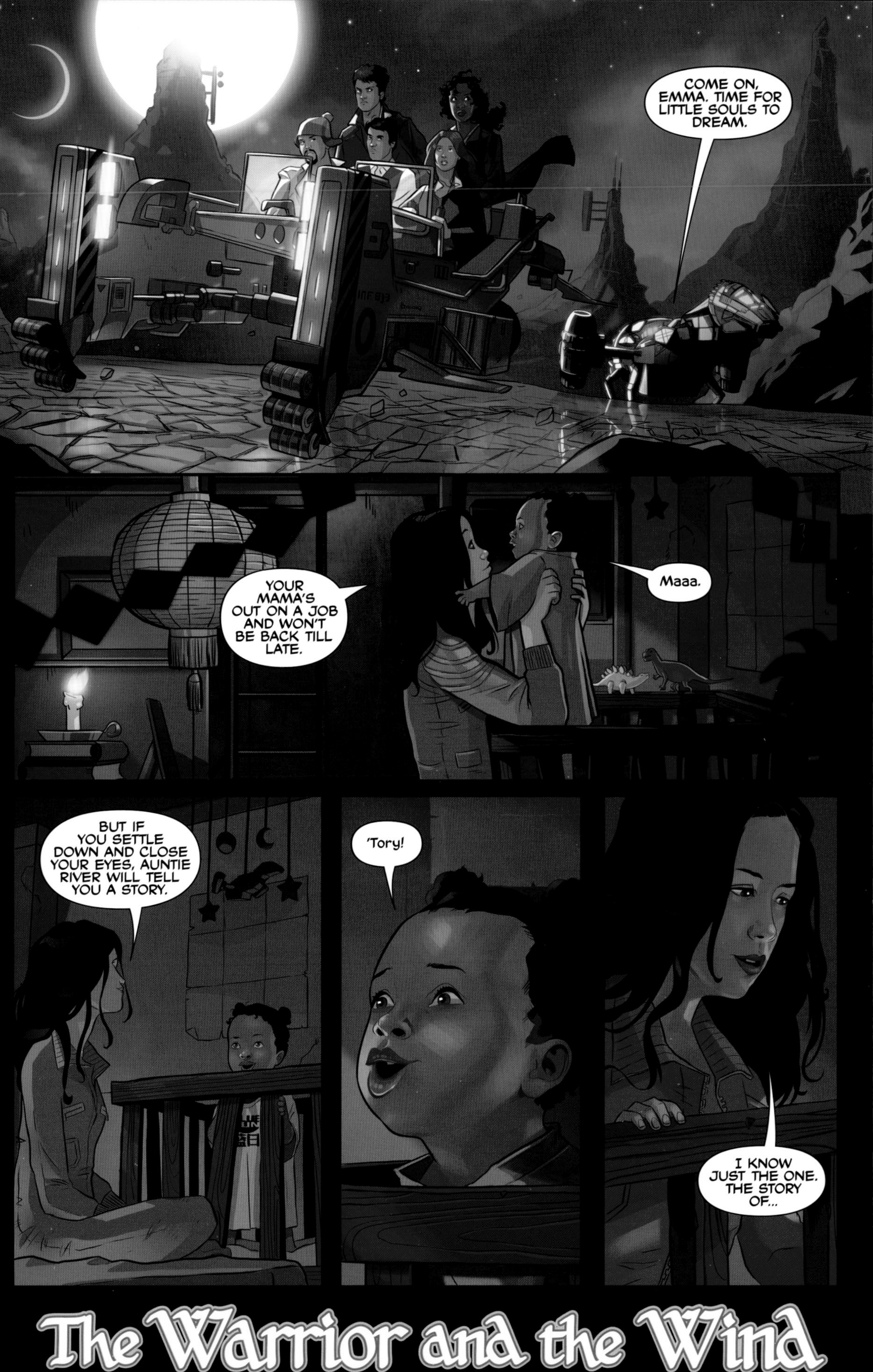
COME ON, EMMA. TIME FOR LITTLE SOULS TO DREAM.
YOUR MAMA'S OUT ON A JOB AND WON'T BE BACK TILL LATE.
Maaa.
BUT IF YOU SETTLE DOWN AND CLOSE YOUR EYES, AUNTIE RIVER WILL TELL YOU A STORY.
'Tory!
I KNOW JUST THE ONE. THE STORY OF...
The Warrior and the Wind

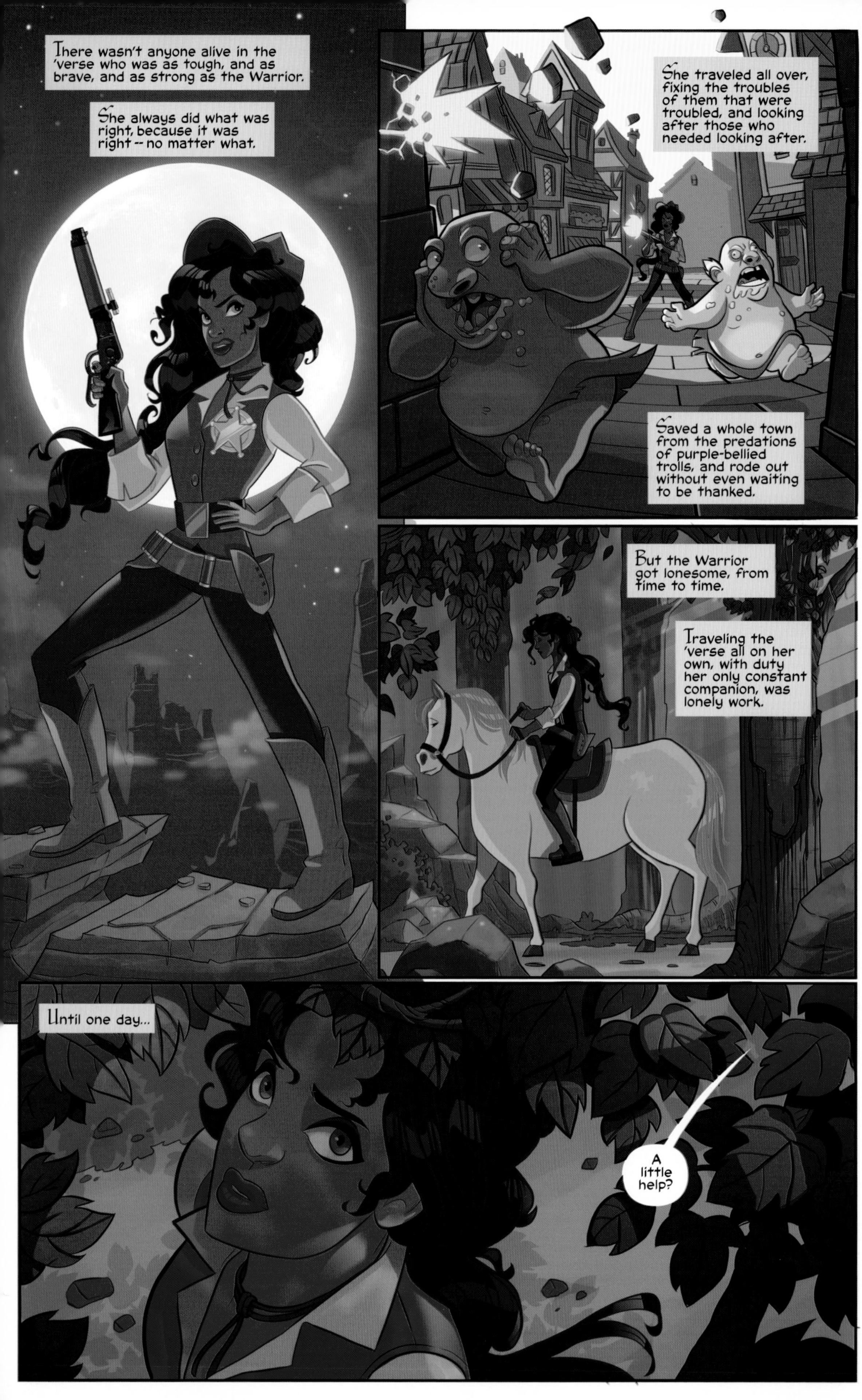

There wasn't anyone alive in the 'verse who was as tough, and as brave, and as strong as the Warrior.
She always did what was right, because it was right -- no matter what.
She traveled all over, fixing the troubles of them that were troubled, and looking after those who needed looking after.
Saved a whole town from the predations of purple-bellied trolls, and rode out without even waiting to be thanked.
But the Warrior got lonesome, from time to time.
Traveling the 'verse all on her own, with duty her only constant companion, was lonely work.
Until one day...
A little help?

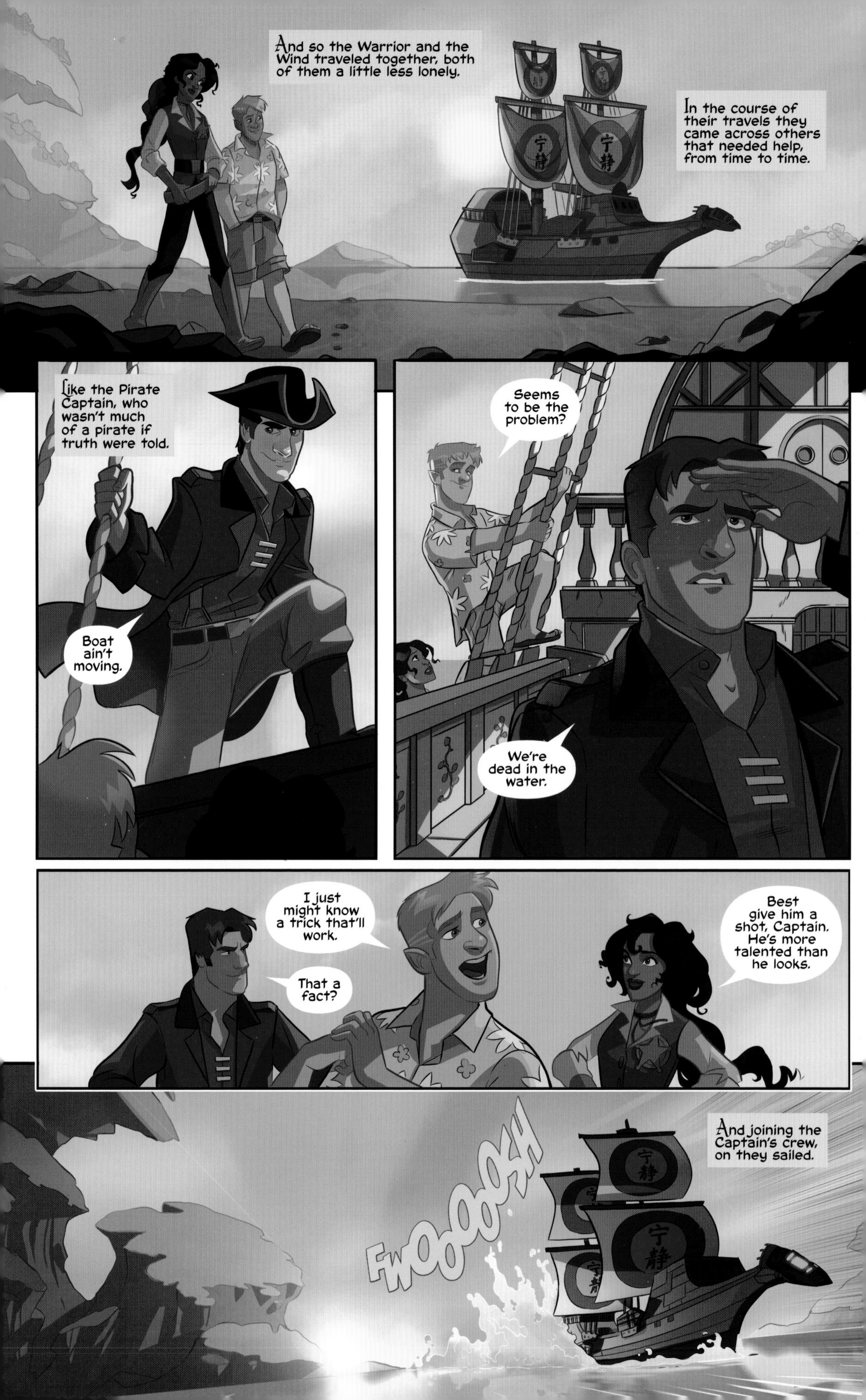
And so the Warrior and the Wind traveled together, both of them a little less lonely.
In the course of their travels they came across others that needed help, from time to time.
Like the Pirate Captain, who wasn't much of a pirate if truth were told.
Boat ain't moving.
Seems to be the problem?
We're dead in the water.
I just might know a trick that'll work.
That a fact?
Best give him a shot, Captain. He's more talented than he looks.
And joining the Captain's crew, on they sailed.
FWOOOOSH

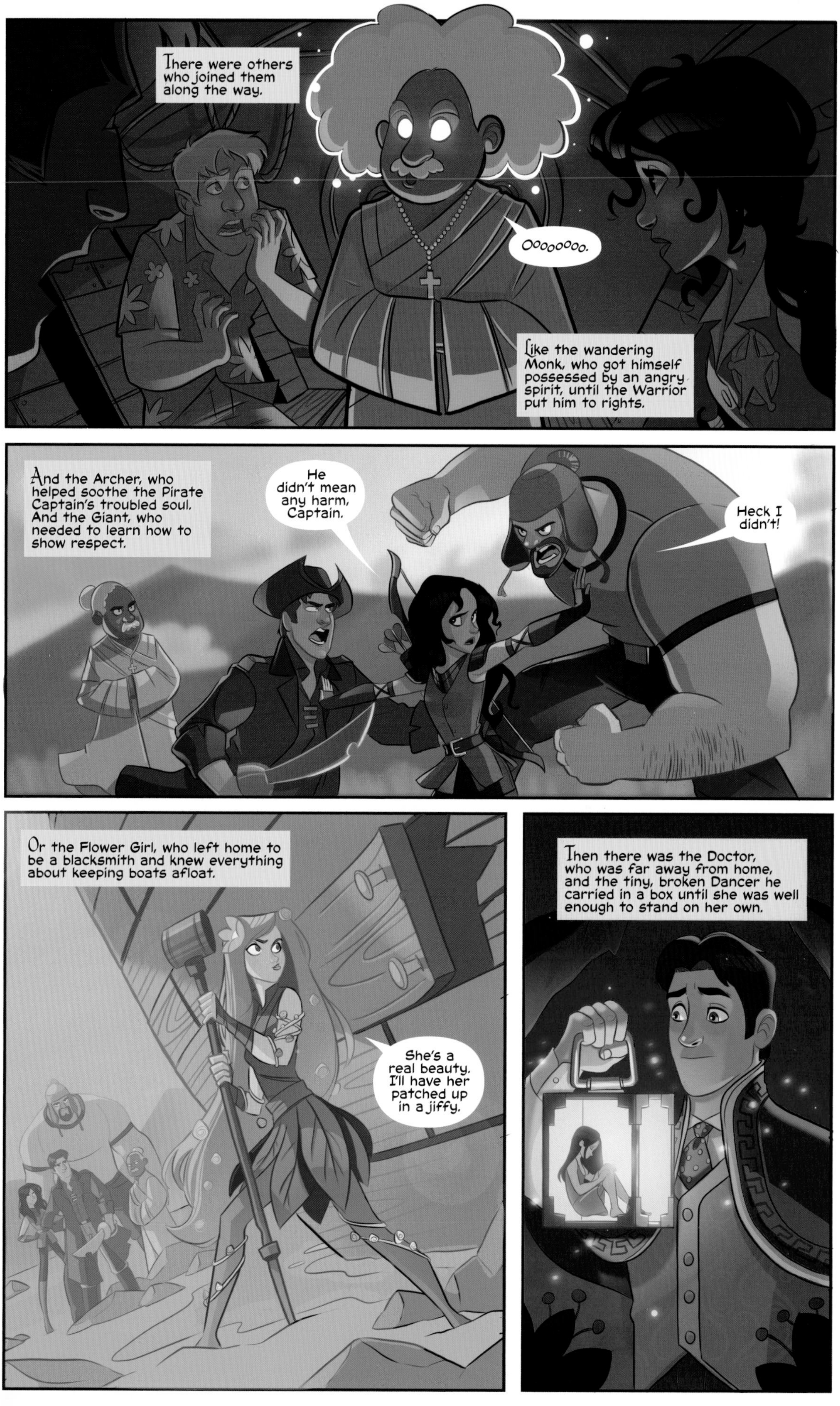
There were others who joined them along the way.
Ooooooo.
Like the wandering Monk, who got himself possessed by an angry spirit, until the Warrior put him to rights.
And the Archer, who helped soothe the Pirate Captain's troubled soul. And the Giant, who needed to learn how to show respect.
He didn't mean any harm, Captain.
Heck I didn't!
Or the Flower Girl, who left home to be a blacksmith and knew everything about keeping boats afloat.
She's a real beauty. I'll have her patched up in a jiffy.
Then there was the Doctor, who was far away from home, and the tiny, broken Dancer he carried in a box until she was well enough to stand on her own.

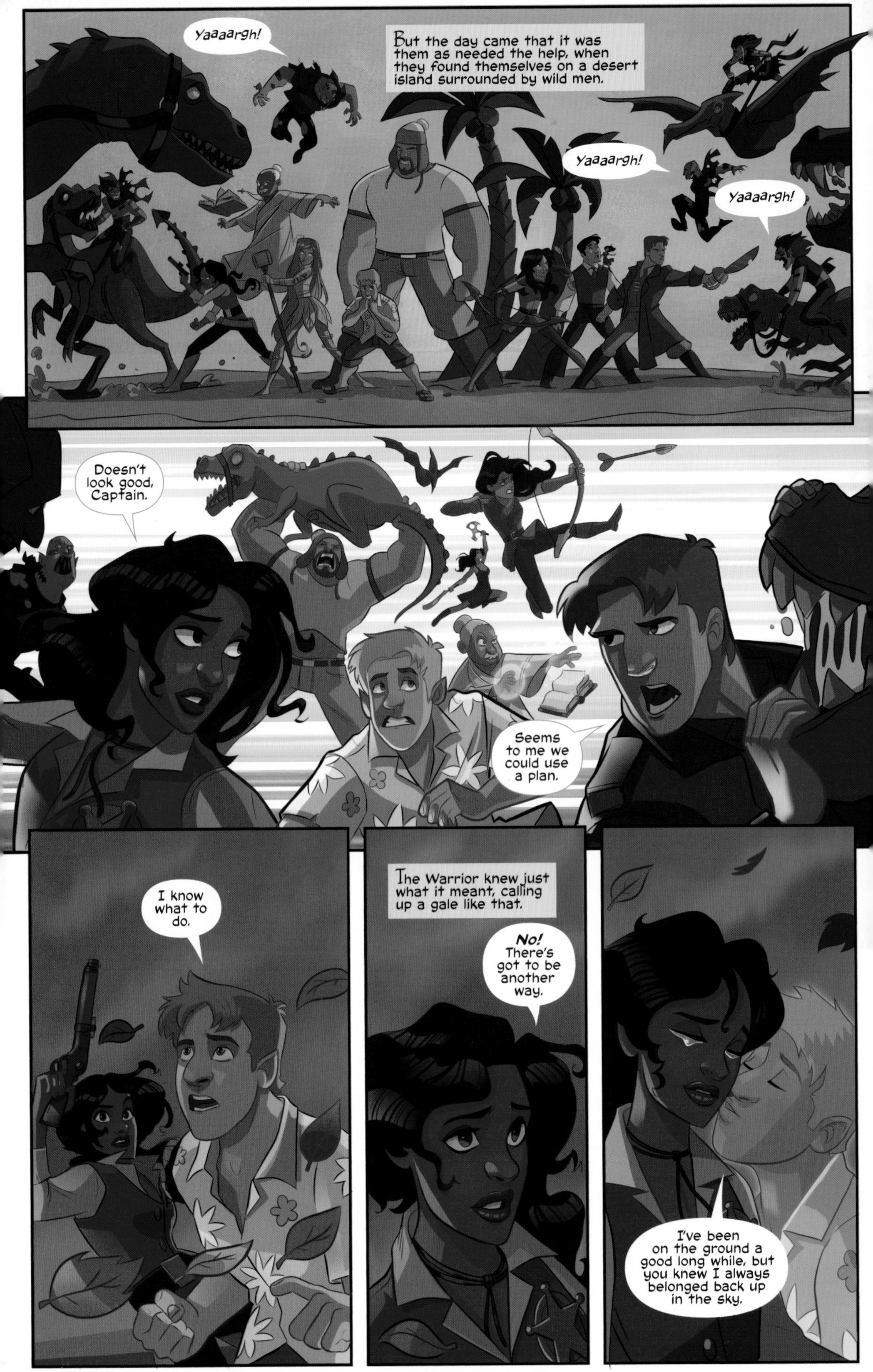
Yaaaargh!
But the day came that it was them as needed the help, when they found themselves on a desert island surrounded by wild men.
Yaaaargh!
Yaaaargh!
Doesn't look good, Captain.
Seems to me we could use a plan.
I know what to do.
The Warrior knew just what it meant, calling up a gale like that.
No! There's got to be another way.
I've been on the ground a good long while, but you knew I always belonged back up in the sky.

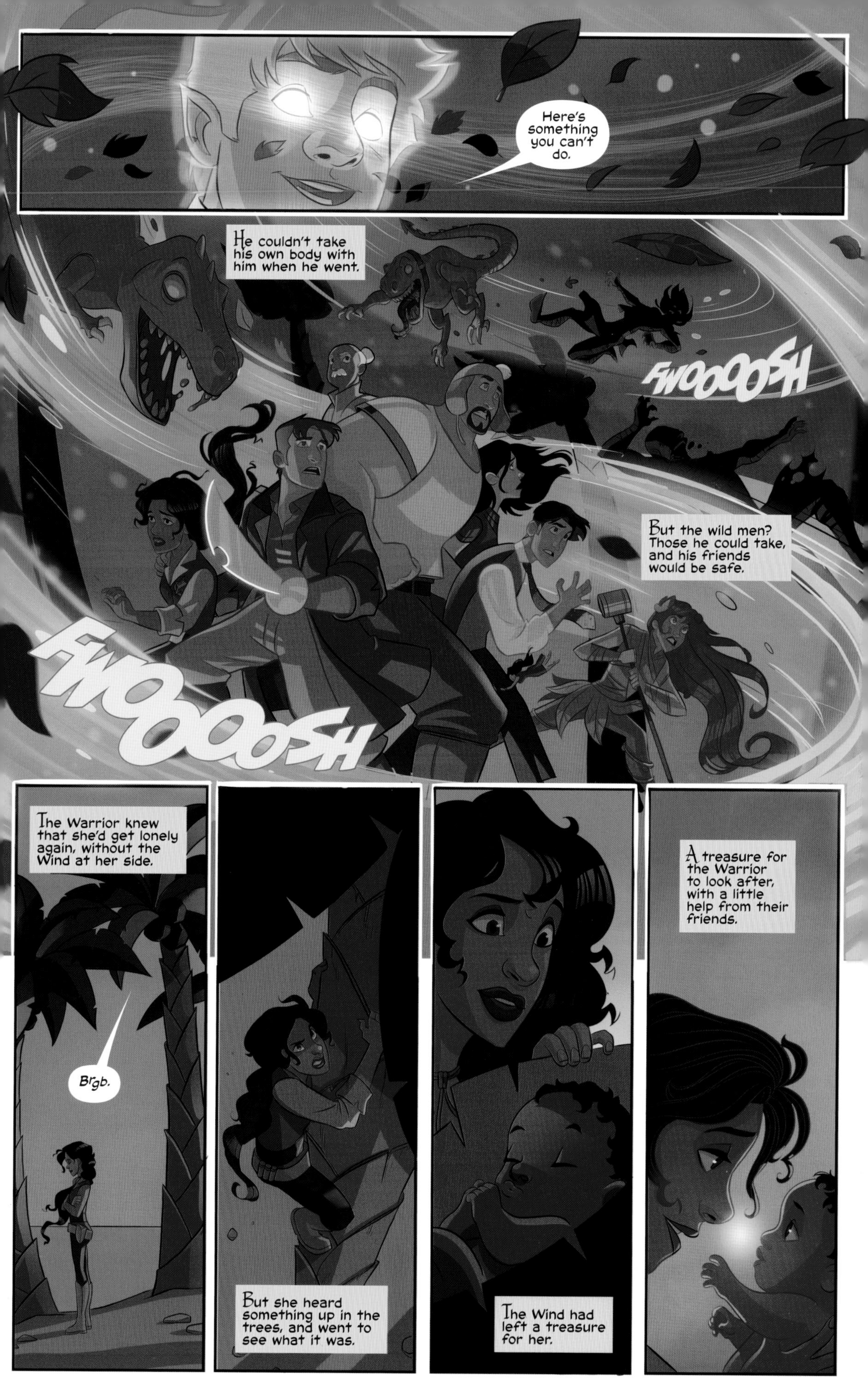
Here's something you can't do.
He couldn't take his own body with him when he went.
FWOOOOSH
But the wild men? Those he could take, and his friends would be safe.
FWOOOOSH
The Warrior knew that she'd get lonely again, without the Wind at her side.
Brgb.
But she heard something up in the trees, and went to see what it was.
The Wind had left a treasure for her.
A treasure for the Warrior to look after, with a little help from their friends.

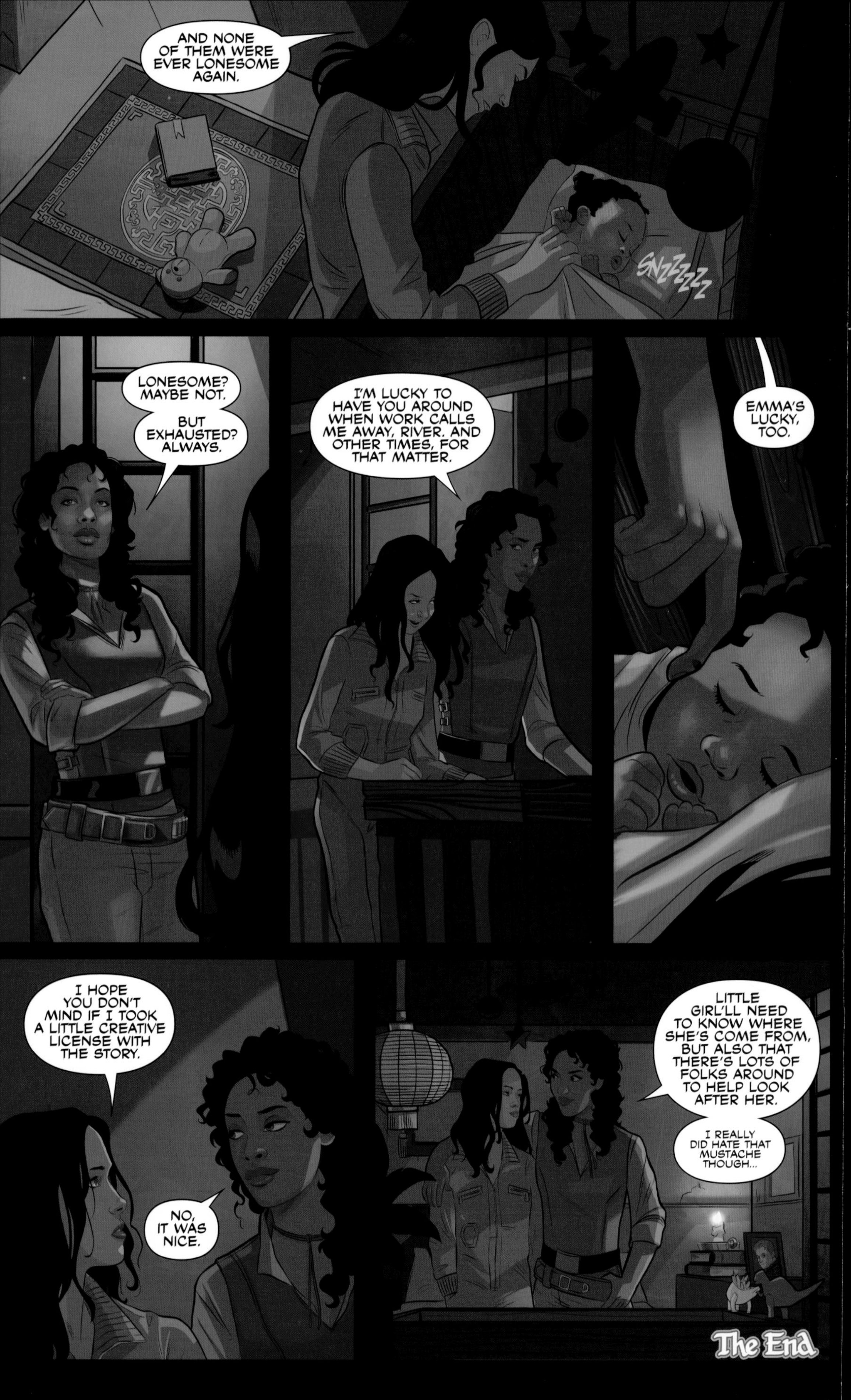
AND NONE OF THEM WERE EVER LONESOME AGAIN.
SNZZZZZZ
LONESOME? MAYBE NOT.
BUT EXHAUSTED? ALWAYS.
I'M LUCKY TO HAVE YOU AROUND WHEN WORK CALLS ME AWAY, RIVER. AND OTHER TIMES, FOR THAT MATTER.
EMMA'S LUCKY, TOO.
I HOPE YOU DON'T MIND IF I TOOK A LITTLE CREATIVE LICENSE WITH THE STORY.
NO, IT WAS NICE.
LITTLE GIRL'LL NEED TO KNOW WHERE SHE'S COME FROM, BUT ALSO THAT THERE'S LOTS OF FOLKS AROUND TO HELP LOOK AFTER HER.
I REALLY DID HATE THAT MUSTACHE THOUGH...
The End

Serenity

宁静 **FIREFLY CLASS 03-K64** ™

COVER GALLERY

Illustration by Georges Jeanty, Karl Story, and Wes Dzioba

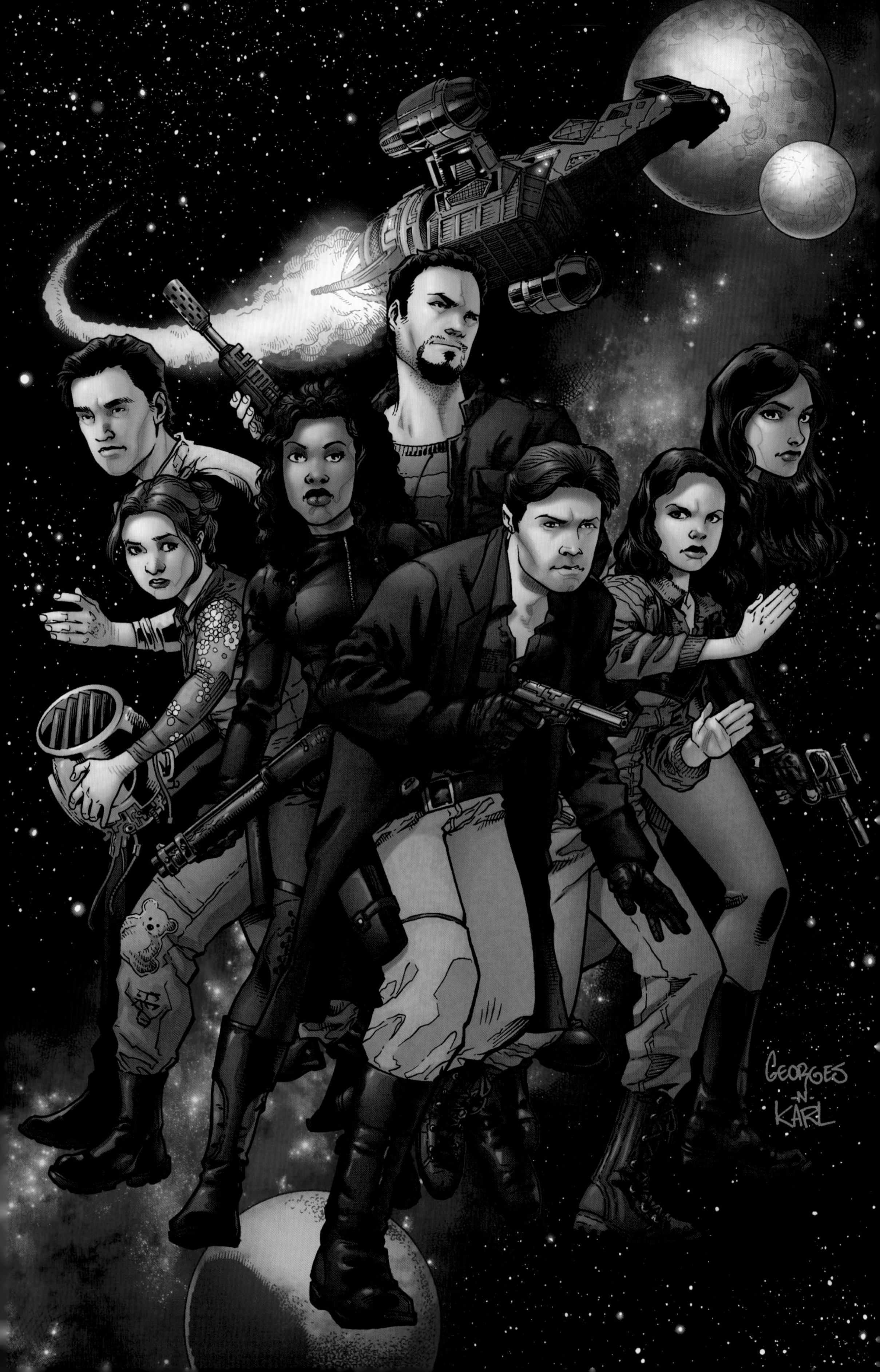
GEORGES -N- KARL

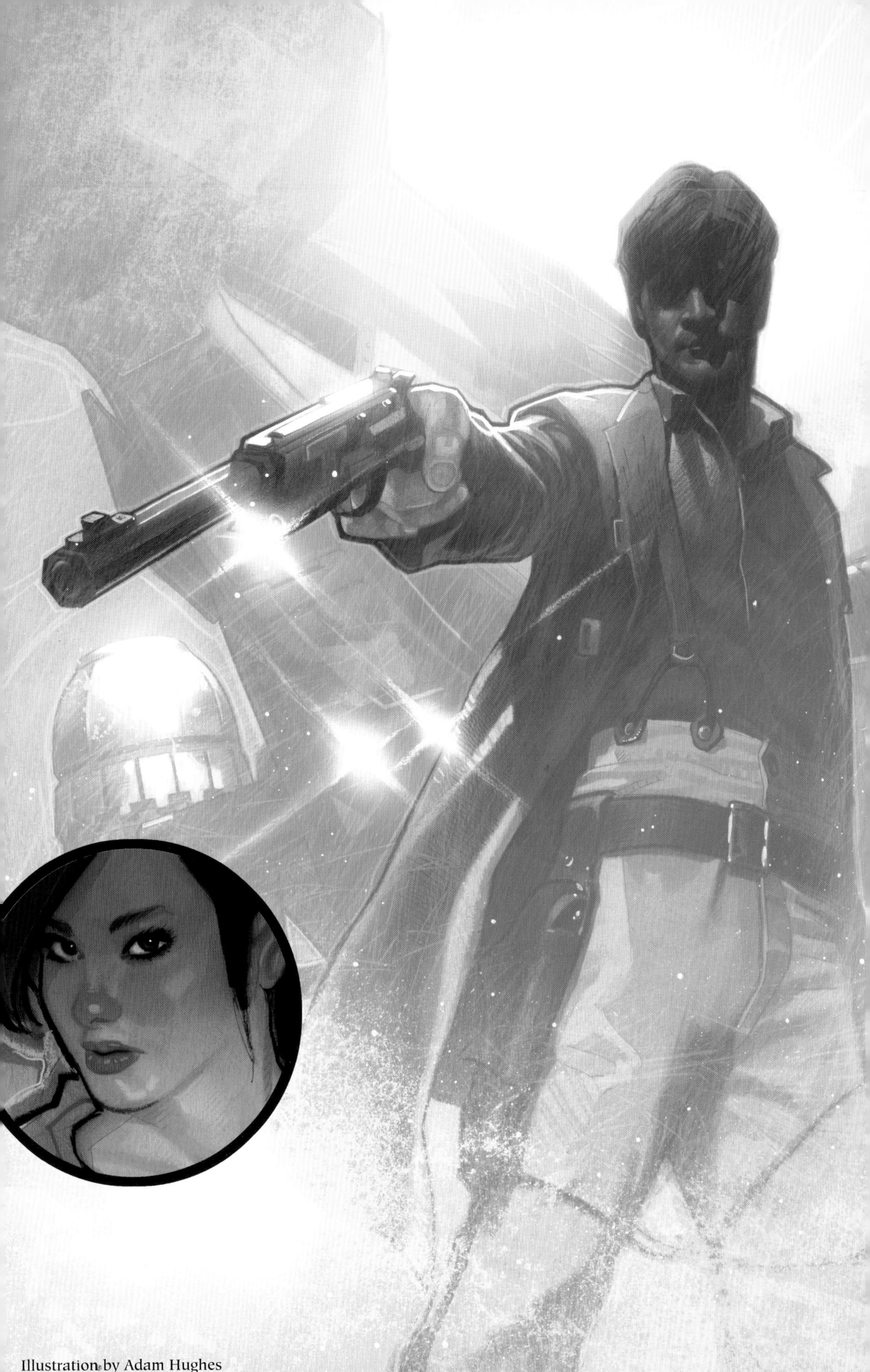

Illustration by Adam Hughes

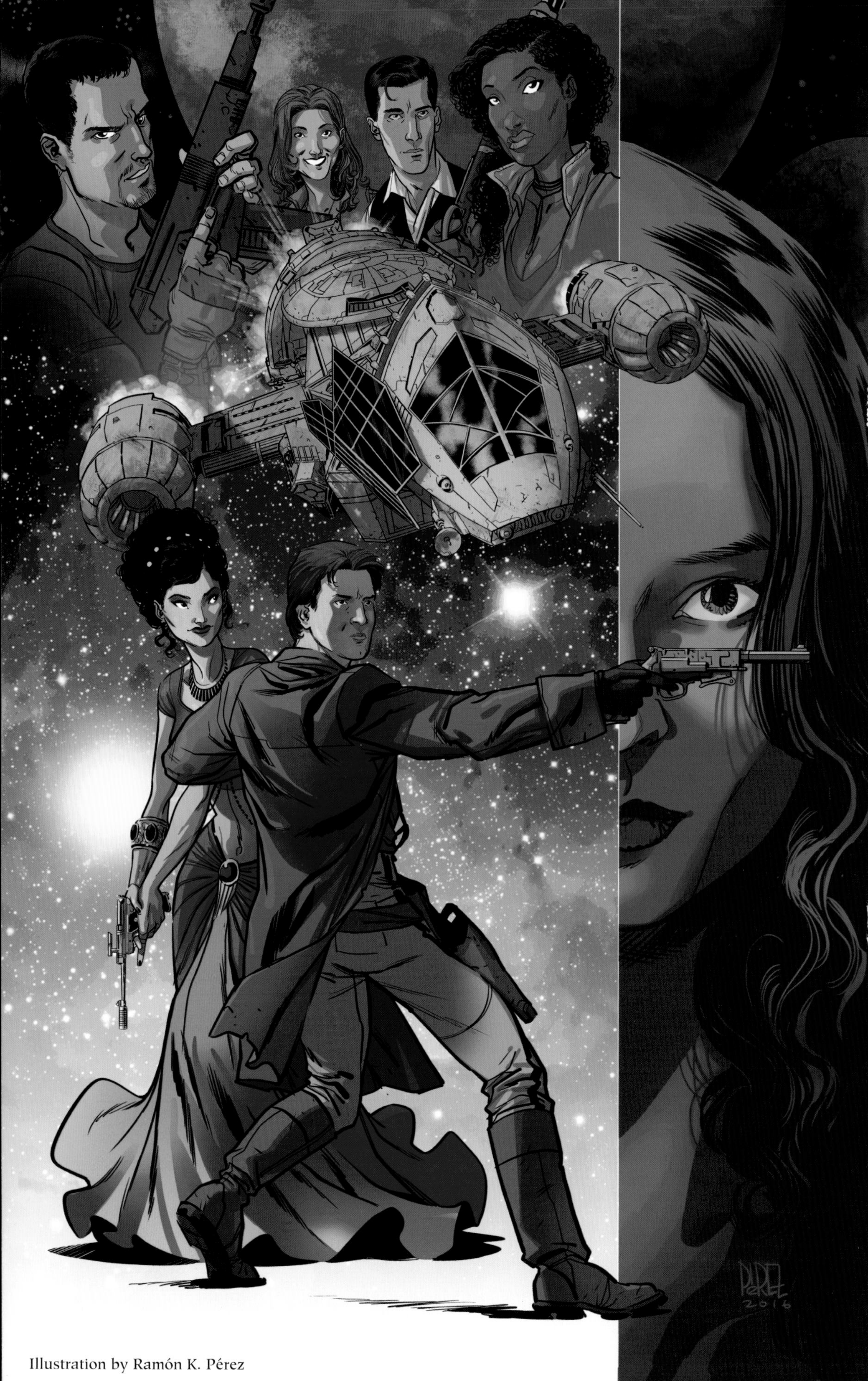

Illustration by Ramón K. Pérez

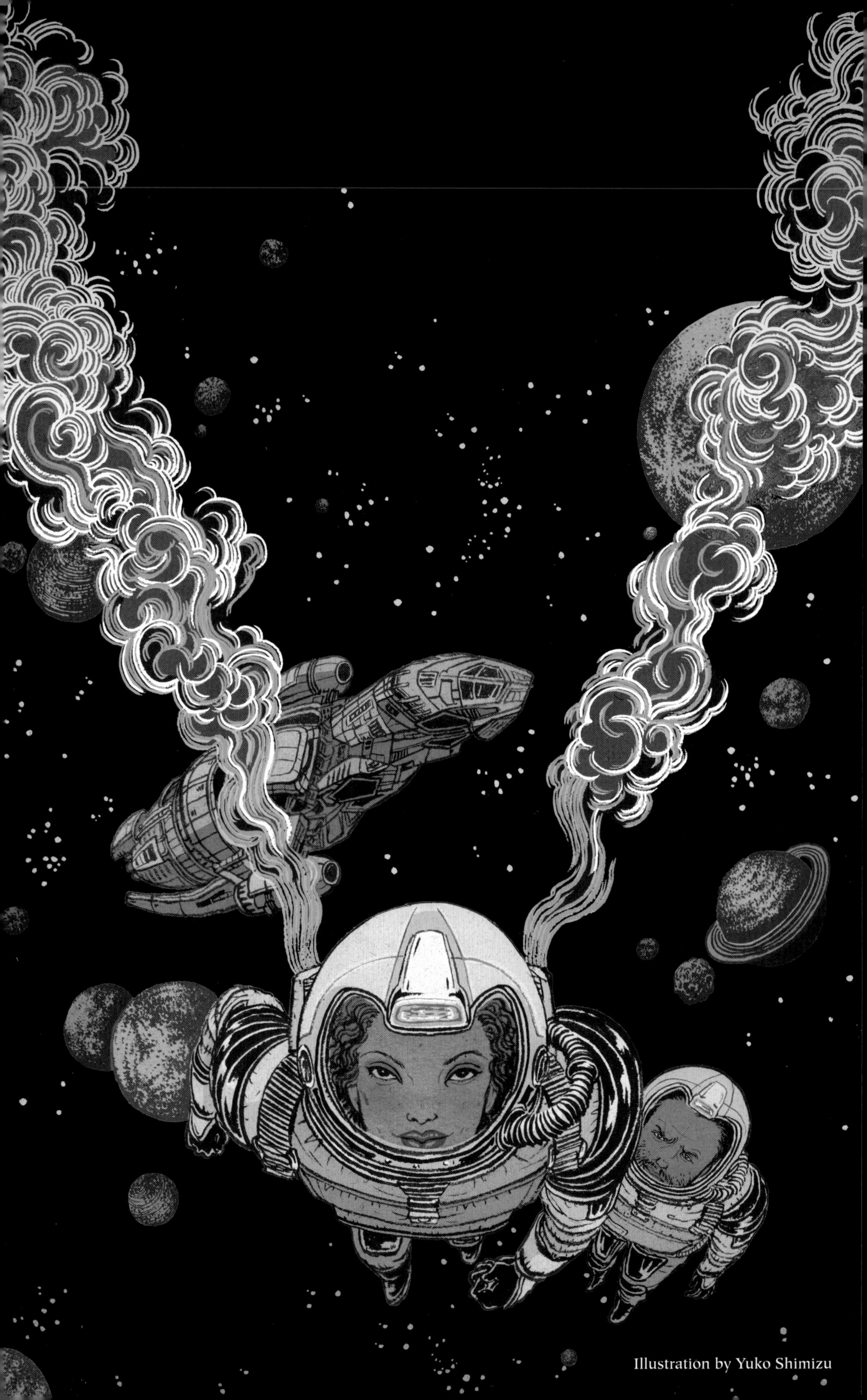

Illustration by Yuko Shimizu

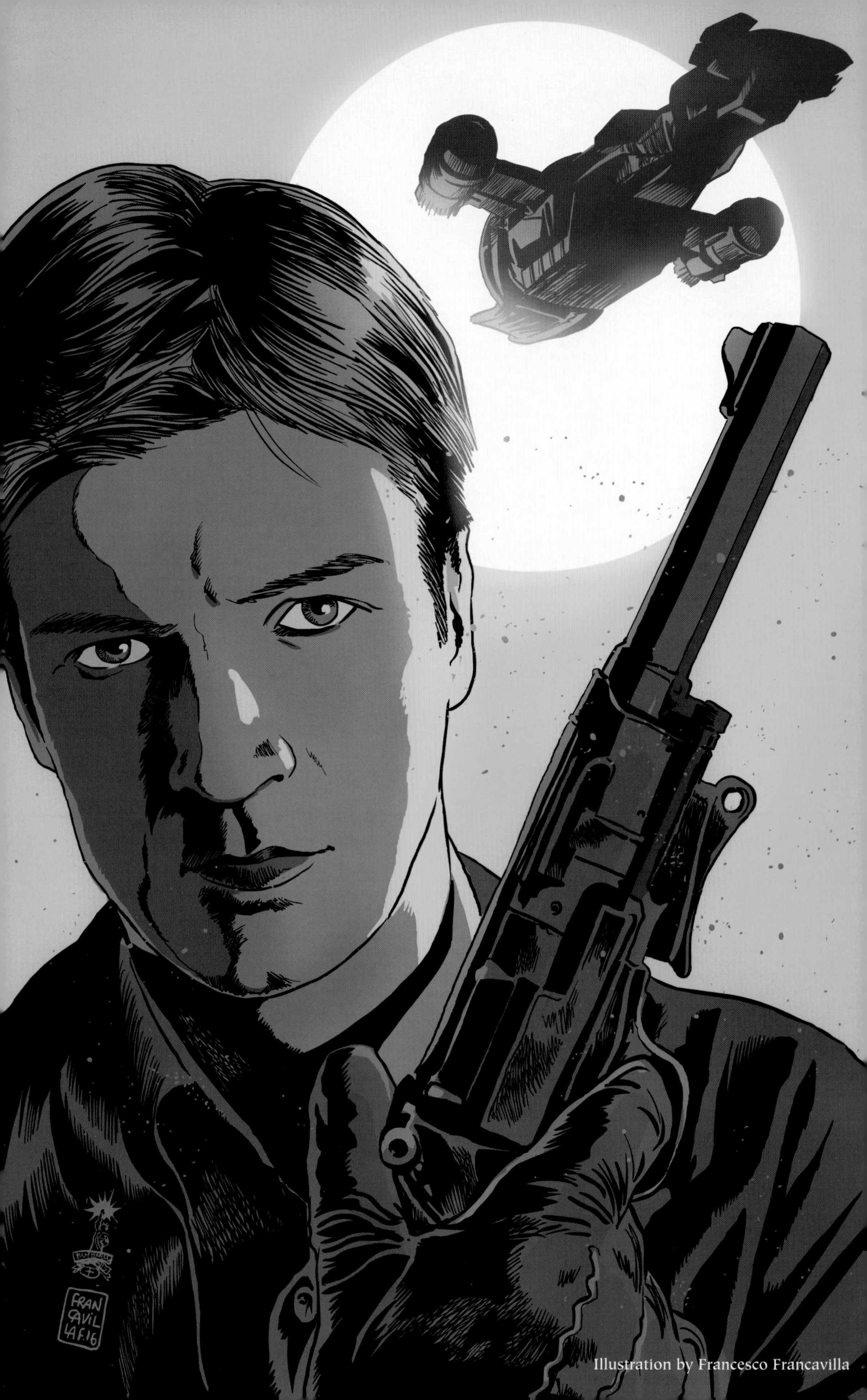
FRAN
CAVIL
LA F.16
Illustration by Francesco Francavilla

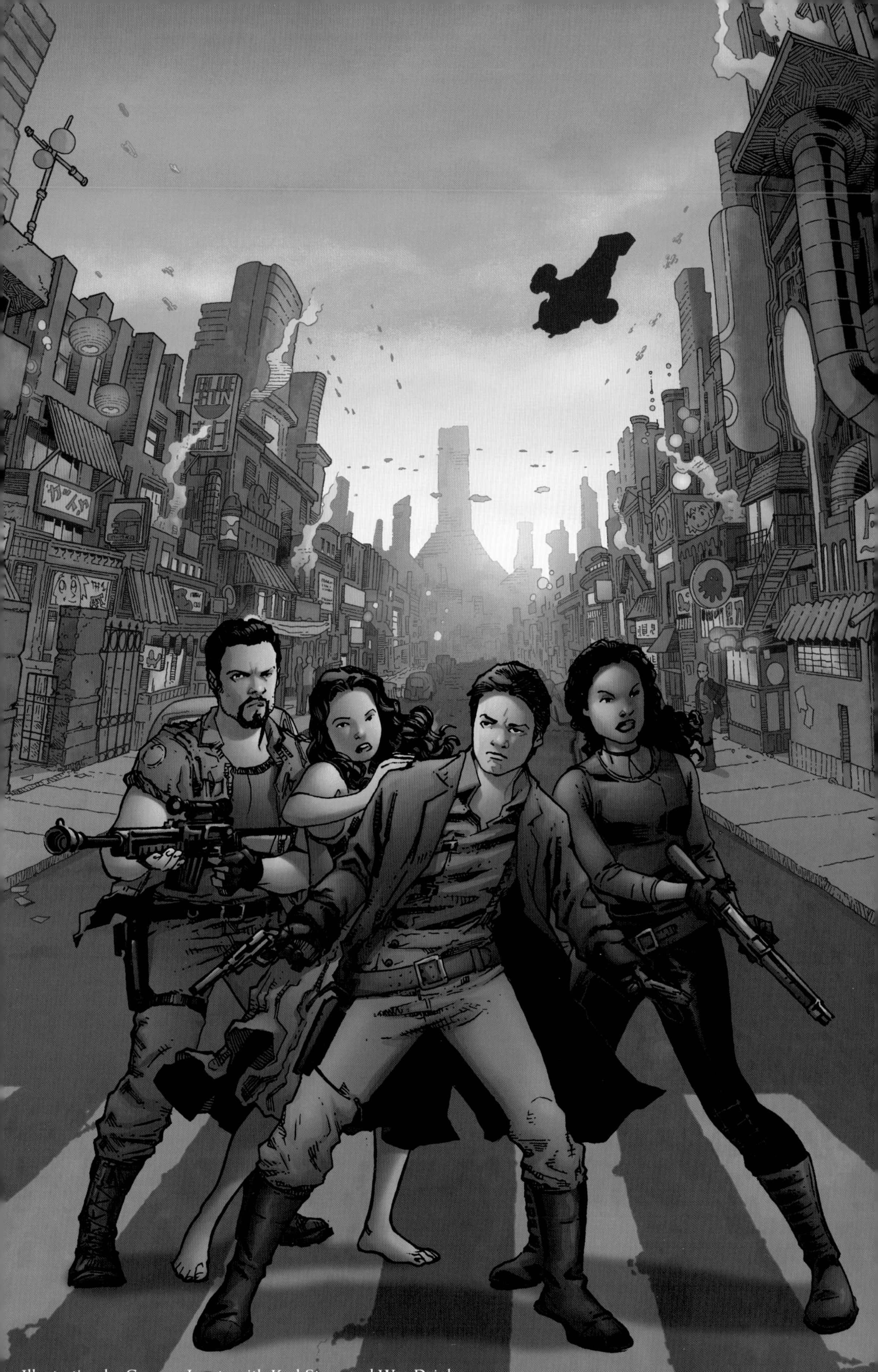
BLUE SUN

Illustration by Georges Jeanty with Karl Story and Wes Dzioba

Illustration by Georges Jeanty with Karl Story and Wes Dzioba

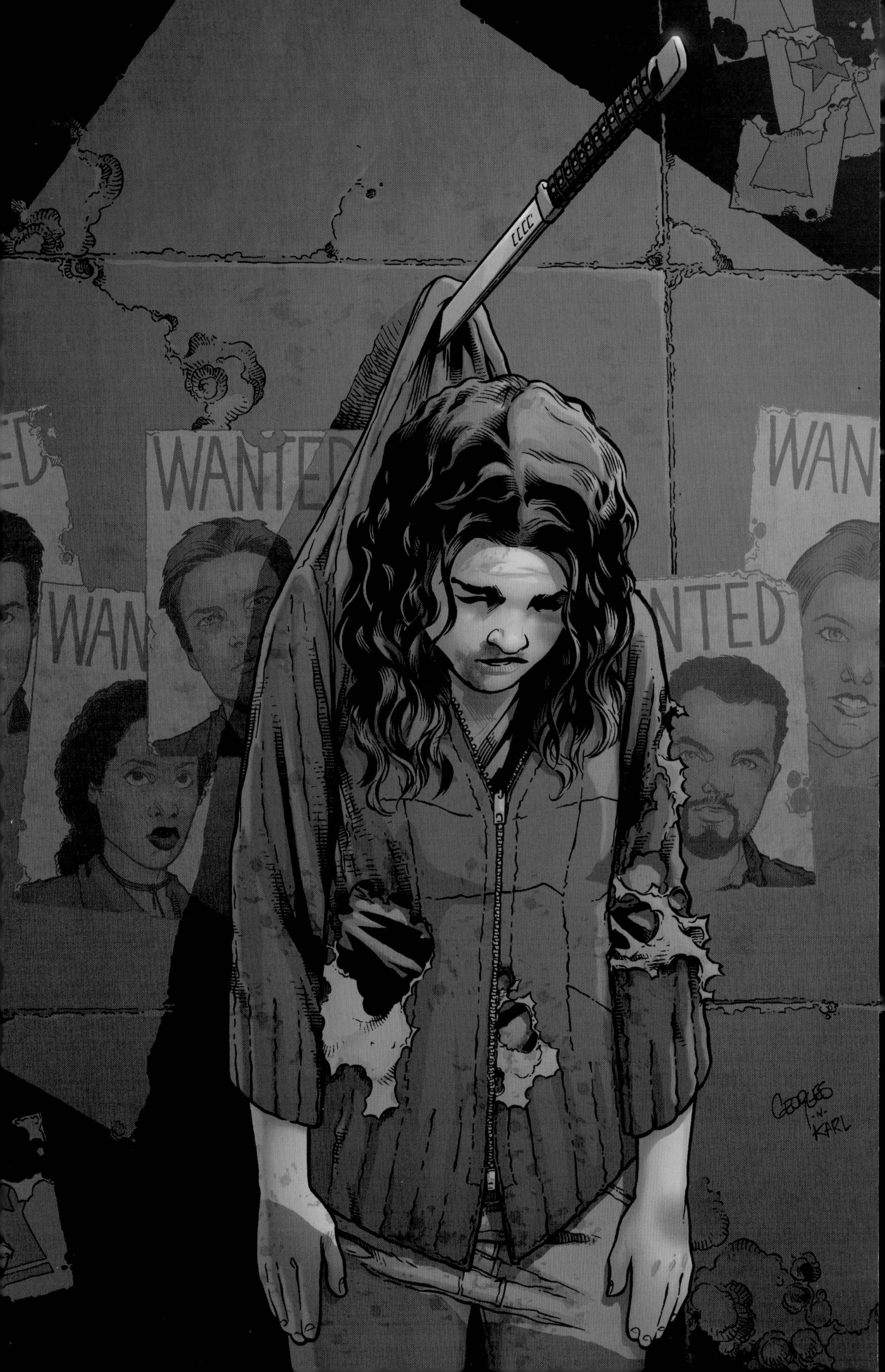
GEORGES
-N-
KARL

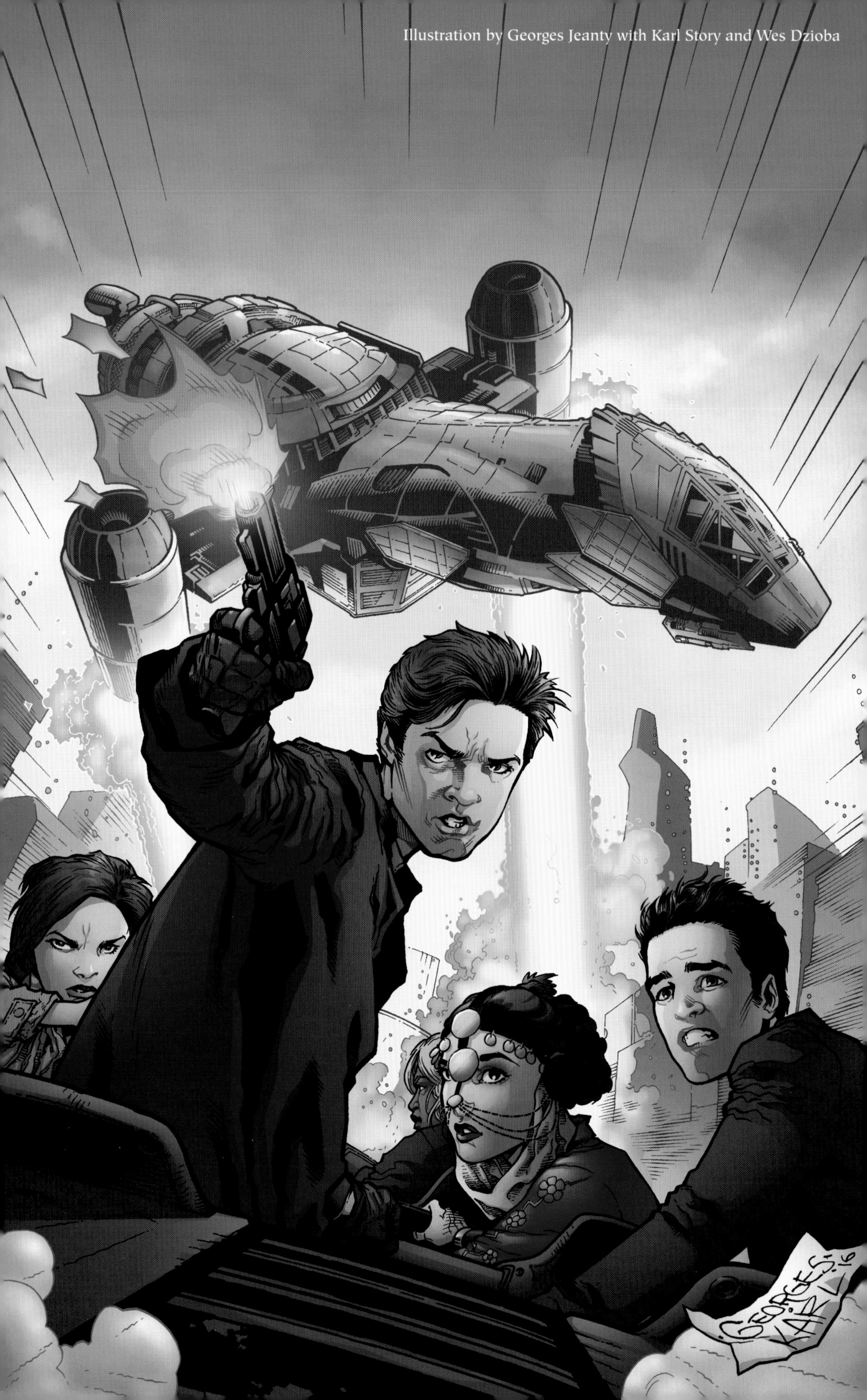

Illustration by Georges Jeanty with Karl Story and Wes Dzioba

Illustration by Georges Jeanty with Karl Story and Wes Dzioba

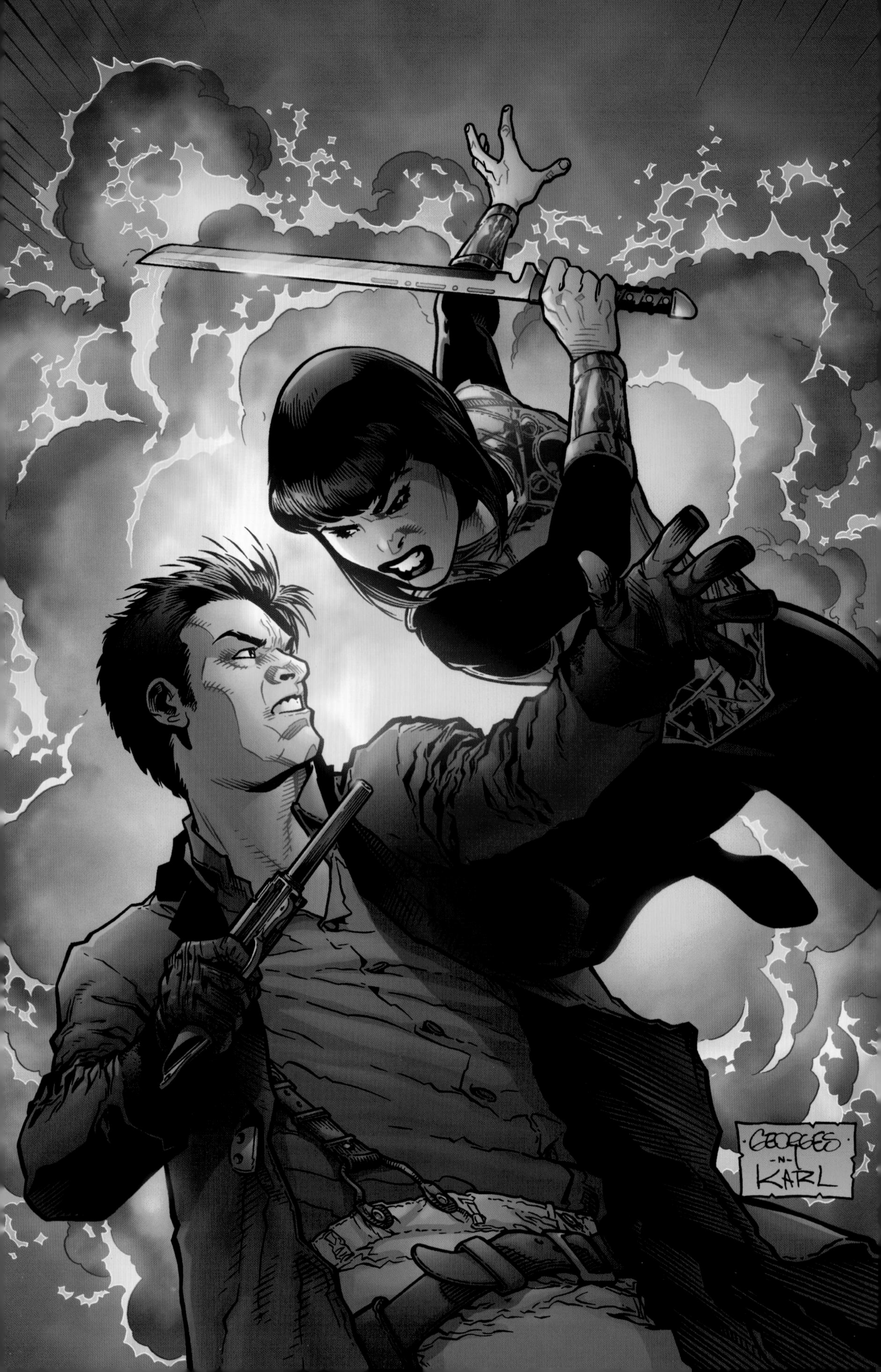
GEORGES
-N-
KARL

Illustration by Georges Jeanty with Karl Story and Wes Dzioba

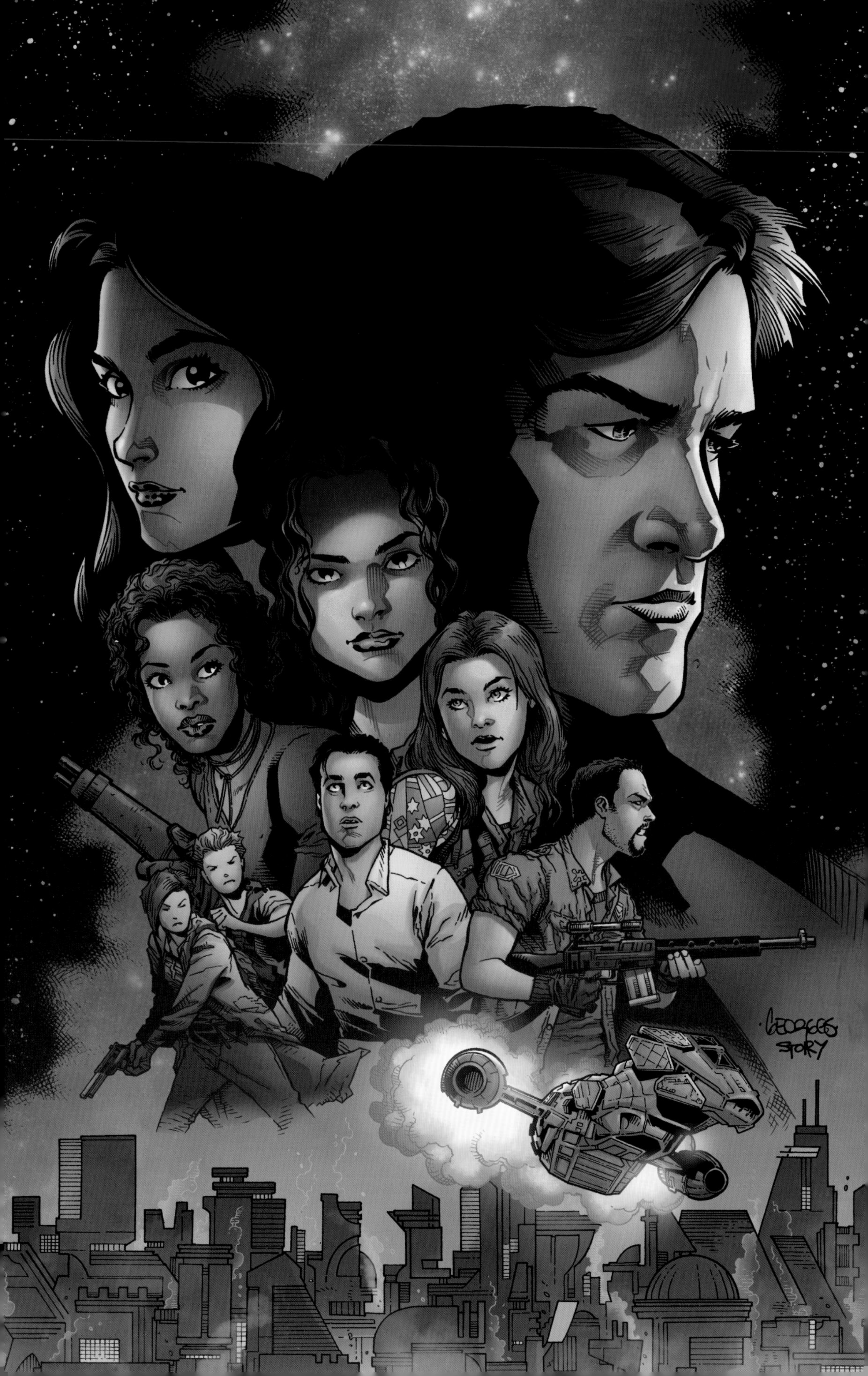
GEORGES
STORY

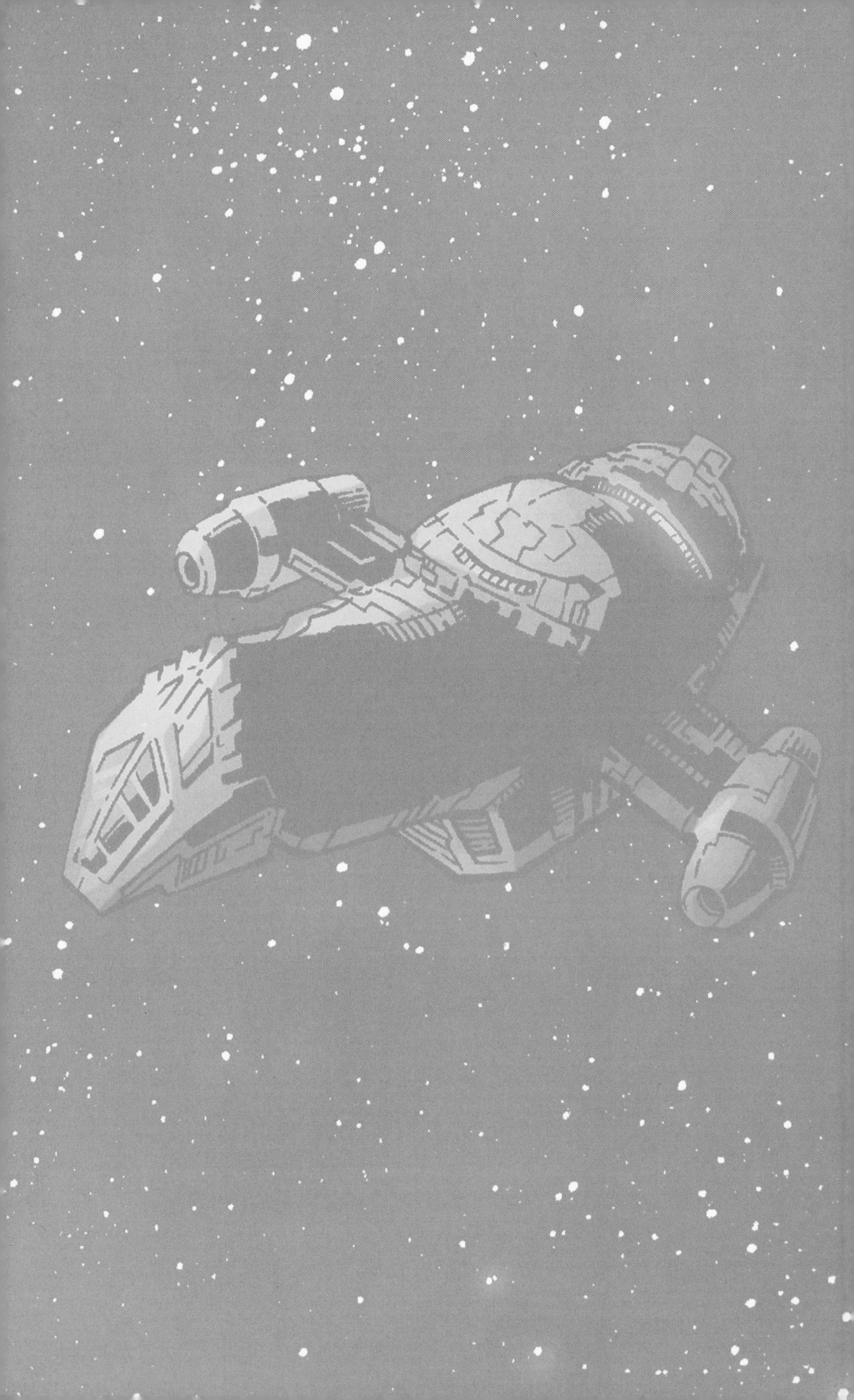

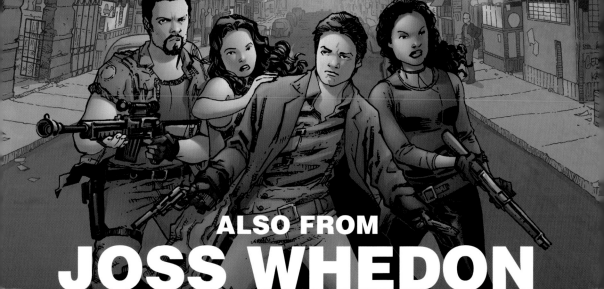

ALSO FROM
JOSS WHEDON

AVAILABLE AT YOUR LOCAL COMICS SHOP OR BOOKSTORE!

DarkHorse.com

 TO FIND A COMICS SHOP IN YOUR AREA, CALL 1-888-266-4226. FOR MORE INFORMATION OR TO ORDER DIRECT VISIT DARKHORSE.COM OR CALL 1-800-862-0052 MON.–FRI. 9 AM TO 5 PM PACIFIC TIME. PRICES AND AVAILABILITY SUBJECT TO CHANGE WITHOUT NOTICE.

Firefly ™ and Serenity: Firefly Class 03-K64™ & © Twentieth Century Fox Film Corporation. Dr. Horrible © Timescience Bloodclub. Buffy the Vampire Slayer™ & © Twentieth Century Fox Film Corporation. All rights reserved. (BL 5035)

Buffy the Vampire Slayer™

BUFFY THE VAMPIRE SLAYER SEASON 8

VOLUME 1: THE LONG WAY HOME
Joss Whedon and Georges Jeanty
ISBN 978-1-59307-822-5 | $15.99

VOLUME 2: NO FUTURE FOR YOU
Brian K. Vaughan, Georges Jeanty, and Joss Whedon
ISBN 978-1-59307-963-5 | $15.99

VOLUME 3: WOLVES AT THE GATE
Drew Goddard, Georges Jeanty, and Joss Whedon
ISBN 978-1-59582-165-2 | $15.99

VOLUME 4: TIME OF YOUR LIFE
Joss Whedon, Jeph Loeb, Georges Jeanty, and others
ISBN 978-1-59582-310-6 | $15.99

VOLUME 5: PREDATORS AND PREY
Joss Whedon, Jane Espenson, Georges Jeanty, Cliff Richards, and others
ISBN 978-1-59582-342-7 | $15.99

VOLUME 6: RETREAT
Joss Whedon, Jane Espenson, Georges Jeanty, Karl Moline, and others
ISBN 978-1-59582-415-8 | $15.99

VOLUME 7: TWILIGHT
Joss Whedon, Brad Meltzer, and Georges Jeanty
ISBN 978-1-59582-558-2 | $16.99

VOLUME 8: LAST GLEAMING
Joss Whedon, Scott Allie, and Georges Jeanty
ISBN 978-1-59582-610-7 | $16.99

BUFFY THE VAMPIRE SLAYER SEASON 8 LIBRARY EDITION

VOLUME 1
ISBN 978-1-59582-888-0 | $29.99

VOLUME 2
ISBN 978-1-59582-935-1 | $29.99

VOLUME 3
ISBN 978-1-59582-978-8 | $29.99

VOLUME 4
ISBN 978-1-61655-127-8 | $29.99

BUFFY THE VAMPIRE SLAYER OMNIBUS: SEASON 8

VOLUME 1
ISBN 978-1-63008-941-2 | $24.99

BUFFY THE VAMPIRE SLAYER SEASON 9

VOLUME 1: FREEFALL
Joss Whedon, Andrew Chambliss, Georges Jeanty, and others
ISBN 978-1-59582-922-1 | $17.99

VOLUME 2: ON YOUR OWN
Andrew Chambliss, Scott Allie, Georges Jeanty, and others
ISBN 978-1-59582-990-0 | $17.99

VOLUME 3: GUARDED
Joss Whedon, Jane Espenson, Drew Z. Greenberg, Georges Jeanty, and others
ISBN 978-1-61655-099-8 | $17.99

VOLUME 4: WELCOME TO THE TEAM
Andrew Chambliss, Georges Jeanty, Karl Moline, and others
ISBN 978-1-61655-166-7 | $17.99

VOLUME 5: THE CORE
Andrew Chambliss, Georges Jeanty, and others
ISBN 978-1-61655-254-1 | $17.99

BUFFY THE VAMPIRE SLAYER SEASON 9 LIBRARY EDITION

VOLUME 1
ISBN 978-1-61655-715-7 | $29.99

VOLUME 2
ISBN 978-1-61655-716-4 | $29.99

VOLUME 3
ISBN 978-1-61655-717-1 | $29.99

BUFFY THE VAMPIRE SLAYER SEASON 10

VOLUME 1: NEW RULES
Christos Gage, Rebekah Isaacs, Nicholas Brendon, and others
ISBN 978-1-61655-490-3 | $18.99

VOLUME 2: I WISH
Christos Gage, Rebekah Isaacs, Nicholas Brendon, and others
ISBN 978-1-61655-600-6 | $18.99

VOLUME 3: LOVE DARES YOU
Christos Gage, Rebekah Isaacs, Nicholas Brendon, and Megan Levens
ISBN 978-1-61655-758-4 | $18.99

VOLUME 4: OLD DEMONS
Christos Gage and Rebekah Isaacs
ISBN 978-1-61655-802-4 | $18.99

VOLUME 5: IN PIECES ON THE GROUND
Christos Gage, Megan Levens, and Rebekah Isaacs
ISBN 978-1-61655-944-1 | $18.99

VOLUME 6: OWN IT
Christos Gage and Rebekah Isaacs
ISBN 978-1-50670-034-2 | $18.99

BUFFY THE VAMPIRE SLAYER SEASON 11

VOLUME 1: THE SPREAD OF THEIR EVIL
Christos Gage and Rebekah Isaacs
ISBN 978-1-50670-274-2 | $19.99

ANGEL & FAITH SEASON 9

VOLUME 1: LIVE THROUGH THIS
Christos Gage, Rebekah Isaacs, and Phil Noto
ISBN 978-1-59582-887-3 | $17.99

VOLUME 2: DADDY ISSUES
Christos Gage, Rebekah Isaacs, and Chris Samnee
ISBN 978-1-59582-960-3 | $17.99

VOLUME 3: FAMILY REUNION
Christos Gage, Rebekah Isaacs, Lee Garbett, and David Lapham
ISBN 978-1-61655-079-0 | $17.99

VOLUME 4: DEATH AND CONSEQUENCES
Christos Gage and Rebekah Isaacs
ISBN 978-1-61655-165-0 | $17.99

VOLUME 5: WHAT YOU WANT, NOT WHAT YOU NEED
Christos Gage and Rebekah Isaacs
ISBN 978-1-61655-253-4 | $17.99

ANGEL & FAITH SEASON 9 LIBRARY EDITION

VOLUME 1
ISBN 978-1-61655-712-6 | $29.99

VOLUME 2
ISBN 978-1-61655-713-3 | $29.99

VOLUME 3
ISBN 978-1-61655-714-0 | $29.99

ANGEL & FAITH SEASON 10

VOLUME 1: WHERE THE RIVER MEETS THE SEA
Victor Gischler, Will Conrad, Derlis Santacruz, and others
ISBN 978-1-61655-503-0 | $18.99

VOLUME 2: LOST AND FOUND
Victor Gischler and Will Conrad
ISBN 978-1-61655-601-3 | $18.99

VOLUME 3: UNITED
Victor Gischler and Will Conrad
ISBN 978-1-61655-766-9 | $18.99

VOLUME 4: A LITTLE MORE THAN KIN
Victor Gischler, Cliff Richards, and Will Conrad
ISBN 978-1-61655-890-1 | $18.99

ANGEL SEASON 11

VOLUME 1: OUT OF THE PAST
Corinna Bechko and Geraldo Borges
ISBN 978-1-50670-346-6 | $17.99

SPIKE

A DARK PLACE
Victor Gischler and Paul Lee
ISBN 978-1-61655-109-4 | $17.99

INTO THE LIGHT
James Marsters and Derlis Santacruz
ISBN 978-1-61655-421-7 | $14.99

WILLOW

WONDERLAND
Jeff Parker, Christos Gage, and Brian Ching
ISBN 978-1-61655-145-2 | $17.99

BUFFY: THE HIGH SCHOOL YEARS

FREAKS AND GEEKS
Faith Erin Hicks and Yishan Li
ISBN 978-1-61655-667-9 | $10.99

GLUTTON FOR PUNISHMENT
Kel McDonald and Yishan Li
ISBN 978-1-50670-115-8 | $10.99

PARENTAL PARASITE
Kel McDonald and Yishan Li
ISBN 978-1-50670-304-6 | $10.99